Sadie

Sadie

a novel by
REBECCA BELLISTON

DESERET
BOOK

Salt Lake City, Utah

To Troy, my forever

Photo on page 71: María Teijeíro/Photodisc/Thinkstock

Deseret Book is a registered trademark of Deseret Book Company.

Visit us at DeseretBook.com

Library of Congress Cataloging-in-Publication Data
Belliston, Rebecca, author.
  Sadie / Rebecca Belliston.
      p. cm.
  ISBN 978-1-60908-060-0 (paperbound)
  1. Abused women—Fiction.   2. Mormons—Fiction.   I. Title.
PS3602.E458S24 2011
813'.6—dc22   2011001534

Printed in the United States of America
Publishers Printing, Salt Lake City, UT
10   9   8   7   6   5   4   3   2   1

The Eve

"You're making a mistake!"

The woman stopped midstride, realizing it should be *them* leaving, not her. "Get out of my room!" she yelled.

Neither agent moved.

"There's a substantial reward involved," the younger one said. "You'll be able to pay off all those school loans."

They know about . . .

Her skin began to crawl. What else did the FBI know about her? She felt researched . . . violated . . . but not coerced. She absolutely refused to feel coerced. "You think I'd betray him for . . . for money!"

"A large chunk of—"

The senior agent held up a hand, cutting off his younger counterpart. "Just be our eyes and ears tonight, Miss Dawson. That's all we're asking."

"And I'm asking you to leave before I call the cops!"

"We are the cops," he pointed out dryly.

Trembling with fury, she grabbed her purse and stormed out of her room. She didn't dare glance over her shoulder as she raced down the hallway, nearly tripping in her high heels. Thankfully, Guillermo's assistant was already waiting for her as she burst through the front doors of the ski lodge. He quickly pulled open the back door of the gleaming Mercedes.

"Is everything all right, Señorita Dawson?" he asked.

"Yes. Fine. Just get me out of here," she replied, sliding in. "Fast!"

As Salvador brought the luxury engine to a soft purr, she pressed her hands against her stomach. Even as they pulled out of the crowded parking lot, her eyes stayed glued on the ski lodge, fully expecting the two agents to break out at any second.

So much for a Merry Christmas.

"Are you sufficiently warm, señorita?" Guillermo's assistant asked.

She glanced at her bare shoulders and cursed. In all the tumult, she'd forgotten her ruby red wrap that matched the rest of her Christmas ensemble. There was no way she was going back for it now. "I'm warm enough," she replied, leaning into the preheated leather. "I'm just anxious to get to the party."

"Guillermo is anxious to see you as well." Salvador's gaze lifted to the rearview mirror. "And if I might say so, you look . . . wow."

She laughed in spite of herself. With the ski lodge fading—and hopefully the last hour as well—she was already feeling much better. "Let's hope so, Salvador. Let's hope."

"A toast!" Guillermo called. "To the most beautiful woman in the world, *mi hermosa.*"

It wasn't until her mom elbowed her that she realized everyone was looking at her. Her cheeks colored, knowing her thoughts hadn't been on her boyfriend or his exaggerated compliment, but instead on the thirty faces around the room. Guillermo's world was lavish, jovial, exciting. And safe. Definitely safe. *The FBI is wrong,* she told herself for the hundredth time. She quickly held up her Argentine wine high with the rest of the room.

Guillermo smiled at her first, then at his guests. "And to her mother. Also a lovely woman who . . ."

His words faded out as her gaze lingered on each face around the room. Two mayors. A few judges. A couple of attorneys with their wives. She shook away her thoughts, refusing to let those agents ruin her Christmas. *It's lies. All of it!*

Guillermo slipped an arm around her waist and pulled her into his side. She studied his waves of cobalt hair, his confident, million-dollar smile, and his black, gentle eyes. It simply couldn't be true.

He held something toward her. "And now, my Christmas present for you."

She stared at his gift. It was a box, a black velvet box. Her breath caught—a *ring?*—though she dismissed the notion almost immediately. The box was too large, too elongated to be a ring. Still, her heart sped up as she gently pried it open.

"Do you like it?" Guillermo asked softly.

She looked up at him and then back at her gift. How could she not? It was a necklace, pure platinum, and every inch around were delicate diamonds. It would have been rude to count, but her bulging eyes did anyway. Twelve diamonds. The necklace wasn't haughty or overdone, but . . . *diamonds!* She hardly dare touch it.

"May I?"

Guillermo grinned as he moved behind her. When he finished with the clasp, he turned and kissed her in front of his thirty distinguished visitors. They responded with grand applause. And with his kiss, the last of her doubt melted away. She didn't deserve him, she never would, but somehow he thought she did.

"*Feliz Navidad, hermosa,*" he whispered in her ear.

She smiled. "Merry Christmas, *amor.*"

Long after the guests had left or retired to their rooms, she sat in front of a full-length mirror admiring her necklace. Her mom had made a comment before leaving, saying she had a "new sparkle" about her. Looking in the mirror, she couldn't see anything different in her face, but her cheeks were tired from smiling. That had to be a good sign.

Leaning forward, she admired her other Christmas gift. A black sweater, hand-knit, gracefully fit around her petite frame, complimenting the diamond necklace perfectly. Her mother had devoted every spare moment since Thanksgiving trying to finish it. Guillermo said the black brought out her dark eyes. She wasn't sure if her eyes stood out any more now than when she'd been wearing her ruby red dress earlier, but all she knew was that she felt happy. And if things went how she hoped and dreamed, this would be only the first of many perfect Christmases. That brought another smile to her lips.

"Augustina?"

Her head came up. "I'm up here, mi amor," she called back.

"AUGUSTINA!"

She whirled at the sound of alarm in Guillermo's voice. She left the mirror and flew through his spacious cabin to meet him and Salvador at the bottom of the spiral staircase. The sight of the two of them, eyes blazing, brought her up short. "What, amor? What is it?"

Guillermo took a menacing step toward her. "What have you done!" he yelled in her face.

Stunned, she fell back. In the two years she had known Guillermo, he'd never, *ever,* raised his voice. "What?" she asked half as loud. "What is it?"

He lunged, hand flashing, and in one powerful move, ripped off the necklace. She cried out as the diamonds tore across her skin. "How could you do this to me!" he roared. He turned and hurled the necklace against the wall.

She stared at the small heap. "What?" her voice quivered, near to tears. "What did I do?"

Suddenly he was searching through a ruby red purse—hers—and in an instant, he shoved something in her face. Frightened and confused, she squinted, trying to make out the small object. It was tiny, the size of a watch battery, only square. She was sure she'd never seen it before. "I don't know wh—"

Her stomach lurched. *The agents!* she breathed.

"What did you do!" he roared again.

She watched Guillermo's fist form around the tiny object, the FBI's listening device. She could see the fury in his eyes, yet she still refused to believe what was coming. *Not Guillermo,* she thought. *Not the man that I—*

Bright lights exploded. She spiraled backward, hit the hard tile, and everything went black.

CHAPTER 1

The Dawn

When she first awoke, she wasn't sure her eyes had opened. A thick blackness surrounded her. She blinked, verifying that indeed her eyes were open, just seeing nothing. The darkness was suffocating and began to drag her in. She battled against it, but suddenly couldn't find air to breathe. Frantic, she thrashed her head. The blackness moved. Feeling a small glimpse of freedom, she shoved a heavy blanket from her face and took in several deep gulps of air.

Her eyes flew through her semidark surroundings, trying to make sense of them. Log walls. A large, dark window. Both unfamiliar. From the bumps pushing painfully into her shoulder, she discerned she was on a couch, albeit a lumpy one.

She struggled to come up with an explanation, but her mind was covered in a thick haze of its own. It was heavy. Sluggish. *Where am I?* she asked, as she blinked slower and slower. *The ski lodge?* A few more blinks. *Too small. A cabin?* Then something registered. Her left eye was only opening halfway with each blink. Not only that, but it throbbed and pulsed painfully.

Something wasn't right . . .

Her eye. The dark, unfamiliar cabin. Her thoughts sped up, remembering the party. The listening device. Guillermo's rage. In a torrent, her memories flooded back. Waking up in the locked room. The storm. The mountain. The truck. All of it rushed back in crystal clear memories. And with the memories came the terror, the blinding terror that sent her running into the blizzard in the first place. She'd only meant to stop a second in the truck, long enough to warm up, but now . . .

Where am I? she asked, heart pounding.

Yet there was an even more terrifying question. *Who found me?* The sound of her pursuers was like wolves hunting for prey, chasing her through that storm.

"You're as good as dead!"

She didn't know who had yelled it—FBI or Guillermo—nor had she stopped to find out. All that mattered was that she'd lost them. At least . . . she thought she had. Now that she was lying in a dark cabin, she was no longer certain. One thing she was certain of, though, was that she had to escape. Fast.

She rolled onto her side and choked back a scream. Pain. Everywhere.

She quickly ran through her damaged parts. Arms, legs, back: all stiff from trudging through the snow. Her stomach was in knots, her shoulder felt out of place—there was no memory for that one—and then there was her face . . . She reached for her left eye, wincing before touching it. She hadn't seen the damage yet, but she could feel it. The memory of Guillermo's blinding rage threatened to swallow her whole, but she shoved it aside to finish her assessment. Her head. Hot. Feverish. And pounding like it never had before.

Pretty bleak, but it could've been worse. She could be in a snowbank with a hole in her head. Or worse, still locked up at Guillermo's. *Yes,* she convinced herself, *it could be a lot worse.* With that knowledge, she ignored all the pain and dizziness, pushed the heavy blanket off, and sat up.

The dark silence was shattered by the sound of an animal scurrying across the floor. Before she could flinch, she was nose to nose with a giant dog, breathing its horrible breath in her face. The dog panted heavily, waiting for her to acknowledge its presence. She didn't move. Didn't breathe.

Don't bark, she begged silently. *Please . . . don't . . . bark.*

As if to spite her, the dog started barking. Her eyes searched the darkness, desperate for an exit, but it was so dark—so ominously dark—and the dog grew louder by the second.

A door cracked open behind her.

She froze, wondering if her life were over. Guillermo was going to attack her again. Or it was the FBI here to arrest her. It didn't matter who was behind that door, she knew it was over. Falling back on the lumpy couch, she smothered herself with the blanket.

"Rocky!" a man whispered urgently. "Come!"

The barking dog left its post. She braced herself for an assault, or at the very least, a barrage of questions from her unknown captor, but the only sound was of the dog's paws clipping across a wooden floor, followed by a door shutting quietly behind both of them.

In the returning silence, she raced through the only options she could find: fight or flight.

So far she'd taken the flight option, breaking out of Guillermo's cabin and running as far and as fast as her frozen body could take her, but was she any better off? She wasn't tied up—or locked up either. But her legs felt thirty pounds heavier than normal. They would be slow. Too slow. *Fight, then?* Even as the idea entered her head she knew it was ridiculous. Physical strength wasn't a quality she possessed even at peak health. And now that she was beaten, bruised, exhausted, and starting what felt like a full-blown fever, there was no way she'd be able to take on anyone, man or beast. *Run it is,* she groaned. *Again.*

Her eyes threatened to spill, but she gritted her teeth. This wasn't the time to fall apart. Instead she convinced herself that she really did have to plunge back into a blinding, freezing blizzard. *I'm stronger than I think. I'm stronger than I think.* And on the third time of chanting it to herself, she began to move. Up. Slowly. All she needed was a door—preferably a back one. With ears pricked for the slightest noise, she rolled up to a sitting position. When all stayed quiet, she scanned the rest of the dark room. It was a large family room of sorts with a kitchen disappearing in the distance. Definitely a cabin. Possibly the one by the truck she'd taken refuge in.

Then she spotted it. A glass door to the outside.

Feeling every damaged part, she pushed herself to stand up. Her head spun, her stomach as well, but she planted her feet, pinched the rim of her nose, and when the room stopped spinning, began to creep toward that door. Inch by painful inch, she slid across the cold, wooden floor, knowing that taking five minutes to escape was better than alerting the beast in the next room and never escaping at all.

Halfway there, she realized her feet were cold—her *bare* feet. She stopped. Between that and the dog, she might as well have been tied up. No one would think she was crazy enough to escape without shoes. Not in knee-deep snow. Little did they know she was beyond crazy . . .

. . . she was surviving.

As she neared the door, she spotted a large pile of something. *Boots!* Even more amazing was that her shoes—her incredibly thin, and probably still soaking wet shoes—were lying on top. Without a thought, she bypassed them for the nearest pair of boots. They were ridiculously big and awkward on her feet, but awkward she could deal with. It was frozen that wasn't much fun.

A smile tugged at the corners of her mouth. She was going to escape again. And this time so easily! The feeling of elation surged adrenaline through her aching muscles.

As she reached for the door handle, a small, green light caught her eye. It was shining from a box that resembled an alarm system. *No!* she corrected, *It is an alarm system!* She read and reread the green screen, trying to make it untrue. Five letters. One blaring message:

ARMED

She whirled around, scrambling for another answer. Windows. Stairs. But each option produced the same ending. The alarm would sound, the dog would outrun her, whoever was holding her captive would come, and then . . . The end of life as she knew it.

Whatever hatred she felt for the dog grew tenfold. Without it, she might have made it, outrun her new captor before help could arrive, but now she was a prisoner. Again.

The defeat was paralyzing. Tears ran down her hot cheeks. Time rewound to the bottom of that spiral staircase, Guillermo's fist cocked, black eyes blazing, and suddenly nothing mattered anymore. All she wanted was sleep.

She followed her path back to the couch, taking half the time, and collapsed into a heap right back where she'd started. The emotions clouding her mind were such that it took a minute lying on that uncomfortable couch before she remembered the awkward boots. The tears that had stopped, started again, but there was no way she was making another long journey. Not for a stupid pair of boots. She yanked them off, pulled the blanket over her head, and welcomed the unconsciousness that quickly followed.

CHAPTER 2

Kevin Hancock watched the nameless girl, curious if she'd ever wake up. She was twenty-something and looked—quite frankly—awful. Not in an ugly sort of way, she was anything but. More like she'd been through a war and then some. Her left eye was swollen blackish-blue, and she had blood smeared over her nose and lower cheek. It was a horribly disturbing image, especially in the full light of morning. He and his buddies had spent half the night speculating what had happened to her, with the general consensus being a drunken boyfriend, but she never woke to confirm or deny their suspicions.

Kevin glanced out the window to what was already a gorgeous day in the Montana mountains. He was the only one up in the cabin, the only morning person of his friends. He didn't mind, though. That gave him time to finish the photo shoot that had been interrupted by the strange girl's appearance yesterday.

Taking the stairs two at a time, he tiptoed into his room and grabbed his camera—his pride and joy—without waking Josh. Coming back down the stairs, he stopped by the sleeping girl again. *That eye!* he cringed. *Yikes!* With camera in hand, he decided to document it. He knew it was a little intrusive, but that kind of thing had never stopped him before. Besides, a little evidence might come in handy some day. She'd thank him later.

He carefully moved the blanket from her face and began snapping pictures. Up shots. Downward angles. Zooms in and out. The whole works.

When he felt he'd done his citizenly duty, he crept past her into the kitchen and reached for his boots. Only they weren't in the pile. He twisted around, but couldn't see them by the front door either. Impatient, he pulled on Josh's, pressed a few buttons on the keypad, and entered the winter wonderland.

The sun was blinding, reflecting off each new flake of snow. He shielded his eyes until they adjusted, then he just stared. The view from Sam's cabin was spectacular, providing a stunning panorama of the mountains just outside of Glacier National Park. The sky was an intense blue, and to contrast the rich color above was the complete absence of it below. Pure white covered everything. Pines. Leafless aspens. Everything had disappeared overnight under a thick blanket of snow. He flipped his camera to wide-screen to fit it all in. He wasn't a good photographer—not yet—but he hoped with a little practice to turn it into a career someday. At least that's what he told his wife, Amy, who somewhat indulged him in his little obsession.

A minute later, Rocky pawed on the glass. Kevin opened the door and Sam's black lab burst outside, running headfirst into the new piles of fluff. Kevin was hit with a strange wave of déjà vu as he watched the dog bound around the side of the cabin. But unlike yesterday, the dog didn't stop at Sam's truck. If it hadn't been for Rocky climbing up the driver's door, Kevin would have never left his photo shoot to investigate and, incidentally, the nameless girl might be frozen inside there even now. Dead.

What was she thinking? Even now, he couldn't make sense of it all. She had no coat. No boots. They probably should have called the cops right away, but they'd only been in Montana a few hours. Plus without a landline at the cabin and that far out of cell phone range, they would've had to drive down to the ski lodge, which none of them were willing to do in the storm. The next logical thing was to bring her inside. At least that way she wouldn't freeze to death.

Speaking of freezing . . .

He blew on his hands. With a few last shots, he slung his camera over his shoulder and went back inside the warm cabin.

"Hey, Kev," Sam called softly from behind the fridge door. "I guess she's still asleep, huh?" For being the brainy, medical student he was, Sam had the tendency to state the obvious. Kevin didn't bother responding.

"What do we do?" Sam asked as he grabbed some things from the fridge.

"Wait." At least, that's what the four of them had decided last night.

Kevin pulled a stool up to the counter and began scanning his photos. When he got to the pictures of the girl, he stopped. "Man. Look at that," he said, showing Sam a particularly gruesome one.

"Periorbital hematoma," Sam said, sounding every bit the med student. "Do you think we should ice it again?"

"Naw. Let her sleep. She's gonna wake up with quite the headache."

Sam frowned as he peeked into the great room. "Yes, she is."

She woke the second time to a coughing spell that shook her head to toe, but once her throat was clear, she was wide-awake. The haze in her head cleared quickly, helped by the bright morning sun, but pain replaced the haze. She had a headache the size of Texas.

Quickly she rechecked her surroundings—definitely an unknown cabin—then listened. There were several voices coming from another room, faint and semicoherent.

Several? she nearly cried. Not good.

"How much longer do we wait?" one was saying. Another responded in an unintelligible mutter. "Maybe we *should* wake her up," a third one said. "She could have people out looking for her."

As they continued discussing her fate, she counted the different voices. There were three at least. All male. None familiar. Suddenly the implication of a newfound danger hit her: locked in a cabin with three unknown men. She had taken a self-defense class in college, but was she really prepared to use it? She brushed her swollen eye. Obviously not. *But I wasn't prepared before,* she told herself. *Now I am.* Somehow that wasn't comforting.

"I say we call the police," one of the men said, bringing her back to the conversation.

No! she yelled silently. *No cops!*

"Either way," a new voice added, "I'm done waiting. I'm outta here."

Four. That made four men. Her silent scream was drowned out by the dog barking outside. It wanted back in. Which meant someone had let it out . . . which meant the alarm . . .

She started to sit just as the conversation stopped abruptly. A door opened, and she heard heavy footsteps coming into the room. But instead of going to the dog like they were supposed to, they headed right toward her. Terrified, she lay motionless as a man came close enough to her couch that she could smell his aftershave. Breathing steadily, she kept her eyes closed as she frantically tried to remember how to incapacitate an attacker.

"Hey." He shook her shoulder a little. "Hey. Wake up."

Faking something between a drug overdose and a coma, she lay perfectly still. The shaking stopped, and she heard his footsteps head into the area she assumed was the kitchen. Another set followed along with quiet whispers. Then she heard the outside door open. With a burst of winter air, the two men left and the dog flew inside. It ran over and jumped up on her feet. She winced, but held her breath, waiting for the last two men to leave. The huge dog quickly made itself at home on her legs. She tried to kick the stupid thing, but it didn't budge, and instead looked to be hibernating for the winter.

Feeling even more trapped, she waited on the lumpy couch, listening. She could hear at least two men in the kitchen, fidgeting quietly behind her.

The longer she waited, the harder it was to keep her mind from wandering. To Christmas. To Guillermo. Still trying to make sense of it all.

Shortly after receiving Guillermo's extravagant Christmas gift, her mom had leaned over and asked one simple question.

"Diamonds, Augustina?"

At the time, she'd tried not to bristle, but it was inevitable. Between the meeting with the agents and trying to play hostess to the upper class of northwestern Montana, she'd been on edge most of dinner. Not to mention, she didn't need any more reminders from her mom about how badly she and Guillermo were mismatched. "Yes, *Mamá,*" she had whispered back. "Be nice, please. Guillermo bought this wine just for you. It's from Argentina, from the year you were born."

"Nineteen-eighty?" her mother had asked in mock innocence.

Though Augustina had laughed, she quickly shot back, "You wish."

Her mom frowned. "Since when do Dawson women wear diamond necklaces, Augustina? Or entertain city officials and drink forty-year-old wine?"

"Fifty-three. You're fifty-three now, Mamá, and there's a first time for everything. Great food, Karina," she had gushed to the passing chef, hoping to derail her mother's bickering. "The *hallaca* is absolutely divine."

Guillermo even left a side conversation to agree with her. "The food is wonderful, is it not? What do you think of the hallaca, Marcela?"

"It's divine," her mom answered, flat as a pancake.

Augustina had kicked her mom under the table—not hard, but hard enough. Yet it hadn't stopped her. As soon as Guillermo was distracted, her mother picked up the lecture where she left off. "Your father couldn't even afford to give me a diamond for our wedding."

"And why exactly did you marry him?"

Even now, she felt bad about the below-the-belt comment, but at the time, comparing Guillermo to her dad had been an insult of the highest order. Her father was a pure-bred, Montana-grown, lousy cowboy of a man. A man neither Dawson woman was very fond of.

Sufficiently squelched, her mother had sat back and pretended to enjoy the hallaca. It wasn't even two bites later when the guilt won out.

Mother and daughter were best friends, had been their whole lives, but sometimes the two sharp-tongued women let their playful banter get out of hand. There was no excuse for that. Not on Christmas.

"Sorry, Mamá," Augustina had whispered. "I just want you to like him."

Her mom smiled warmly. "I do, *hija mia.* I really do."

Lying on the uncomfortable couch, it was easy to get lost in the memories, wondering if her mom would answer the same way if she had known what would happen to her daughter a mere hour later.

Mamá, she cried silently, *I'm in trouble.*

Infuriated by her sudden weakness, she decided it was time to quit whining about her life and do something. The men were still puttering quietly behind her, but she was sure that with the element of surprise, she could bolt out that door before they knew what hit them. If only the stupid dog would forget about her and quit licking her hand . . .

She flicked its drippy nose. By the time she realized her mistake, it was too late. The heavy dog jumped onto her chest and started barking excitedly. *If I had a gun right now—s*he didn't have time to finish that thought. Footsteps were back, coming at an alarming speed, though they were quickly drowned out by the pounding of her heart and the hyper-ventilating canine crushing her ribs.

"Rocky!" a man shouted next to her. "Get off her! Sam, grab your dog. I think she's awake."

There was a loud whistle, followed by immediate relief as the monstrous dog leaped off.

"Hey," the man said a little louder. "Hey, are you awake?"

There was no hiding her consciousness. Her face had contorted in pain as she tried not to be mauled by the dog, and this man had witnessed it. Slowly, her right eye fluttered open followed by her swollen left. Everything was a blur for a moment before she found a face close to her own.

The face smiled. "Well, it's about time."

CHAPTER 3

The man kneeling in front of her looked twenty-something, a little younger than she was, with dark hair and blue questioning eyes. "Are you okay?" he asked.

Part of her wanted to punch him and run, reverting back to the fight or flight method of dealing with things. Fight *and* flight, she corrected, with the *and* being a dreadfully blunt word. As he waited for her response, she sized him up. The guy was big, but not huge. Tall, maybe. But that still left the other one and he could be a sumo wrestler for all she knew.

His smile began to fade. "You okay? We've been worried about you."

She needed to sit, to check her surroundings. Slowly she pushed herself up, then instantly regretted it as her head screamed at her for making it change positions. It punished her further by making the room spin violently around his face.

Then, like a broken record, he asked again, "Are you okay?"

What do you think! She was being hunted, was now lost, and her head felt like it had been hit with a bulldozer, leaving little room to find any solution to it all. Her eyes found the front door of the cabin, but it was fifteen long feet away. She'd never make it before someone stopped her.

Out of options, she did something completely juvenile.

"*Lo siento,*" she said softly. "*No comprendo inglés.*" The shock registered on his face, but she kept going, keeping her voice as innocent as possible. "*Dónde estoy?*"

"Uh . . . you speak Spanish." It wasn't a question. The dark-haired guy glanced sideways. "Say something to her, Sam."

Only then did she notice a blond guy crouched next to the other. "*Hola, me llamo Sam,*" he greeted warmly. "*Este es Josh,*" he added, introducing the first guy as well.

No! she cried silently, *NO!* She had banked on the fact that they wouldn't understand her, helping her avoid all questions and sneak out without them calling the cops. Now what?

The blond's face clouded in concern. "*Estas bien? Qué pasó?*"

Mourning the loss of her cover, it took her a minute to answer: *What happened?* Deciding to keep it simple, she said, "*Me perdí.*"

The dark-haired one looked to his friend for translation.

"She got lost," Sam explained before turning back to her. "*Donde quieres ir? Tenemos una camioneta. No tenemos un teléfono aquí, pero hay uno bajo la montaña.*"

Her eyes widened. *No phone here?* She worked to keep her face impassive, but eliminating all calls to the cops had her soaring. Maybe escape was possible after all. She was smaller than the two guys, but she was fast. Fast was good.

"What are you saying?" the dark-haired guy asked impatiently.

"I offered to take her somewhere," Sam said. "I told her that we have a truck."

"I think she remembers the truck."

"Right." Sam gave her a brief, apologetic smile before finishing. "I told her we don't have a phone at the cabin, but we can take her to one down the mountain."

"And?"

Sam shrugged and both turned back to wait for her answer. But with the pounding headache, she couldn't think straight to respond. The two guys looked harmless enough at the moment. It was tempting to take them up on their offer. A ride somewhere—without calls—she just had to decide where. Unfortunately, each option was worse than the one before. Truth was, she had no idea where to go or who to call. Not the cops— they'd alert the FBI. Not the ski lodge—they'd alert Guillermo. Not back to her apartment. Not even to her mom's. Guillermo knew it all. And even if he didn't, the feds would.

Then something strange happened. She started to cry. It was odd for her to cry in front of strangers—another sign she wasn't at full capacity—but she couldn't help it. Her head screamed under the new emotion. Squeezing her eyes shut, she willed the tears to stop. It took a second for them to obey, but once they did, she opened them again, ready to respond. Yet her poor observers were even more dumbfounded than before.

"*Lo siento,*" she apologized quickly, "*Estoy muy cansada . . . y pienso que estoy enferma. Necesito ayuda. Pienso . . .*" She stopped herself, begging for a plan, a story, anything at all. How she got lost, where she needed to go.

While she was struggling to think, the dog sat up, ears pointed forward and, straight from her worst nightmare, the other two other men walked back in. They were in their early twenties like the others. One guy was tall and lanky, the other short and stocky with wild curly hair.

"We forgot our—Hey!" the tall one interrupted himself, "You woke up! How are ya?" He didn't look nearly as concerned as the first two were as he smiled at her. "I betcha got yourself a nasty headache, right?"

She didn't respond since she wasn't supposed to understand—not that she would have anyway.

"She doesn't speak English," the dark-haired guy said for her. "Sam's talking to her."

The tall guy laughed, but not at her. "So your mission paid off after all, eh, Sam?"

Ignoring the dig, Sam introduced them. "*Estes son Kevin y Trevor. Nuestros amigos.*"

She blinked at each of the new faces, somewhat acknowledging them. Four friends. Four voices. How many more were coming?

"*Cómo te llamas?*" Sam asked her.

My name? she repeated silently. It was a simple enough question, although it could potentially lead her back into trouble. She was speaking Spanish, but wasn't sure she wanted them to have the name Guillermo used. But would the feds use her American name when looking for her?

While Sam waited for her answer, the other three glanced back and forth between her—the woman who refused to answer the simplest of questions—and each other. Her tears welled up again, but there was no way she was going to let them escape again. *Focus,* she begged. *A name. Maybe just a first name.*

"My name is Augustina," she said softly. "Uh, I mean, Sadie."

Shock appeared simultaneously on the four faces.

Her heart stopped. *They know!* Guillermo had already come hunting her, or the FBI had, and now they were going to turn her over for a hefty reward.

The dark-haired guy was the first to recover. "Wait. You speak English?"

Her lashes lowered to her hot cheeks. Spanish and English flowed so naturally through her head, she barely noticed when she switched back and forth. It took several seconds before she could meet their stunned faces and then the wall of windows spun as a new dizziness set in.

"Uh, Sadie, was it?" the tall, lanky one said. "You want something to eat? You don't look so good."

She shook her head, only adding to the shifting movements in her vision. Unable to stay upright, she lay back down. The uncomfortable couch no longer felt so uncomfortable as she tried to hide herself in its folds.

"Seriously," he pressed, "you look like you're gonna pass out. Water, maybe?"

"No," she whispered. "I'm fine."

"Can we call someone for you then?" the dark-haired one asked, still hovering just inches away. "The cops, maybe? It looks like you got beat up," he added softly.

"No," she moaned. "Please, no."

He stole a nervous glance at the others. "Can we take you somewhere then, or call someone for you? We can drive you down to the lodge."

Sadie hid behind her eyelids, trying to force a solution out of her jumbled thoughts. But shutting her eyes focused all her pain to her temples, and the haze from before began to seep back in. And through it all, she could only see one object. A tiny object. The one that had ruined her life. *Mamá,* she cried again, *I'm in trouble.*

Somewhere through the fog she heard one of them say, "I think she's asleep again," and taking the path of least resistance, she returned to sweet oblivion.

CHAPTER 4

Josh Young volunteered to stay behind. His friends didn't want to miss any more potential slope time—girl or no girl, they had a lot of skiing to fit into their all-too-short week—and had taken off soon after she conked out. But Josh had been the first one Sadie had seen, the first to talk to her, and now he wanted to make sure that when she woke again—whenever that would be—he was there to help.

He spent some time working on some MBA applications in the kitchen, but tired of that quickly and headed over to the couch opposite Sadie. Placing his stockinged feet on the coffee table in front of him, he propped his laptop on his chest and searched for something to listen to. He had a wide variety of music on his laptop, from The Beatles to Harry Connick Jr., from the Mormon Tabernacle Choir to John Mayer. Not a lick of country, though. That was one genre gone bad in his opinion. Two days after Christmas he was also done with holiday music, so he settled on Rachmaninoff's Piano Concerto No. 2, wanting something relaxing—and wordless—so he could keep churning out his essays. Josh nearly grabbed his headphones, but decided that with all the other noise Sadie had slept through, it wouldn't matter. If anything, a little music might rouse her.

He found it strange that they still knew so little about the girl asleep on Sam's couch. Trevor, being typical Trevor, had gone on and on about her: her long, dark, curly hair, her "deep, mysterious eyes." She was beautiful, no question, but Josh was only interested in that left cheek. The logical explanation was that she had been attacked by someone, though it could have been caused by something less violent, like hitting it against something. However, from all her other odd behavior, he highly doubted it. It was repulsive to think of someone hitting her. A boyfriend? An angry boss? A complete stranger for all they knew.

A disturbing picture suddenly popped in his mind. His girlfriend, Megan, with a bruised eye like Sadie's. It was an extremely disconcerting image—and one that thankfully didn't exist in reality—and he quickly shook it off, wondering what Megan was doing right then. Probably hitting all the after-Christmas sales with her mom. Josh felt guilty leaving her the day after Christmas when they already had so little time together, but Megan understood this annual ski trip he took with his buddies. The four guys had been best friends since the fourth grade, and Megan had accepted that they were a package deal. Now that Kevin's wife was making an effort to hang out with her, Josh hoped the package was easier to live with.

A brief coughing spell from the other couch brought his head around. He jumped, nearly dropping his laptop when he saw Sadie awake and staring right at him.

"Hey," he said, sitting up quickly.

Her coughing grew more pronounced. Setting aside his laptop, Josh ran into the kitchen and grabbed a glass of water. "You want some medicine or something?" he asked as he handed it to her. "That cough sounds pretty bad."

"No, thanks," she replied softly. The water seemed to help calm down the cough.

Though he knew he was staring, he couldn't seem to look away. Sadie looked a lot worse when she was awake, showing just how swollen that left eye was. Unaware of his scrutiny, her dark eyes stayed on the front door.

"Can I drive you somewhere?" he asked again. "You said you were lost. We're just about three miles from the ski lodge. Where were you headed?"

She didn't respond and, for a moment, he wondered how well she understood English. Then he remembered she'd spoken without any accent before, so he tried again. "The other guys have the truck right now, but they'll be back from skiing in a minute and then we can take you wherever you need. The lodge, maybe? Or a friend's cabin?" he tried when she still said nothing. Even then, the next closest cabin was almost a half a mile down the road. She really was lost.

Her gaze lowered to her hands. They were scratched, dirty, and slightly bloody like the rest of her, but for some reason she looked surprised to see them in such disarray.

"You want to wash up while we wait?" he offered. "There's a bathroom down there."

She nodded, though she winced as well. "Actually, my head is killing me. Do you have any ibuprofen?"

"Yeah, I'm sure there's some around." He kept talking as he went into the kitchen. "Sam's dad is a doctor and keeps a stash of medicine up here. This is Sam's cabin by the way—his family's cabin. Sam's the blond guy with spiked hair. Great guy. Great family. I'm Josh, by the way," he added, as he came back with a couple of bottles—cough medicine and ibuprofen.

Sadie took it from him and motioned to his computer. "What are you listening to?"

He had forgotten his music was still playing. "Oh, it's a piano concerto. One of Rachmaninoff's. The second—and best—actually."

One of her dark eyebrows rose slightly.

"I . . . was in the mood for some classical music," he tried to explain. It sounded lame, even to him. "My mom plays a lot of classical music around the house. It kinda grows on you after awhile." Wondering how he got so off-topic, he shut down the music and refocused.

He didn't want to pry, but at the same time, he couldn't help himself.

"I know it's none of my business, but . . . it looks like you got beat up. Can we call the cops or—"

Her head snapped up. "You're right. It *is* none of your business."

"I—I'm sorry," he stuttered. "I didn't mean . . ."

She sighed, her eyes dropping to her filthy hands again. "It's okay. It's just . . . I'm not really sure where to go or who to call. The person that . . ." She chewed her bottom lip. "He knows where I live, my family, and friends, and . . . I . . . I'm just kind of . . ."

Though she struggled to admit it, Sadie confirmed his suspicions. She wasn't lost. She was running. Maybe what she really needed was a restraining order. His dad was a cop and could easily help her set one up if needed, but for now . . . "The bathroom's over that way," he pointed again. "If you want to get cleaned up first, we can talk."

Sadie nodded and then tried to stand. She didn't get far. Josh stepped forward and grabbed her damp arm to help her up. Once she was standing, he realized just how tiny she was, maybe five feet tall, with a petite figure at that, making her seem even more fragile than before.

Damp? he suddenly realized. Sure enough, Sadie's black sweater was damp, and she was shivering. When they'd brought her in from Sam's truck, she'd been wet head to toe—not surprising since she wasn't wearing any gear to shield her from the blizzard. At the time, they'd taken off her wet shoes and socks and thrown the heaviest blanket on top of her, hoping to warm her up. Then Sam had cranked up the heat, making a miserable night for the rest of them. But apparently it hadn't worked. She was still wet, and Josh felt horrible.

"I'll go grab you something to change into," he said as he ran up to the loft.

He searched through his things, not really sure what to grab. He checked Trevor's stuff as well—the shortest of the bunch—but found nothing. By the time he made it downstairs with a pair of his own gray sweatpants and hoodie, Sadie was halfway to the bathroom.

"You sure?" she asked, hesitantly taking the sweats from him.

"Yeah. You're cold enough. You need to get dry."

She tried to smile, but it showed more of her fatigue than she probably realized.

Once in the bathroom, Sadie set the pile of sweats aside, sat on the toilet lid, and laid her head on the nearest counter, wondering how long before the medicine kicked in. Her plan no longer involved escape. Not only were the four guys not holding her hostage, or making any calls, they seemed anxious to help her get wherever she wanted—wherever that was—or call whomever she needed, or . . .

Please, her brain begged, *don't make me think anymore.* So she sat somewhat comatose and took herself to the most soothing, relaxing place she could think of. Her lake. Whitefish. She imagined the surrounding pines swaying gently in the wind, the soft breeze cooling her feverish skin, and she pictured herself washing her swollen face with the icy glacier-fed water. With each detail, more of the pain dissipated just like she knew it would. Whenever she needed solace and comfort, Whitefish Lake had been there, offering its healing power, and it was that same lake that now brought her the calm serenity so severely lacking in her life.

When the pounding in her head was reduced to a mild thumping, she sat up and glanced around the large bathroom. It was a beautiful bathroom. Kind of a strange thing to think, considering, but with the fancy stone etching, ornate mahogany cabinetry, and a huge Jacuzzi tub, it looked like something from *Better Homes and Gardens.* The bathroom matched the rest of the cabin, spacious in feel, luxurious in décor. It was obvious that Sam's family had a lot of money. Not that it surprised her. This part of Montana sported an abundance of beautiful cabins. The most beautiful of all being—

Guillermo's face popped in her mind, and suddenly she hated the bathroom, she hated fancy cabins, and most especially she hated money— money that made the FBI suspicious and that gave rich people the right to act any way they pleased. *I do love medicine, however,* she mused. She felt her fight coming back, and it felt good.

Ready to clean up and get on with her life, she stood and turned on the sink. Then she looked up and gasped. *That can't be me!* The face staring back at her was yellow—sallow actually—with a large red welt on her upper cheek. But even worse was above that. Her entire left eye was encompassed in dark purple. She knew the bruise was bad, but seeing it herself made her sick. And if her eye was that bad . . . She lifted her now-filthy black sweater to check on the injury she suspected on the couch. Sure enough, just below the shoulder blade was an enormous bruise, but unlike her eye, she couldn't remember how she got it.

She leaned over the sink and traced a small red scratch at the base of her neck. It was a lot smaller than she thought it would be. Apparently Guillermo ripping off the necklace caused more emotional damage than physical.

Sighing and near tears, she examined her hair. It was pitiful. A ragged, plastered, sweaty mess. She combed the dark snarls with her fingers, trying to work out the knots, but in its current state, she didn't make any progress. Quietly, she cracked open a few bathroom drawers. The first drawer held guy stuff—razors, shaving cream, aftershave—reminding her that she was intruding on someone's privacy. The second produced a brush. That was it. There was no makeup, nothing that could hide the violence on her face. She ran the brush through her hair several times. It helped a little. A very little.

The Jacuzzi called to her. If using a brush was intrusive, using someone's expensive tub went well beyond, but in her present state she no longer cared. She wanted as few reminders from Christmas as possible, which meant returning to a stronger, cleaner version of herself. Crossing the room, she turned the water to the hottest setting.

The three friends hadn't skied for long, just a couple of hours, but Sam was anxious to get back and check on things. Specifically Sadie. One step inside the cabin, however, and his face fell. "She left?"

Josh looked up from his laptop. "No. She's still here. Just in the bathroom. I think she's showering or something because she's been in there awhile." Then he motioned to the pile of gear Kevin dumped by the front door. "How's the snow?"

"Perfect!" Trevor answered for all of them. "Tons of fresh powder. You missed out."

Josh shrugged and went back to work. Sam pulled up a chair next to him, intensely curious. "So did you talk to her? Did she say anything else?"

"Not really. Whoever did that to her has her too scared to say much. Every time I offered to help she clammed up, like she has nowhere to go, nowhere to run. My gut instinct is to call the cops."

"Typical Josh comment," Trevor snorted as he walked to the fridge and pulled out the milk. Thankfully he also pulled out a glass. Some habits were hard to break with Trevor, even after all these years. Then he poured himself a bowl of Lucky Charms, oblivious to the fact that he was eating cereal at four in the afternoon.

"Well, what would you have her do?" Josh asked Trevor in return. "Go back to whoever attacked her?"

"No." Trevor shoved a huge bite in his mouth. "Let her stay here for a while. I'll take good care of her. Trevor takes good care of all the ladies," he added with a grin.

"Typical Trevor comment," Josh muttered.

"His idea isn't half-bad actually," Kevin said, jumping into the conversation. "Sadie's obviously running from someone, and if she doesn't want the cops involved, maybe she could hide out here."

Josh shook his head. "No. No way. In case you've forgotten, we're guests of the Jacksons and there are certain rules we've all agreed to and—"

"No beer," Trevor cut in. "Thanks a lot, Sam."

Sam ignored him. So did Josh as he continued, "—the 'No Women' rule is pretty much at the top of the list. Besides, Sadie needs help. Real help."

"Exactly," Kevin pressed, "so let's help. I don't think Sam's parents would mind if we let her stay; in fact, I bet they'd do the same. Besides, it's not like she's a girlfriend of any of you losers, so I think letting her stay here is harmless. Right, Trevor?"

Trevor crossed his heart exaggeratedly. "Right."

Josh rolled his eyes. "What I meant, is Sadie needs some help, some long-lasting, permanent help, so something like this doesn't happen again. If she's uncomfortable talking to the police, I was thinking my dad could hook her up with a lawyer who can work up a restraining order or something. He could even set her up with someone she can talk to for support."

"It's a freaking black eye!" Trevor cried. "Now suddenly she needs a cop, a lawyer, *and* a shrink? I'm telling you, all she needs is a place to hide out and a few karate lessons."

Josh sighed. "What do you think, Sam?"

Sam shrugged. It was his cabin and therefore, in a way, his decision. He wanted to help Sadie, yet there was something intimidating about her. He wasn't sure if it was the eye or the beautiful woman beneath, but having her there made the walls of his cabin shrink. And really, they didn't know if she wanted a place to—

"Oh, Sam doesn't know anything," Trevor said. "And Josh takes everything too seriously. I say we let her hang with us for awhile. It would be"—he grinned—"the Christian thing to do."

"Since when have you cared about the Christian thing?" Josh pointed out.

"I just converted."

Kevin laughed. "I doubt you'd be such a Christian if she had a wart on her nose and a couple of long hairs growing out of her chin."

Trevor took another bite of cereal. "True. Good thing she doesn't or we'd have to turn her over to the cops like Josh wants to. But I say leave the cops, lawyers, and shrinks out of it. I say we keep her. Right, Sam? Good, Christian, loving, Mormon-of-a—"

"Sadie!" Josh called suddenly.

As one, they turned to see her standing in the hallway, her long, curly hair dripping down a pair of oversized-sweats. She was staring at the four of them. Wide-eyed. White-faced.

Sam quickly rewound the conversation wondering how much she'd heard. Obviously enough. He wanted to kick himself and his stupid friends for being so careless!

For several seconds, she didn't move and neither did they. Then totally and without warning, she took off. She flew through the kitchen past the four of them and was out the back door in a blur. Sam stared at the door. Just like that, she was gone.

Josh pushed away from the table, grabbed a pair of boots, and yelled, "Grab my coat!"

CHAPTER 5

She's crazy! That's all Josh could think as he ran after Sadie. Her hair was soaking wet, and she was running barefoot through two feet of snow. *Barefoot! She's insane! And fast!* Already she was off the deck and halfway around the cabin. Thankfully his long legs were clearing the snow faster than her short ones could. "Sadie, stop!"

In the second she slowed to check on him, he caught her by the arm. "Please. You can't—"

Her fist caught him in the gut. It wasn't a hard blow, but it certainly got his attention. And set her free. She took off again, but he stayed put, not wanting to scare her further. "Please!" he called. "It's fine if you leave, just please . . . take some boots. And my coat . . ." Josh turned just as Kevin came up behind him, heavy coat in hand. Josh waved both in a flag of surrender. "Please, Sadie. You'll freeze to death without something on your feet."

She slowed to a stop on the snow-covered driveway.

Seeing a small window of opportunity, Josh approached her, boots and coat still high in the air. He stopped five nonthreatening feet away. His friends moved past him to form a circle around her, but he quickly waved them back, knowing from his dad how aggressive that could be perceived by someone in her frame of mind. She was in survival mode and obviously not thinking clearly.

"We want to help you, Sadie," he continued carefully. "Just come back inside. Come on, your hair is wet and you're barefoot!" Even his enormous gray sweats looked pitifully thin against the frigid air. He shook his head, unable to comprehend the amount of fear to make a person do something like that. Already his feet were seizing up, and he was wearing thick socks.

"Josh is right," Sam said behind him. "Hypothermia will set in after ten minutes. Probably sooner. There's nothing around for a half a mile. Just let us help."

She turned then to face them. Her dark eyes, somewhat glazed over, stayed on Josh and his offering. "Please," he begged.

After what felt like an eternity, she finally stepped through the snow and took his stuff.

Seeing a bit of reasoning return to her, he decided to push. "Just let us take you somewhere. Sam's truck is back now so we can take you anywhere you want to go."

"Anywhere," Kevin added behind Josh. "You name it. Las Vegas . . . Zimbabwe . . . Seriously, we just want to help. Whatever we said in there—whatever *I* said in there—you have to know we didn't mean it. We're just being idiots. Especially this guy here."

Trevor was quick to agree. "Seriously. I was just messin' around in there. I didn't mean any of it. Don't listen to me. I'm just an idiot."

Sam was nodding vigorously. "He is. Trust me."

Her large eyes moved from person to person—not blinking, barely even focusing on their faces. Her breaths came in short, white puffs, but seemed to be slowing. "You don't understand," she whispered.

"I'm sure we don't," Josh agreed wholeheartedly, as he stood knee-deep in snow with a woman half-crazed with fear, willing to risk her life just to escape it. "Which is why we'll do whatever you tell us. Just don't hurt yourself, Sadie."

"Come on!" Kevin whined, bouncing from foot to foot. "I'm freezin' here! Unless you got some Ice Woman super powers, you gotta be cold, too."

She looked at Sam's cabin again and then nodded slowly.

Kevin watched Sadie curl up on a kitchen chair, knees to her chin and a heavy blanket wrapped around her shoulders. "I really am a normal person," she was saying quietly. "At least . . . I used to be."

No one was going to argue with her now. Not with all the eggshells they were walking on. Six months of marriage and Kevin knew when to talk to a woman and when to just plain shut up. And emotional female outbursts were *definitely* a time for a man to buckle down and shut his trap.

"I know it's probably hard to believe, I mean"—she sniffed back a few tears—"look at me."

She didn't have to tell them. They already were. Josh was on the chair next to her, also wrapped in a blanket, Sam was on a stool next to Kevin looking—quite frankly—scared to death. Trevor, however, was back at his spot with his bowl of Lucky Charms, watching Sadie like someone watches a Saturday night movie.

"You must think I'm crazy, but if you only knew me before . . ." She laid her head on her knees. "Maybe it wouldn't matter. Maybe you'd still think I was crazy. How else could I have ended up with someone like him? In a mess like this?"

"Do you need a place to stay?" Kevin asked without permission. Thankfully Sam immediately nodded his approval.

"No," she said into her knees.

The friends looked at each other. It was her move next. Kevin had expected her to come inside with a plan. Instead she had come inside and fallen apart. Not only that, but she was a walking contradiction. Beautiful woman behind an ugly eye. Sheer stubborn willpower that crumpled into unexpected hysteria. She didn't want to stay, and yet they couldn't get her to leave, and for four college guys, it was a little overwhelming.

"Don't you think you should change again?" Josh ventured. "My toes feel like they're going to fall off. You have to be freezing. I'm sure we can find something else for you."

Kevin wanted to warn his buddy that he was entering female land-mine territory—she'd already told him no twice—but he just kept his mouth shut. He'd have to learn the hard way.

"No, really. I'm not cold." Her head came up with a faraway look. "I wasn't cold before either. Running through the storm, I mean. I was scared, terrified . . . but not cold. Just like now." She tightened the heavy blanket around her, contradicting herself once again.

Kevin waited for his nerdy, soon-to-be-doctor friend to come up with an explanation, but Sam looked as dumbfounded by her as the rest of them were—if not more so.

"But the second I felt safe," she went on, "like, literally, the very second I thought I had finally escaped them for good, it was like a bucket of ice water had been poured over my head. I started shaking uncontrollably and couldn't stop."

"Escaped?" Kevin blurted out.

"Them?" Josh asked at the same time. "More than one person did that to you?"

Her dark eyes pooled. "No. Just one. He . . ." She swallowed hard. "Just him."

The only sound in the cabin was the crackling fire. Even Rocky felt the heaviness of the subject and lay silently at her feet. Kevin kept trying to piece her story together, then something else clicked. Sadie *still* didn't feel safe. Even now she was in survival mode, otherwise she would be as cold as the rest of them were. "Maybe you should change," he said, joining Josh's argument. "I have some shorts or . . ." His mind churned, calculating his six-foot-four body to her five-foot-nothing body.

"No. I'm not cold. Really. It's just weird."

Yeah, Kevin agreed. *Freaky weird.*

"So how'd you end up here?" Trevor asked.

"I really don't know. One minute I was in the middle of trees and snow and more trees, and the next I was standing by your truck. I saw it was unlocked and climbed inside. I only meant to stay for a minute to warm up and stop shaking, but I must have passed out."

She rubbed her forehead. "Oh, man, I think my headache's coming back." And with that announcement came another onslaught of tears. "Why did he do this to me?" she whispered.

Kevin didn't know who "he" was, but they were getting a clearer picture of what "this" was, and it wasn't pretty. "Do you need a place to stay, Sadie?" he tried again. "You're welcome to stay if you want to hide out. Besides, I betcha don't know it, but our specialty is fugitives."

"We're also good at beating up jerks," Trevor added. Then with a glance around the table, he amended, "Well, most of us would be anyway."

Her eyes lifted slowly. "I don't know. Are you sure—"

"Yes," Sam said. "Very."

She took a deep breath. "Maybe. Just until I figure out what to do."

"As long as you need," Kevin insisted. "We're here until January second."

"Thanks." And with another cleansing breath, she stood. "Maybe I should lie down for awhile. I'm sorry, but I just don't feel like myself right now. Then maybe I'll know what to do."

She was headed for the couch, but Sam quickly intercepted her. "Take my room. We should have put you in there the first time, but we didn't realize how long you were going to . . ." His sentence faded before he prudently redirected. "Anyway, if you need anything, just holler."

Sadie left the four guys and entered the large bedroom knowing full well she wouldn't be able to sleep. Every time she closed her eyes, Guillermo's face was waiting for her. Instead she wandered over to the bay window and watched the sun descend in the western sky, scattering a lovely pink across the rigid mountains. The view looked so harmless, a far cry from the mountainside that almost killed her. It was impossible to trace her path through the snow, but she tried anyway. Her sense of direction was bad enough she'd never find her way back to Guillermo's. Not that she wanted to. She would never go back there again.

Her eyelids grew heavy and before she could force them open, she caught another glimpse of that face. Not the one she'd fallen in love with, but the one right before he hit her. It barely resembled the man she'd known for two years; it was as if a completely different person had been standing at the bottom of those stairs.

A lump settled in the back of her throat. *He hates me.*

What an awful feeling to have the love of your life despise you. Yet something else was gnawing at her, something hidden in his expression. Something that could only be described as fear. *Him? Afraid of me?* she questioned. It was almost laughable. Her boyfriend was the confident, charismatic one. What could he possibly fear from her? Nothing. Not unless . . .

She shook it off. It was lies. All of it. The FBI was trained to intimidate, each claim about Guillermo was made to scare her into submission: investment fraud, bribing government officials, even going so far as to suggest drug trafficking and violent tendencies. The last one was a little easier to believe, but the rest was preposterous. She was perfectly acquainted with Guillermo and his associates. They were kind, respectable, well-educated people, and she had been around enough crackheads to know they weren't involved in drugs either. Right from the beginning, he'd told her about the FBI's investigations. He purposely made his whole life open to them, just to put a stop to it. "They're just after my money, Augustina," he had told her. She believed him then. She believed him even now.

Two days of pent-up anger exploded. *What right did those agents have?* she fumed. *I said I wouldn't spy on him. I told them no!* But he was guilty in their minds, giving them liberty to trample the laws under their feet.

She hated the FBI. Even more than Guillermo. In a strange way, she was grateful he'd found out about her meeting, even if it had almost cost her her life.

Her body shuddered in sudden remembrance. *"You're as good as dead!"* She still wasn't sure who had shouted it through the snow—whether Guillermo's men or the FBI agents who had followed her to his cabin— but she didn't think they were referring to the storm.

Her system began to overload, no longer able to handle the memories. And then, as if there were a switch, her memories shut off completely, and she turned her attention back to the pink mountains.

Guillermo studied the pink mountains. Almost two full days of searching and there was still no sign of Augustina. Not a footprint. Not a phone call. Nothing. Normally he was an even-tempered man but this had pushed him to his limit. "What is taking so long?" he said quietly.

His younger brother stayed silent as he sat across from him at their table in the lodge, smart enough to know that some questions weren't to be answered. At least not by him.

"Imbéciles!" Guillermo shouted with a fist on the table. "I should have heard something by now, but I've heard nothing. Nothing!" Again he pounded the table, attracting several nervous glances from around the dining hall.

"Maybe you should go back to the cabin," Manuel dared to suggest.

Guillermo put his fingers on his temples. "No, Manuel. No. I will wait here for Salvador and Luis. They will be back soon. *They* will know what happened to my Augustina." It was a dig, and Manuel didn't miss it. Guillermo thought his little brother was useless, and both of them knew it.

Guillermo left their table and wandered over to the floor-to-ceiling windows. The view from the lodge was stunning, but that's not where his thoughts took him. He was reliving his last moments with Augustina, devastated by the truth he now knew. She was completely innocent. A pawn. Not even a pawn, an innocent bystander. The FBI planted the bug in her purse against her wishes. *Against her wishes,* he echoed, feeling the weight of those words. The stunned look on her face had been genuine. Not an act of deception.

It is their fault I hit her! he seethed.

And mine, he relented. *Definitely mine.* After all, he was the one that had jumped to conclusions, feeling a lifetime of betrayals personified in that one act. And now that mistake was one he could be paying for the rest of his life.

I have to find her. First. I have to tell her . . . Apologize . . . Beg . . .

His head fell against the window. *Oh, Augustina. What have I done?*

Chapter 6

Trevor was bored. Bored and irritated. Over twenty-four hours in Montana and they'd wasted most of it sitting around. Josh was typing away in the kitchen, Sam was studying on one couch, and Kevin was half-asleep on the other. With no TV in the cabin—or any technology whatsoever—Trevor was left thinking about the perfectly unutilized snow outside. But none of his friends wanted to leave. Not with the girl there.

He left his spot to scrounge up something to eat. He rummaged around and found a bag of chips and a can of Sprite—*Sprite!* He was getting too old to hang out with a bunch of Mormons. He didn't know how Kevin put up with it. He never complained.

Tearing into the bag, he sat by Josh, still typing away on his laptop. "Is that seriously what you came up here to do?"

Josh frowned. "I have to finish these MBA applications before school starts up again."

"What about BYU?" Sam asked from the great room.

"I haven't heard back yet. Their program is pretty competitive. I'd like some other options, just in case." Josh leaned back in his chair. "Man, I absolutely despise essays."

"Man, I absolutely despise this trip," Trevor muttered under his breath.

With his Sprite, he wandered into the great room and waited for Kevin to move his big feet out of the way so he could sit. When he didn't, Trevor sat anyway. Bad move. Kevin threw a foot in Trevor's side, knocking him to the floor. As far as pecking order went, Trevor was low-man on the proverbial totem pole. Then the cabin was silent again. Absolutely, pitifully silent.

"Night boarding, Sam?" Trevor asked.

"Maybe later."

"Skiing, Kev?"

He didn't even get a response. The only thing he could figure was keeping them cabin-bound was Sadie, like they were waiting around for a glimpse of her. But even she had been a no-show for the last hour. Not that he totally blamed them. Those dark eye lashes . . . and olive skin . . . and . . .

"By the way," he called, "y'all know the girl's mine, right?"

That got their attention. "Don't even think about it, Trevor," Josh growled.

"Well, she's obviously not Mormon, knocking you and Sam from the running, and poor Kev's tied to the old ball and chain, so that leaves me and me alone to heal her aching heart."

With a nervous glance down the hallway, Josh made his way to the others. "Seriously Trevor, could you please restrain yourself? You're the last thing Sadie needs."

"And what? You are?"

"Trevor," Josh hissed.

Trevor laughed, no longer bored. He'd found himself a new form of entertainment. Bugging Josh. "Actually, I think I'm just what Sadie needs."

Josh turned. "Come on, Kev . . . Sam . . . help me out here."

Kevin spoke from behind closed eyelids. "Sadie will never give him the time of day. Chicks like her aren't interested in guys like us."

That one stung a little. "That's okay," Trevor said, recovering quickly. "I like a good challenge."

"Seriously, Trevor," Josh said again. "This isn't about you or me or any of us. None of us know what Sadie's been through. We're all going to behave, right?"

Trevor sighed. Game over. "Fine. But she's something to look at."

"That's beside the point," Josh insisted. "She's off limits."

Trevor looked at his other friends. Both were in obvious agreement with his nemesis. "Man, when did you guys become such downers? Why should I have to suffer because you all have women?"

"Technically," Kevin yawned, "I'm the only one with a woman. The others just pretend."

"How is Amy, anyway?" Sam asked.

As his buddies began discussing the women in their lives—all predictably boring—Trevor lay on the rug. With Kevin married and Josh soon to be, that left him and Sam as the last standing bachelors, and Sam wasn't nearly as fun as he used to be.

"Trevor?" Sam said for the second time.

His head came up. "Yeah?"

"Kevin wants to bring wives next year. What do you think? Any chance you'll ever settle down and get married?"

"Oh, man. Let's hope not."

Sadie woke to a sudden burst of laughter. She gingerly got off the bed and slid into the hallway. She stayed behind the corner, hoping for a minute to study the four guys, but the dog—always the dog—came bounding over to her with a loud bark. They all looked up.

"Oh, hey," Lanky said in surprise. "Did we wake you?"

"No. I couldn't sleep."

Sam slid off one of the couches to sit on the floor by Curly, making room for her. She curled up into the corner, tucking her feet underneath her, and decided the couch wasn't nearly as uncomfortable now that her bruised shoulder wasn't pushing into it. The big, black—and incidentally quite smelly—beast jumped up after her and snuggled itself into her hip. Then there was dead silence in the massive cabin. She'd killed the mood. Even jovial Lanky was watching her stoically. *Lanky? Curly?* she repeated.

"I know I should remember," she said, "but what are your names again?"

"I'm Kevin," Lanky started, "but you can call me Kev."

Sadie nodded, committing his name to memory. Kevin was the tallest of the group, made even more so by his long, spindly body. With his straight brown hair and long face, he looked like a teenager who'd outpaced his body. From the little she'd seen of Kevin, she guessed he wore a smile, and his camera, round-the-clock.

Curly spoke from the floor. "I'm Trevor, but you can just call me Stud."

Sadie smiled, but Kevin smacked him on the head. Trevor was the complete opposite of Kevin. Short and stocky. And his curly, light brown hair was completely wild—almost like a Chia Pet.

"I'm Josh." This came from the dark-haired guy by the fireplace.

Josh? The name jolted her. It was Josh's face she had woken to both times, his over-sized gray sweats she wore, and his calm face the sole reason she wasn't an ice sculpture outside somewhere. However, it was his name that had sent her running from the cabin in the first place. Trevor said Josh wanted to turn her over to the cops. For all she knew, he still did.

"Josh," she repeated, suddenly wary.

"And I'm Sam." For some reason she remembered his name. Maybe because it was his cabin and truck that had sheltered her. Or because he had been her translator and introduced himself first. "What about you?" Sam asked in return. "What was that other name you said?"

Only then did she remember her humiliating Spanish introduction. "Oh, Augustina? That's what my mom calls me. She was born in Argentina, but moved to the States when she was twenty. She met my dad here in Montana. When I was born, they couldn't agree on a name. My dad liked Sarah and, being kind of bossy, he picked my first name, so

Augustina became my middle name. When my dad left, my mom went back to calling me the name she liked."

Sam's face squinted in confusion. "I thought your name was Sadie, not Sarah."

She knew she was babbling, but she couldn't seem to stop herself. "My last name is Dawson, and in grade school, a few boys figured out my unfortunate initials are S. A. D." She drew each letter in the air for emphasis. "So they started calling me Saddy, which I, of course, hated." *Saddy?* she repeated. At the time the name was the antithesis to her bubbly personality, but she wondered if these four guys would think it fitting. "Anyway, somehow it evolved into Sadie and just kind of stuck."

"Sadie," Kevin said, mulling it over. "I like it."

"Thanks. And by the way, I'm *really* sorry about the whole Spanish thing. I just wasn't ready to explain myself to anyone"—*I'm still not, actually*—"and I hoped that if no one could understand me, I could slip out without any questions."

"It's good Sam knows Spanish then," Josh replied easily.

Sadie looked at him. It almost sounded like he was happy she stayed. So maybe he didn't want to turn her over to the cops after all. "Speaking of Spanish," she said, turning to Sam, "Where did you learn to speak like that? You barely have an accent."

"I spent two years on a mission for my church in Peru."

"Two years?" she cried. "Wow. *Hablas muy bien.*"

Sam grinned at the compliment. "*Gracias. Me encanta español. Es una—*"

"Hey!" Trevor called out. "Only English here."

And with that the silence returned. As did their undivided attention. It was like they'd never seen a woman before—*like they'd never seen a black eye before,* she corrected.

She twisted a ring on her pinky. "So . . . where are you guys from?"

"We're all from Spokane," Kevin answered.

"Spokane? Isn't that a long drive?"

"It is when you let a grandma like Sam drive," Trevor snickered at the same time Sam tried to drown him out with an explanation.

"It's only about four hours. My dad used to come to this part of Montana as a kid, so he and my mom built this cabin here. They think it's the best-kept secret for skiing and hiking."

"True," Sadie agreed, at least that's what Guillermo told her. He was convinced northwest Montana was the hidden gem of America, ready to boom out of obscurity. Because of that, he'd invested in the ski resort, several businesses in the area, and who knew what else. He was quite the entrepreneur, building up a large empire for one so young.

Empire? Her thoughts skidded to a halt. That's the same word the FBI agents used, only with them, they had attached the word "drug" onto it. Realizing where her thoughts were, she asked a little more urgently, "You guys in school?"

This time Josh answered for the group. "I have another semester of engineering at Washington State, Sam's in medical school at Stanford, Trevor's at UW getting who-knows-what kind of degree, and Kevin's a working fool, running deliveries in Spokane. He keeps telling us he makes good money, but I've never seen any of it."

Kevin chucked a pillow across the room.

"In fact," Josh smiled, catching the pillow and sending it sailing back, "I don't even think his wife's seen any of it 'cause he's such a tightwad."

Sadie glanced at Kevin's left hand, surprised to see a wedding ring there. She tried to check out the left hands of the rest of the men, but couldn't really tell. Her best guess was that the four of them were a little younger than her. At twenty-six, she considered herself too young to marry. Even Guillermo, who was nine years her senior, considered her too young. *A ring? How could I have been so blind?*

She groaned audibly. She couldn't even go thirty seconds without thinking about him. But try as she might, her thoughts always wound back to him. Like an obsession. Or an addict going back for the next hit. *I hate him. I hate that I can't escape him. Not even in my mind.*

Desperate for distraction, she left the couch and stood near the warm fire. She studied the family picture hanging above the mantle of the two-story fireplace. Like everything else in the cabin, it was huge and not just in size. There were probably twenty-five people in the picture.

"That's Sam's family," Josh said, standing beside her.

It took a moment, but she found Sam's blond hair in the back left corner. "Wow. You have a big family, Sam," she noted.

Sam smiled. "I'm the youngest of five kids. The only one not married with kids."

Still, it was a lot of people, a lot of little kids. The portrait was taken in front of the cabin and was actually quite stunning, considering the amount of people. "It's beautiful," she said.

"Thanks," Kevin said. "I took it."

"Really? But it looks so professional."

"Ouch!" Trevor laughed. "I think she just slammed you, Kev."

Though she should have explained herself, she couldn't take her eyes off the picture. Taken in the full height of fall, the colors were spectacular, yet that wasn't where the true beauty lay. Everyone looked so happy. Genuinely so. Even the little kids. It was depressing actually, and instead of distracting her from her problems, it only compounded them. Now she missed her mom fiercely. Her mom, who could make her laugh at the craziest moments, would have unloaded buckets of advice at a time like this—where to go, what to say, what to do—but right now, Sadie felt entirely alone. And staring into the happy faces only made her feel more so.

"So what's your story, Sadie?" Kevin asked. "Are you working? School?"

She left the happy faces and curled back up on her couch. The dog was even nice enough to give her a few inches of personal space as she told them a little about her life. Growing up in Whitefish. Being food service manager at the ski lodge. The guys perked up at the mention of the lodge, but once she mentioned that she didn't ski—at all—Trevor nearly jumped out of his skin.

"How can you not ski?" he cried. "Don't they give you free lift passes?"

"No. Actually," she sighed, "my boss probably hates me right now. I'm supposed to be at work right now. This is the busiest time of year and usually—" She stopped, suddenly wondering if she even had a job anymore. Indirectly, Guillermo was her boss's boss.

When the cabin grew painfully quiet again, she looked up. It was obvious the guys wanted an explanation for her odd behavior, though some of it they must have guessed already. Things like her face were impossible to hide—even from herself.

With a quick breath she began, keeping it as brief as possible. "Two men came to me on Christmas Day, wanting me to spy on my boyfriend. They said they were . . . from the FBI." Josh's head whipped up in surprise, but she rushed on. "I wouldn't do it. I had no reason to. But . . . well . . . long story short, my boyfriend found a bug in my purse and assumed I was spying after all. He got mad and"—she shrugged—"I'm here."

"Why would the FBI want you to spy on your boyfriend?" Josh asked quietly.

"He's rich, from Venezuela. And . . . so . . ." She winced at the words. They sounded horrible. "They think he's involved in organized crime. Like a cartel or something."

"Is he?" Trevor asked, looking up.

"No!" she snapped, then instantly softened. "I wouldn't get involved with someone like that. He just invested in some international real estate and got lucky."

"International real estate?" Kevin echoed.

"Yes!" Once again, her temper got the better of her. She backed down, feeling stupid for being so defensive, but it was the same question her mother had asked a dozen times. "He and his family aren't involved in drugs or anything. They're not like that. They're incredibly nice."

"So nice they beat their girlfriends," Josh said under his breath.

It hadn't been meant for her ears, but she had heard it anyway. She closed her eyes, trying to push his comment back out. When she couldn't, she felt the need to defend herself. And her boyfriend.

"I can't imagine what he felt, thinking I was capable of that kind of deception. I never got the chance to explain what really happened. I got scared after he . . ." Her breath caught, unable to say what his rage felt like. Unable to describe what it felt like to wake up locked in a room, waiting for him to let her out, yet at the same time terrified of the moment he would. "So I just ran. Someone chased me for awhile, but I don't know if it was him and his assistants or if it was the FBI. All had reason to, I guess. But I lost them in the storm."

There it was. Laid out on the line. FBI? Drug cartels? Surely this wasn't her life.

When she finally got the courage to look up, she found four identical expressions: a look of shock, mixed with concern, but mostly pity. The thing she absolutely loathed. "I'm going to be fine," she said quickly. "Really. I'm happy you'll let me stay until I figure out what to do."

"Do you think they're still looking for you?" Sam asked quietly.

The thought sent a chill down her spine. "I don't know."

Marcela Dawson threw her keys across the kitchen counter. Normally she worked the nine-to-nine shift at a department store in Kalispell restocking merchandise, but with the holiday crowds she'd spent the entire day doing returns. It had been a long day. She was exhausted. And hungry. She wandered to the freezer and took out a prepackaged meal. It was supposedly healthy, but, as with most foods, healthy usually meant tasteless. She cracked open a corner and doused the chicken with salt and butter flakes. In her mind, those things didn't really count, and she congratulated herself for sticking to her diet.

Once her dinner was cooking in the microwave, she picked up the phone. It was kind of late, but Augustina was a night owl. She dialed her daughter's number and began counting the rings, hoping this time would be different. Even when the two of them fought, they still found a way to talk every day. Now it had been two days and not a word. Whatever she'd said about Augustina's boyfriend had made her furious this time.

"This is Sadie," the phone answered. "You know what to do."

Marcela's heart fell. "Hi, sweetie. I just . . . I'm really, *really* sorry about Christmas. I thought by the end of the night you knew I had changed my mind about Guillermo. Please, don't be mad at me. I like him, really. He's a generous man and his family is so kind. Please, let's talk. I miss you," she added sadly. "Call me when you get this. I'll be up late."

Marcela held the phone long after she hung up, hoping for a quick call back. When it didn't come, she kept it with her as she walked to the TV. She flipped on her favorite crime drama, hoping she'd still get that call before her dinner was done.

It was while sitting there that the strangest feeling came over her. It felt like someone was watching her. She ignored it a moment, but her sixth sense kicked in. She could almost feel eyes trained on her back. Quickly, she scanned her small apartment. It was empty, of course, but that didn't do anything to alleviate the feeling. Her pulse picked up.

The curtains were open even though the sun had set hours ago. She rushed over and shut every one, hoping it would help. It didn't. *Someone is watching me.* Somehow she was certain.

Her hands gripped the phone. If they weren't outside, that meant . . .

Calm down, she scolded herself. Though her feet were hesitant, she forced herself to search under the table and behind the couch. Nothing. That left the coat closet. Silently, with skin crawling, she crept over to the door. Holding her breath, she turned the handle slowly to find coats, a few board games, and an old vacuum. Everything as it should be.

A loud beeping echoed through the apartment. Marcela jumped a foot in the air.

"The microwave," she said, with her hand over her heart. After several slow breaths, she walked into the kitchen. The tray trembled in her hands, every instinct telling her to run back to her couch and call the police. Instead she set her food aside and mustered up the courage to check the last few spots. Bathroom. Bedroom. Linen closet. Empty. Empty. Empty.

The absurdity of the moment hit her. *It's like I'm six years old or something.* She chuckled, though she could still hear the fear in her thoughts. *I just saw something like this on TV. That's all.* She quickly flipped the channel to a mindless sitcom. It helped. Some.

No one is here. No one is here, she kept telling herself, and while she believed it, she no longer felt like eating. Instead she clutched the phone and waited for her only daughter to call.

CHAPTER 7

Sadie looked from somber face to somber face, cursing herself for ever leaving Sam's room. She hadn't meant to ruin their evening. These guys were on vacation, but instead of them pulling her out of her depression, she'd only dragged them into hers.

"Sadie, is the FBI looking for you?" Josh asked, nearly repeating Sam's previous question. "Right now?"

She looked out the dark window, hugging herself. "Probably."

Josh's eyes shot to Kevin before coming back to her. "My dad is a cop, Sadie. If you've done something illegal, we can't get involved. We can't hide you from the FBI."

Josh's dad is a . . .

She searched their faces again as a thousand questions leaped into her mind. What if this was a setup? What if the feds followed her, bribed them, and were listening even now? *And here I am spilling my guts. About Guillermo . . . About everything! Josh's dad is a cop!*

"You're one of them," she whispered, standing slowly. "Aren't you? You told them I'm here, and now you're just keeping me hostage until they can take me away."

"What?" Josh cried. "No!"

Her eyes began to burn. Trevor had been right before. Josh wanted to turn her over to the cops. She truly had nowhere safe to hide. Nowhere to run.

She started backing away from him—away from all of them.

"I don't work for the police department," Josh explained. "My dad does. All I'm saying is, we can't help you if you're running from the law. We can take you back to the lodge if you need, but beyond that, I'm sorry."

These men wanted to take her back to the lodge. Back to *Guillermo's* lodge! The place where the feds broke into her room, questioned her, and jammed a bug in her purse without her knowing. Her breaths came in short bursts. "You promised . . ." In the snow. But it was just another lie. Just another man with another lie.

She searched the nearest window wondering how much time she had and to what lengths they would go to hold her captive. She scanned the room for something and grabbed the poker for the fire. "Leave me alone," she warned, waving it in front of her.

Josh was on his feet now—they all were. "Hold on, Sadie. I was just saying—"

"Stay back," she said, inching her way to the front door.

Kevin jumped in front of her, blocking Josh from her view. "Whoa, calm down. No one's coming for you, no one knows where you are, and we aren't turning you in. Are we, Josh?"

Josh shook his head. "We don't know anything, Kev. We don't know the whole story. If she's running from the feds then—"

"Don't you get it?" she shrieked. "I'm not a criminal! I'm *evidence!*"

"Evidence?" Josh and Kevin repeated.

She pointed to her eye. "They've been waiting for a chance to nail him . . . They've begged me . . . hunted me . . . at the lodge. In the storm. And now I can't . . . I can't . . . Please . . ." Her limbs were giving out. Her voice as well. "You promised . . ."

"Evidence," Josh said again, like he was trying to digest it. Then slowly, almost imperceptibly, he nodded. "Okay."

He and Sadie were in a deadlock stare down. She didn't trust him. He didn't trust her. And neither was willing to turn their back on the other.

Kevin stepped cautiously forward and pried the poker from Sadie's hand. "Okay . . . wow. That was fun." Then he glared at Josh like she did. "Now what?"

When no one answered, Trevor did. "Let's eat."

"Seriously, Trevor!" Sam exploded. "At a time like this, that's all you can think of?"

"What? Maybe she's hungry. I know I am. When was the last time you ate, Sadie? It had to be before you got here, at least."

She blinked slowly. "Hallaca."

"Ah-what-ka?"

She could picture it so clearly. The hallaca. The Argentine wine. Her mother complaining. The room laughing. The diamonds nestled against her neck. And the kiss. The kiss that melted away the last of her doubt. *How blind!* she thought. *How naïve!* And yet in that one moment, how utterly and blissfully happy she had been. "Christmas," she whispered.

"Christmas!" Trevor cried. "No wonder you're acting all crazy. You gotta eat." And before she could refuse, he dragged her into the kitchen.

Special Agent Stephen Dubois heard his stomach growl in the empty room. Not very professional considering what the government paid him. Yet he hadn't eaten in twelve hours, and more than just his stomach knew it. His temper was rising as he waited for his arrogant partner.

He'd worked hard to get to where he was, which at the moment was in a room, alone, doing nothing. As far as he was concerned, the task assigned to him was one at which he couldn't fail. Not if he expected his career to go in the direction he wanted. Up. Fast. That meant he had to find the girl—the same one who refused to help them on Christmas Day, the same one that eluded him in the storm. She'd been a thorn in his side from the beginning, a woman completely naïve about men like Guillermo Vasquez—probably why he picked her in the first place.

"What about your girlfriend?" Dubois remembered taunting the sleek Venezuelan. "What would she think if she knew everything you're involved in?"

Guillermo Vasquez had laughed in his face. "You mean everything you have accused me of? Go ahead. Try."

Dubois had. Christmas Day. But just as Vasquez had predicted, she didn't believe a word. *Stupid, idiotic woman!* he fumed. If she were dead somewhere, it was her own fault. Yet in all fairness, Dubois didn't completely blame her. He blamed his partner. If Agent Madsen had just let him run things on Christmas, he would have found a way to get what they wanted.

For now, he was still convinced Augustina could help them bring Vasquez down once and for all—assuming she was still alive. Dead, she was worthless. But he still believed she was the one way to break into the iron-clad Vasquez organization—possibly beyond. Judges, politicians, and who knew who else. After all, beautiful women had been the downfall of many of history's powerful men. And now Vasquez's million-dollar feathers had been ruffled. Whatever he'd done to make her leave was enough to have him covering every base. It was bad. Illegal certainly. And now it was a race to find her.

But without her, it would take years to find the evidence needed. Vasquez knew all the laws in America a little too well. He knew how a little red tape and paperwork could bog down an organization like the FBI. It was ironic really. The laws that made America great were also the same laws that tied the hands of the authorities from locking up a slimeball like him. Any other country and Vasquez would have been slammed in prison years earlier. But no. He and his attorneys knew the system and laughed in their faces as they muddled through it. Yet Dubois didn't lack confidence. Vasquez was his man. But first, he had to find that girl!

He paced the empty room again until Madsen finally stormed in.

Madsen looked twenty years older than he was, making Dubois wonder if that's where he himself was headed—a guy who practically slept in his business suit.

"What do you have, Dubois?" Madsen said in his typical cool greeting.

"Vasquez's man is still watching Dawson's apartment, and her mother's. He also has surveillance on the ski lodge and the club."

"And?"

"Nothing. Her apartment's empty, and she hasn't contacted her roommate."

Madsen stroked his neatly trimmed goatee. "What other relatives does she have? Friends she could hide out with?"

"None in the area we haven't searched. We're still working on those out of state."

"Work faster," Madsen said. "How do we know this isn't just a ruse, a way of throwing us off his tracks? How do we know Vasquez hasn't stashed her body somewhere?"

"Because he's beside himself," Dubois answered with confidence. "Whatever he did to make her leave is enough to have broken through his thick skin. Even his own men can't stand him right now—that's a first. We've been waiting for him to make a wrong move, and this is it. She knows something and now he has to find her before we do."

Agent Madsen turned to leave and then stopped. "One last thing, Dubois. Have you found out how Vasquez knew about our meeting with her on Christmas Day?"

Dubois flinched at the accusation and then recovered quickly, realizing it hadn't been an accusation at all. It was a dangerous game he was playing. With Vasquez *and* the FBI. "No," he said, "but I'll make it a priority to find out."

CHAPTER 8

"So whatcha in the mood for?" Kevin asked, with his head inside the fridge. "We've got pastrami, hot dogs, cold pizza . . . no wait . . . cold pizza's gone."

"Nothing," Sadie said. "I'm fine, really. I just need to sleep."

As Josh pulled up a chair next to her, she visibly recoiled. He sat anyway, feeling horrible. Nothing like calling a victim the perpetrator. Her words still haunted him: *I'm evidence.* No judge looking at that eye could deny what had transpired between her and her boyfriend. His dad had talked about working with victims of violence, but hearing Sadie say it that way sobered him to the core. She didn't want to talk to the cops. He hoped that would change with time, but for now she was still in self-defense mode. That was understandable.

"Come on," Trevor said. "You gotta be starving. How about I make you something. Anything you want. Just name it."

Her dark eyes closed briefly. "Actually . . . I could really use a cup of coffee. It might clear my head a little."

Before Trevor could get in a snide remark, Josh said, "No coffee here. Something else, though, like . . . uh . . . ." Kevin shook his head behind the fridge. Sam just shrugged. That left Trevor. "Lucky Charms, maybe?" Josh suggested weakly.

She watched Trevor pour himself another bowl and nearly smiled. "Tempting, but no. May I look?"

Kevin held the fridge open for her, but unfortunately, grocery shopping wasn't something the guys excelled at. Especially real food groceries. Sadie ended up back at the table with a slice of bread and a glass of water. As if she were their prisoner.

Then the silence was back, hovering over every part of the cabin. Josh tried to think of something to help smooth things, but before he could, she pushed away from the table. "Thanks for the food. I think I'm going to try to sleep again."

Josh watched her walk away. Not quite the relaxing week he had hoped for. In reality, he felt considerably more wound up now than he had been during finals.

"Maybe one of us should go shopping," Kevin said at last. "This is pathetic."

Josh sighed. "I'll go."

In the morning, Sadie took her time getting up and ready. Her body ached from one side to the other, and twice she'd woken with nightmares, horrifying moments of Guillermo chasing her through the snow, even though she was certain it hadn't been his voice calling her name. Each time left her trembling and worn out. So she lay there in the massive bed, long after her eyes opened. Normally she was an avid journaler, and at times like this she would have spent the day solving her problems on paper. As it was, she just stayed there, spinning useless circles in her mind.

Once the double dose of ibuprofen kicked in, she climbed out of the massive bed. Instantly she was aware of Josh's gray sweats hanging on her body. Not something she wanted to wear twice if she could help it. There was a large mahogany dresser in the corner and she made another decision to snoop. Unfortunately, the only clothes she found were guy clothes. Sam's. From the look of things, he was a nice dresser, but she wasn't about to wear any more male clothing, so she continued to the walk-in closet, hoping his mom kept some clothes at the cabin. She did. One rack had ski clothing and equipment, the other had women's sweatshirts, sweaters, and even a few pants. None of the clothes were Sadie's style or size, but then again, neither were Josh's huge sweats. She quickly donned an over-sized sweatshirt with Glacier National Park sprawled across the front, then worked on pants. Though it was harder, she found a pair of light blue jogging pants that were still too long and baggy, but fit better than Josh's.

That helped her determine to wash her own still-damp clothes in the Jacuzzi tub. With a little effort, she had the black hand-knit sweater drying over the shower door and her sleek black skinny pants draped over the edge of the Jacuzzi. Then, no longer able to put off the inevitable, she made her way to the mirror.

It didn't matter how many times she saw it, the bruise was hideously gruesome. And instead of fading like she hoped, it had deepened in color: something between purple, lime-green, and brown. It was easy in front of the mirror to hate Guillermo, and she stayed a few minutes letting the hatred fester. Finally with a sigh, she ran the brush through her long hair.

She slipped out of Sam's bedroom and braced herself for a slobber attack by the obnoxious dog. By some miracle, the hallway stayed dog-free, so she wandered into the kitchen. Sam was at the table reading a textbook, the others were nowhere in sight. Sadie pulled out one of the heavy chairs and sat next to him. His head came up in surprise.

"Oh, morning, Sadie. Did you sleep well?" Sam gave her a nice, friendly smile, as if he were genuinely happy she was ruining their ski vacation.

"Yes. Thank you. And thanks for the bed. I hope you didn't end up on a couch."

"No. There are a bunch of bedrooms in the loft."

"Oh, good." Sadie glanced around the quiet cabin. "Where are the others?"

"Snowshoeing. I stayed behind to study—*Cellular Physiology*." Sam shifted his book to show her, but something in the way he had said it made it sound like studying wasn't the real reason he'd stayed. Then she remembered Josh had stayed behind yesterday. Sadie wasn't sure whether to feel grateful or annoyed to have round-the-clock bodyguards. In her present condition, she chose the first.

"Oh, I forgot," Sam said, standing. "Trevor made pancakes. You want some?"

Sadie nodded, surprised at how hungry she actually felt. While she preferred her morning coffee—surely a little latte would fix her persistent migraine—she made herself content with a banana she hadn't noticed on the table last night.

While Sam warmed up her pancakes, Sadie noticed the light from the nearest window seemed off. "What time is it?" she asked.

"Around eleven thirty, I think."

"Really?" Her cheeks flushed. "Sorry."

"Why? You've been through a lot. Sleep is the best thing you could do right now."

Sadie didn't bother telling him that she could easily have slept just as long without an excuse. She liked that Sam had given her the benefit of the doubt.

"Actually," he said, leaning against the counter, "I was just reading about this study they did at Stanford—my school—with fruit flies. I know they're not that biologically similar to humans, but their phagocytes work similar to our own white blood cells. They injected these fruit flies with various illnesses and observed what happened, and the ones that were allowed to sleep were much more likely to recuperate from their illness than those they kept awake—which, how you keep a fruit fly awake is beyond me—but, anyway, that proves that sleep truly aids in recuperation. Isn't that cool?"

"Uh . . ." Sadie wasn't sure how to respond.

It was Sam's turn to blush. "Sorry. I just meant that I'm glad you were able to sleep for a while. Speaking of healing . . ." he rushed on, "it sounds like your voice is better."

Sadie rotated her bad shoulder, blinked a few times, and cleared her scratchy throat, checking all her damaged parts. "Yeah. I'm definitely on the mend."

"Good." Sam handed her the warm plate and sat by his textbooks, only he didn't go back to studying. At least not *Cellular Physiology.* "Don't worry," he said, "we already blessed it."

"Okay . . ." Whatever that was supposed to mean. But that wasn't her concern. She didn't particularly enjoy eating with an audience. She took her first bite quickly and said, "Mmm. Very good." Thankfully Sam went back to his books.

The front door opened and Sam's black lab came flying across the great room, leaving a trail of snow behind. Sadie cringed as it jumped up, wet paws and all, on her newly acquired jogging pants. It panted and wagged its tail excitedly as it waited for her to respond.

"Rocky likes you," Sam said with a smile.

"Hmm." *Be nice,* she scolded herself. Still, she couldn't bring herself to touch the mangy hair. Especially since she was still eating breakfast.

"You're not a dog person, are you?"

Her dad was. She wasn't. "Not really," she admitted. "Sorry."

"That's okay," he said, though his expression said otherwise. "Rocky! Come!"

Sadie choked on her pancake. That was the same voice that saved her from the beast the first night. It was strange putting Sam behind it. She had pictured someone more commanding, more dangerous. Not quiet, shy Sam.

"Mornin', Sadie," Kevin called, the first inside. "Or should I say 'Good afternoon'?"

Sadie tucked a dark curl behind her ear. *Why isn't there a clock in the bedroom?*

Kevin laughed as he and his friends dumped their gear by the door. "I was just teasing. I'm glad you wasted a perfectly beautiful day in bed."

"Thanks. In my defense, Sam said fruit flies would've done the same."

"I did?" Sam asked at the same time Kevin and the others burst out laughing.

The three guys joined her and Sam in the kitchen, with Josh taking the chair next to her again. "Is there something wrong with my clothes?" he asked.

Sadie looked at the Glacier National Park sweatshirt, suddenly worried she was making it worse with Josh. For all she knew, he'd spent the morning convincing Kevin and Trevor to kick her out. But then he smiled. "Relax. I was just teasing."

Great. More teasing. Something she wasn't used to. Guillermo didn't have much of a sense of humor, nor did he appreciate it much in others.

From the little she knew of these guys, she guessed that wasn't the only thing different about them. Guillermo at least used a fork when he ate. And a plate. Trevor picked up another pancake and shoved it in his mouth.

"Hey, Sadie," he said mid-chew, "you ever been snowshoeing?"

"Snowshoeing? No."

"Today's your lucky day, then. We came in to get you guys."

Sam shut his book. "Snowshoeing is awesome. You'll love it. It's as easy as walking."

Sadie could think of a hundred reasons to decline the invitation, first and foremost that she'd experienced enough freezing weather to last a lifetime. Only slightly behind that was she wasn't sure if anyone was still hunting for her.

"How long have I been here?" she asked suddenly. "I mean, here at the cabin."

"Day and a half," Josh answered, "Why?"

Sadie nodded, churning on that. Without trying to, she'd found a place to hide that no one could have anticipated. Including her.

"So . . . you coming?" Sam pressed, looking anxious to join his friends—practically wagging his tail like his dog. She didn't want him to have to stay behind and babysit her again. Plus, it seemed like a very normal thing to do. Normal was good.

Walking on snow? she mused. *How bad can it be?*

Kevin slung his camera over his shoulder. "You should come. There's a natural trail that runs through the pines behind Sam's cabin. It's not very steep, so it's perfect for hiking."

"Yeah, I remember," she said, still deciding.

Everything in the kitchen screeched to a halt. She looked up.

"Right," Kevin said softly. "Sorry. I forgot."

Way to kill the mood again! She forced herself to smile. "It might be nice to try it out in the day. I didn't get to"—she struggled for the right word—"*appreciate* the beauty last time."

Kevin perked up, grateful for the escape she'd offered. "All right! The lady wants to see the trail by daylight."

CHAPTER 9

The sky was starting to cloud over. The temperature was dropping, and with the brisk Montana wind, it felt even colder. Josh glanced over at Sadie, who didn't look nearly warm enough. The only winter gear she found was a bright green coat and matching gloves—both Sam's mom's. No hat. No snow pants. "Are you sure you're warm enough?"

She nodded even as the wind swirled dark hair around her face. "I'm not cold."

"Ice Woman!" Kevin called out.

She rolled her eyes. "I'm a little cold, just not *that* cold. If it gets unbearable, I'll head back inside."

Sam stayed close to her as they tromped through the snow—they all were near, like she was a magnet for twenty-something males. "I thought my mom had more gear up here than just a coat and gloves."

"She does, but I'm fine. Really."

For the next hour, the five of them tromped around the slope behind Sam's cabin. It was steep enough to provide an amazing view, but not so steep as to make it treacherous. Rocky raced around them, inadvertently tripping them up at times and leaping after snowballs at other times. Even in her subpar condition, Sadie had no problem keeping up with the guys. And not just physically. "What is he doing?" she asked at one point.

When Josh realized who she was looking at—Kevin arched backward as far as he could go, face inverted, snapping pictures of the underside of a tree—he shrugged. "Don't ask."

Sadie continued watching Kevin though. "Can't he just turn the camera upside-down?"

Josh smiled. "Yeah. I guess he could."

"Or . . ." she said a little louder, "just rotate it on the computer like a normal person?"

Josh hooted, but Kevin wasn't about to be bested. "Oh-ho-ho," he called out from his awkward position. "How little you people know about photography.

"Apparently we aren't the only ones," Sadie muttered.

"That's it." Kevin tucked his camera away. "Race to the bottom of the hill."

"No," Sadie said with a firm shake of her head. "Nope. I was just kidding. You can take upside-down pictures all you want. I'll shut up."

Josh looked at Sam, who nodded in return. Without any warning, the two of them took off down the hill. Kevin's reaction time was slow, but his competitive nature had him sprinting to catch up. The three of them whizzed past Trevor who immediately took up the chase, trying to close the distance with his short legs. All of them ran—or rather half-clomped, half-stumbled—down the hill, trying to get their knees high enough to clear the fresh powder.

With only ten feet to go and his subsequent victory speech prepared, Josh was unexpectedly shoved out of the way. He went down, face first, and got a mouthful of the freezing powder. Recovering quickly, he swung around in time to sideswipe Kevin. Kevin stumbled, but somehow covered the last ten feet unmarred, after which he declared himself the winner with a ridiculous victory dance. Josh ended the dance with a snowball, aimed squarely at Kevin's chest.

"So that's the only way you can win, Kev?" he huffed. "To cheat?"

Kevin grinned. "So says the loser."

He offered Josh a hand up. Josh grabbed it and yanked hard, giving his buddy a chance to eat snow. Kevin came up white-faced, but his mouth split into a wide grin. "You've always been jealous of me. Admit it."

Josh laughed, but chucked another hunk of snow, hitting him upside the head, which erupted into a full-blown, entirely adolescent snowball fight.

Sadie caught up to the four guys, shook her head, and said simply, "Men."

The five of them talked about school, families, and breakfast cereals. Sam bored them with stories of Lewis and Clark's adventures through Montana, and Trevor bored them with stories of his feats of strength. Mostly though, they laughed. At themselves. At each other. Josh even caught Sadie laughing a few times, which all things considered, he figured was pretty good. But after an hour, the wind picked up, the snow started, and Sadie began to cough. Her cheeks and nose were rosy, and her dark hair was quickly turning white in the heavy snow.

"I think we should head back inside," Josh suggested.

"What?" Trevor cried. "We haven't even left Sam's property."

Kevin looked at Sadie and then at Josh and nodded. "I think I'm done. How about you, Sadie?"

"Sure." She cleared her throat with another cough. "Whatever you guys want."

"Race to the top then?" Trevor suggested. "Last one up makes lunch."

Only three guys took off the second time. Not Josh. *Idiots!* he wanted to yell after them. They'd nearly left Sadie outside alone. When he turned to check on her, she was restraining a smile. He followed her gaze and watched his buddies scramble to the top of the hill. Running in snowshoes wasn't very graceful. Or pretty.

"What's with you men?" she asked. "Always goading each other into competition? I don't get it."

"Me neither. Trevor can get pretty out of control with it."

"Trevor. Uh-huh. I'm sure he's the only one, too. I'm sure if you hadn't

64

felt the need to stay behind with me, you wouldn't have taken off with the others, right?"

Josh smiled, caught. "Maybe. But if I had, I guarantee I wouldn't have looked like that."

Sadie laughed and the two of them started slowly up the hill. She tucked her face into her green coat and Josh did the same to avoid the worst of the bitter wind.

"Just so you guys know," she said after a minute, "I'm a big girl. I can take care of myself. You guys can stop posting bodyguards."

"Bodyguards?"

She rolled her dark eyes. "Yes. But thank you." And with a little sigh, she hugged herself. "What would your dad say if he knew you were harboring an FBI fugitive?"

"I don't know," he said truthfully. "He would probably offer to help if you needed it, but not much else. I think he would understand the situation."

She seemed to take that in for a moment. "And do you?"

His gaze went to her left eye without meaning to. *I'm evidence.* "I think so."

She gave him a little smile. "Thanks." She glanced back up the long hill. "So, I guess we're making lunch?"

"I'll let you in on a secret, Sadie. Trevor's making lunch right now—he always does—and I bet if we slow down, it'll be done by the time we get inside."

They didn't slow down, though. Now that they were heading uphill, the storm was blowing directly into their faces. Josh picked up his speed and Sadie matched it easily. The Jacksons owned a few acres on the mountain, but it wasn't until they trudged in snowshoes from one corner of the property to the other that he realized just how big that really was.

"This is a little familiar," Sadie said quietly.

Josh glanced from the trail below up to what was quickly turning into a blizzard. "I'm sorry, Sadie. We never should have brought you out here."

For some reason she smiled. "No. I'm enjoying myself—something I definitely wasn't doing last time. And besides, I have boots this time. And a coat. Makes for warmer hiking."

Josh stopped and stared at her. "What?" she asked, stopping as well.

"Just that you can still find something to laugh about after all you've been through."

"Well," she shrugged, "it's either laugh or cry, and I think I've done a little of both."

By the time they made it inside, the cabin was filled with the aroma of tomato soup and grilled cheese sandwiches—Trevor's specialty. Josh draped his parka over the back of a kitchen chair, and then moved the chair closer to the fireplace, hoping his clothes would dry faster. It was a wet snow out there and his coat was soaked. Sadie followed suit, then tossed her hair around, shaking off the large flakes. When she was done, she twisted it out of the way and proceeded to brush the snow from her pants, completely unaware of the male attention she was drawing.

Josh smacked Trevor as he passed him in the kitchen. The guy looked ridiculous, following her every move. After a quick glare, Trevor went back to making lunch.

Kevin handed her a mug filled to the brim with hot chocolate. She pulled it close to her face and let the steam dance on her rosy cheeks. "Thanks, Kev. This is perfect. I'm freezing."

"Interesting," Kevin said, though he looked at Josh. Earlier, the two of them had discussed Sadie's internal thermostat and the emotional implications of never feeling cold. It was nice to think that she finally felt safe.

"Well, enjoy," Trevor added from the stove. "It's my special recipe."

"Yeah," Josh snickered. "Nestlé."

Josh went to a side cupboard, felt around, and found the bag of marshmallows. He kept it somewhat hidden as he went over to the large stone fireplace. Several hot coals were simmering in the bottom, and Josh tore open the bag excitedly.

Sadie sat on the hearth next to him, mug still close to her face. "You're going to roast marshmallows? Inside?"

"Of course." Josh slid a couple of marshmallows onto a roasting stick and lowered them two precise inches above the hot coals. "You know," he said, turning the stick slowly, "the trick to roasting marshmallows is patience. People always rush it and end up burning the tip, leaving the inside completely neglected. That's a crying shame, if you ask me. The inside is the best part. So you have to wait. Wait and turn. Then you have to wait again."

"Wow." She smiled as she took a sip of hot liquid. "You really know your marshmallows, Josh."

She was mocking him, openly. He didn't mind. Most people did. At first. "It's true," he replied. "I was born to roast marshmallows. It goes back in my family many generations."

"Really? Well, then, I feel honored to be in your presence."

Josh chuckled, enjoying her quick wit again. Pulling out the stick, he inspected his work. *Perfect.* He held the marshmallows in front of her.

Her brows furrowed. "They're not done."

An obvious amateur. He pushed the marshmallows closer. "Try it."

"But they're barely even brown," she insisted.

"Just try it."

She pulled off the top one, leaving behind a trail of white goo, and bit into it slowly. For a moment her face was pensive and then her shoulders slumped. "Okay, it's good. Very good."

"Ha! I told you!" He pulled off the other and popped it in his mouth. "Perfect," he mumbled.

"You know, you're not a very humble marshmallow roaster."

"Hey, I can't help it. With so few talents, I have to flaunt the ones I have."

Kevin plopped down on the nearest couch. "Make me a couple, would ya?"

"I'll take some, too," Sam called from the kitchen.

Josh looked at Sadie, smug that his friends had just validated his ability. Sadie just shook her head as he slipped several more over the red coals.

"You guys aren't like other guys, are you?" she said.

Kevin snorted. "There's the understatement of the century." But Josh wasn't about to let her comment go.

"What? You think we're weird or something?"

Sadie laughed. "Yeah. Basically."

"Hear that, Trevor?" Josh said loudly. "Sadie thinks you're weird."

"Who, me?" He flipped a grilled cheese sandwich high into the air, did a perfect three-sixty, and caught it back on the spatula. At least that had been the plan. In actuality the sandwich landed on the floor with a soft thud. Trevor picked it up, dusted it off, and bit off the corner.

"Oh, come on," Sadie said back to Josh.

"Well, so maybe *he's* a little strange," Josh conceded, "but the rest of us are—"

Rocky jumped off the couch and ran to the window, ears cocked forward. Curious, Josh stopped to listen as well. A small engine, not quite loud enough to be a car, was making its way up the road. With the ski lodge three miles away, it was rare to have people on the road in front of Sam's cabin. But even more strange was to hear the engine cut just outside on the driveway. Rocky started barking excitedly.

"Are you expecting someone, Sam?" Josh asked.

Sam shook his head, looking just as surprised as everyone else. Josh leaned forward to peer out the window, but from his spot on the hearth he couldn't see anything.

Then he noticed Sadie. The color had drained from her face. Her eyes, wide with fear, darted around the room in panic. She obviously didn't want to be seen by whomever it was.

"Why don't you wait in Sam's room until we see who it is?" he suggested softly.

She didn't answer. She just stood and walked swiftly to the back hallway.

CHAPTER 10

Rocky was practically climbing the door by the time the knock came. Sam waited until Sadie disappeared, but as he reached for the lock, Josh realized Rocky wasn't the only dog barking. A dog on the other side was going just as crazy. Josh grabbed Rocky out of the way so Sam could open the door. It was no use. Once Rocky spotted the other dog, he threw his weight down, broke free, and ran forward, snarling. The other dog stood its ground, growling right back.

Josh ignored the dogs long enough to examine the man standing in the doorway. He wore a heavy, olive green coat over matching uniform. Josh wasn't able to make out the insignia, but it was obvious this wasn't a social visit.

As he glanced back toward Sam's room, the man whistled loudly over the snarling dogs. His German shepherd immediately dropped to its haunches. With the other dog under control, Josh grabbed Rocky and dragged him out of the way.

"Sorry about that," Sam said, glaring at Rocky. "Can we help you with something?"

"I hope so," the man answered. "My name is Doug Walker. I'm a law enforcement officer with the Forest Service. I'm sorry to interrupt your afternoon, but we've had a woman go missing on the mountain."

Josh's stomach dropped, but Sam managed to keep his face impassive.

The officer pulled out a small picture and held it up. "Have any of you seen this woman?"

The friends didn't need to see the photo to know who it would be, but they crowded in anyway. It was the first time they'd seen Sadie's face as it should have been: perfectly unblemished. She wasn't alone in the picture; she was tucked under the arm of someone. *The boyfriend?* Josh suddenly wondered, but the person had been cropped out of the photo.

"Nope," Trevor answered. "Never seen her. Sorry."

Josh whipped around. Giving Sadie a place to stay was one thing, but lying to an officer—even if he was nothing more than a glorified park ranger—was unacceptable. Yet the officer accepted Trevor's statement without question. He put the small colored picture away and pulled out a white paper with a close-up of the same photo, only in black and white. Below the photo was all of Sadie's personal information.

"She's been missing almost three days now," the officer continued, "and her family is worried. There's a phone number there." He pointed below the picture. "Could you please call if you see or hear anything that might help?"

"Sure," Trevor answered as if they actually would.

Josh was done with the lies. "Actually, we—"

A low growl escaped the German shepherd. The officer tapped his dog's nose in warning. Too late. The message had been delivered. Rocky charged forward, nearly ripping Josh's arm from the socket. Josh held strong to his collar as Sam yelled at Rocky to knock it off. The officer whistled again and his dog dropped to the snow for a second time. Rocky, however, picked up volume.

"Let him go!" the officer said over the chaos.

Are you nuts? Josh thought, but he did anyway. Rocky jumped the last two feet and barked in the face of the German shepherd. In perfect obedience, the other dog remained perfectly still—not happy, but motionless.

Sarah (Sadie) Augustina Dawson

Age: 26 years

Height: 59 inches

Weight: 102 pounds

Hair color: Dark brown

Eye color: Dark brown

Complexion: Olive

Last seen Christmas Day wearing black sweater and black pants at the Blue Ridge Lodge.

Please call 406-872-4002 with any information.

It looked up at its master as if to say, *You're killin' me here!* But one fierce glare from the officer, and the dog's head snapped back in place.

If Josh hadn't been so wound up, he might have been impressed. Normally Rocky didn't have issues with other dogs. Josh guessed from the way the officer had glared at his own, it normally didn't—

He froze. There was only one reason that officer brought a dog with him. Smell. And Josh had no doubt that the police dog had just caught hold of Sadie's scent. Whether Trevor lied or Sadie hid, that officer was moments away from knowing exactly where she was.

Instinctively, he moved closer to Rocky with no more thought of retreat, but instead of standing the line. He just couldn't let that dog sniff her out like some animal. Rocky tired of the one-sided dog fight and stopped barking, but he still kept a dominant stance over the other. Josh couldn't help but do the same.

The officer was talking again, and Josh had to focus to catch what he was saying.

". . . group of volunteers are gathering in the morning to search for Miss Dawson. We're meeting outside of the lodge at eight o'clock and would be grateful if you could help us out. Even a few hours would be much appreciated. It would mean a lot to the Dawson family."

"Sure," Sam said. "We'd be glad to help."

The lies were coming easily now.

The ranger tipped his hat slightly. "Great. See you in the morning. Come on, girl."

His dog didn't move.

Josh could only imagine the thoughts running through that dog's head. She was trained for obedience, and yet she was also trained to hunt. Right now she couldn't do both. Josh held his breath waiting to see which she would choose.

"Come on, girl," the officer said again.

She whined in response. The ranger's eyes suddenly flew behind the four guys to the great room. In another second, he would put two and two together.

Josh didn't give him the chance.

Grabbing Rocky's collar, he yanked hard. "Come on, boy. Stop being a brute. Let her go." He looked up at the officer. "Sorry. He doesn't have the manners yours does."

The officer smiled as he patted her back. "She's worth her weight in gold."

With another whistle, he finally got his dog's attention, and the two of them stepped off the front porch. Sam shut the door in time for Josh to slump against it.

While his three friends pored over the missing person flyer, Josh rewound the last three minutes. Lying to an officer. Hiding Sadie from the FBI. There's no way his dad would back them up on this one.

"Now what?" Sam asked softly.

"We all go to prison," Josh said, rubbing his eyes.

Kevin scanned the paper. "People could get hurt looking for her. She has to tell someone."

"*We* should have told him," Josh corrected. "What were you thinking, Trevor?" *What was I thinking!* he added, head spinning.

"Hey," Trevor fought back, "Sadie's an adult. If she doesn't want the world knowing where she is, then it's nobody's business but hers."

"It's her family's business!" Sam countered. "She should have let them know where she is. They must be worried sick."

"And then what? Let her boyfriend take her down again?"

Trevor was right. But Sam was right, too. Then again so were Kevin and Josh for that matter. All Josh could think was that if it hadn't been for Sam's dog, they wouldn't even be having this conversation. They would be saying good-bye to Sadie. Rocky's paws were on the frosted window watching the snowmobile disappear down the road.

"What?" Kevin asked, following Josh's gaze.

Josh blew out his breath. "Rocky just kept that dog from finding Sadie."

Trevor stopped mid-yell to stare at him. "Do you think that guy . . . ?"

Josh shook his head quickly. "No. If the ranger thought we had her, he would never have left. He would have found a way to come in and search the place."

"Oh, wow . . . ," Kevin said for all of them.

For a minute no one spoke. Finally, Josh took the paper from Kevin and walked to the back bedroom. "Sadie?" he called softly.

She opened the door hesitantly, eyes going to the front door. Josh, however, stared down at the black-and-white photo of her, struck by the happy and confident woman looking up at him. It was in such contrast to the frightened and vulnerable one in Sam's doorway. It made him sick.

He handed her the missing person sign, then watched the remaining color drain from her face. She read it, reread it, then buried her face in her hands and sank to the ground.

CHAPTER 11

Sadie waited until the cabin was silent before she crept out of Sam's room. She was alone, sort of. The dog was on a couch and she could see Sam and Josh outside on the deck, shoveling the still-falling snow. It wasn't complete privacy, but probably as close as she was going to get. The black lab looked up and then lay right back down, no longer expecting a greeting from her. After everything, though, she felt some obligation to him. She wandered into the two-story great room and knelt in front of him.

For a long time the two just stared at each other, before she managed a simple, "Thanks."

Rocky laid his chin on his paws in acknowledgement.

With that taken care of, Sadie went to the stone fireplace, studying Sam's family picture again. It still amazed her that all those people were from one family. Couples were grouped together with matching outfits right down to the socks, but one couple stood out from the rest. Sam's parents. They were in their early sixties and quite handsome. Yet the thing that struck her was their faces, like they were lit from the inside with joy. The light seemed to radiate to the others, as if every family member were perfectly happy. It was just a façade, though. Sadie knew that kind of happiness didn't exist in the real world.

Her gaze dropped to the flyer of herself, thinking she'd been happy once as well. That, too, was a façade. The photo, not even a week old, disgusted her. Because for the briefest, tiniest moment, she missed him.

She tore the paper into tiny pieces and threw it and all thoughts of Guillermo into the dying fire. Both were consumed before she made it back to the couch.

As the sun set and the room darkened, her thoughts settled on her mom and the agony she must be in. Her only daughter, missing. Knowing her mom's tendency toward the dramatic, she wondered how she'd taken the news, but that thought led to a more distressing thought. Who told her? Guillermo? The FBI? And if so, did any of them have the guts to tell her why?

Sadie didn't stop the thoughts as they crashed against her one after another. It wasn't fair for her to be living in this façade of snowshoes and marshmallows when everyone else in her life was desperately awaiting news of her.

Rocky stretched and jumped off the couch, heading for the back door. As the dog went out, one of the guys came back in. She didn't check to see which one, not really caring. She was headed down a dangerous path called Regret and she didn't want to be interrupted while she explored it.

A voice was whispering to her that she should have stayed at Guillermo's. She should have worked things out with him instead of running away. Then she could have spared her mom all the anguish she was now in. *But then what?* she wondered. How long would he have left her locked up? It was hard to know how forgiving he was when she'd never seen him with a need to forgive. *Still,* she reasoned, *what's the worst that could have happened?* He would have cooled down, she would have explained her complete innocence, and they would be together again.

Maybe.

It wasn't until Josh got up to poke the dying fire that she remembered she wasn't alone. She should have guessed it was him sitting on the couch opposite her. Sam would have tried to bombard her with happy thoughts, but Josh was content to let her sit in private remorse. He got a decent flame going before returning to his spot. Still, he said nothing, leaving her time to throw herself a full-blown pity party.

She didn't deserve what had happened to her. She had done nothing wrong—other than walk out on the FBI, and even that couldn't be very illegal. But, then again, her mom didn't deserve the torture she was probably going through either.

Suddenly she was furious at herself. At first the depressing thoughts brought her comfort, but now she could see they were useless. She needed to be doing, not thinking. That was the only way to help her mom. Which meant one thing . . .

It was time to go back.

She let the idea simmer a moment, knowing it was the right thing to do. Frightening, but right. With a deep breath, she turned to make her announcement. But Josh wasn't watching the fire like she had been. He was watching her across the dimly lit room. Only his eyes appeared to be staring through her, not at her.

Distracted, she asked, "What has you so lost in thought?"

He blinked hard, coming back into focus. "Sorry. I was thinking about my mom, actually. It's her birthday today."

"Oh?" In an instant, Sadie swapped her dramatic solution for a less devastating one. "Are you going down the mountain to call her?"

He hesitated. "No."

"Are you sure? I bet she'd love a call." *As would my mom,* she added desperately.

"Actually . . . I haven't seen her in awhile. It's kind of a long story."

She waited, but when he didn't elaborate further, she realized what he was really saying. No phone call. Her shoulders slumped. Now she had no choice. She had to go back.

She tried to envision the moment she would see Guillermo again, wondering if he would kiss her or punch her? Then she was stuck deciding which was worse.

"You remind me of her a little bit actually," Josh said quietly, which explained why he was still staring at her. "She had dark, curly hair. Deep, brown eyes." He finally turned back to the fire. "She was very pretty." Sadie wasn't sure how to respond, but he went on, oblivious to the fact he'd shut down his story seconds ago. "My dad remarried when I was seven and my stepmom is my mom in every sense of the word. I'm not sure why I still think about my real mom anymore. Seems a little pathetic."

"Not really," she countered. "When I was a baby, my dad decided he was done with the whole family thing and took off. I saw him a few times as a kid and less and less after that. Now he's out of my life completely. Crazy thing is, even though he's a jerk, I still miss him sometimes. So maybe we just miss what they could have been." She shook her head. "What they *should* have been."

"Yeah."

As Josh fell silent again, Sadie knew it was time. "Well, I need to let my mom know I'm okay. I can't believe I didn't do it sooner. And I guess I should call the ranger station, too," she sighed. "And the lodge and everyone else . . ." For all she knew, everyone in northwestern Montana was looking for her. "But . . ." A familiar, suffocating pain hit her. "I'm just not ready to see him yet."

"Then don't go back. Trevor and Kevin will be back with dinner in a minute, and then I can drive you down to where you can get reception on my cell phone. That way you can let your mom and the authorities know you're okay, without having to see . . . *him*. We're here until the second. You're welcome to stay as long as you need."

The solution was so tempting, so easy to accept, yet at the same time . . . "Aren't you guys sick of having a psychotic fifth wheel hanging around?"

"Doesn't bother me, and knowing the others, it doesn't bother them, either. Actually," he added with a smile, "I think Trevor likes having a pretty girl hanging around."

Sadie's lashes lowered. Josh was being generous—they all were. She considered his offer. A call to her mom, a chance to end the searching, and a safe place to hide from it all.

She nodded. "Okay. Thank you. But kick me out any time."

"Not likely, but if anyone gets sick of you, I'll let you know."

She studied him. Josh had an honesty about him—for better or worse. He'd been blunt enough before, she was sure he was telling it to her straight now. "Thanks," she said again, and feeling a tremendous weight lifted, she leaned back into the couch.

With help in the works for her mom, the next round of thoughts was less dismal. She just wondered where she'd be right now if those FBI agents hadn't shown up and ruined her life. Sipping Argentine wine. Stroking diamonds.

"Does it still hurt?" Josh asked.

No need to ask what "it" was. He was staring at "it" like he had been for two days. "Not really," she said. "It's my shoulder that kills."

"What happened to your shoulder?"

"Another bruise, but it's huge. It hurts a ton."

Josh's eyes narrowed. "Also from him?"

"Honestly, I don't remember. I didn't notice it until after I got here." She wanted to say that someone else had "given" that bruise to her— Salvador maybe—but for all she knew it was Guillermo as well. "I sort of blacked out after the first one."

Josh leaned forward. "You blacked out?"

"Yeah. Instead of punching him back, I passed out. Pretty pathetic, isn't it?"

"No," he growled. "Pathetic is the low-life male who knocked you out cold."

"True," she conceded quietly. "Very true."

"What happened after that?"

Sadie glanced sideways. Suddenly, answering Josh's questions didn't seem like such a good idea. He wasn't reacting very well. His hands were balled into fists and his jaw was clenched tight. One part of her was yelling at herself to shut up, but the other was grateful for a chance to talk through things.

"Well, I woke up in a different room—*locked* in a different room, actually. I could hear someone on the other side of the door, so I pounded on it for awhile, yelling at them to let me out. Nobody did, so . . ." Her shoulders lifted. "I climbed out the window."

"Really?"

"Yeah," she said, still somewhat proud of herself. "I don't think they expected that since the window was so small. But then again"—she smiled weakly—"so am I."

Josh wasn't smiling, though. He didn't look amused in the least. She heard him mutter something about how her boyfriend should have been the one locked up. "Locked up" was a little harsh, but she wouldn't have minded seeing Guillermo with a black eye—or two—of his own.

"Sad thing is," she continued, "I took a self-defense class in college. A lot of good it did me." She closed her eyes, the left one throbbing in memory. "I guess in his mind I deserved it."

"No girl deserves to get hit. No matter what she did."

"Even if he thought—"

"Yes," Josh cut in. "Even if."

"—he thought I betrayed him?" she continued, ignoring his disruption. "He thought I had stabbed him in the back, Josh. That I actually believed everything the feds told me. I mean, he thought I was their spy. Me! Harmless little Sadie! Ready to turn him in like a common criminal. I can't even imagine what that must have felt like."

"That's no excuse, Sadie. Real men don't hit women. Period."

"I know," she said. "I know. But Guillermo's not the kind of guy to hit a girl normally."

"Normally? *Normally?*" Josh said, voice rising. "Do you even hear yourself?"

She had no response. Her argument was weak, and she knew it. But she'd spent the last two days trying to understand what had sparked such rage in such a benevolent man. All she could figure was that she had hurt Guillermo at a depth she couldn't even begin to understand.

Josh sat forward, elbows on his knees. "Sadie, what kind of real estate investors have the federal government trying to bug their cabin?"

Her eyes narrowed. "He's not involved in drugs if that's what you're getting at. I would know. I'm not stupid."

"I didn't say you were, just . . . maybe after you call your mom, you should call the FBI."

"The FBI? *The FBI!*" She shot to her feet. "The FBI tried to kill me!"

Josh reared back. "What do you mean?"

"In the storm. They were the ones chasing me. They said that if I didn't stop, I was as good as dead."

He shook his head. "That can't be right. The FBI doesn't threaten innocent people."

"Yeah? Well, maybe they don't know I'm innocent!"

"No," he insisted. "No way. You must have heard them wrong, or maybe they were talking about the storm—which very nearly killed you. Or maybe it wasn't even them. I thought you said it could have been your boyfriend's friends."

Sadie threw her hands up. "I don't know. I don't care. It doesn't matter anyway. If the FBI would have left me alone in the first place, none of this would've happened. This is their fault as much as it is his!" she cried, pointing to her eye. Josh shot her an incredulous look, but she wasn't about to be derailed. "I told them to stay away from me. I told them I wanted nothing to do with it, but they planted the bug anyway. I said no and look where it got me! They're still hunting me, only now they're sending cops door to door. They'll never quit!"

She stopped, realizing she'd lost it. Josh just watched her, his expression unreadable in the dim light. So she began again, pleading for understanding. "The FBI is wrong about Guillermo. He's a good person, Josh. He really is. He's so kind and generous to everyone. If you only knew him . . ." Her voice cracked as her emotions began to take over. "He loves me," she whispered. *Or he did.*

The only sound in the room was the crackling fire. Josh stood slowly and came toward her. Sadie kept her eyes on his feet, refusing to let him see the pooling tears. She was mad at him for butting into her life, mad at him for dredging up more pain, and even more mad at herself for letting him.

When he lifted her chin to look at him, his expression was no longer one of frustration, but one of pure sadness. And pity. Pity that she loathed more than life itself. "*That,*" he said, softly touching her bruise, "is not love, Sadie."

A few tears escaped. She couldn't help it.

"I would never hurt my girlfriend, Sadie, regardless of what she had done. And no man who deserves the title of man would ever treat a woman like this. Ever."

She scooted away from him, no longer caring who was right or wrong, but just wanting to be done. She grasped wildly for the switch in her mind to shut off the pain but couldn't find it. If she had her way in that moment, she would never spend another second with another man. Ever.

"My dad tells me stories," he pressed, "women who think it's just a one-time thing and end up dead a week later. You can't kid yourself think-ing—"

Her chin came up. "I'd like you to leave," she said calmly. "Please."

Josh's brows shot up in surprise. He studied her a long minute, then nodded softly and made his way back outside.

Only after the door shut did it occur to her that it should be *her* leaving. Not him.

CHAPTER 12

"Don't you want your coat?"

Josh looked down at his shirt and scowled. "Believe me, the weather out here is a lot warmer than in there."

Sam looked through the window. Sadie was staring straight ahead, her somber profile lit by the nearly nonexistent fire. "What happened in there?" he asked softly. "Is she going to call?"

"She's calling her mom and the authorities when Kevin and Trevor get back. By the way, she thinks that ranger was from the FBI."

That was new to Sam. "Was he?"

"I doubt it. I don't think the FBI would hide who they were."

"Is that why you guys were arguing?"

"No." Josh picked up his shovel and began working on the endless piles of snow. "Sadie started defending her abusive boyfriend."

Sam shook his head. "She's had a rough couple of days. Go easy on her."

"That's the point!" he exploded. "Do you know she has a huge bruise on her shoulder she can't even remember getting? Or that her boyfriend hit her hard enough she passed out cold?" His face twisted as if in pain. "Is it possible to get a concussion from something like that?"

Sam sifted through six months of medical school. "I haven't studied head trauma yet, but she was pretty confused and out of it the first day. I don't know. Maybe."

Josh loaded his shovel with twice the snow it was built to handle. "I can't believe she would defend that jerk. She seems smarter than that. If she even thinks about going back . . ."

Sam stared at his buddy. "Hey, you're not . . . uh . . . you know?"

"Not what?"

"Interested? In . . . Sadie?"

Josh's head whipped up and around. "Are you crazy?"

"Right. No. Sorry. I just thought . . ." But Sam should have known better. Josh and Megan were as steady as Kevin and Amy were—minus the marriage. Plus, Sadie wasn't Mormon. Sam kicked himself that his thoughts ever went that direction, especially with Josh glaring at him.

"Just because Sadie's attract-*ive,* doesn't mean I'm attract-*ed.* I'm not. At all."

"I know. Sorry," Sam said again. He turned and watched Sadie through the glass, thinking that if anyone was attracted it was him. He shook it off. He had Elizabeth back in California—well, not really, but some day he was going to get up the nerve to ask her out.

Josh elbowed him. "Wait a sec, Sam. Are you?"

"I don't know. Maybe. A little."

"Look, the *last* thing she needs right now is a couple of guys going gaga over her. Trevor's bad enough. Give her some space."

"Geez, don't overreact. I'm just a little—I don't know—mesmerized, that's all. It's hard not to be."

"Being *mesmerized* is one thing. Being serious about it is another. Besides, she's not your type."

Sam bristled. "And what's that supposed to mean?"

Josh leaned against his shovel. "Sorry. I didn't realize you're into girl-friends of rich, wanted-by-the-FBI drug lords—especially the type that are quick to defend their abusive boyfriends. Or that you'd gone back on our pact: no nonmember girls. Come on. We both know that 'To look once is human. To look twice is . . . '"

"'. . . asking for trouble,'" Sam finished for him, hating that he was right.

"That motto has gotten us this far. You can't quit on me now. What happened to that sweet-little-blonde-*Mormon*-girl in California you keep yapping about?"

"Who? Elizabeth?" Sam smiled in sudden remembrance. Elizabeth was brainy, spiritual, *and* beautiful. And like Josh pointed out, Mormon. But sadly, Sam had said more to Sadie than he ever had to Elizabeth. "I have issues," he sighed.

Josh threw a pile of snow his way with a laugh. "Yes, you do. Just ask her out. It's not that hard."

"Easy for you to say. How do I know she won't turn me down?"

"You won't until you try."

"Gee, thanks. Maybe if you could meet Elizabeth, you could tell me what you think. I think she's perfect."

Josh's expression darkened. "Then why are you letting a pretty little thing like Sadie distract you?"

"I'm not."

"Good."

"Good," Sam echoed. Both of them stole one last glance at Sadie before going back to shoveling. By the time they finished shoveling the deck around the side of the cabin, Kevin and Trevor pulled up.

"Chinese, anyone?" Trevor called out.

Josh rolled his eyes. "Only Trevor could find Chinese takeout in a Montana blizzard."

Dinner was uncomfortably quiet. Sadie barely touched her food even though she insisted she loved cheap Chinese food. Sam asked her a few questions about her job at the lodge to which she gave one-word answers.

After a little bit of that, even he gave up and started talking basketball with Kevin and Trevor. Josh kept stealing glances across the table, waiting for Sadie to look back, but she never did. In fact, as dinner wore on, it became obvious she was avoiding him—quite a feat considering he was seated directly across from her.

As the conversation turned from indoor sports to outdoor, Trevor suggested it was the perfect night for snowboarding with the fresh snow and warm temperatures that came in behind the storm. Trevor just about had them convinced when Sadie cut him off mid-sentence.

"Hey, Sam, before you guys go, would you mind driving me down the hill? I need to call . . ." she blew out her breath, ". . . everyone."

"Uh, sure." Sam looked just as surprised as Josh by the sudden change in conversation.

"Do you have a phone I could use?" she continued. "I really don't want to go back to the lodge just yet."

"My phone gets the best reception up here," Kevin said. "Once you're around the first ridge you should be able to make your calls."

"Thanks. And is it okay if I stay here a little bit longer?" Then she added softly, "I know it has to be weird for you guys to have me here."

"Stay as long as you need," Sam assured her.

She looked around the table, gaze stopping just short of Josh. "All of you are being so generous. Thanks."

Josh sat back, contemplating the dark-haired enigma. He had seriously offended Sadie, that much was obvious, but he wasn't about to apologize for what he'd said. Someone had to remind her that her boyfriend was a creep. Yet, he couldn't help but notice that hidden in her eyes was a deep, penetrating sadness. Part of that was his fault for bluntly shoving reality down her throat, and for that he was truly sorry.

"Do you want to go now?" Sam asked.

"Yeah, I think so." Her voice wavered a little, but her face was calmly resolute.

"Okay. Just let me grab my wallet."

"Wait," Trevor said, jumping back in the conversation, "How about we all ride down together and go snowboarding after you make your calls, Sadie? That'll save Sam a trip down the mountain, and then I can show you how fun night boarding is."

She shook her head. "I'm not in the mood. Plus I don't know how to snowboard."

"No prob. I'll teach you."

"No really. Not interested. I don't have any gear anyway."

"Sam's mom always keeps stuff here. And besides, snowboarding isn't that hard." Little did Sadie know, Trevor had a stubborn streak all his own.

"Come on," Kevin said, piling on, "It wouldn't hurt to get outside this cabin for a bit."

In an attempt at reconciliation, Josh finally spoke up. "Hey, guys, Sadie obviously doesn't want to go. Sam can just bring her back here after she makes her calls—or I can," he added with a look of truce across the table. "I don't mind. Really. And I'm sorry about before. I was out of line."

She blinked, and a little of the ice melted. "He's right," she said to the others. "I really don't want to go. Besides, I'm not ready to go back to the ski lodge. My boyfriend owns part of it, so I'm sure I'd—"

"Whoa, whoa, whoa!" Trevor interrupted. "Your boyfriend *owns* the ski lodge?"

"Part owner," she admitted begrudgingly.

Kevin whistled softly. "Talk about your international real estate."

Sam straightened in his chair. "Wait, what did you say his name was?"

"Guillermo . . . Vasquez."

"Mr. Vasquez?" Sam shook his head. "Oh man, I know him. My parents and I met him at the lodge when he bought it a few years back. I can't believe it. *That's* your boyfriend? That guy is loaded." At Sadie's frown, he quickly amended, "and very nice," though he winced at his second choice of words as well.

"*An-y-way,*" she said, "I really don't want to see him, or any of his friends, or the FBI, or anyone at all, actually. So you guys go do your snowboarding thing without me. I should probably just sleep anyway."

"You're worried about people finding you, right?" Trevor asked. When she nodded, he continued, "And your boyfriend knows you don't snow-board or ski, right?"

"Yes."

"Then where's the last place anyone will look for you?"

Josh had to admit, Trevor's logic was sound. First time.

Trevor plowed on with a full grin. "So let's head over to Deer Basin. It's less than an hour away and their night boarding's just as good. Then you can make your calls and forget about everything else."

Sadie looked from person to person until she came to Josh, almost pleading for help.

"I can stay behind if you don't want to go," he suggested. "I have a couple of essays to work on anyway."

But his words seemed to have the opposite effect. "No, I'll go," she said, making it perfectly clear that she didn't want to be stuck alone with him for another one of his lectures.

Chapter 13

Sadie watched the guys throw their gear into the back of Sam's truck, still working on an excuse. Her best option was to not hold back the tears that were sure to flow once she talked to her mom. The crying would scare off the guys, and they'd go without her. In the meantime, she wasn't thrilled to climb back into that truck. The memory of the last time was still too fresh. But she had no choice. Her mom needed her, so she piled in with them.

The extended cab really wasn't meant for five adults, four of whom were grown men. At six-foot four, Kevin got the coveted front seat. Josh was only a few inches shy of that, but Sam insisted on driving his own truck. Trevor was the shortest, giving him no chance whatsoever, which meant Sadie—poor, vertically challenged Sadie—was shoved in between him and Josh in the back seat. It was a good thing she was so short because their legs took up all the room.

She braced herself for another rebuke from Josh, especially now that she was literally stuck next to him, but he said nothing as they climbed in, nor as they started their slow descent down the hill. Her curiosity got the better of her and she stole a peek around her long curls. Josh was leaned against the seat half asleep, but as soon as he noticed her, he gave a little smile. Apparently he'd forgiven her for her bad behavior, making it easier to forgive his, and she settled in more comfortably in the less-than-comfortable quarters.

Sam put Kevin in charge of picking out the music, and instantly she wished he hadn't. Not only did Kevin have lousy taste in music, but he turned the volume up way too high. He started dancing around the front seat, oblivious. Even Trevor's leg bounced next to hers.

She marveled at how different four friends could be and yet still get along so well—"best friends since the fourth grade." Sam was the quiet intellectual. Kevin was the class clown. Trevor was . . . well, just Trevor—self-absorbed and slightly obnoxious. And Josh—who'd been virtually silent since their earlier conversation—was still a puzzle. Sometimes quick to make her laugh, and other times, so aggravating.

The winding road began to wreck havoc with her stomach. Thankfully it was a short drive to the ski village—her home away from home—and Sam slowed to a stop just on the outskirts. Kevin handed her his phone over the seat. "It should work fine here."

Sadie held onto it awkwardly. The four of them were waiting for her to make the calls, but in such close proximity, it seemed strange. She was expecting a wild emotional outburst from her mom—if not worse. "Do you mind if I get out?" she asked.

"Oh. Right. Sure," Sam said, pulling over.

Both Josh and Sam had to climb out before she was able to get out of the truck. Once she was free, she walked a little ways into the headlights.

"Maybe I'll call Amy while we're here," Kevin said as the guys watched her.

"No way," Trevor whined. "You talked to her yesterday. Call her on your own time."

"The mountain's not going anywhere, Trevor."

"And Amy is? You don't hear Josh moaning about Megan, do you? Call her when we get to Deer Basin, and I'm on the slopes."

The guys grew silent as they watched Sadie. Twice during her call she looked up at the truck. She wasn't crying. She wasn't even smiling. She looked . . . worried, almost confused.

"What do you think is wrong?" Kevin asked.

"I'll go check," Josh offered.

By the time he made it to her, Sadie was no longer talking into the phone, but clutching it tightly in her hand. "How'd it go with your mom?" he asked carefully.

"She didn't know I was missing."

"Wait. What?"

She nodded with a blank stare. "My mom had no idea I was gone."

"But . . . that . . . can't . . ." He struggled to compute. "How?"

"I don't know," she whispered, hugging herself against the night air. "She thought I was just mad at her or something and that's why I hadn't returned her calls."

Josh's mind raced through the conversation with the ranger, trying to make sense of it all. "But the guy specifically said your family was worried. Could he mean somebody else?"

"No. It's just me and my mom. My brother lives in San Diego and none of my aunts or uncles live around here."

"But that doesn't make any sense!"

"I know."

For a moment, neither spoke, too confused to do anything else. Then Josh asked, "Did you tell her where you are or what happened?"

"Only that something happened with Guillermo and I wanted to take a breather for a few days. She was more worried at the end of the conversation than she was at the beginning. I tried to assure her that I'm okay."

"And are you?"

She smiled weakly. "I will be after the next call."

Josh went back to the truck window to report and to give her some privacy. The other guys couldn't make any sense of it either. Nothing in this whole Sadie thing made sense.

"Why wouldn't they have started the search at her mom's place?" Kevin asked.

"They would have," Josh said. "That's what's so disturbing."

He stayed outside the truck, straining to hear her next call. Sadie was spelling out her name—first, middle, and last, plus her nickname. Then with a look of pure disbelief, she slowly shook her head.

A pit dug itself in Josh's stomach. "Something's seriously wrong, and I have the feeling it has something to do with her jerk of a boyfriend."

He left the truck with his buddies following in time to catch the last part of her conversation. "Are you sure?" she was saying. "I thought that . . . okay . . . right. Sorry to bother you, officer. I must have been given the wrong information."

She closed the phone and stared up at the stars. "What am I supposed to think now? They didn't know—" Her voice caught. "I can't believe this."

"Why would that ranger say to call then?" Kevin asked. "Did you talk to him specifically?"

"Well . . . no. I kind of burned the paper with his number on it, but I called information and got the National Forest Service Station."

"That's it, then," Sam burst in relief. "They just gave you the wrong number."

Sadie was already shaking her head. "They said that even if it had been called into another department—fire, police, or anywhere—they would have a record of it in their office."

The gravity of her words settled around them. Her mom. The police. The ranger.

Josh's next words came carefully, knowing he was treading on thin ice. "Maybe you should call the FBI."

Her expression hardened. "No!"

"Josh is right," Kevin added. "You're in way over your head." Then he shot Josh a look saying she wasn't the only one.

"No. No way! Not after what they did."

"Then let Josh call his dad," Sam suggested. "He can tell you what to do."

"Yes," Josh said, wondering why he hadn't thought of it sooner. "He was promoted to detective a few years back. He could make a few calls and figure out what's going on."

"No." She took a deep breath. "No, it's okay. I can handle this. I just need to think for a minute. You said the search starts at the ski lodge in the morning. So . . . I'll just call there. Maybe they know what's going on."

She walked out of the protection of the headlights. The four men watched her, too overwhelmed to do any more speculating. It quickly became apparent that the third call was different from the others. Within seconds she was nodding her head, and after another minute she flashed them a smile. Once the call was done, she came back to report. "Well, at least *they* knew what I was talking about. The lodge has my sign plastered everywhere—so embarrassing—but I told the guy at the desk I was completely safe. He said he'd pass that message on to everyone."

"Oh. Good," Sam said, but Josh was still wary.

"Did he say why the authorities hadn't been alerted? Why they had no record you were missing, or why nobody thought to ask your mom?"

It took a moment for Sadie to answer, and suddenly her eyes were glistening in the headlights. "The police said I hadn't been missing long enough, so Guillermo . . . he . . ." She swallowed hard. "He started a search on his own. He hired people on his own dime—including that ranger—to do whatever it took to find me."

"Oh," Trevor replied. "I guess that makes sense."

"Yes," she whispered. "Maybe he still loves me after all."

CHAPTER 14

For the next forty minutes, Sadie went from depressed to relieved to almost happy. Her mom was okay. Guillermo had been so worried that he struck out on his own and organized a private search party. That could only mean one thing: he wanted her back. She wasn't sure what that meant for her or her future, but in the meantime, her spirits were lifted tremendously. Almost enough to distract her from what lay ahead.

Almost.

As they neared Deer Basin, her emotions began to freefall again. She twisted the ring on her pinky trying to think up an excuse to get out of snowboarding now that she didn't need to be cheered up. In all her twenty-six years, she'd never ventured over to Deer Basin. Of course, if it hadn't been for her good-paying job, she never would have gone to Blue Ridge either.

Sam pulled into the parking lot, and Sadie glanced at the clock. Just after eight, and the parking lot was still packed. She'd only been skiing twice in her lifetime—both times, failing miserably. And this wasn't even skiing. This was snowboarding! Add to it the darkness that obscured things like trees, boulders, and cliffs, and she figured she might end up a missing person after all.

A hand went on her knee—Trevor's—letting her know that her knee wasn't the only one she was bouncing in the close quarters. "Sorry," she muttered. "I really don't want to do this."

"Don't worry," he said with a smile. "I can teach anyone to snowboard, and I've got Josh here to prove it."

That didn't calm her nerves. Her pinky grew raw under the constant ring-twisting.

Then she spotted it, her salvation. A huge bonfire glowed outside the lodge, shining like a beacon in the night. And surrounding the bonfire were scores of people having a wonderfully safe evening.

"Hey, guys," she said as they began unloading, "I'm going to sit over there while you enjoy your skiing or boarding or whatever it is you do. That way I won't slow you down."

"No way," Trevor said. "You promised. You can come willingly or over my shoulder like a sack of potatoes—and believe me, I'm good enough to board with you over my shoulder."

"You wouldn't dare," she said, even as Trevor started toward her with a grin. She threw her hands up in surrender, but not before throwing out a few Spanish insults.

Sam laughed, understanding more than he should, and said, "I'll go buy your lift pass."

Sadie sighed. Yet another reason she shouldn't have come. Somehow in her flight for life, she'd neglected to grab her purse from Guillermo's cabin, leaving her subject to Sam's generosity. And another reason was about to be revealed.

Out of the corner of her eye she saw a flash of green. Kevin handed her a bundle of clothes, and she groaned. For whatever reason, Sam's mom had an affinity for green. And not just any green, either. A glaring, neon green. From the gloves to the snow pants, every piece was the same garish hideous green. The clothes were bound to reflect every artificial light on the mountain, and with each piece of gear she put on, she felt more and more ridiculous. By the time she put on the hat—also green—she passed all hope of retaining any dignity. The guys were all wearing dark, subtle colors, looking great in their snow gear. She just looked like a bright green snow beast.

As if to confirm it, Josh turned, raised an eyebrow, and simply said, "Nice."

She began shedding the gloves. "I don't know how you expect me to move in all this. I'm already sweating. Besides, I look stupid."

"No. You look good." But he wasn't fooling her. His eyes were laughing hysterically.

Kevin walked over and put an arm around her shoulder. "What's wrong, Kermit?"

That did it. He and Josh busted up. The hat and scarf came off as well, as Sadie determined she would spend the rest of the night in front of that bonfire.

"Wait, wait, wait." Josh grabbed her before she could break free of the coat as well. "We can't have you getting sick again, can we? It's cold."

"Not by the fire," she pointed out.

Ignoring her comment, he put her left glove on followed by the right, then tied the scarf snuggly around her neck. The whole time he repressed a smile. Sadie had the overwhelming desire for a laser, one that could pierce through thick skulls. "Much better," he said, fixing her hat as well. As he turned to leave, he sung softly—but not quite softly enough—"It's not easy being green."

Kevin slapped him on the shoulder, and the two of them erupted in another round of juvenile laughter.

Sadie smiled in spite of herself. They were ridiculous—both of them. With a roll of her eyes, she wandered off to find Trevor, who was scouting out a gentle slope to teach her on. Thankfully he didn't comment on her outfit, but instead began a discourse in snowboardese about the "intricate" sport of night boarding.

It didn't take long for her to tune him out and drift back to Guillermo. Until that moment, it never dawned on her that while he'd invested in the ski resort, she'd never actually seen her boyfriend ski or snowboard. *No wonder I love him.*

Loved! she caught herself. *Loved.*

"Are you listening?" Trevor asked over his shoulder.

"Yes," she lied. "But don't you guys ever ski?" she asked. At least then she would have two boards beneath her, not one.

"The other guys like skiing better, but I like boarding. So we switch off."

Just her luck. *I'm gonna die,* she groaned, noting the irony, considering how close she'd come recently. So she really tried to listen. Bending, leaning. Toes, heels. Fall backward on the hill, not forward. Good to know. It was more helpful to watch Trevor than listen.

Surprisingly, he was being extremely patient with her—not really a word she would have picked out for Trevor. He was also easily distracted. One little, "How exactly does the heel thingy work again?" and she bought herself another ten minutes of nonboarding time. But the December night air soon caught up with her. Her face was freezing, her toes were burning, and she was ready to humiliate herself just to get to that fire.

"All right, I think I'm ready," she said finally.

"Great! Are you right or left-handed?"

"Left."

"Goofy," he said, kneeling down to strap her into the contraption.

"Thanks," she said, though she couldn't exactly disagree. These guys kept pushing her outside her comfort zone and she didn't like it. Guillermo not only made her feel comfortable, but he made her feel elegant, sophisticated, and beautiful, oftentimes caring more about how she looked than she did. She was sure he'd drop dead at the sight of her now. Goofy indeed.

Trevor laughed. "Goofy is a snowboarding term for lefties."

Whether it was or not, she still felt it.

When she was sufficiently strapped in, Trevor gave her a little push, and she started down the short hill. He trotted alongside her, shouting help as needed. She fell half a dozen times on the way down, but like he taught her, she fell back on the mountain instead of face-planting it all the way down. When they reached the bottom alive *and* unharmed, she was thoroughly ecstatic.

So was he.

"Way to go, girl!" he said with a congratulatory hug.

"Thanks. You really *are* a good teacher, Trevor."

She waited for him to release her from the hug. After another second, she finally gave him a gentle push. He didn't go far, though, and kept one arm draped around her.

"You know, for a first-timer you did great—and I'm not just saying that. You did great!"

There was something in the way he was looking at her, something that said, *Caution: brain off. Going on pure instinct now, baby.* She hoped she'd just read him wrong.

Fat chance.

He brushed a strand of hair from her cheek. "You know, good-looking chicks like you always choose the wrong guy. I bet your rich boyfriend never knew what he had. You deserve someone better." Then he winked.

Sadie was dumbfounded. She couldn't tell if Trevor was joking around or if he was really coming on to her—stud man indeed—but she wasn't about to stick around to find out. She stepped away from him and changed the subject. "Does your girlfriend snowboard?"

That's all it took. He was off again about how his girlfriend did a completely different style, easily dominating the rest of the conversation while she frantically searched the hill for help. By some miracle, she spotted Sam across the way. "Sam!" she shouted.

He looked around and ran over to them. "Hey. How'd the lesson go?"

"Sadie did awesome!" Trevor said. "I had no idea what a pro we had under our roof."

Now Trevor was being absurd. She moved closer to Sam. "Actually, it wasn't that—"

"Hey, Gumby!" came a loud shout. There was no mistaking Kevin's boisterous voice.

Sadie spun around in time to see him and Josh laughing uncontrollably. Again. Somehow in the midst of Trevor, she had forgotten about her unfortunate outfit. Apparently they hadn't.

Luckily neither saw the snowball coming. It hit Josh squarely on the back.

Nice shot, Dawson! she said to herself. Three years of softball paid off.

"Hey!" Josh cried. "What was that for? Kevin said it."

"Yeah, but you laughed. A lot." Plus he was closer by ten feet.

"Oh, come on. You gotta admit you look very . . ." She picked up another chunk, daring him to say it. "Very nice," Josh said quickly. "You look very nice."

"Thank you. Now if you don't mind, I'm going to sit by the fire." And without waiting, she turned on heel and marched off.

"I'll come with you," Sam said, racing after her.

Guillermo listened to Salvador's report, feeling his heart fracture into a million pieces. Augustina was alive *and* safe. But not coming back.

"I told you," Manuel crowed. "I told you!"

"Shut up!" Guillermo exploded. "Just shut up. Get him out of here!"

Luis stood. Manuel didn't even bother fighting the huge guy.

With his little brother taken care of, Guillermo raced through everything he'd just learned. "Who is the phone registered to?"

"A Kevin Hancock," Salvador answered. "It's a Spokane number."

"Spokane? Augustina is in Washington?"

"No. The call was placed not too far from here."

"Augustina is here. With a Kevin Hancock." Guillermo couldn't believe it. His life was spiraling out of control. "Are there any agents by that name? Old friends? Relatives?"

"No, no, and no. He may be a nobody, sir. A stranger with a phone, perhaps."

"Or he may be a somebody." Guillermo ran his finger along the rim of his coffee. Something had to happen fast if he had any prayer of salvaging his relationship, his life, or his business. Already he could feel the vultures swarming.

He took a deep breath, brushed down his suit, and said, "Get my phone."

CHAPTER 15

"How noticeable is my eye?"

Sam's eyes flickered to Sadie as they approached the bonfire, careful not to look at her too long. "It's not that bad. It just looks like part of your face is in the shadows."

She nodded, but still took a bench on the edge of the crowd. Sam sat next to her, close, but not too close. He wanted to give her—and himself for that matter—enough personal space. Sadie gave him the jitters, like the kind he got on a first date, only worse. Not that she would think this was a date, but having her all to himself was kind of exciting. And scary. And—

He shot to his feet. "You want some hot chocolate?" He needed a second to regroup.

"Sure. Thanks."

Sam left her and moved quickly into the lodge, trying to clear her from his thoughts. Yet even after waiting in line and emerging five minutes later, he had to stop. Sadie looked stunning by the bonfire: long curls dancing in the wind, delicate features glowing in the firelight. And like he guessed, she no longer wore a single speck of green.

She turned and spotted him with a wave. Flushing like a kid caught with his hand in the cookie jar, he quickly ran the two steaming cups over to her.

"Thanks," she said. "You know, I envy you, Sam."

He sat a friendly two feet away. "Me? Why?"

"Having all this time with your friends. My best friend lives in New York now; she's studying at Julliard. I'm happy for her, but sad for me. We hardly talk anymore."

"Long distances are hard," he agreed. "With me in California, and the other three guys in different corners of Washington State, we hardly see each other anymore. The last time we were together was at Kevin's wedding last summer."

Sadie shook her head with a smile. "It's weird to think of Kevin married."

"That's only because you don't know Amy. She's awesome. She keeps Kevin in line, believe it or not."

"Hmm." She took a sip, tucked a strand of hair behind her ear, and asked, "What about Trevor? What's his girlfriend like?"

"I don't know. He has a new girlfriend each month. It's hard to keep up."

"He does seem like a bit of a player. He's . . . uh . . ." She smiled. ". . . quite the flirt."

"Yes. He is." Sam turned back to the slopes. *Trevor*, he scowled. *What did you do?*

"And Josh?" she continued. "Does he have a girlfriend?"

Sam was still fuming about Trevor when he answered. "Megan. They've dated off and on since high school. I think Megan's ready to be married, but Josh wants to finish grad school first. Seriously though, I don't know what he's waiting for."

Sadie twisted around to face him head on. "Aren't you guys a little young to be talking so much about marriage? I mean, no offense, but it's weird. Especially coming from guys."

The question caught him off guard. Or maybe it was that she was staring at him so intently. It took him a moment before he could think straight to answer. "Well, we're all twenty-four or soon to be, and—"

"See!" she cut in. "That is young! I'm twenty-six and I can't imagine talking about marriage with my boyfriend, and he's thirty-five."

"I don't know. I think we just envy what Kevin and Amy have. Kevin's a lucky guy."

He wasn't sure if his answer was a good one, but Sadie turned back to the bonfire, silent for a time. The wind blew another dark strand in front of her face, but instead of tucking it behind her ear, she played with it mindlessly. "And where does Josh go to school?" she asked.

"Washington State—about two hours from home. He graduates this spring, so he'll be somewhere else by the end of summer. Probably Utah, if he gets into BYU." He sighed. "Then we'll be even more spread apart."

"Utah?" She sat up. "That reminds me, are you guys Mormon?"

Sam smiled. "Yeah—I mean, just Josh and I are. How'd you guess?"

"Let's see . . ." She began ticking items on her fingers. "A mission for your church, no coffee, no cussing—except Trevor a few times—BYU. Although the biggest giveaway was that four college guys weren't drinking themselves silly over the holiday. It's . . . different."

Weird. That's the word she used before. It wasn't the first time someone thought his religion was weird, but with Sadie it stung a little.

"My aunt and uncle joined a Mormon church awhile ago," she amended. "It's easy to recognize the rules once you know them. I think my uncle watches every BYU football game ever. He's obsessed."

Aunt and uncle? "Are you religious?" Sam blurted.

"Do you count going to church on Easter and Christmas as religious?"

"Well . . . uh . . ."

She smiled, releasing him. "That's okay. I don't consider myself religious. I grew up going to church—my mom's still devout and all—but I stopped going once I moved out."

He nodded, not sure if he was disappointed or not.

"To be honest," she went on, "I've always had a hard time with the concept of God. I mean, I've always believed there is a God—He made the earth and the universe and everything—but I guess that's where my problem is."

"How so?"

"Well . . . I'm just a short, little, food service manager at a ski resort in Montana, going about my pathetic life. It's hard to believe I would interest someone like Him. I mean, churches always say that God cares about us—about me—but really, how could He? Even for a human, I'm nothing. Especially when you think about the thousands of orphans in Africa with AIDS. I'm nothing compared with those kids—and that's assuming He even cares about *them.*"

"I personally think God cares about humans—about us—very much," he countered. "Even you, Sadie."

She rolled her eyes. "The standard answer. If you ask me, it's like ants."

"Ants?" he repeated, confused.

Her eyes lit up. "Yeah. Maybe they aren't as cool as fruit flies, but I've always had a thing for ants. I did a project on them once in elementary school—how they form lines and work together in groups. They're very interesting. But anyway, just because I enjoy watching ants outside from time to time doesn't mean I care about them personally. Like, if I were to accidentally step on one, it wouldn't bother me in the least."

Sam smiled, enjoying her imagery.

"Or," she continued, only partially serious now, "if Sadie ant stole Sammy ant's food, I wouldn't care either. In fact, I'd probably find it kinda funny. But the minute the ants are out of sight, I don't give them a second thought. To me, it's the same way with God. We may entertain Him, may give Him cause to chuckle from time to time, but that's it. Does that make sense?"

Her eyes, normally the color of dark chocolate, were blazing a beautiful amber in the firelight, and Sam had to drop his gaze to focus. "Yeah, but I think it's different in this case. God is more than just our Creator, He's our Heavenly *Father.* Think of your dad, for instance, how—"

"I don't really have a dad," she interrupted.

"Oh. Sorry." Sam's ears went hot. "Maybe your mom, then. Or any great parent figure."

Sadie smiled easily. "My mom. Definitely."

"Okay. Think about how much your mom cares about you. All the trivial things in your life that shouldn't really matter to her, but do, simply because she's your mom. I think it's the same with God, only with Him, He's not just a parent to us, He's a *perfect* parent to us. Perfect love. Perfect interest in every aspect of our life. That's so much more than even your mom—or my dad, or whoever—can offer."

Her brows were pulled down, really considering what he was saying, so he took it one step further. "The way I figure, as our *Father* and not just our *Creator,* God cares about us more than we'll ever know. There's a scripture that says that God's whole work and glory is to bring about *our* eternal life, meaning everything He does is for *us.*"

"Hmm. I've never thought of it that way." She cocked her head to one side and studied him. "Wow, Sam. I wouldn't have taken you for a theologian. I'm impressed."

He wasn't sure if that was a compliment or an insult, so he waited for her to say more. Religion, even more than medicine, was his favorite topic of conversation. The two years he'd spent in Peru had been the happiest of his life, but there was a delicate balance when talking religion, and with someone like Sadie, he didn't want to push too hard. So he bit his tongue and tried to let her guide the discussion. But after the silence stretched on, he couldn't stand it. He wasn't a missionary anymore. He didn't have Josh's ease with doctrine—or women for that matter—and things were suddenly uncomfortable.

Noticing her empty cup, he asked, "Do you want some more?"

"I prayed," she answered softly.

"Huh?"

"In the storm . . . when I was running. I was standing in the middle of a million pine trees and a massive blizzard. I was all alone and freezing and terrified. I knew I was going to die. So . . ." She shrugged. "I prayed. I don't know why. Maybe it was because I thought I was about to meet God and all, but it was my first real prayer since I was a little girl. The second I opened my eyes—like, literally, the very second—I was standing by your truck."

Sam was too stunned to speak.

"I would call it a miracle," she continued quietly, "except I didn't deserve one. Not after ignoring Him all these years. But . . . I just don't know how else to explain it. Crazy, huh?"

Sam shook his head, feeling the burning from within. "Not crazy, Sadie. That's amazing. Awesome. Like I said, God loves every one of us—you included." He paused a moment to keep his emotions in check. "And if you ask me, I don't think you were alone in that storm."

She blinked rapidly, spilling a few tears. "Thanks," she whispered.

Neither said anything for a time. Finally she sat up, wiped her eyes, and said, "I'd love some more hot chocolate. Do you mind?"

By the time Sam came back out, he could hear Kevin's distinctive laugh from across the way. The guys were back. Trevor was on one side of Sadie and Josh on the other. But before Sam could think too much about it, he reminded himself that they'd brought Sadie here to cheer her up. And from the sound of her laughter floating softly toward him, he knew she was definitely cheered up.

He joined his friends and handed Sadie her new cup.

"Hey," Kevin whined. "Where's mine?"

Sam looked at his own, still untouched. "Here," he said.

"Man, you're way too nice. I was just messing with ya." Kevin turned to Josh and Trevor. "You guys want one?"

Josh shook his head, but Trevor jumped off the bench. "No, but maybe I'll find something else to warm me up. Hey, Sadie," he added quickly, "can I buy you a drink?"

Sam nearly slugged him, but Sadie just smiled. "No thanks, Trevor. This is perfect."

CHAPTER 16

Even with the huge bonfire, the cold began to seep through the Glacier Park sweatshirt. Sadie was freezing. She thought about moving closer to the fire, but that meant leaving her spot in between Josh and Sam. At the moment, the two of them were catching up on people from their high school, almost as if she weren't there. She didn't mind though, it made it seem like she was more friend than intruder.

Friend, she repeated, liking the sound of it. Guillermo had been many things to her: admirer, boyfriend, even confidant. He was charismatic, he was entertaining, but he wasn't necessarily her friend, and it was nice to have friends again.

A gust of wind came off the mountain, and an involuntary shiver ran down her spine. She hugged herself and hunkered down. Josh shifted on the bench next to her, and instantly she was being surrounded by the warmth of his coat. "You look cold," he noted.

His coat was still warm, making it hard to resist. "I am. You sure?"

He nodded, smiled, and went back to his conversation with Sam.

As the conversation moved on to people from their church, Sadie studied the guys on either side of her. Sam, with his kind, green eyes and blond hair that was a little on the wild side without his hat, and Josh, with his thoughtful, blue eyes, and hair almost as dark as hers, which somehow was still perfectly in place. It suddenly occurred to her that both of them were quite good-looking. Not like Guillermo, who had more of a *GQ* look about him, but Sam and Josh had more natural attractiveness. Even after a long night of snowboarding.

She ran her fingers through her own tangled mess, wondering what they thought of her in return. Without a hat, she probably had strays going every which way. Then she decided anything was better than the green snow beast.

Josh nudged her. "What are you smiling about?"

Her smile grew. "Kermit."

He looked at her pile of gear down the bench and grinned as well. "You mean Gumby?"

"I don't know. I think Kermit is more fitting. My mom always told me I had scrawny little frog legs."

Josh laughed heartily—Sam, too—pleased to have her join in the fun. Then Josh quickly added, "It's nice to see you smiling again, Sadie."

"It's nice to be smiling again," she admitted, and then she added, "And in case you're wondering, it really isn't easy being green."

Josh and Sam erupted for a second time with Sadie. Their laughter was suddenly cut off by a blinding flash. Sadie blinked in time to see Kevin adjust something on his camera.

"Say cheese," he called, and without waiting, he began snapping pictures of the three of them on the bench. Sadie only smiled for the first dozen, until she realized Josh and Sam weren't being nearly as cooperative. Once she stopped, Kevin gave up and joined them on the bench.

"Oh, I almost forgot, Sadie. You have a message on my phone. It's from some guy named Gee-yer—"

Sadie leaped to her feet. "Guillermo?"

"Don't worry," Kevin said, punching in his voice mail, "I didn't listen to *all* of it."

Pulse racing, she sped away from the others, already anticipating the sound of Guillermo's deep voice.

The second the message started, her heart melted. It was completely in Spanish, so Kevin couldn't have understood much.

"When I got the call that you were safe," Guillermo was saying, "I was beside myself with relief. And now I am beside myself with grief. If there was a way to go back and change that moment, hermosa, I would. Please believe I have killed myself for what happened between us. You did not deserve my wrath. I know that now. I know what truly happened on Christmas, and I"—His voice cracked—"I know I do not deserve for you to come back to me, but please come back anyway. You are my life. Please give me a chance to make things right. I love you, hermosa. I always have, and now I know that I always will. You may be doubting my love right now, but that is why I am asking for you to return. Let me show you my sadness, how I have worried night and day for you. What happened happened, but I cannot change the past. So let me make the future right. Do not let those agents tear us apart. Please. Please. Please."

The message was too short. She hit replay, once, then twice, as hot tears streamed down her cheeks. *He loves me.*

Once she had his words committed to memory, she held onto the phone, wondering if she should call him back right then. Unfortunately, some conversations had to happen in person. So she listened to the message once more and then walked over to share her news.

"I'm going back," she announced.

The three guys just stared at her.

"Not right now," she amended, since it was nearing midnight, "but in the morning." She could barely believe it herself.

Josh started shaking his head furiously, but she hurried on, speaking mostly to him. "I can't hide forever, and Guillermo's obviously not angry anymore. I want a chance to explain what happened with the FBI."

"You don't have to do that, Sadie."

"Yes, I do. I want him to know that I didn't stab him in the back. That I still love him."

"Love him?" His eyes narrowed. "Have you forgotten what he did to you? Do you want me to get a mirror?"

The comment knocked the air from her lungs.

"Let it go, Josh," Kevin said quietly.

Sadie forced herself to breathe slowly and deeply. "No. It's okay. Josh is right." She stepped closer to him so he could see her face clearly. She wanted him to see that she was healing, both physically and emotionally. "I know what it must look like to you—what *I* must look like," she added softly, "but it's not what it seems, okay?"

"Was he drinking when he hit you?"

"Well . . ." She tried to remember back to Christmas and the Argentine wine. He may have had some, but not much. Guillermo had never been a big drinker. "No. Not really."

"Then it's exactly what it seems. And how do you expect to anticipate that kind of temper the next time? What will it be that sets him off? How do you know it won't be more than your eye or shoulder?"

"He won't . . ." Her voice cracked. She closed her eyes briefly and tried again. "It won't happen again. I've known Guillermo for two years, and he's not like that. You don't know him. He's extremely kind and gentle to everyone. Ask anyone he knows."

Josh shook his head angrily. "Are you guys seriously buying this?"

Sam said nothing, but Kevin jumped in. "He's right, Sadie. Just because this is the first time your boyfriend hit you doesn't mean it's the only time."

"And what about the drug and organized crime thing," Josh added. "If he's who the FBI say he is, then you could be putting yourself in an extremely dangerous situation—which I'm sure is what the feds were trying to tell you on Christmas."

Kevin was nodding in agreement. Sam stayed uncommitted.

"I can't believe this," she said softly. It was tempting to snap at Josh, but she wanted to show him she'd thought this through, that she wasn't just going back blindly. If the message hadn't been in Spanish, she would've played it for him so he could hear Guillermo's remorse for himself. As it was, she said, "You're a Christian, right, Josh? What about forgiveness?"

He leaned forward. "What you're talking about is *not* forgiveness. It's about excusing the behavior, or worse, ignoring it all together. There's a place for forgiveness, don't get me wrong, but that place doesn't put you in harm's way."

"Right, but . . . haven't you made a mistake you'd give anything to go back and change?"

"Absolutely. And I've paid the consequence for every one. Look, Sadie, whether your boyfriend meant to hit you or not is beside the point. There are serious consequences for what he did to you, and you can't negate those consequences by crying Christian compassion."

Consequences, she repeated. Up until five minutes ago, it felt like she was the only one paying for Guillermo's rage. But then she had heard his voice. He was in as much agony as she was. They had both paid for the mistakes of others and now the consequences needed to be placed where they truly belonged. The FBI. "You're only seeing a small piece of a larger picture," she insisted, "And that piece isn't representative of the whole."

Josh just stared at her.

Desperate, she turned to Sam. "What about you? You know Guillermo, right?" Sam looked startled by the sudden attention, but she needed him right now. "You said yourself he was really nice. Do you think he's capable of everything those agents said?"

"I don't know him that well, but it's hard to imagine him involved in drugs and—"

"Not just involved," Josh countered, "but heading it up. A whole business, with people who guard any prisoners he—"

"Josh!" she snapped and then turned to wait for Sam.

"It seems hard to believe," Sam finished softly.

"See!" Sadie said.

"Sam doesn't count," Josh countered. "He doesn't have a mean bone in his body. He thinks everyone in the world is like him, as nice as they appear to be on the surface. It's hard for Sam to comprehend that there are truly evil people in the world, people that hurt other people, including those they love. But it's not reality, Sadie."

"I don't think I'm naïve, though," Sam shot back. "Look," he said back to Sadie, "I really don't know Mr. Vasquez that well. He *seems* like a good guy, but . . . I wouldn't have thought him capable of *that* either."

Sadie felt every gaze shift to her eye. "Me neither," she whispered. And just that fast, she could feel her sanity slipping through her fingers. Her mom. Her job. Her life. It wasn't fair. She wanted her life back. She needed it back. For better or worse.

"It was just extenuating circumstances," she whispered.

Josh exhaled heavily. "Sadie, look at us guys for a sec, okay? Me. Kevin. Sam. Trevor. There's not a single circumstance—*not one!*—in which any one of us would ever hit you. Not. One. Not. Ever. Do you get that? Or after what's happened, can you even believe it's true?"

He was right. As much as she hated him for it, she knew that none of them would have done to her what Guillermo had. Not even under extenuating circumstances.

Her eyes lowered, her breathing sped up, and suddenly it was Christmas night. She was on the floor of Guillermo's cabin, wounded, beaten. Nothing. She felt herself falling into that black hole, becoming the nothingness she had become on that cold, dark floor. She fought against it, frantic. She couldn't—she wouldn't—be nothing again.

Her eyes locked on Josh. "I have to go back. Please try to understand."

He put his elbows on his knees and stared into the large bonfire. He wasn't going to understand. He wasn't going to even try. She turned to the others, but even Kevin and Sam refused to meet her eyes.

She took a different seat as they all let the subject drop.

CHAPTER 17

The ride back to the cabin was a quiet one. In an act of pure chivalry, Kevin offered Sadie the front seat. The last thing she wanted was to be shoved in between Josh and Trevor for the long ride back. But she didn't want to torture lanky Kevin by making him sit in the back. It would have been better to walk, but that wasn't going to happen either. So she took up her former position. Squashed.

Trevor fell asleep against the side window almost immediately. Kevin was quick to follow, but not Josh. He stared mindlessly out his window as Sam drove back, probably thinking what a horribly disturbed person she was. A victim. She cringed. What an awful and incredibly insulting word.

Fine, she thought. *I know what I am and what I'm not.*

The dark winding roads began messing with her stomach again. Closing her eyes, she imagined the most amazing reunion for her and Guillermo. He would drop to the floor and wrap his arms around her knees. She'd stroke his black hair . . . allowing him to finish the last of his remorse. They would kiss and move on. She yawned, enjoying the vision . . . one that felt more dream than reality . . . but she didn't mind. She was ready . . . ready to be back in his arms . . .

"Man, some guys have all the luck."

Trevor hopped out of the truck and slammed the door. Sadie didn't move.

Josh was amused that Trevor, of all people, was jealous of him. It didn't happen often and he certainly hadn't earned the jealousy, but still . . . it was amusing.

He tried rousing her again. "We're back, Sadie."

Nothing.

It was impossible to stay mad at her when she looked so peaceful— her face lit by soft moonlight, her thick lashes resting peacefully on her cheeks. By the time he'd gotten his thoughts cooled enough for the next round, she'd already conked out. And then her head sagged against his shoulder, dissolving any residual anger. It was tempting to stare at her awhile longer—she really was something to look at—but instead he nudged her sleeping head with his shoulder, using more force than before.

Her eyes fluttered open slowly, then her head snapped up, wide awake. With a look of horror, she glanced from his face, to his shoulder, and back again. He smiled to let her know it was okay. A person who is furious with you doesn't intentionally use your shoulder as a pillow—which is what he'd already assured Trevor. She'd fallen asleep and her head had simply slumped to one side. It just happened to be his. Strangely, he was disappointed.

"Sorry," she finally said.

"Don't be. It was my pleasure."

Sadie quickly took in their surroundings: empty truck, Sam unloading the last of the gear, and no sign of Kevin or Trevor anywhere. She groaned. "Oh, man. I'm a deep sleeper."

"You really are. I was about ready to carry you inside the cabin again."

"Again?" she repeated.

Josh nodded, remembering the last time he'd seen her asleep in the truck. While his friends had argued about what to do with the unknown woman, he'd merely picked her up and carried her into the cabin, deciding that whoever she was, she didn't need to freeze while they figured it out. How little he'd known then of what was to come.

As she caught up to his thoughts, her eyes widened and she added another quiet, "Sorry."

In spite of her stubborn will, in spite of her complete naïveté and the dangerous choice she was making, he smiled again. "My pleasure," he assured her again.

Her face had such a wide range of emotions, most of which played over it now. It was quite entertaining to watch.

"Aren't you getting out?" she asked, with a touch of irritation, signaling the end of the teasing, but before Josh could answer she realized why he hadn't moved. He was wedged in, with her leaning heavily against him. Ducking her chin, she quickly slid into Trevor's spot as she apologized yet again. He laughed that time.

He pushed Sam's seat forward and then stopped, remembering one last thing. "Hey, what does '*La Bella Durmiente*' mean?"

From the way her eyes popped open, he figured his Spanish was close enough. Her mouth opened to respond, then clamped shut.

With another laugh, he climbed out of the truck. He offered Sadie a hand, but she purposely bypassed it for the door handle. Once she was free of the truck—and him—she walked swiftly past him to the cabin.

"Good night, Sleeping Beauty," he called quickly.

She stopped and turned, a hint of a smile playing at the corners of her mouth. "I thought you didn't know what it meant."

"Lucky guess."

Her full smile finally broke through. And with a shake of her head, she walked inside.

It was the smell that woke Sadie—the hearty smell of bacon and eggs—yet it was the sound that made her smile. Sizzling grease, mixed with terribly out-of-tune whistling. Trevor. It had been years since she'd eaten a home-cooked breakfast and she jumped out of bed uncharacteristically fast.

In the bathroom, she splashed her face with cold water—the fastest way to wake up without coffee—then braced herself for the first look of the day. The mirror, honest as ever, showed that the bruise was healing nicely, which meant it looked hideous. More greenish-brown than purple. She was certain that with a little creative makeup job, the last of it could easily be hidden. In a few more hours, she would have just such makeup.

The most exciting thing, however, was putting on her own clothes. The lovely, form-fitting sweater, the skinny black pants. It was like finding a part of herself. After folding up the Glacier Park sweatshirt and blue running pants, she gave a quick look around. She was leaving.

Trevor and Josh were the only ones in the kitchen. And the dog—always the dog—followed Trevor around, waiting for a piece of bacon to be thrown its way.

Sadie sat in her spot at the table. "Something smells good, Trevor."

Both turned in surprise, though Josh frowned. "What makes you think he's the cook?"

"Because Sadie knows I do everything around here," Trevor replied. "Bunch of lazies."

Josh pointed down to a pitcher of orange juice. "What do you call this?"

"Pathetic."

Sadie laughed. She was going to miss these guys. "Do you guys need any help? I'm not a fabulous cook but I know enough to get by."

"No." Trevor wagged a finger at her. "Nobody messes with my cooking. I already surrendered the OJ, but alas . . . no more." He plopped another piece of bacon into the grease.

"By the way, Sadie," Josh added as he stirred, "if you thought my marshmallows were amazing, you should try my orange juice."

"Wow," she smiled. "I can't wait."

She sat back, thrilled that Josh wasn't mad at her anymore. That could only mean that he understood her side of things. Finally.

While Trevor whistled and Josh stirred, she studied them, taking a last mental picture before she left. Trevor was in shorts and a T-shirt even though it was the dead of winter. His curly hair stuck out of a baseball cap in every which direction. Josh, however, was in jeans and a navy hoodie that had "Cougars" sprawled across the back. There was something about the way his dark hair curled up in the back that made her smile. She guessed it drove his personality nuts, trying to get it to lie flat, but it was actually kinda cute. She could picture his blue eyes, knowing they would stand out against the navy sweatshirt. He was a half a foot taller than Trevor and more solidly built, and for a brief second she wondered what he would look like in a T-shirt and shorts.

Sadie! she suddenly choked. *You're totally checking him out!* The thought made her laugh out, which she tried—not so smoothly—to cover up with a few coughs.

The two of them threw her a curious glance. "You okay?" Josh asked. *Oh man, am I blushing?* "Yeah."

Clearing her throat, she quickly diverted her attention to the snow-covered deck. It didn't work for long, though. Her thoughts found their way back to Josh. Crazy as it was, she was glad it was *his* shoulder and not Trevor's she'd fallen asleep against. She could handle Josh's teasing. Who knew how Trevor would have exploited it.

"Are you sure you want to go back today, Sadie?" Trevor asked. "Today's skiing."

Conflicting emotions engulfed her, especially as Josh stopped stirring to look at her. But she was resolved. "Yeah. It's time to get back to my life. And my own clothes."

Trevor glanced over her outfit. "Are you sure? I personally thought you looked hot in Mrs. Jackson's running pants."

"Trevor . . . ," Josh said, rolling his eyes.

"What?" Trevor said as he winked at Sadie across the kitchen. "It's true. Although I gotta say, I'm digging you in this black sweater thing. It brings out your beautiful eyes."

"Trevor!" Josh shouted. "Seriously!" Then he turned to Sadie. "Sorry."

"It's okay," she said with a laugh. "Most girls like compliments."

"Depends on who it's coming from," Josh noted as he went back to his juice.

She felt her cheeks flush again in memory of Josh's "lucky guess."

True. She smiled. *Very true.*

"Just be glad I came downstairs when I did," Josh added. "Otherwise you'd be stuck alone down here with Trevor."

Sadie grimaced in jest. "Oh, man. Yes. Thank you."

"*Buenos días,* Sadie," Sam called from the stairs. Kevin wasn't far behind.

"*Buenos días,*" she said back. "*Como estas hoy?*"

"*Bien, bien.*" He took the seat next to her. "*Soñé que estaba volando. Fue—*"

"Hey!" Trevor interrupted, "I thought we already discussed this. English, poor fa-vor."

"You know, Trevor," she chided, "it's comments like that that keep two beautiful cultures apart. You really should educate yourself. Or get a life—whichever comes first." Of course, all of it went over his head since she reprimanded him completely in Spanish.

Sam burst out laughing. Trevor smacked him on the arm. "What? What'd she say?"

"She said she likes your hair," Sam snickered.

"Really?" Trevor swept off his hat and patted his outrageous curls. "Thanks."

Josh set the orange juice down and sat across from Sadie. "I speak less Spanish than you do and even I know that wasn't the translation. Nobody likes your hair, moron."

"Are you kidding! Chicks dig my hair. Right, Sadie?"

She just smiled. "Let's eat."

Trevor set the last of the food on the table, and Sadie reached for the toast. It smelled great. It looked even better. But Josh said, "I'll pray," and she quickly set it back down. She kept forgetting these guys did that. She watched each of their heads lower before she did the same.

Josh began his prayer thanking God—or Heavenly Father like Sam pointed out—for good food, friends, and the new-fallen snow—which Trevor muttered a loud "amen" to. Josh prayed for their families back home, for the four of them on the trip.

"And for Sadie . . . ," he continued. Her head snapped up. She looked at his head, but he just kept going, eyes closed. "We're grateful for Thy care in bringing her safely to Sam's truck, for protecting her through the storm, and leading her away from danger and harm."

Dumbfounded, Sadie just stared at him.

"And as she prepares to leave, we pray for Thy continued care over her. We ask Thee to bless her with wisdom and knowledge to keep her safe and protected from evil."

That was it. He ended the prayer and all of them dug into breakfast.

All, except Sadie.

She couldn't move. It was as though Josh actually believed God cared about her. Not only cared about her, but was responsible for getting her to Sam's truck—and willing to help her even now. She couldn't help but wonder if it was true. Sam believed God was with her in the storm. Obviously Josh did as well. Listening to this heartfelt plea, it was easy to think maybe—

"Hey!" Trevor waved a hand in front of her. "Hello. I thought you were hungry."

Her eyes came back into focus, which for some reason were still on Josh. Only he was staring back with eyebrows raised. She smiled weakly. "I am. Pass the toast."

Sadie ate her last meal at the cabin in sheer bliss. The food was excellent and she made sure to compliment the chef. The orange juice also received a rave review. There was a down-to-earth atmosphere around these guys she had grown to love. They were real and she could be real around them. She cherished the few days she had spent with them. But as breakfast ended, she knew the time had come.

She looked around the table, feeling the emotions rise in her throat as she thought of all they had done for her. Taking her in. Putting up with her neurotic behavior. Giving her a reason to laugh again and again. And then again. All with no thought of return—which was providential since she had nothing to offer them. Her gratitude began taking the form of tears, and she panicked. That was the last thing they wanted to see. Instead, she forced herself to smile.

"Thanks for everything, you guys. You're the best."

None of them responded. They all just looked at her.

She lowered her eyes and picked at an invisible piece of lint on her black sweater. "You have to come see me at the lodge before you head back to Spokane, okay?"

"Definitely," Trevor said for all of them.

"We're gonna miss you, girl," Kevin added softly.

That did it. Her throat swelled. Her eyes began to burn. She blinked rapidly, trying to find a sufficient reply. In the end, she could only nod.

Finally, Sam stood. "Well . . . I'll get my keys."

Josh was on his feet just as fast. "That's okay. I'll drive her down. I need to call my sister anyway. It's her birthday."

"Oh. Okay."

Trevor walked over and gave Sadie a big hug. The others quickly followed.

"Take care of yourself, okay?" Kevin whispered in her ear.

Though her heart was heavy, she worked to keep her voice light. "I will. See ya around."

"Don't forget to keep up the snowboarding," Trevor called.

"Yeah, good luck with that one," she quipped over her shoulder.

It was weird for Sadie to leave the cabin empty-handed. Not a bag or a purse. Not even a coat. Josh offered his again, but she assured him she was warm enough.

After opening the passenger door for her, he took a minute to brush off the windshield with his sleeve. She couldn't help but watch him, allowing herself a final mental picture. There was something about Josh that kept drawing her in. An attraction of sorts, but not necessarily that strong. Not that he wasn't attractive. He was. Great hair. Great eyes. Great smile. It was more that he was intriguing. Different. Even more than the others.

Maybe it's just the morning, she decided. Between his unexpected prayer, a perfect breakfast, and knowing she was leaving it all for the unknown realm of Guillermo, her thoughts were a little erratic.

"So your sister's birthday is close to your mom's?" she asked as he joined her in the cold truck.

He glanced sideways. "Actually, no. Katie's is in September, Lauren's in October."

As understanding hit, Sadie started to smile. "Oh." Josh had gone out of his way to take her back to the lodge himself. He wasn't the most creative liar, but it definitely notched him up in the intrigue department. "I thought Mormons weren't supposed to lie," she pointed out happily.

He brought the truck engine to a roar. "Funny. I didn't think the Bible singled us out."

As they started down the mountain, Sadie smiled at the passing pines. There was just something about Josh. Something . . .

"Truthfully," he said, "I wanted to drive you down"—his eyes flickered to hers—"in case you changed your mind."

. . . annoying!

Things started clicking into place. There was a sudden stab of disappointment followed by a flood of anger. "I see. You wanted to take me yourself to see if *you* could change my mind."

"Yes."

Her head fell against the seat. It was so frustrating trying to make him understand. She glared out the window. Josh was a pain. That's what that "something" was. A royal pain in the—

"Sadie, I've just got this bad feeling about your situation. It seems dangerous to me and I know it's none of my business, but I keep thinking of all the strange things that have happened."

"Like what?" she asked, working to keep her temper in check.

"Like how a ranger showed up on our doorstep and happened to be the only one in the police system who knew you were gone?"

"I already told you. Guillermo hired him to help with the search."

He shot her a withering look. "Then explain why the only people looking for you were limited to a three-mile radius. Why wouldn't they have started at your mom's place?"

Okay. That was strange. But—

"Or the fact that your boyfriend searched your purse for a listening device, as if he knew it would be there? What kind of guy snoops in his girlfriend's purse? How would he even know what it was anyway?"

She opened her mouth, but nothing came out.

"Or how about the fact that your rich boyfriend has a whole organization around him, with attack dogs and men who guard any prisoners he decides to take? He locked you in a room, Sadie! Then sent men after you when you escaped."

"That was the FBI," she said softly. "I'm sure of it."

"The FBI? Exactly! He has the *Federal Bureau of In-ves-ti-ga-tions* breathing down his throat."

"Yeah? Well, maybe the FBI has a hidden agenda?" she fought back.

His grip tightened on the steering wheel. "Like what?"

"Guillermo's extremely wealthy. If they can claim he earned his money illegally, they would reap the benefits."

"It doesn't work that way. I grew up with a tremendous respect for law enforcements, let alone the FBI. You've got to be crazy to think that your boyfriend is the moral, honest one and they're the corrupt ones."

"Well, in my limited experience, the FBI are the corrupt ones. They were the ones who broke into my room at the lodge. They were the ones who used every tactic to manipulate me into helping them spy on my boyfriend. They were the ones who said they wouldn't put a bug in my purse and then did anyway! I'm sorry if I find it hard to believe they are the *moral, honest* people you think they are."

Josh's jaw tightened. "Why can't you just go back to your apartment, or your mom's, or anywhere else in the world? Why the lodge? Why can't you give it more time?"

She sighed. "Because I don't want to run anymore."

"There's nothing wrong with running, Sadie," he said gently.

That's because Josh had never been the one running. Running was the most terrifying feeling in the world. There was no control in running. It was pure instinct. Pure victim.

"Look," she tried, "I appreciate your concern. I really do. What if I tell you I'll be more careful, more watchful than before, okay? If I suspect anything is going on with Guillermo, or the FBI, or whatever, then I'll leave and go back to my apartment. I was only staying up here another week. Then we'll be through the holidays, and my hours will cut back to normal."

Josh pulled up to the ski lodge and let Sam's truck idle while he considered everything. There were mobs of people going in and out of the ski lodge, stirring Sadie's pulse. On the other side of those doors were a whole lot of people with a whole lot of questions. She wasn't looking forward to the answers.

He finally faced her. "I really can't change your mind?"

"No, but I'll be okay. Really. And if I have any problems, I'll just punch *him* this time."

Instantly, he froze. "No, Sadie. If your boyfriend tries anything, and I mean anything at all, you run. Okay?"

"Fair enough," she promised. "I'll run back to the cabin."

Josh laid his head back against the seat, eyes closed in quiet frustration.

She studied him one last time, wondering if she'd ever see him or the others again.

"Try to wear boots next time," he said at last. "And a coat."

She smiled. "I will. Thanks, Josh. For everything."

Sadie climbed out of the truck and shut the door with a wave. It wasn't until she was all the way inside that she heard Sam's truck pull away.

CHAPTER 18

Guillermo sat in an oversized chair outside of a dressing room as he waited patiently for Augustina to emerge. He had picked out two dresses for her to try on, both chosen specifically to accentuate her dark features and petite figure. He had dated many women in his thirty-five years—all great beauties—but there was something more to Augustina. While he was excited to show her off at the party, he was even more anxious to acquaint her with his business associates.

The days she was missing had been absolute torture for him. In one short week he'd been given a glimpse of his life without her. It wasn't pretty. He deeply regretted hitting her in his fit of fury. Her body still showed the results. It had been wrong, entirely wrong, and he vowed never to lose his temper with her again.

She still refused to tell him where she had been. That bothered him. A lot. Obsessively a lot. His nature was to distrust everyone and everything. Yet he knew if he was going to build a lasting relationship with Augustina, he was going to have to start somewhere. She had proven her loyalty to him. The FBI was furious. Guillermo had won. And now it was time to give her a piece of his heart.

The door to the dressing room finally opened and she walked out, do-ing a little twirl to show off the black, strapless gown. Guillermo's mouth fell open. *Increíble!* It was as if the designer had made the dress with her in mind. The color, pure ebony, not only showed off her honey-luster skin, but added depth to her beautiful eyes. And the way it hugged her body . . . He nodded vigorously as he stood up next to her.

"This is definitely the dress you must wear. *Es perfecto!*" He looked her over head to toe. "You are the most beautiful thing I have ever seen. Truly."

She smiled at his praise, only adding to her beauty. "I like the dress, too. I was thinking I should wear my hair up, something like this . . ." She reached up and piled her long hair onto the top of her head. "What do you think?"

He kissed several spots along the nape of her neck, eliciting a giggle from her. "Yes. You must definitely wear your hair up for the party."

Her expression fell abruptly. "I'm excited for the New Year's Eve party, I really am, but does it really have to be about me?"

"Amor . . . ," he whispered. He stroked the skin of her shoulder where his final blow was still visible. His fingertips trailed the olive skin up to her cheek. The bruise there was barely noticeable under her makeup, but still undeniable. The whole time he caressed his wrongdoing, she refused to meet his eyes, breaking his heart. Whether she would admit it or not, she still harbored feelings about Christmas.

He lifted her chin, forcing her eyes upward. "I will spend the rest of my life making up what I did to you. This party is only the beginning."

Her arms slid around his waist and her head collapsed on his chest. "Don't torture yourself anymore, amor. It's done and forgotten. Let's just move forward."

Forward. Yes. He slipped a hand into his suit pocket, and for several elongated seconds he waited, wondering if she was ready. Then slowly, carefully, he pulled out the diamond necklace—now repaired—and held it toward her.

Her dark eyes widened, almost in horror. Her hand reached for it, then stopped short. "I'm not ready," she whispered. "I'm so sorry." Closing his hand around the necklace, she pushed it away.

"I understand," he said. And he did. More than he wanted to. Her words before meant nothing. It was not done. She had not forgotten. "It is I . . . that . . ." His words caught in his throat, ". . . am sorry. So immensely . . ." He clenched the necklace. The diamonds, cold and hard, cut notches in his skin like her words cut notches in his heart.

He fell back and slumped in the chair, wanting to hurl the necklace again. She had rejected him. Him. Guillermo Vasquez. The most powerful man in Montana. His shoulders sagged, his head hung, refusing to let her see her power over him. It was unfathomable. But then again . . . he knew he deserved it. "I—I am so, so sorry," he stammered. "So, incredibly . . ." The tears flowed with no effort whatsoever. "Beyond any words . . . You cannot imagine how . . ."

She knelt in front of him, black gown and all, and took his hands in hers. She, too, was crying. For a long time they stayed that way, letting their sorrows flow freely. Life had pushed them painfully off course. It wasn't right. It wasn't fair.

But then something miraculous happened. Augustina gently opened his hand. He looked up, not daring to believe. In an act of sweet forgiveness, the necklace suddenly lay in the palm of her hand, stretched toward him. "I'm ready now," she whispered.

He looked at her a long moment. Then with reverential ritual, he took the diamonds and laid them around her delicate neck. Seeing them nestled against her skin made him smile unabashedly. Now it was truly done.

He grabbed her to him and held her tight, breathing in her rose-scented hair, tracing the soft curves of her back. Never before had he considered marriage to anyone, not even Augustina, but ironically the events of the past week pushed his thoughts in that direction. She had proven her loyalty, and now it was his turn to prove his. Guillermo wanted her to be his.

Permanently.

With a final squeeze, he took her hand and pulled her out of the private dressing room. "Come. Let us find you some earrings to match."

The boys ended up at the Blue Ridge Lodge for breakfast the next day—Sam's request. However, Sam wasn't the only one searching for the dark-haired beauty. Josh was torn between needing to make sure Sadie was safe and knowing her safety wasn't the only reason he wanted to see her again. His feelings toward her were turning dangerous, yet he couldn't stop searching the crowds. If she was truly okay, then he was mad at her for being so forgiving. And if she wasn't . . . then he would personally find a way to make her boyfriend pay. But Sadie was nowhere to be found. Even after lunch and dinner again at the lodge, they never caught a glimpse of her. Sam even peeked into the ski club after skiing, but to no avail. She surfaced several times in Josh's nightmares that night—horrible versions of her running in the snow—but in the real world, her posters were down and all signs of her had vanished. That only upped his anxiety.

After another disappointing breakfast at the lodge the next morning, the guys drove back to the cabin to grab their gear.

As they pulled up, Trevor said, "What's that?" and jumped out of the truck. By the time Josh and the others caught up to him, Trevor pulled a small envelope off the front door. It read "To my friends" on the outside in definite female handwriting. Josh tried to grab the envelope from him. There was only one female any of them knew within two hundred miles, but Trevor just hunched his stocky body, blocking his friends as he tore it open.

"We probably just missed her," Sam said, searching the road.

Trevor pulled out a card with gold ribbons. "An invitation?" Trevor and Josh said in unison.

Josh left the others and wandered into the cabin. Kevin and Sam followed, but Trevor stayed on the porch, skimming the contents.

"Ooooh, it's a party. At the club."

"A party?" Sam repeated.

"Yeah," Trevor continued through the doorway. "Looks like Sadie's boyfriend is hosting a New Year's Eve bash in honor of her safe return, and we are all invited."

Josh threw his coat over the couch. "How nice for them."

"Wait! New Year's Eve?" Sam cried. "That's tonight!"

Trevor waved the invitation high in the air. "There's a note on the bottom from Sadie."

Josh crossed the room in two giant steps and yanked the card from Trevor's gasp. He skipped all the fancy gold lettering, going straight to the handwriting at the bottom.

Hey guys,
All is well with me. Everything is forgiven and forgotten.
Thanks again for everything! I hope you'll ALL come.
Ice Woman

"I'm in," Trevor announced instantly.

"All right," Kevin shrugged. "Why not?"

"Why not?" Josh could think of a hundred reasons. He settled on the most obvious. "This is at the ski club, Trevor—hosted by the *owner* of the ski club. The napkins will cost more than your entire wardrobe. Believe me, this isn't going to be the drink fest you think it is."

"Sure it will, only these drinks will be worth drinking."

"The invitation says it's black tie," Sam added.

"Black tie, as in a tux," Josh clarified to Trevor, the man who'd rather shave his head bald than wear a button-down shirt.

Trevor grimaced. "A tux? What kind of party is that?"

"The kind of party people like us don't go to," Josh said.

"I'll find something to put on," Kevin said. "Come on, we have to go. Sadie went out of her way to invite us. *All* of us. Besides, don't you want to see if she is really okay?"

Sam sighed. "All right. I'm in."

Josh reread her note. Forgiven and forgotten. Her very words. The whole idea was revolting. As if throwing her a huge party negated everything Guillermo had done to her.

"So?" Trevor asked impatiently, looking straight at Josh.

Josh glanced up. His three buddies were watching him, waiting. "What?"

Kevin rolled his eyes. "He'll come."

Chapter 19

The foursome showed up to the party around nine, Josh dragging his feet the entire way. They had spent the day skiing, which should have put him in a better mood, but he couldn't stop thinking about the events of the week and how quickly what had started out as a battered, half-frozen, strange woman in Sam's truck had so quickly resolved itself into a gold-lettered invitation with a flippant All-is-fine-with-me note. It didn't seem right by any stretch of the imagination. So he took his frustrations out on the hill, being more aggressive than usual in his skiing. His body had taken a beating, yet he would have kept skiing all day and into the night if that meant he didn't have to go to that party. Now he was stuck.

One step inside the large ballroom, though, and he wasn't the only one wondering if they should turn around. Everything spoke of the high society to which they didn't belong. The twenty or so tables lining the perimeter of the large ballroom were covered in black tablecloths with six place settings each, white with gold trim and flatware. At the center of each table was an ornate, three-foot-high centerpiece, filled to overflowing with white roses. And the entire room was lit solely by a thousand candles, casting a golden aura over the lavish party.

Equally fancy were the people: tuxes, evening gowns, and enough jewels to support a small country. Josh glanced over the four of them. It was ridiculous. Kevin and Trevor were in button-down shirts and jeans, the nicest clothes they had brought to Montana. He and Sam were only slightly better, having packed for church. Josh wore a navy sports coat over a gray oxford shirt, while Sam donned a full suit and tie. Even so, it was obvious they were all sorely underdressed.

Kevin elbowed Josh. "A little fancier than we're used to back on the farm, eh?"

"I tried to warn you. We don't belong here."

"It's fine. Nobody will care."

"I care," Josh muttered under his breath.

Most of the guests were socializing in the center of the room, champagne in one hand, superficially greeting with the other. Josh found a table in a far corner by the live band, determined to avoid Sadie and her boyfriend as much as he could. He told himself it was because he didn't want to ruin her nice evening with his lousy attitude, but in all honesty, he was scared of her, scared of how she had monopolized his thoughts since she left. It wasn't good. So while his buddies commented on the rest of the party, he studied his fancy napkin.

His resolve didn't last long.

Trevor let out a low whistle. "Would ya take a look at that!"

Josh's neck overpowered him and instantly he found her. Sadie stood in the middle of the room, the center of attention. She wore a floor-length, strapless black gown, which left her shoulders and the majority of her back bare. Her long hair was swept off her neck in a low bun, except a few dark curls that had escaped onto skin that glowed a soft satin under the candlelight.

"Man," Trevor crowed. "She. Is. Gorgeous!"

"Gorgeous" was a gross understatement. She looked perfect. *A little too perfect,* he realized. It bothered him—though maybe it shouldn't—that there wasn't a hint of a bruise anywhere. Not under her eye. Not on her bare shoulder. Almost as if nothing had happened on Christmas. Maybe in her mind, nothing had.

Josh broke his steady gaze to glare at the man beside her. Guillermo kept a hold of her tiny waist, signifying his claim over her as they spoke to their guests. He looked older than her by a decade, but had similar coloring. Like her, everything he wore was black, from the eight-hundred dollar shoes to the eight-thousand dollar suit. His tie, not quite tightened around his black shirt, gave him the look of complete and utter arrogance.

Josh wasn't really sure what he expected, but in all fairness, Guillermo didn't look like the drug-pushing brute he had imagined. Haughty maybe, but nothing more.

"She said he was *tall,* dark, and handsome," Sam said. "He doesn't look very tall to me."

"He is compared to Sadie," Kevin noted, "but who cares. He's rich instead. Which do you think she'd rather have?" After another second he added, "Man, I think even *I* would date him."

"Well, isn't he the kinda guy you would expect her to be with?" Trevor said. "Though it hardly seems fair he gets the looks, the money, *and* the girl."

Kevin held up a finger. "You forgot the ski resort, the Ferrari, the house in Paris, the island in the Bahamas, *and* the girl."

The four of them let out a collective sigh. The handsome couple looked like something off the cover of a magazine as they greeted the people coming in. And it wasn't just the four friends that were awestruck. They held every eye in the room.

"Okay," Kevin finally relented, "We really do stick out."

Josh nodded. "Exactly. So why are we here?"

"Free food and liquor," Trevor said bluntly.

"We're here," Sam said, "because Sadie wants us to be . . . I think."

As if hearing her name, she glanced over her bare shoulder. Her face lit up as soon as she spotted them in the far corner. She whispered something to Guillermo and then glided gracefully across the floor toward their table. With each step she took, she grew more beautiful. Josh's leg began to bounce nervously under the table. He wasn't ready for her.

"You came!" she called.

Kevin stood and kissed her on the cheek. "Wow, girl, you sure clean up good."

She laughed. "Thanks. So do you."

Trevor followed suit, lingering longer with his kiss than Kevin had. Then he held out her hands as he inspected her head to toe. "Man, Sadie, you look smokin' hot!"

Josh rolled his eyes. It was ridiculous they were standing around, mouths hanging open in her presence—himself included. She was still the same person as before.

"Thanks," she said again. "Sometimes I feel like a doll Guillermo likes to dress up, but it's kind of fun. These are real, you know," she said, pointing to diamond-drop earrings that hung down to the matching necklace.

Diamonds, Josh nodded. *An abusive man's best friend.*

"Well, you look great," Sam answered for all of them.

"Thank you."

Then, as if to inspect them, she looked around the table, locking eyes with Josh briefly. She smiled in approval of what she saw. "I must say you boys look pretty great as well."

Kevin tugged on his shirt. "Don't you think we're a little underdressed?"

A little? Josh scoffed, but Sadie waved a hand in dismissal. "No. Most of these people are just trying to keep up with him." She motioned back to Guillermo, still the center of activity.

Sam lowered his voice. "So I guess everything worked out okay for you two?"

Josh didn't miss the flicker in her eyes. The flicker of the Sadie they first knew, the sadness, the pain. Yet her words said otherwise. "Yes," she said softly. "When I got back, he begged for my forgiveness. I didn't even have to explain about the FBI. He had already figured it out. So I forgave him, and he forgave me."

"Just like that?" Josh asked. He hadn't meant to let the thought slip out, and he regretted letting it come out so sharply. He was supposed to behave.

Sadie turned. "Yes," she said in a more amiable tone than he'd offered her.

"So why hadn't he called your mom?"

"He knew I was mad at him and probably just wanted to give me some space. He didn't want to worry my mom unless he knew for sure I was really in trouble."

That only made her boyfriend seem more shady in Josh's mind, but looking into those dark eyes, he suddenly had no more power to fight her.

"Well, this is a nice party," Sam said. "Thanks for inviting us."

"Sure," she said, but she wasn't looking at Sam. Her large eyes stayed on Josh, begging for mercy. "I'm glad you *all* came. I really wanted to see you again."

Josh should have nodded. For two days he'd been hoping for a glimpse of her, to know she was safe, yet, now that she was barely two feet away and not only safe, but seemingly happy as well, he couldn't think of a thing to say.

Finally, she released her gaze and gave the others a quick smile. "Well . . . I'd better get back. I'll see you guys in a little bit." And then she was gone, swallowed up in the crowd.

Josh watched her go, unable to do otherwise. Guillermo immediately took her back without even a single glance in their direction, as if they weren't worthy of his notice.

"What the heck was that?" Kevin whispered next to Josh.

"What?"

"She really wanted to see *you* again? What are the rest of us? Pond scum?"

Josh pulled his eyes back to their table. Sam and Trevor were still staring hopelessly after Sadie. "She was talking to all of us," he whispered back.

"Didn't seem that way to me."

"Yeah, well, you're crazy."

"True," Kevin conceded, and with a slap on the back, added, "but I'm not the only one. You need to loosen up, buddy. It's over. Bruises fade. Let it go."

Josh rubbed his eyes, feeling every hour of sleep lost on Sadie's behalf. "Maybe they shouldn't."

"Hey," Trevor called over the live band, "Do you think Guillermo would punch *me* if I asked Sadie to dance?"

Josh and Kevin exchanged a look before they answered together. "Go for it."

"I'll be back in a minute, amor."

Guillermo broke away from the judge momentarily. "Is something wrong?"

Sadie smiled. "No. I just need some fresh air."

"Oh. Then I shall come with you. Excuse us, please."

"No," Sadie said quickly. "That's okay. You stay and finish the story. They haven't even heard the Isla de Vieques part yet," she added for the benefit of the judge, his wife, and the other four men who had been hanging on Guillermo's every word for the last twenty minutes. Guillermo had the charisma of a politician and the grace of an actor, and while Sadie had always known people adored him, it wasn't until this party that she realized to what extent. But after an hour and a half of person after person, in three-inch heels, no less—Guillermo's choice—she needed a break. Not to mention, she needed a moment alone to find someone. Someone who had disappeared from the dark table in the corner.

"You have to finish," the judge agreed. "I have a bet riding on this one."

Guillermo laughed and took Sadie by the waist. "I shall finish the story first, and then we can find some fresh air together."

"No, really," she said, fanning her face with her hand. "You finish.

I'll be back in just a minute." And without waiting, she slipped out of his grasp and into the hall.

The hallway outside the large chestnut doors was quiet. And cold. Without all the warm bodies, her arms were chilled, making her wish she'd brought her black wrap with her. But as she wound farther away from the party, she realized the hallway wasn't entirely quiet. There was faint music coming from down by the dining room—piano music. She followed it around a corner and stopped outside the large dining room. It was semidark inside, lit only by the lights shining through the wall of glass. Even then, she recognized the piano player immediately.

Her eyes raised in pleasant surprise. *Well, well, well . . .*

She listened a moment in complete amazement. The prelude he played was incredibly difficult, having more sharps than a composer should be allowed to throw on a page, yet he played the monstrous chords effortlessly.

Quietly, so as not to disturb him, she cracked the door open and squeezed through. With his back to her, Josh remained unaware and kept the music flowing. She was grateful she had persevered through three failed attempts and had figured out the way back to Sam's cabin to deliver the invitation. At the time, her best hope was that all four would come tonight, but deep down she feared they wouldn't—*especially* Josh. But he *had* come. And shown up looking so . . .

She grinned. With his navy sports coat and dark waves, he nearly disappeared into the black baby grand. And with each grandiose measure he played, her smile grew. But the piece he was playing was almost done, making her wish she'd left the party much, much sooner.

Each of the chords grew softer than the previous as the prelude began to die out. By the time the last chord sounded, it was barely audible across the room.

Josh's hands stayed a moment longer in reverential silence before finally dropping.

"Wow . . . ," Sadie said, clapping softly. "That was fantastic!"

He whirled, his blue eyes narrowing as he spotted her against the dark wood of the room. "How long have you been there?"

She smiled. "Not long enough. I missed my favorite part."

"You know, it's not nice to eavesdrop on people."

"Actually, sometimes it is." Her smile grew. "I'm seriously impressed, Josh. Not only can you play 'Prelude in C-Sharp Minor,' but you played it so well!"

His expression finally softened. "Ah? Dost the lady know Rachmaninoff?"

"Yes. And again, wow. Why didn't you tell me you played the piano?"

He watched her another moment before twisting back around. He rubbed the polished wood the way Guillermo rubbed his sports car. "I don't—at least, I haven't much since I moved away from home. It's hard to find pianos on campus. When I found this deserted baby grand, I couldn't resist. Sorry. I thought I was playing soft enough I wouldn't disturb anyone."

"Oh, don't worry. I wasn't disturbed," she assured him.

She made her way over and sat next to him on the familiar bench, still shocked by this bit of news. He stiffened as her bare arm brushed his suit coat and quickly slid over to give her plenty of room.

"So you're a fan of Rachmaninoff?" he asked, staring straight ahead.

She thought back to her first day in the cabin, and Josh's laptop music. She should have guessed it back then. "You know, you're not the only one who enjoys classical music. I happen to enjoy a good piano concerto myself every once in awhile."

"Really?" He finally faced her with a smile of his own. "I wouldn't have guessed."

"Well, listening to classical music isn't something I admit to very often. It . . . uh . . . doesn't do much for my social life."

"Ah," he nodded. "That would explain my problem."

Sadie laughed, doubting Josh had any problems with his social life.

"It's like being a *Star Trek* fan," he added. "You can't admit it to anyone unless you know they're Trekkies, too—like a secret club or something. You *are* a Trekky, right?"

"No. I'm not *quite* that nerdy."

Ouch, he mouthed, though his eyes danced. Eyes, she noticed, that changed to match the color of his shirt. Blue-gray, with a few specks of gold. Eyes that suddenly questioned why she was staring at him so intently.

"So are you going to play me one of Rachmaninoff's concertos?" she asked quickly. "Which one were you listening to? The second—and best—if I remember right?"

He smiled. "Why didn't you tell me you liked it? I would have left it playing."

"I was a little distracted at the time."

Josh's face clouded in sudden remembrance. Sadie wanted to kick herself. She didn't want him to remember those dark days. They were in the past. She was too interested in the present. "You could play it for me now," she suggested.

"Nah. I'd never do it justice. I never really learned to perfect a song. But I can lend you my laptop if you're that desperate."

"Hmm. I wish you would have offered it on the way to Deer Basin. Kevin has lousy taste in music."

Josh laughed again. "Yes, he does. But don't tell him that."

The two of them grew silent, even though Josh's left hand traced a few notes on the piano. She studied his fingers, trying to decipher which song was playing in his head. She wished he'd just give in and play it.

"So, Josh, you play the piano, snowboard, *and* roast marshmallows to perfection. What other hidden talents do you have?" *Dancing maybe?* she hoped silently.

"I speak Klingon."

"Huh?"

He rolled his eyes. "You know, you really should watch *Star Trek* sometime."

She elbowed him lightly. "I don't think that's going to happen."

His eyes flickered to her arm, suddenly aware—as she now was—that she was openly flirting with him. Not good! Blushing, she decided to get to the point of why she needed fresh air in the first place. "Why aren't you in with the others at the party?"

His fingers dropped away from the piano. "I'm really not in a social mood. Plus it's not that fun watching people get drunk."

A weak excuse, but better than what she had feared earlier—that he was avoiding her. "Sure it is," she countered. "I bet Trevor's a lot of fun with a few drinks."

"You'd think so, but actually Kevin's the entertaining one. He gets giggly."

A giggly Kevin popped in Sadie's head, making her giggle in turn. "Oh, come on. That's not worth going back for?"

A sudden shadow crossed the piano, and both of them turned as someone opened the door. Josh shot to his feet, recognizing the person immediately. Sadie stood as well, though more slowly. Earlier she had debated whether or not to introduce Guillermo to her new friends—especially knowing how Josh felt about her boyfriend. Now she had no choice.

CHAPTER 20

"Ah, there you are, hermosa," Guillermo said. He crossed the room with a smile, wrapped an arm around Sadie's waist, and kissed her forehead. "I was looking for you."

"Sorry, amor," she said. "I found a friend." With a quick breath of courage, she added, "Guillermo, this is my friend, Josh. And Josh . . ." She turned, catching her first glimpse of Josh. The open hostility rolling off him cut her volume in half. "This is Guillermo."

Guillermo reached his hand out in friendly greeting, completely unaware of the one-sided revulsion. "It is a pleasure to meet you, Josh."

Josh shook his hand but didn't return the compliment.

She should have expected such a response, but still . . . it was disappointing. She had hoped tonight Josh would be able to see how well Guillermo treated her, how he spoiled her, and most of all, how he loved her. But looking into those blazing, blue eyes, she saw the impossibility of ever changing his mind.

"So," Guillermo said, "was my Augustina playing one of her songs for you? She has such talent for creating masterpieces."

Sadie's mouth fell open, blood rushing to her face. Her music wasn't something she was going to admit to Josh, especially not after hearing him play so well.

He broke off his icy glare to look at her, his expression suddenly full of surprise. "No. I didn't realize Sadie played the piano *or* wrote music."

"Ah," Guillermo gave her a little squeeze, "My Augustina is wonderful. Her music is the sound of a beautiful spring morning. Her voice . . . a cool mountain breeze." He began pushing her toward the piano. "Play us one of your songs, hermosa."

She clung to his suit coat. "Not right now, amor. Actually, Josh also plays the piano."

"Wonderful, wonderful," Guillermo responded, having eyes only for her. "I would love to learn a talent such as that someday."

"Someday," she agreed.

While all of her outward attention was focused on Guillermo, inside she was dying to know Josh's thoughts. He must think her such a fool.

Guillermo leaned down and kissed her still-hot cheek. "If you will not play, then will you come back to the party, amor? There are still many people I would like for you to meet."

"Sure. I'll be there in a minute."

Guillermo's eyes widened a fraction, then flew to Josh, taking a moment to appraise Sadie's "friend." Flattered by the small display of jealousy, Sadie went on tiptoe and gave him a quick kiss of reassurance. She just needed a moment alone with Josh to smooth over the last of his hostility, maybe even convince him to go back to the party. The kiss worked. Guillermo relaxed, kissed her back—quite forcefully—and walked out of the room.

Josh focused all his energy outside. The floor-to-ceiling windows offered a beautiful view of the moonlit mountains, and with the heavy snow, the pines hung in random, strange shapes, casting strange shadows across the snow. And yet, his thoughts really weren't on the pines. Or their shadows. They were on the woman who now stood close by. *Too close,* he breathed. *Way too close!* And with her high heels, her face was close enough to make out every feature. Her deep, beautiful eyes . . . her cheekbones . . .

Pines, he insisted. *Look at the stupid pine trees!*

There were so many things Josh had wanted to say to Sadie's boyfriend and even more he had wanted to do. He had a dozen images of Sadie emblazoned in his memory: bruised, unconscious, half-frozen, half-crazed. And those were only his memories. Sadie probably had a dozen more horrifying, all at that man's doing. However, acting on impulse would have gone against his better judgment—not to mention knocking Sadie's boyfriend flat on his back probably would have ticked her off—so he'd bitten his tongue and tried to behave. But when Sadie reached up to kiss her "amor," Josh went to the window, unable to stomach any affection between the two. But then she had sent him away and was now standing close enough he could smell her perfume.

Shadows! he begged. *Snow. Anything. Focus!*

After a moment she tipped her head back. "So?"

The two-letter question was fully loaded and he knew it. He chose his words carefully. "So, that's him?"

Her dark eyes sparkled, rewarding him for his good behavior. "Yes. I'm really glad you got to meet Guillermo. He's wonderful."

"Wonderful" was a bit nauseating, but Josh continued diplomatically. "He seems nice."

Sadie didn't miss it. *"Seems?"*

Josh sighed. It was a never-ending battle between them, but he didn't want to fight. Not now. And with a smile he realized her good-for-nothing boyfriend had been good for one thing. "So Sadie, you play piano, sing, *and* write music? What other hidden talents do *you* have?"

Her lashes lowered, but there was no way he was letting her escape this one. He motioned to the piano. "Shall we?"

She followed him, though she didn't sit on the bench. "I really don't have any other talents. Seriously. I don't ski *or* snowboard. I can't cook or roast marshmallows to save my life. It's pathetic, really. I majored in music thinking—"

"You what?" he interrupted. "Wow. You really have been holding out. Which area?"

"Composition." Her hand flew up to stop further comment from him. "I'm not that good. My best friend got into Julliard. I didn't. That should tell you about my abilities."

"Not really," he tried to counter, but she continued over him.

"Anyway, I majored in music thinking I could do something with it. Turns out there's not much a mediocre composition major can do to bring home a decent paycheck. I played this piano at the club, which is how I met Guillermo. Then he helped me get my job now."

A musician. Great. He was in over his head, but he plunged himself deeper, too curious. "I think it's only fair I get to hear one of your songs since you already heard me play."

"No way. Nope." She shook her head. "Guillermo's waiting for me."

Wrong excuse. "He can wait." Josh motioned again to the piano. "Go on. Play."

Typically stubborn, she still didn't move, but he wasn't about to give in. "Hey, you snuck in on a very private jam session. That deserves at least one song."

"Fine." She turned. "Tell you what, I'll play on two conditions."

It felt like a trap, but he said, "Okay. What?"

"First off, you can't laugh."

"That's all? Easy. And second?"

Her dark eyes flashed. "Hold on. I mean it. No laughing." She shoved a finger in his face. "Not even one tiny little snicker."

Maybe not so easy. He bit his cheeks to keep from smiling. "Got it. And second?"

"Second . . ." she hesitated. "You come back to the party."

And there was the trap. He was done watching Guillermo parade her around for his guests, like she was some sort of prize. But the fact that she wanted him back, was personally inviting him back, was curiously enough to persuade him. "Okay."

"You mean it? You'll come back? And stay? No sneaking off again?"

He nodded.

Sadie smiled. "All right, then." She waltzed over to the bench and sat, smoothing out her black gown in the process. Then she cocked her head to one side, throwing a few curls onto her bare shoulder. He wondered if she had any idea what a thing like that could do to a guy like him.

"Do you want me to play Guillermo's favorite song or my mom's?"

"How about you play *your* favorite," he countered.

"My favorite? I can't. It's not finished. It doesn't even have lyrics yet. Just a melody."

"That's okay. I like a good melody."

She sighed. "Fine. But I don't play nearly as well as you do and remember, you can't laugh. Not even a teeny, tiny bit. And if you don't like it, you have to lie and tell me it's wonderful anyway, okay?"

Josh smiled. She was adorable. There was no other word for her. "Just play."

After what he guessed was a nice-sized Spanish insult, she brought her hands to the keys and closed her eyes in quiet concentration.

When her music started it was slow and gentle, mostly soft chords filled with a haunting sadness found only in the minor key she'd chosen. Then her voice came in, humming a soft, lilting melody that fit perfectly with the rest. The whole time she kept her eyes closed, leaving Josh open access to admire her.

She was, without question, the most beautiful thing he'd ever seen. Even in the faint light he had her memorized: dark lashes resting peacefully on her cheeks; lips humming softly; and delicate curls swaying gently to the music.

Before he was aware, he was sitting next to her on the bench again. He was careful not to touch her, not wanting to disturb the trance she'd fallen into.

Her song began to build both in dynamics and notes, and her hands glided over the keys. The verses flowed into a powerful chorus, and Josh suddenly wished for lyrics that would unleash the full power of her voice. Her fingers glowed in the faint light and his gaze traced the soft, olive skin up to her shoulder. In every sense he knew it was wrong, but the desire to stroke her skin was overpowering. He forced his eyes back to her hands, noticing for the first time that, in spite of her fancy getup, her nails were short. A true musician.

But her unfinished song was short—way too short—and the music began to wind down the same way it started, with a few minor chords and the same enchanting melody.

Feeling time slipping away, he seized one last chance to capture the vision next to him, committing everything in that moment to memory. And with one final soft chord, the song was over. Her hands dropped from the piano, and her eyes opened.

"That's as much as I've finished," she said. "It's still in the rough stages and . . ."

Josh hardly heard her words as his mind fought an internal battle. She was so close and yet not nearly close enough. Sadie had grown silent, her beautiful eyes locking on his, and he could feel himself leaning toward her. How easy it would be to just . . .

His gaze flickered to her lips. It had only been for a fraction of a second, but her eyes widened in surprise. He'd been caught. He wanted to kiss Sadie. He knew it . . .

. . . and now she knew it.

Josh jumped to his feet and took himself a safe distance away. *What are you doing!* he yelled at himself. First, for trying to kiss Sadie—then for not. Already part of him was plotting a way to go back and recapture the moment.

"Aren't you going to say anything?" Sadie asked softly.

He didn't dare look at her. Not yet. Not until he recovered some amount of self-control. All the while he reminded himself of who he was—and who *she* was! He was a guest of hers, a guest of her *boyfriend's!* He felt himself flush in shame, in embarrassment. What must she think of him? Making a move on her two minutes after Guillermo left the room. Making a move on her at *all!* He wasn't that kind of guy. He was a friend and nothing more. *Nothing more,* he insisted, even as his heart took a small dive.

"Remember," she said in a voice now lacking in confidence, "you were supposed to say my song was wonderful, even if it wasn't."

He tried to convince himself that she hadn't really noticed, that she didn't know how close he'd come to kissing her. Yet, whether she noticed or not, she deserved an apology.

He finally turned back to her. "I'm sorry, Sadie. I was . . ." He struggled for the right word. *Enchanted. Mesmerized. A complete idiot!* Nothing sounded sufficient.

Her face fell. "You hated it."

"No. No!" He cleared his throat, coming out of his stupor. "I loved your song. I just—"

"That's okay. I understand," she said, trying to smile.

"No. That's not what I meant. I loved your song. Really. A lot." *A little too much,* he added silently. It had him thinking crazy things.

"Really? Great. Thanks." And with an exaggerated sigh of relief, she swung her legs around to face him. "Okay. Now I'm ready. What did you *really* think? And this time, no lies. Just give it to me straight. One musician to another. I can take it."

"Sadie, I was serious. Your song is beautiful and . . ." Again, he couldn't think straight, ". . . enchanting. I like the key. G minor is awesome. I love your chord progression, especially where it goes to major. The melody is great—all of it's great! You have a real talent."

Her face lit up. "Thanks. It still needs words, and the chorus is rough, and—"

"It's perfect," he broke in. "Don't change a thing."

"But it's not even finished."

"Yes, it is."

A smile played at the corners of her mouth. "So you think I should leave my song the way it is? *Without* lyrics? A song someone . . . *hums* to?"

It was odd, he admitted. How many songs were hummed? None he could think of. So he took another moment to be honest as requested. One musician to another. But it didn't take long to know there was nothing he would change about the song. Or Sadie.

He looked into her anxious face. "Yes."

She cocked her head to the side, throwing another curl on her shoulder. "You really are an odd one, Josh."

To look once . . . In an instant, the very words he'd flung at Sam came hurling back to slap him in the face. He had not only looked twice, but a third, and a fourth just to cement Sadie in his memory.

Megan! he suddenly remembered. He forced his eyes to the floor. Why hadn't *she* consumed his thoughts for the past two days? The past two minutes? The shame engulfed him.

"I was just kidding," Sadie said, misinterpreting his sudden mood change. "You're not that odd. Well," she smiled, "except the *Star Trek* thing."

"No. Right. Sorry. I was thinking about something else."

When he didn't give any more explanation, she shrugged. "Well, thanks for the advice anyway, even if it was a little strange." Again she smiled her large smile at him. He didn't return it though. He couldn't have for the world.

Her own began to fade as she studied him.

She sighed finally. "We should probably get back to the party. Guillermo's going to wonder where I am. So is my mom—she's here by the way. I should introduce you to her. She's awesome, and you'll see what I mean by short. I'm a giant compared to her."

Josh nodded, only partially listening as she started toward the door. After a few lonely steps she turned. "Aren't you coming? You promised, remember?"

"Right."

He kept his distance as he followed her through the cold, quiet hallway. Sadie glanced at him a few times, curious, but he had nothing left to say. Not to her. Or himself.

As they neared the large chestnut doors, an older gentleman stepped in front of them. "May I speak with you a minute, Miss Dawson?" He looked over at Josh. "Alone?"

Grateful for any excuse to escape Sadie, Josh reached for the door. That is, until he saw her face. Then he froze.

Chapter 21

"What are you doing here?" Sadie hissed. "Get out of my way!"

Josh looked back and forth between Sadie and the older man, trying to figure out who had her suddenly so terrified. The man was dressed in a suit and tie like everyone else at the party, yet somehow Josh knew he wasn't one of the guests.

"There's a room over this way, Miss Dawson," he said calmly. "If you don't mind, I'd just like a minute to speak to you. Only a minute, I promise."

"Excuse me," she said, trying to move around him.

The man sidestepped, moving quickly to block the chestnut doors. Josh's hand shot out and grabbed his arm, firm enough to make his message clear. "I think Miss Dawson wants some space," Josh warned.

"I'm afraid she doesn't have a choice. And if you don't let go of me, sir"—a gold badge flashed in Josh's face—"you'll be spending New Year's Eve in a very cold cell."

Josh fell back. *The FBI?* He looked at her for confirmation, but she was staring at the floor.

"Shall we?" the FBI agent said to her.

"No," she whispered, barely audible over the roaring party.

In that moment, everything shifted for Josh. The FBI—finally. Just that fast, he completely trusted the man in the dark suit. "Go talk to him, Sadie," he suggested softly. "Just for a minute."

Her face whipped up so fast and furious, he flinched. "No! Leave me alone! Both of you!" She grabbed the door handle but only got it halfway open before the man slammed it shut.

"Miss Dawson, I'm only here to help you."

"That's what you said last time, and you just about got me killed!"

"That wasn't me trying to kill you," he said calmly, "which is why we need to speak."

"No." Her eyes, swimming with emotion, went back to Josh. "Please . . ."

Josh felt like he was being ripped in two. Everything that agent represented could only mean protection for Sadie and retribution for Guillermo. But seeing her terrified, on the verge of tears, and looking to him for help from it all . . . *I'm evidence,* her expression begged. Bruise or not, Josh knew of a photo that was evidence enough. But not here. Not now. "I'm sorry," he said to the man. "This isn't a good time for—"

The agent didn't even give him a glance of recognition. "If you had returned my phone calls, Miss Dawson, we could have taken care of this earlier, but you didn't. And this is a conversation that needs to happen."

"Fine," she said, voice hardening. "Let's talk. Right here. Right now. Or not at all."

"If you don't mind, there are some things I'd rather not discuss in public."

Josh looked up at the same time Sadie did. A few people had stopped in the hallway, witnessing the little episode. The people scattered instantly, but the point was well taken.

Josh moved closer to her, blocking the agent from her view. "I'll go with you," he quietly offered. "Then you wouldn't have to be alone. That way you can say what needs to be—"

The chestnut doors burst open, knocking Josh backward. "Excuse me, *por favor!*" Guillermo's loud voice interrupted. "Excuse me!"

By the time Josh steadied himself, Guillermo was by Sadie, a protective arm around her shoulders, and Josh had been shoved to the side.

"Señor Madsen," Guillermo greeted cheerfully. "How nice to see you again. You have arrived at our party at last."

Sadie whirled. "You know him?"

"Know him?" Guillermo smiled. "I invited him. Did I not, Señor Madsen?"

The FBI agent folded his arms, unimpressed by Guillermo's bravado. "Yes."

Sadie's eyes darted from one man to the other until, with a look of absolute betrayal, she started backing away from both. "*You* . . . invited *him*!"

Guillermo kept pace with her. "Yes. You see, I invited Agent Madsen tonight because he and I are good friends."

"Friends?" she shrieked.

"Yes. Good friends for some time now. His little sidekick as well. Tell me, Señor Madsen, where is Señor Dubois tonight? I am sure his name was on the invitation, no?"

"You . . ." Sadie reared back and for a second Josh thought she was going to punch Guillermo. "How could you?"

Guillermo stroked her cheek, unrepentant. "I am friends with many people in your government, hermosa. You know that." All smiles, he turned back to Madsen. "What can we help you with tonight, my friend?"

Before Agent Madsen could answer, Guillermo spotted Josh off to the side. In a split second, his expression hardened to cold steel. "You!" He spun back to the agent. "So this is your new game? Harass her with a new agent?"

Guillermo dropped his arm from Sadie and started toward Josh, seething with unexpected fury. "What did you do to her!" he shouted in Josh's face.

Josh fell back, stunned more than frightened. Recovering quickly, he planted both feet on the ground and let the adrenaline surge. *Bring it on.*

Sadie grabbed Guillermo's arm. "Stop!"

Guillermo whirled on her. "Why did you not tell me he was a fed! I would never have left you alone!"

Josh had seen enough. He plowed forward and pushed his way into the small space between them, his body becoming the barrier she needed. "Leave her alone," he warned.

The look Guillermo gave him was pure murder. "Step aside, little agent, before you can step no more."

"I don't think so." Josh figured he had Guillermo by six inches and thirty pounds. Add to it a week's worth of unrealized anger and it would be no match whatsoever. He hoped it wouldn't come to that, so he took two steps back, forcing Sadie back as well. At the same time he searched for an exit. One way or another, he was getting her out of there.

She tried to get around him. "Please, Guillermo!" she cried. "He's . . . he's not . . ."

"He's not one of *mine*," the FBI agent finished for her. "I thought he was one of yours."

"No. He is not mine." Guillermo stopped his tirade in confusion. He looked from the agent to Sadie, then back to Josh. "Who are you?" he asked, point blank.

For the first time in his life, Josh wished for his father's badge. "I'm—"

"—my friend," Sadie cut in swiftly. She pushed her way past Josh and ran back into Guillermo's arms. "Like I said before, he's just a friend."

"Friend?" Guillermo repeated. Then quick as a snake, sly as a fox, he relaxed into a smile. He took a deep breath and ran a hand through his jet-black hair. "Oh dear. My mistake. I am very sorry," he said to Josh. "After she got lost this week, I am slightly protective of my little one. I am sure you can understand why."

My little one? Lost? Josh felt sick.

Guillermo walked forward and extended a hand of friendship like he had once before, but unlike before, Josh refused to take it. Guillermo frowned. "Hmm. You see"—he motioned to the agent—"Señor Madsen and I have our moments. Do we not, friend?"

"Thousands," Madsen replied wryly.

Guillermo spoke again to Josh, this time more penitently. "I am truly sorry. I did not mean to accuse you. Any friend of mi hermosa is a friend of mine. Forgive me. I only wish to keep her safe."

Safe? Josh's pulse was thick in his neck, his fists balled. He was confused, shaking in anger, and completely overwhelmed. And if *he* was feeling this way, he could only imagine how Sadie felt. Guillermo wasn't interested in her safety now, nor would he ever be.

Sadie left Guillermo and came back to Josh's side. "Maybe you should go," she said softly.

Josh stared at her. "What?"

"Just go back to the party. I'll be there in a minute."

"But . . ." Josh looked around. He couldn't leave her. Not now! And yet, he had no right to stay. She didn't want him there. Guillermo certainly didn't want him there. Not even the FBI agent wanted him there. He was just caught in the cross fire. But then again, so was she, which is why he couldn't move. Not without Sadie. She didn't belong in this dangerous duel. He just had to find a way to convince her.

"Please," she said, eyes pleading. "Just go."

Crushed, Josh moved away. He was too wound up to return to the party, and instead walked down a short hallway. His feet were heavy as he left Sadie. In consequence, he rounded a corner and stopped, lurking in the shadows. He perched on the balls of his feet and listened. "And now," the agent's voice carried, "if you don't mind, Mr. Vasquez, I would like a minute to talk to Miss Dawson. Alone."

"I do not mind at all," Guillermo said easily. "Would you like to speak to Señor Madsen, hermosa?"

Please, Josh begged her silently. *Just go.*

"No," came her soft, but stubborn reply.

Josh's head fell against the wall. "As you can see," Guillermo said with a smile in his voice, "I have no problem with you speaking to her, but she does. And unfortunately for you, her lawyer could not make it tonight, so if you do not mind . . ."

After a long, torturous silence, the agent said stiffly, "You know my number, Miss Dawson. I'm always here to help. And when you're ready to talk about what happened Christmas evening, give me a call anytime, day or night. I'd hate to *lose* you again."

Hearing heavy footsteps approaching, Josh slunk into the nearest crevice. As the agent stormed past, Josh hit rock bottom. It was worse than seeing her run blindly into the snow, worse than seeing her walk back into that lodge. She had chosen to stay. She had chosen Guillermo.

"*Estas bien?*" he heard Guillermo ask softly.

Even at rock bottom, Josh couldn't leave her alone with him. He inched to the corner and peered around. Guillermo had her by the shoulders, looking down into her visibly shaken face.

"Why did you invite them?" she asked softly. "They're the ones who started everything."

"Because I have nothing to hide, amor. The sooner they understand that, the sooner they'll leave me—and *you*—alone." Guillermo lifted her chin. "Come now . . . this party is for you. Do not give them another thought. Do not let them spoil this night for us—for you."

Her head bobbed up and down, though she still didn't look up.

"Oh, hermosa." He pulled her in for a long hug. "I am so sorry. This is the price of wealth, I am afraid. But do not let it upset you." He stepped away from her. "Come now, let me see a smile. There are many guests who wait to see your beautiful smile. Let me see . . ."

She did as commanded, though her smile was weak and terribly frightened. Even now.

"Ah, there is my girl," he said anyway. "Now, let us return to the party, yes?"

"Yes." She quickly wiped her eyes.

"Good. Good. But first . . ." He leaned down to study her face closely.

"Perhaps you should freshen up a moment. I will have someone bring your purse to you. Then we may enjoy the last hour of this year in happiness and prepare for a wonderful new year to come." He kissed her forehead and added what Josh guessed more than actually heard. "The first of many."

As Guillermo returned through the chestnut doors, Sadie stayed in place, eyes on the carpet. Josh stayed hidden, eyes on her. Regardless of what she said, she wasn't doing well. He knew he had no business getting more involved, but neither could he stand back and watch her suffer alone. Not when he could do something about it.

The door cracked open, and a woman handed out her purse. Sadie thanked her and started toward the nearest bathroom, in the opposite direction of Josh.

"Sadie?" he called softly.

She turned. "You're still here?" It wasn't spoken in anger, just quiet surprise.

"I couldn't leave you."

The statement was truer than he cared to admit.

She nodded quickly. Then her chin lowered, her breathing sped up, and she started to cry.

CHAPTER 22

Josh strode forward and swallowed Sadie up in his arms. Even with her high heels, she only came to his chest, and it was against his chest she collapsed, bathing his gray oxford in tears. It felt natural to wrap her up in the safety of his arms, but unfortunately, the embrace was short-lived. She backed away after only a minute.

"Sorry about that," she sniffed.

"Don't be." He had needed it more than she did. His arms felt unsteady without her.

"So you heard . . ."

He nodded, too honest to do otherwise.

Her eyes filled again. "Why can't he just leave me alone? I hate him."

"Me, too," Josh responded, knowing full well they were speaking about two different men. He had never hated anyone before. It was such a powerful emotion—one he wasn't proud to admit—yet it was the only word to describe his feelings for the man who continued to hurt Sadie. And the longer the tears ran down her face, the hotter the hatred burned.

She pulled a tissue from her purse and dabbed her eyes. It did a better job of stopping the tears than his hug had, and within seconds, she was back in control. "I can't believe I dragged you into this mess again. I'm sorry, Josh."

"I don't mind."

She shot him a quizzical look. "Yeah, right. Who wouldn't love this?"

A man wandered out of the party, laughing and unaware. Sadie kept her face hidden until he was past and then looked up at Josh with a sigh. "I should clean up and get back in there. I need to put on my happy face before someone sees what a mess I really am."

"You don't have to pretend to be happy, Sadie, and you don't have to go back there."

She smiled weakly. "I have a room full of guests who disagree with you, but it's okay. I'm fine now." And she was. He could tell. It was unfathomable how she could be—his blood still felt hot in his veins—but all the fear and anxiety was wiped from her beautiful face. "Thanks for staying with me, Josh."

Josh tried to nod, but he felt himself pulled in by the power of her eyes.

She smiled the kind of smile someone has when they have a secret. "Well, I'd better freshen up. Wait for me here."

Freshen up? His sluggish mind finally caught up. Guillermo. Her purse. He bent low and examined her left eye like Guillermo had. Just that fast, the stomach-churning rage was back. Her flawless skin no longer looked so flawless now. Her tears had washed away her makeup. No wonder Guillermo was so intent on having her "freshen up."

"You can see it again," she whispered, "can't you?"

Josh nodded slowly.

Her eyes liquefied as she scanned the plush hallway. "I have to get out of here."

Finally! "Where do you want to go?" he asked, mind racing. "Back to the cabin? Or maybe your mom's? Wherever you think, I can take you there. You have your purse, but do you have a coat? Never mind. Just take mine. I'll go grab Sam's keys and—"

"What?" she cried. "I meant I have to get out of the hallway before someone sees me like this. I can't leave, Josh. Are you crazy?"

For a moment he was too stunned. Then he was just mad. "Can't or *won't*, Sadie?"

Her silence carried her painful answer.

"I see," Josh said, even though he really didn't.

"Please," she whispered, "don't do this. Just give me a minute and then we can talk."

But as she turned toward the bathroom, the breath went out of him completely. Though she'd told him about it before, he'd never realized the magnitude of it. The bruise on her shoulder was concealed well, but his eyes still found the outline. He was blown away by its size. It was huge. Significantly larger than a fist. Delivered after she'd already blacked out.

"How can you go back to him?" he whispered.

For a long time she didn't answer. Josh waited for her to lash out at him, but she just watched him over her shoulder, expression unreadable, almost calm. "Can you give me a reason why I shouldn't?" she asked softly.

"I can give you two just looking at you. And I bet that agent has a thousand more."

She nodded imperceptibly. "Any other?"

What other reason was there? Wasn't that enough? Wasn't that why she ran from Guillermo's in the first place! Then his head jerked up, panicked. *Does she mean . . . ?*

He shook his head, trying to clear it. Was there another reason he didn't want her to go back? Of course there was. Jealousy. Pure, love-induced jealousy. That was her real question. She was finally calling him out on the kiss that almost was.

"I understand," she said. Then it came. The hurt, the anger, and the betrayal all flashed in her dark eyes without him saying a single word. "I better go," she said, backing away, and just that fast, she slipped through the door to the women's restroom.

Kevin was surprised to see Josh wander back to the party, having given him up for dead. Although on closer examination, Kevin wondered if he was dead after all. The guy looked like he'd been hit by a bus. "Where'd you disappear to?" Kevin asked. "You're missing all the fun."

Josh collapsed into a chair. "I found a piano."

"Oh, that sounds fun. And here I was worried you might get bored."

"Bored?" Josh choked. "More like besieged."

"Huh?"

"Never mind."

Kevin twirled one of the gold-plated forks as the rest of the room twirled around them. The live band was good—of course it was good; rich people had no tolerance for bad music—and had Amy been there, he would've spent the night on his feet. As it was, he sat with Sam, fork-twirling, deciding that this was his last vacation without his wife.

Trevor came up behind them with a perky redhead in tow. "Why are y'all sitting around? There's girls enough for all you losers. Come on. Dance!"

"No, thanks," Josh muttered.

Trevor slapped him on the back. "What's wrong, Joshy boy. Isn't there a girl pretty enough to tempt you? Megan wouldn't even have to know. Or maybe none of the ladies will give you the time of day? Is that it?"

Josh's head dropped onto the table. Not quite the reaction Kevin expected. Usually his buddy had a good comeback for Trevor, something like . . . well . . . Kevin couldn't think of one. That's why he had Josh. But Trevor whisked his newest fling away before either got a chance.

"Finally," Sam burst out, bringing Josh's head up again.

When Kevin realized why, he nearly chucked his fork at him. Sadie was back. "You know," he said for Sam's benefit, "being good-looking has got to be such a drag for chicks. I bet Sadie hates having guys hang on her all the time. Maybe not Guillermo, which is good, 'cause the guy never lets go of her. Not even to scratch his ear. It's like he owns her or something."

Josh's head fell back on the table. Kevin wondered if he was sick,

160

hoping if so, it wasn't from the bluish hors d'oeuvre things, since he'd pounded a tray of them earlier.

"She looks happy, though," Sam said. "Although who wouldn't be? This is Montana's elite here and they all love her."

Kevin watched Sadie and Guillermo make the rounds with each of the eighty guests. She smiled warmly, shook hands like a pro, laughed, conversed, and then moved on. With the four—well, three—of them sitting in the far corner, she and her boyfriend were bound to reach them sometime soon. Kevin had never met a millionaire before—except Sam's dad, but he didn't count; too nice—and he quickly brushed off his jeans in preparation.

"That's why she always goes back, isn't it?" Josh said, upright again. He was like an oil rig, with the whole up-down thing. Now he had a red circle on his forehead. Not very becoming for a guy who was about to meet a millionaire. "And she always will. How disgusting."

"What?" Sam asked. "Who goes back? Where?"

"Nothing. Never mind. Just ignore me."

"We usually do," Kevin quipped.

A waiter came around with a tray of champagne. "None for me," Sam said. Josh waved a hand as well, but Kevin ignored them both and took three glasses, overjoyed to have two Mormon friends. He took a sip out of the first and sat back with a sigh. "I don't know how you guys do it. Even after all these years I still don't get it."

"See if you feel that way in the morning," Josh muttered.

Kevin slammed his glass down. "Hey, what's your problem anyway?"

Josh frowned. "Nothing."

"No, seriously. You've been on one all day. Skiing. Disappearing for an hour. The up-down head thing. What's with you anyway?"

Josh didn't answer, but Kevin didn't miss the glance he stole toward the center of the room. Kevin looked back and forth between the handsome couple and Josh, trying to figure out what he'd missed. Until it occurred to him. Sadie had vanished from the party . . . around the same time as . . .

Things continued to click in place. Sadie only wanting to see Josh. Josh driving her to the lodge. Sadie and Josh.

Josh and . . .

"Ohhhh," he said long and slow. Was it possible? Steady, reliable Josh? Crushing on Sadie? The last time Kevin saw Josh crushing on anyone was in the tenth grade, and that was Megan. But Josh was miserable, and the only thing that made a man that miserable was a woman. Sadie.

Kevin grinned. "No way! You sly dog. When'd that happen?"

"I'm heading back to the cabin," Josh announced suddenly.

Sam sat up. "You're going back? Now? Don't you want to wait until midnight? You know . . . the whole point of New Year's Eve?"

"No. I'm leaving now."

"Oh, come on," Kevin said, fully laughing now, "You can't leave now. Not when I'm onto something." But Josh was on his feet, scrambling to escape.

"Do you want me to drive you up?" Sam offered, clueless as usual.

"No. I'll walk. You stay and be the de-sig-na . . . ted . . ." Josh trailed off as Sadie turned and looked their way. Surprisingly, the smile she had for every one of her other guests faded into nothingness. "Nice," Josh said. "See you at the cabin." Then he disappeared into the crowd.

Suddenly, Kevin understood. Josh and Sadie weren't crushing on each other. They were fighting. And it didn't take a genius to figure out who won. Kevin should've known better. Josh would never fall for someone outside his religion. He could see Sam getting distracted, losing focus, but Josh never lost focus on anything. From the time he was a kid, Josh had planned out his entire life, and Kevin had yet to see him take a single detour. Sadie would have been more than a detour. She would have been a complete derail. It was impossible. For a second Kevin was disappointed, but then he drank Josh's expensive champagne and got over it.

"A toast!" Guillermo called. Sam raised his Sprite high in the air, making Kevin roll his eyes. "To all of our wonderful friends, may I wish you a successful and prosperous new year." A few people clapped, but Guillermo's expression sobered as he looked at Sadie. "And to mi hermosa, my beautiful one, who once was lost but now is found. I love you," he added reverently. "Happy New Year."

Everyone gave a cheer as the happy couple interlocked arms and drank their champagne. Then Guillermo kissed Sadie soundly on the lips, eliciting another cheer from the crowd.

Kevin snorted. "That's one fancy dance of words. I wonder what his fan club would think if they knew the real story behind her disappearance."

"What makes you think they don't?" Sam asked.

"Oh, they don't. Trust me."

The live band started up and Guillermo waltzed Sadie to the middle of the dance floor. Other couples quickly joined them. Kevin scanned the crowd for Trevor, but instead found Josh in the back of the room. Still at the party. Still watching the couple in the center of the room. There was only one way to explain the tortured look on his buddy's face, and that was to believe the impossible.

Josh had fallen for Sadie.

CHAPTER 23

Josh burst out of the ski lodge, determined to never return. Yet there was this nagging fear but desperate hope that if he'd simply answered Sadie's question with what she already suspected, it might be enough to get her to leave Guillermo. Even now. So he kept pushing up the freezing, snowy road, trying to come up with every reason he shouldn't turn around and do just that. For all he could figure there were three: Guillermo, Megan, and his religion—though not necessarily in that order.

Any of the three reasons should have scared him off, but put them together and it was ridiculous he'd allowed his feelings to go so far. But for the sake of resolution, for one brief moment he allowed himself to eliminate the first two reasons just to see where that left him on the third. If he and Sadie weren't dating other people, would he make a move? But it wasn't even worth asking. He knew he wasn't willing to risk a life divided between someone he loved and his commitment to God. He had promised himself as a kid that he would accept nothing less than a temple marriage, and that meant only dating women firmly rooted in the gospel. But Sadie wasn't firmly rooted in the gospel. She was firmly rooted in the world—Guillermo's world.

Josh blew warm air on his hands, coming to terms with it. Reason three was a deal breaker. Sadie had made her choice. Now, so had he.

He picked up his speed, trudging onward and upward. His fingers were icicles, his lungs and legs were burning from exertion, yet he didn't stop.

Halfway to the cabin, he heard the fireworks go off, signaling the New Year. A sign, he figured. Alone on New Year's, alone for the rest of the year—at least, he deserved to be. Megan was going to hate him—which she should. *Kissing Sadie?* He was tempted to call her right then and get it over with, but that wouldn't have been fair to her. He needed to talk to her face to face, yet he dreaded the moment he would break her heart—not that it was the first time.

He thought back to when he had returned from his mission, when he tried in vain to break up with her. At the time, he'd felt that they both needed some space. He'd changed in the two years he'd been gone. So had she. Yet the guilt had been too much then. "What did I do wrong?" Megan asked simply. When Josh couldn't pinpoint anything, it ended the discussion. And that had been almost two years ago! His step slowed, relishing the frigid temperature even more. The way he figured, freezing to death might solve all his problems. But then thinking about freezing to death only led him back to thoughts of Sadie.

Why did this happen to me? he asked the snow. He'd always been a good Mormon boy, steering clear of drugs and alcohol and all the traps others fell into. He went to church every week, had been deacon's quorum president and early-morning seminary class president, said his prayers, and read his scriptures. So it didn't seem fair that he ended up in the very trap he'd tried to avoid. It all felt so out of character, he didn't even know which way was up anymore. *But,* he decided with resolve, *in another thirty-six hours, I'll be out of Montana and Sadie's life forever.* Then he could pick up the pieces of his life and see if there was a way to salvage a relationship with Megan—if that's what he even wanted anymore.

Thirty-six hours, he echoed. It didn't sound so bad.

By the time Sam's truck pulled up to the cabin, Josh was seated at the kitchen counter with a knife and a block of cheese. He wrapped it up quickly, trying to make a quick escape, but Trevor was through the door before he could shut the fridge. "You're still up?"

Josh looked at the clock. Just after one. "Yeah. How was the rest of the party?"

"Ah . . . great chicks, great music, great drinks." Trevor fell into the nearest couch. "My kind of party. Let's get ourselves more rich friends."

No thanks.

Sam wasn't far behind, also raving about the party, but it wasn't until Kevin came in that Josh knew he should have gone to bed when he had the chance. "What the heck was all that?" he asked, coming right toward him.

Josh started inching toward the stairs. Kevin was way too perceptive. "What?"

"Sadie came over and started asking about you, wondering why you left?"

"Didn't we all," Trevor muttered from the couch.

"She was ticked," Kevin went on, looking pretty mad himself. "Something about not saying good-bye to her . . . about how you promised her you'd stay . . ."

"Oh no!" Josh hit his head. Condition number two. "She's going to hate me."

"Oh don't worry. She already does. What's with you two anyway?"

Josh fell into the couch, mirroring Trevor's drunken slouch. "Nothing. Absolutely nothing at all." He could feel Kevin's eyes on the back of his head, challenging his answer. "So did you guys say good-bye to her?" he asked, making it clear he had.

"Sam got her number," Trevor said, rolling his eyes.

"You did?" Josh asked. That's more than he had.

Sam shrugged. "So we can keep in touch. All of us."

"Oh." Keeping in touch. Something Josh wouldn't be doing.

He sunk lower into the couch as Sam and Trevor launched into a discussion about Guillermo, his assets, his arrogance, and the kind of cars he must drive. The whole time, Josh wondered when those blazing eyes of his would turn against Sadie next. But when the conversation drifted back to Sadie, with Trevor spending an unnecessary amount of time discussing the way she looked, he was done. He left his friends and wandered up to his room.

Tossing his sports coat over a chair, he lay on top of the blankets. It took a second to realize what song was playing in the back of his mind. Sadie's. He quickly grabbed his laptop and searched for something to distract him. But every song he found was either a love song or classical music. Sadie ruined both. He nearly shut his laptop, but her voice refused to leave him, so he quickly picked the first song and pushed the volume to full.

By the time he realized the lyrics, he no longer had the strength to shut it off.

> *I've been sitting here all night with you,*
> *And I've been saying things, and though they're all true,*
> *They're not the ones need saying.*
> *So I'm sitting here all night with you.*
> *I'm only asking that you will see through*
> *This game we both are playing.*
> *And if you'll take the time in only reading my mind*
> *You could break down the walls I can't get through.*
> *If you'll look past the words to what I'm saying.*
> *Look past the words to what I need.*
> *If you look past the words you'll see me aching*
> *For the right time to tell you how I feel.*

The surface of Whitefish Lake was untouched glass, a flawless mirror reflecting the deep blue above. The emerald pines surrounding Sadie's favorite lake whispered for her to take a closer look. She did, with a deep, cleansing breath, cherishing this glorious summer day. The sharp rocks along the shore crunched painlessly under her bare feet, making her vaguely aware she was dreaming. But she didn't question the how or the why; she just enjoyed the moment for what it was.

Her mom was there somewhere, contentedly reading a romance novel. Her older brother was there as well, though he, too, was unseen. Then someone took her hand. She didn't have to look over to know who it was, nor did she wonder why Josh was in her dream. It only seemed right that he was part of her little utopia.

When the two of them reached the stairs that led away from her lake, her feet stopped. He stepped in front of her, also reticent to leave. His blue eyes were pulled down, as if searching for something on her face. It wasn't until he started to smile, that she realized what. Her lips. Her breath caught. His eyes closed, and so did hers. Then she waited for it. Josh. Yes. Finally.

Something struck her, shoving her backward and knocking her flat onto the stairs. Her eyes flew open in time to see Josh fall forward, face clenched in pain. She grabbed his shirt trying to break his fall, but his weight was too much for her. The two fell backward, shattering the wooden planks.

Wind rushed in her ears, and she panicked. They were still falling, plummeting beyond into a huge, black void. The dark nothingness started swallowing up her utopia. First the pines. Then the lake. Everything was disappearing rapidly, leaving nothing but black. Terrified, she reached for Josh's hand. She found air. She whipped around, searching for his hand and found it clutching the front of his gray oxford.

No! she screamed without sound.

She watched as a gaping red hole grew where his hand was. He had been shot. She spun around, searching for the shooter but finding nothing. She wanted to warn Josh that it wasn't over, but like before, the scream couldn't find a voice. In horror, she watched the wound grow until his entire shirt was stained deep scarlet.

Then, suddenly, his weight was gone. Josh was nowhere. Like

everything else, he had disappeared into the nothingness, leaving no one in the suffocating darkness but her and the shooter. That time the scream made it past her lips. "Josh!"

His voice answered from far away with one, frantic word. "Run!"

She tried. Nothing happened. Her feet were paralyzed, trapped in deep snow. She knew the shooter was coming, could feel Guillermo's footsteps behind her, but her legs wouldn't obey.

"Please!" she begged her body, but everything refused her command. Her eyes. Hands. Feet, neck, voice. No matter what she tried, nothing moved.

Guillermo's footsteps matched her beating heart. Heavy. Oppressive. And growing like the roar of thunder.

Then everything stopped. For one brief, terrifying second there was utter silence. Sadie couldn't turn her head. She had nothing but black for sight. And all she could do was wait.

There was a giant explosion of noise. The bullet hit just below her shoulder—a new wound on old. With the shot, her body was released. She spun around and found the face that had haunted her dreams for a week, ferocious, frightening, and the last thing with her in the dark.

"Why, hermosa?" he asked simply. "Why?"

"This is just a dream!" she shouted at herself. "Wake up!"

His gun rose a second time.

She screamed even louder knowing the next time would end it all. "Sadie! WAKE UP!"

Her eyes finally obeyed, flying open. She frantically searched around her, fully expecting Guillermo to be hovered over her, gun in hand. But he was nowhere in sight. And she was no longer in darkness.

CHAPTER 24

Just a dream. Just a dream. Just a dream, Sadie chanted. Yet her heart continued to pound, not knowing the difference between dreams and reality. She rolled over and screamed into her pillow, letting the adrenaline rush out of her as she came back to the world around her: her room at the lodge, the bright morning sun, and the knowledge that Guillermo was not a killer.

With one last groan, she stared at the clock. Just after ten. Yet she felt more exhausted than when she'd dropped into bed after the party at three—or four maybe. All because of a dream. Another stupid nightmare. Only a week, and they were getting old. But this dream was different than the others. The gun was a new addition, though she knew why. The setting was new as well—which really wasn't fair since Whitefish Lake had always been her safe haven. And the last thing different . . . was Josh.

She struggled to get back to the part of her consciousness where dreams live and Josh loved her, but Josh was gone—in the imaginary world and the real.

She kicked the blanket off her legs, mad at herself more than him. *Can you give me a reason?* she cringed. He'd been so shocked by her insinuation—him, having romantic feelings for her?—he couldn't even respond. A simple shake of the head. That's all she got in his brutal rejection. But things weren't supposed to end that way for them. Even as friends, Josh meant too much to her now. If he'd just given her a chance, she would have fixed things. She'd come out of the bathroom prepared to repair their friendship. Instead she'd come out to an empty hallway. Even then, she was convinced that if they could just find a quiet minute together, she could mend things before he left Montana and walked out of her life forever. And now . . .

She stared at the ceiling. She wished she had work to turn to, but Guillermo had cleared her work schedule for the week, saying she needed more time to recuperate.

With a yawn, she slowly sat up. Instantly her eyes were drawn to the dresser, where several dozen white roses sat adorned in vases. They hadn't been there when she'd drifted to sleep, which meant Guillermo had snuck them into her room sometime after that—the hopeless romantic.

She inhaled deeply, trying to catch their scent. White roses were her absolute favorite, and Guillermo had covered the party with them. Forcing her tired body out of bed, she grabbed the small envelope attached to the closest vase. His note was short:

Hermosa,

I am yours forever and always. I carry with me today the vision of you last night. Please forgive me for I have some business that calls me away for the day. I will hold your face in my mind until I return. Dinner at Mariposas: six o'clock.

Con todo mi amor, G.

Poor Guillermo. That's all she could think. He'd spent the last few days throwing himself and his money into that party, yet she'd spent the majority of it thinking about another man.

She set the letter back with her roses and took her journal from her nightstand. Throughout the years, her journal had become her unpaid therapist, helping her work out seemingly unsolvable problems. She'd spent the better half of yesterday catching up the last week—*The Good, the Bad, and the Ugly,* as she had entitled her long Christmas saga—but so much had happened in the last twenty-four hours, she needed time to hash out the party with her inanimate friend.

Her pen couldn't write fast enough. The party. The agent. The crowds. Josh. And, as always happened, things began to clarify in her mind. Namely how completely opposite the two men were that shared her heart.

Guillermo is charismatic and friendly, and everyone loves him for it—made all the more evident at the party. Josh is friendly too, but in a completely different way. There's an honesty about him, not just in words, but in his expressions. When he smiles, he's genuinely happy. And when he's mad, there's no doubt about it. But with Guillermo, I can't tell what he's thinking. He always looks happy to me. The only time I haven't seen him perfectly happy was a time I'd rather forget. It's like it was a different person Christmas night, and the longer it goes, the easier it is to believe that person doesn't exist.

She stopped writing a moment with a sudden chill.

Except in my dreams where he exists in full force.

She paused again.

And in the hallway last night.

It had been so brief, but seeing him go after Josh brought her fears back in abundance. Guillermo's temper still existed whether she wanted to admit it or not. Josh had seen it, too, which made it even worse. She had tried to dismiss it as her boyfriend's protectiveness of her, and maybe if it hadn't been Josh he had lashed out at, she could have. But she couldn't forget. Nor could she ever forget the way Josh stepped in front of her. She lay back on her bed. *I'm doomed.*

It took a moment of laying there before she realized something. Sitting up again, she wrote even faster.

It's me! I'm the problem. I mirror whichever guy I'm with, and now it's like I have to choose which part of me I like better.

Around Guillermo, I feel poised, sophisticated, and maybe even a little charming. I like being those things—what girl wouldn't?—but with Josh, I'm real. Laughing or crying, depressed or ridiculous, none of it's an act. It's just me. And the crazy thing is that he accepts me, neurotic behavior and all, messed up face and all. Not only accepts me, but cares for me. Possibly even romantically . . .

Even as a smile crept up on her, she shoved it aside. While Josh might have been leaning in to kiss her one minute, he was running the next. *Maybe I just read him wrong at the piano.* But then she remembered . . . the flicker of his eyes. It had been so fast, down to the lips and back. For however brief a moment, he had wanted to kiss her. She was sure. And in that moment, she had wanted him to as well.

Oh, Josh, she scribbled heavily, *WHY DID YOU LEAVE?*

Throwing her pen down, she crossed her room and looked out the frosted window. Her room had a perfect view of the slopes where it seemed as though everyone in the world was enjoying New Year's Day instead of wasting it like she was. But without work—and now Guillermo—she was left with nothing to do, which was making for a long, lonely holiday.

The first thought that popped in her head wasn't a good one. She couldn't go back to the cabin. Whether she wanted it or not, her new friends had all said their good-byes last night—one without even saying the words. They were all heading back to their real lives, and she wasn't part of it. Instead she took her time showering and straightening her long, thick hair. Even then, she still had five or six hours to kill. Still, she held strong.

Needing another friend—and hopefully a more helpful one—she grabbed her phone. Before she could dial her mom's number, she saw a blinking message.

Her heart leaped into her throat—*Josh?* It was sad how quickly her hopes soared. But for more than one reason, she knew it wouldn't be him.

When she saw who it actually was, she almost threw her phone.

Why won't they leave me alone!

Last night she thought Guillermo ended the FBI thing once and for all, but no! They were never going to leave her alone. They'd been leaving messages all week. *Maybe it's time to get a new number,* she fumed as she deleted yet another message without listening to it. *Or better yet . . . a restraining order.* "Wait . . ." she said aloud, "can I even get a restraining order on the FBI?" The thought made her smile as she dialed her mom.

"*Feliz año nuevo,* Augustina," her mom greeted. "How was the rest of the party?"

Because of the roads and the crowds, her mom had left the party early. Sadie spent the next ten minutes explaining everything, sparing no details. She even told her mom about the strange dream, although she left out the part about the gun. Her mom would read more into the Guillermo-gun thing than was really there.

"I wish I could have met this Josh," her mom said supportively. "Why did he leave?"

"I don't know," Sadie said. "I don't know! I must have scared him off or he's mad at me or . . . I don't know. I'll never see him again and he didn't even say good-bye."

"Maybe he doesn't think it was a good-bye," her mom offered.

Sadie sat up on her bed. "You think so?"

Her mom laughed. "You're really serious about this boy, aren't you?"

Sadie sighed without answering.

"So where does this leave you and Guillermo?" her mom asked.

Looking at her beautiful roses, she shrugged. "I don't know. I think . . . maybe . . . I just don't know anything anymore, Mom."

"Hmm."

Sadie read her dark tone easily. It was the I'm-not-going-to-butt-in-but-I-really-want-to tone. Her mom hadn't been so quick to forgive Guillermo after hearing the real reason her only daughter had disappeared. She'd barely said two civil sentences to him last night. Sadie braced herself for another lecture about how you can tell more about a person's character from their flaws than their strengths, but her mom didn't say anything. In fact, she realized her mom had been uncharacteristically quiet during the whole conversation.

"Are you okay, Mamá?"

"Just tired. So do you think Josh returns your feelings?"

Sadie wanted to answer the question but she couldn't quite shake the feeling that something wasn't right. Last night, she attributed it to the long, emotional week, but now she wasn't so sure. "Are you sure, Mom? You sound worried."

"It's nothing. I've just been on edge the past few days. That's all."

"About what, me leaving again? Because I already told you that won't happen."

"It's not that. I've just been a little spooked lately. It's nothing really."

"Spooked?" Sadie repeated, growing concerned. It wasn't normal for her to have to pry information out of her mom. Marcela Dawson was an open book—one you often couldn't shut, even if you wanted to. Something definitely was wrong. "Like what, Mamá?"

"Like . . . the other day, our family photo album was out on the table. And . . ."

"And?"

"And I don't remember taking it out. I haven't looked at it in years."

"Maybe you meant to look at it, but never did," Sadie suggested.

"Yes. I'm sure that is it. Like I said, it's nothing."

Although her mom had a tendency to overreact, even be superstitious at times, this was different. She sounded genuinely frightened. "*Qué más?* What else?"

"Well, you're going to think your mother is losing it—and maybe I am—but . . . have you ever felt like you're being watched?"

"What? I don't know. I guess maybe a few times. Why?"

"It just feels like someone is always here. In the house. At work. At the store. No one ever is, of course. I'm sure it is just in my head."

"Or maybe you've been watching too many crime dramas," Sadie suggested. "Or reading too much? You know you have a thing for creepy stories."

"Yes. That's it, I bet." Marcela forced a laugh. "But enough about me. You didn't answer my question. Do you think Josh returns your feelings?"

Sadie thought back to the piano, then to the indisputable shake of his head in the hallway. "I don't know. I thought he did, but . . . maybe not. All I know is I really, *really* want to see him again. Does that make me a bad person?"

"No. That makes you a woman."

Sadie laughed, loving that she would never be able to tarnish herself in her mother's eyes.

"Hey, *querida,* can we chat later? I am walking with Gerri in a minute."

"Sure, Mom. I'll call you tonight."

Sadie set aside her phone and looked at the clock. Barely noon. There was a pile of clothes waiting, but there was no way she was doing laundry on a holiday. Which left only one thing to do. Find the boys. One in particular, though she knew it was probably a bad idea. She justified it by telling herself that she missed hanging out with them—*all* of them—and if, by some miracle, they hadn't left for Spokane yet, she wanted as much time with them as she could.

She grabbed her purse and headed out into the lobby. It was packed. Seemed like everyone but her was going skiing for the day. Probably even . . . Her step slowed . . . *No!* she cried. Even if the guys hadn't left for home, they wouldn't be at the cabin. They would be skiing or snow-boarding like everyone else in Montana. While driving a few miles to their cabin didn't seem too bad, driving an hour to Deer Basin seemed desperate—which she was, but not publicly.

Defeated, she slumped into the nearest chair. She was only there a second before she remembered something. They only went to Deer Basin for her. Normally they went . . .

Jumping up, she ran to the nearest window and searched the over-flowing parking lot. There were at least a dozen silver F-150s, but it didn't matter. She knew one of them was Sam's. And with a grin that overtook her face, she ran back to her room for her boots.

CHAPTER 25

The sun was blinding, reflecting off the new snow like a mirror. Sadie scrambled for her sunglasses and then searched the hills. Not only was New Year's Day one of the busiest ski days of the year, but the weather was supposed to reach the low forties. With all the recent snowstorms, skiing just couldn't get any better—or so eighty people had told her the night before.

She walked slowly around, scanning every face. Too many people. She tried to remember what the guys' coats looked like, but sadly, she could only remember Josh's. While he'd offered its warmth to her at the bonfire, she was stuck thinking of another time he'd offered it to her, on the driveway in a moment of pure insanity. Even more desperate, she doubled her search. Unfortunately, Josh's coat was plain blue like a million others on the blasted mountain.

The minutes passed slowly as she searched for any sign of them. She got several weird looks from people wondering why she was wandering around without skis. Still, she was determined, even if it took every last minute of her six hours.

Finally she spotted a tall, lanky guy with a distinctive red stripe across his coat. Kevin. Her stomach did excited flips as she watched him ski to the bottom of the hill. He was a good skier—of course he was, they probably all were—but as soon as he made it to flat ground, he began skiing in the opposite direction from her.

"Kevin!" she yelled, waving a frantic arm over her head and running after him. "Kevin!"

He turned and lifted his goggles to see who was running after him like a maniac. With a smile of recognition, he yelled back, "Ice Woman!"

Sadie was out of breath by the time she reached him, both from exertion and sheer excitement at having found them, even if "them" at the moment was just Kevin.

"How are you today?" he asked.

"Great!" she huffed. "You?"

He frowned, an expression she'd rarely seen on Kevin. "Kinda depressed, actually. We head home in the morning. I'm more than ready to get back to my wife, just not the rest of life."

Sadie nodded. Tomorrow. A whole lot better than today.

Feeling every second ticking by, she searched the hill behind him.

"So what are you up to today?" he asked. "We figured you'd be out with your boyfriend eating caviar or buying limos or something."

She rolled her eyes. "Nice. No, Guillermo's working."

"On New Year's? Isn't he his own boss?"

"Yeah." It was lame, what could she say. But right now she really didn't care about Guillermo. And with any luck, in a minute she'd care about him even less. "So . . . where's the rest of the gang?" she asked.

"Oh, them? I left them in a trail of powder up the hill. They'll be along soon."

"Sadie!" Sam called on cue. He skied up behind Kevin with Trevor right behind.

Three down. One to go.

Trevor said something to her, but she didn't exactly catch it. Even while Kevin explained to them how lame her boyfriend was, there was still no blue coat.

"No boyfriend today?" Trevor said. "Perfect. You want to come skiing with us?"

"No." She shook her head vigorously. "I don't"—her heart dropped—"ski." *On no! How am I supposed to hang out with them now?* Her brilliant plan no longer seemed so brilliant.

"Oh, come on," Trevor said. "Just ski. You'll love it. I promise."

"No. I've humiliated myself enough for one winter break." Thoroughly depressed, she checked the masses again. "So, where's Josh?" she asked, no longer hiding her interest.

Sam looked around with her. "I don't know. He was with us a second ago."

"Oh, he's coming," Trevor said. "He's just slow. Very . . . *ver-y* . . . slow."

"I'm not that slow," a voice said from behind her.

Sadie brushed down the front of her coat, feeling jittery and nervous. She and Josh hadn't exactly parted well, and she had no idea what to expect from him today.

"Oh, sorry," Trevor responded, less than apologetically. "I didn't see you there."

"Right," Josh drawled. "Just like you didn't see me when you nearly ran me off that cliff."

Trevor grinned. "Exactly."

Josh skied up beside Sadie, and she finally looked at him. He was smiling down at her. "I'm surprised to see you here. How are you today?"

His face, a window to his emotions, looked genuinely happy to see her. That's all she needed. "I'm good. I'm great!"

"Convince her to come skiing with us," Trevor said.

Josh gave her outfit a once-over. "She's not exactly dressed for skiing, and I have the feeling she already told you 'no.'"

"Yes, I did," she replied, though for once she wished she wasn't such a wimp. *Now what?* she asked herself, scrambling.

"You want to have lunch with us, then?" Kevin offered.

Thank you, Kev! "Yeah. Lunch sounds great! I haven't even had breakfast yet."

"Breakfast?" Kevin smirked. "You just wake up or something?"

She ducked her chin. "Sort of. I'm not much of a morning person."

"Yeah," Josh said with a quick smile. "I think we remember."

Though she blushed, she was too thrilled to be bothered by their teasing. She'd found the guys. Even better, she'd found Josh. Happier than she'd been in a long time, she followed him and the others into the lodge.

The ski lodge had two main restaurants: The Blue Moose, which was open to anyone, anytime; and Mariposas, which was expensive and exclusive—and Sadie's place of employment. Mariposas also had a beautiful baby grand piano with a newly cherished memory attached to it. However, Sadie didn't want to be inundated by questions from her coworkers, Guillermo's friends, and a hundred other regulars she knew, so she herded the guys to The Blue Moose.

They stood outside the restaurant waiting for a table to open up. The crowded restaurant was decorated around its namesake. Huge antlers adorned the blue walls and even the chandeliers. It was a fun, relaxed atmosphere. Yet in truth, she couldn't care less about the restaurant, the lodge, or anything else. Every time she looked at Josh, his eyes were on her, yet he hadn't said more than two words in the twenty minutes they'd been waiting. There was a conversation they needed to have, but at the moment, Trevor was monopolizing her time. Finally the five were led to a booth in the back of the crowded restaurant.

Sadie sat first, sliding in all the way. She hoped Josh would slide in after her. No such luck. Trevor followed and plopped his coat next to him, leaving Josh, Kevin, and Sam to squish in the other side. But all was not lost. Josh sat directly across from her.

She grabbed a menu, yet couldn't seem to focus on the words. Josh was watching her again, the corners of his mouth turned up. Her curiosity won out and she looked up. "What?"

His gaze dropped to his own menu. "Nothing. I'm still not used to seeing you in clothes actually meant for you. It's . . . different."

It wasn't a compliment, but it might as well have been. He liked what he saw. Still not catching any words, she smiled behind her menu, wondering how to get out of dinner with Guillermo—and a relationship, for that matter.

Trevor rubbed his stomach exaggeratedly. "Man . . . I'm so hungry I could eat a moose."

"Ha-ha," Josh said, without emotion. "That joke gets funnier every year."

"Doesn't it, though?"

Sadie laughed. She had missed hanging out with these guys. Her eyes scanned the room, recognizing a few people, and noticing a few others. One in particular. A man watching her from a few booths down. There was something familiar about his face, though she couldn't place him. Probably from the club. He was watching her curiously, though, which meant he probably knew Guillermo, which meant he probably wondered why she was hanging out with four other men. Sadie slid down in her seat, deciding it was time to actually read the menu. The waiter would be by soon and she had no idea what to order. Nothing looked like it could calm a fluttery stomach.

"I can't wait to get back to Amy," Kevin said. "This week was *way* too long. Next year, though. I'm warning you guys now, so get working on it."

"Better check with Amy before you invite her," Trevor retorted. "She told me Christmas break's her favorite week of the year. I bet she's got her feet kicked up at the spa right now."

Kevin made a face. "She said something about a spa yesterday. Thanks a lot, Trevor."

He grinned. "Anytime."

"What about you, Josh?" Sam asked. "I haven't heard you talk about Megan at all. Are you up for Kevin's challenge?"

It took all of Sadie's willpower to keep her eyes on the menu. There was a long, torturous silence, followed by his soft, but undeniable answer.

"Def-i-nite-ly."

Sadie couldn't move. Couldn't think.

"So what's Megan going to do if you get into BYU? That's quite a drive for a Friday night date."

Josh folded his menu and set it aside. "Actually . . . I'm hoping she'll move down there with me." He let that sink in a moment, then added, "I think it's time I popped the question."

Sadie felt the floor drop out from under her. She lowered her menu enough to catch a glimpse of him. Josh wasn't grinning like she expected him to be, he was barely even smiling, but it didn't matter. All the pieces were fitting into place. His odd behavior. His sudden mood changes. It all made sense. Megan. Of course a guy like Josh had someone else, but Sadie had deluded herself into thinking it was a one-sided relationship. That all of the interest was from Megan. She'd actually deluded herself into thinking that Josh cared for . . .

She swallowed hard. *Obviously not.*

The more she thought of their strange encounters, the worse it got. At the piano. In the hallway. Anytime she let her flirting get out of control, Josh backed off, giving her crystal-clear signals. He hadn't been leaning in at the piano, she had. While she was coming onto him in the hall, he had been planning a proposal. To Megan. She hid behind the menu, eyes burning.

An onslaught of comments flew around the table, most barely registering. Sam started: "You mean it? That's awesome! I knew you'd never be able to wait until after grad school."

Kevin threw in a "You can't be serious. Now? After all this time, you chose *right now?*"

And Trevor finished with the simple, "When?"

Josh sat back. "Assuming things go well, I was thinking about Valentine's."

"Valentine's?" Trevor grimaced. "Everyone proposes on Valentine's. You gotta catch her off guard—like maybe Groundhog Day. Now there's a holiday for proposing. She'll never see it coming. You could pop out of the ground, ring in hand."

Josh rolled his eyes. "Nice. I think I'll stick with Valentine's."

"But it's such a copout."

Sadie quickly jumped back into the conversation. "No. She'll love it." Then she forced herself to smile across the table like the mature adult she was. Josh loved Megan. Guillermo loved her. End of story.

Josh barely acknowledged her. "I hope so. I have a lot of work to do before then. As for you guys . . ." He pointed around the table, "keep your big mouths shut. Especially you, Kev."

"Me? What'd I do now?"

"Megan and Amy talk all the time. It'll slip out."

Kevin grunted. "Amy will kill me if she finds out I knew before her. Plus, there's no way you're ready. You need time to—"

"Time?" Sam cried. "How much more time does a guy need? I thought he was going to propose the second he got home from his mission. I say it's about time. I just can't believe it. Megan's officially gonna be one of us."

"Yeah," Josh quipped. "Poor her."

It was like Sadie was watching a movie. She heard the words, but felt completely detached. Josh loved Megan.

"Looks like you might get your wish after all, Kevin," Sam said, really warming to the subject. "Wives next year. That just leaves Trevor and me to find someone."

"I don't know if Megan will survive a week with you guys," Josh said. "Skiing or not."

"We'll be nice," Sam said. "Plus she'll be with Amy and whoever Trevor and I—"

"No way!" Trevor said, nearly rising in his seat. "No how! Over my dead body! This is guy time—our only time! Five years and going strong. I say no women allowed next year or any year after." He glanced sideways suddenly, as if he'd forgotten someone was sitting beside him. "Except you, Sadie. You can come anytime."

She sunk lower in her seat. *Thanks, Trevor. Thanks for drawing attention to me right now. Thanks for making me feel like a bigger fool. Christmas with Josh and his new wife? Over my dead body, indeed.*

The waiter showed up, interrupting the painful conversation. Unfortunately, he asked for Sadie's order first. Unable to think past Josh's surprise announcement, she chose the first thing saw. Antler soup. Then she called out, "By the way, this one's on me, guys." That brought a round of protests, but she went on quickly. "Seriously. I owe you so much. All of you." Her eyes went back to Josh, which they probably shouldn't have, but she wanted him to know that she owed him the most. Right from the beginning in Sam's truck, clear until last night. "You saved me," she whispered.

He blinked slowly and then dropped his eyes.

"You're right," Trevor said. "Buying us lunch ought to even the score."

Sadie chucked her napkin at him.

"Well, if Sadie's buying," Kevin said to the waiter, "that changes what I'm gonna order. Come to me last."

CHAPTER 26

The food took an extraordinarily long time to come out, which was fine with Sadie. It gave her more time with her boys. *My boys,* she repeated. That's what they had become. But as her antler soup came, she felt her time slipping away. The dumb jokes. The Lucky Charms. The roasted marshmallows and endless teasing. Even Trevor's obnoxious hair. She finally had friends again—real, genuine friends—and they were leaving.

"I'm gonna miss you guys," she said softly.

"Come visit then," Sam suggested. "Spokane isn't that far away and we have plenty of room at my house if you need a place to stay."

"Don't you leave for California right after you get back?" Josh noted.

"Well . . . yeah."

"You can stay with Amy and me in our mansion on the hill," Kevin offered with a wink.

She tried to smile. While it was tempting, she knew it wasn't realistic. She had work to get back to—not to mention life. And with Josh's newest revelation, things weren't quite what she hoped for. She pushed some crackers around her soup, no longer hungry.

Out of the corner of her eye, she saw Josh peering at her again, smiling—again. She tried to ignore him, too tired to play friend-that-he-loves-to-tease, but he wouldn't look away. Finally she met his gaze. He locked eyes with her briefly and then stretched his neck as if searching the restaurant for something. "Hey, guys. Did you know that Sadie writes music?"

Her spoon dropped, splashing red soup on her new pink blouse. At the same time she grabbed her napkin, she scanned The Blue Moose for a piano. There wasn't one, thankfully. Now, more than ever, she was grateful to have steered them away from the club.

"Really?" Trevor said. "What kind? 'Cause I rock at electric guitar."

"It's nothing. Just some dumb songs." She looked at Josh, pleading with her eyes for him to stop. For some reason that only made him smile more.

"Can we hear one of your songs?" Sam asked eagerly.

"Yes," Josh said. "I'm sure there's a piano around here somewhere."

"Oh, so you're a piano player?" Kevin asked, now looking between the two of them. "How interesting. So is Josh, but I bet you knew that already."

"Yes." There wasn't a whole lot more she could say without digging herself deeper into the pit Josh had so willingly dug for her.

"Supposedly," Josh continued, really enjoying himself now, "there's a song she wrote for Guillermo, but I haven't heard it. *Yet.*"

She kicked him under the table. "I said it was his favorite, not that I wrote it for him."

He ignored her. "Hey, Sam, do you know if there's a piano anywhere in the lodge?"

"Umm . . . there might be one in the club."

"Really?" he asked in mock surprise.

Sadie glared at him, about ready to hurl her soup across the table. In a way, this teasing thing was good. She no longer cared that he had some stupid girl back home.

"Yeah, I remember now," Sam said. "There's a beautiful grand piano in there. Maybe we can go there after lunch and you can play us some of your songs, Sadie."

Josh looked back at Sadie. "That is a great idea."

"No," she growled. "It's not."

"Just one?" Trevor asked.

"Come on, you know you're going to give in," Kevin added. "You always do. So show us what you've got."

When she shook her head, Trevor nudged her. "Either play us one of your songs or come skiing with us. We all know your boyfriend's gone for the day, so no excuses there. And obviously you'll have no problem getting us into the club. So . . . which will it be?"

Sadie studied her soup, debating. Skiing with them would be a disaster. A song was shorter, but so much more painful. Out of the corner of her eye she saw Josh settle back in his seat, arms folded triumphantly. There was no way she would give him the satisfaction of winning again. Not after the stunt he pulled last night. "Fine," she heard herself say. "I'll ski."

Josh sat up. "You're serious? You'd rather ski than play us one of your songs?"

"Yes," she said, happy to have denied him what he wanted.

"But I thought you hated skiing."

"I do, thank you very much."

"Wow." He shook his head, his blue eyes dancing. "Stubborn little thing, aren't you?"

Sadie didn't say much for the rest of lunch except to ask for the bill, which somehow had already been paid.

"There you guys are!" Kevin ducked under the rope to join Sam and Sadie in the long line. "Thanks for holding my spot."

The lady behind them shot Sadie a dirty look as if it were her fault Kevin made her two kids wait that much longer for the ski lift. Personally Sadie didn't mind waiting in the long line. It had been the same when she'd rented her gear. It just meant time wasted without her making a fool of herself. But Sam—who offered to stay behind and help her get set up with the right gear—looked thrilled to have Kevin join them. She felt bad. She hadn't been much company the past hour, even though Sam had tried; he asked about her family, growing up in Montana, her work, and if she'd ever given any thought to going back to church. But her answers kept getting shorter and shorter until he just stopped trying altogether. Poor guy. He was the sweetest of the bunch and she'd just ruined his last ski day. Now he was stuck taking her on one of the easiest runs. Kevin as well, apparently.

"So where are the others?" Sam asked.

"Trevor took off after some girl. But Josh"—Kevin pointed—"is back there."

Sadie turned to see Josh at the end of the same long line, unwilling to cut like Kevin had. Seeing an opportunity, she said, "Hey, Kev, how about you take my spot and I'll take yours." And before he could argue, she smiled at the lady behind them and ducked under the ropes.

She pushed her way past the scores of children waiting in line and then stopped before reaching Josh, wondering if she had the courage to go through with it. She tucked her scarf and her gloves into her pockets and took a deep breath. With the temperatures climbing and her black outfit attracting the sun, she was feeling uncomfortably warm. Maybe it was just the anticipation of being alone with Josh and muddling her way through what needed to be said.

He still hadn't noticed her, so she took one last opportunity to enjoy him from a distance. He was in a trance—his deep blue eyes staring at a sky of the same color—but from her standpoint, he was perfect. *Be an adult,* she reminded herself. They were still friends, regardless of her little crush. And with that, she pushed herself awkwardly forward.

"Hey, can I join you?"

His head snapped up in surprise. "Oh . . . hey. Yeah. Sure. Why aren't you up there with Kevin and Sam? I would've caught up."

"I figure it's better to waste the day standing in line than in a hospital with a broken leg."

He smiled. "Well, if that's the case, maybe your luck will hold out and Trevor will get in line just as we get to the ski lift, then you can cut back with him."

"Oh, I really hope so," she said, already searching for the wild hair. But Trevor was nowhere and while she had Josh alone, she decided to plunge in. "Also, I"—she bit her lower lip—"never really thanked you for last night. I mean, I tried, but . . . I don't know, I just . . ." Josh began to fidget with his poles and she rushed on, wanting to have it said. "I still feel awful you were dragged into that whole FBI mess, but you were there when I needed you. You . . . stayed, and, and . . . I don't know. I . . ." Her words began to tumble over themselves, remembering how he'd jumped in front of Guillermo, remembering how she'd fallen apart against his chest. His gray shirt probably had permanent mascara stains. "It just meant a lot to me, I guess, and I wanted to say thanks."

She wasn't sure what to expect from him. She really didn't want to talk about Guillermo, the FBI, or anything having to do with that side of her life, but neither did she have the courage to apologize for her poorly timed question afterward when she'd practically begged him to love her—which is probably what he was waiting for. Thankfully, he let her off with a simple nod. After that, he did the next best thing. He changed the subject.

"I really wanted to hear another of your songs today."

"I know."

He shook his head and they inched forward in line. "Am I that bad? Worth skiing for?"

"Yes," she said without hesitation.

He smiled. "Well, I'm sorry. You didn't have to come. I would have left you alone."

She held up a hand to block the bright sun intruding on her view of him. "You're telling me that now?"

He laughed heartily. Then he glanced over her black outfit. "So . . . no Kermit today?"

"You're never going to let me live that down, are you?"

"No, I don't think I will."

"Well, I decided black is a little less . . ."

"Obnoxious?" he offered.

It was her turn to laugh. "No. I was thinking a little less conspicuous."

"I don't know. I kind of liked you in neon green. It made it easy to pick you out of the crowd. Think how handy that'd be on a day like today. In fact, I think Deer Basin should hire you full time."

"Why?" she asked, leery.

His eyes twinkled, the way they always did when he was teasing her. "You can light up the slopes at night. Think of all the money they'd save."

She smacked his coat. "Be nice. Sam's mom probably loves that outfit."

"Oh, all right," he conceded, though it didn't wipe the smirk off his face, and for another minute afterward he continued to grin. It wasn't until she realized why he was smiling so much today that it hurt. Megan.

"So, you're in a particularly good mood," she noted, trying to keep her voice light.

"I guess I am," he said, though his smile faded some. "I did some serious life-pondering this morning and finally got some things figured out. Now that I've decided what I need to do, I feel much, much better."

"About Megan, you mean?" She hoped her voice wasn't as shaky as it sounded.

"Yeah . . ."

It seemed as though he wanted to say more, but when he didn't, she quickly said, "That's great," before things could get awkward. "Megan's a lucky lady. You're quite the catch."

Josh turned in surprise. "Uh . . . thanks."

Quite the catch? she cringed. *Did I really just say that?* She began playing with her zipper. So much for not letting things get awkward. So much for being real around him. Real stupid. And lame! Not to mention the all-powerful cliché. *You're quite the catch?* What a winner that was! But whenever she was around him, it was like she was a runaway train en route to Flirtville, and no matter the cost to her pride, she couldn't stop herself. It was pathetic.

Both of them pretended to watch the people in line around them as a heavy silence hung in the air. A few times Sadie glanced at the lodge, wondering if she should just go back and do laundry. Unfortunately, Sam had already paid for her lift pass and gear while she was trying on boots. It would be a waste of his money.

Wanting to kick herself, she just stood there until a little girl caught her attention. She was standing right in front of them in the long line. Sadie probably wouldn't have noticed her, except the small blonde kept stealing glances at Josh around her father's leg. Dressed in pink, head to toe, the little girl was adorable, with large green eyes that followed his every move.

At first it seemed that Josh hadn't noticed her because he never looked her direction, but the next time the girl poked her head around, he raised a few fingers, sending the five-year-old blushing behind her father's leg. Sadie waited. Sure enough, two seconds later she was back, peeking, and waiting for him to give some small sign that he was aware of her.

For the next few minutes the two of them played their little game: her peeking, Josh waving. He kept his face like a statue, seemingly uninterested, while the little girl waited for the smallest flicker of his hand.

The irony of the situation hit Sadie. *I'm the little girl, completely obsessed with getting his attention—even if just a tiny portion. And when he finally gives it, I shy away, blushing like a school girl with her first crush.* Sadie sighed. *Pathetic, pathetic, pathetic.*

Josh glanced sideways. "What has you so lost in thought?"

The little girl frowned. She'd lost his attention. She didn't give up though; she just waited, hoping he would return. Sadie understood completely.

"I was just thinking that sometimes I still feel like a little kid," she said.

The child suddenly realized she had had an audience. Embarrassed, she hid again. Sadie crouched down to her level, and when the girl re-appeared, she whispered quickly, "I like your coat. It's very pretty." The blonde didn't move. Didn't blink. "I love pink, too," Sadie added. "See . . ." She unzipped her coat enough to show off her pink blouse.

"Did you get it for Christmas?" Josh asked, joining Sadie at the child's height.

The large eyes shifted, no longer caring one bit about Sadie. Then slowly her blonde head bounced up and down and she pointed to the matching pink hat. "Ah. That too?" he asked. "It's very pretty." And with a wink that could break the heart of any woman, he added, "And so are you."

The girl pursed her lips, but a giggle burst out before she could hide again. Her father turned, finally aware people were talking to his daughter. "Sophie's shy," he explained as he rubbed her back.

Sadie straightened, as did Josh. "She's adorable," she said.

"Thanks."

Sophie's dad went back to his conversation with his friend. A moment later, Sophie peeked her head around so she and Josh could begin their game again. Sadie watched affectionately, growing more and more jealous of the little girl. And Megan.

"She reminds me of my youngest sister," Josh said with another wave. "She was a little towhead like that one."

"How many siblings do you have?" Sadie asked.

"I'm the oldest of six."

"Six?" she cried. "How do you keep track of them all?"

"Well . . . I recite their names each morning and twice on Saturday just to be sure."

Sadie elbowed him softly. "That's not what I meant. That's just a lot of kids." And he was the oldest. It actually explained a lot. Big brother Josh. "So how old are they?"

He moved forward another few inches. "My brother, Jake, is twenty and on a mission for our church in Nebraska."

"Nebraska? I thought mission people went overseas, a third world country or something. Didn't Sam live in Peru?"

"Yeah, but missionaries can be sent just about anywhere."

Sadie's eyes widened with a sudden thought. "Wait, were you a missionary?"

His face answered before he did. "Yep! Best two years of my life."

For some reason that seemed really weird to her. He didn't fit her picture of a missionary. He was too . . . manly, or something. "Did you preach in Nebraska like your brother?"

"No. I served in Scotland, actually."

"Scotland?" She was starting to sound like an idiot, repeating everything he said, but it was all so unexpected. "I bet it's beautiful there," she offered quickly.

"Aye," he said in a thick Scottish brogue. "The soomers be green lek ya ne'er seen. 'Tis luv'ly, Lassie. Truly luv'ly." He pulled off his hat and finished with a little bow.

Sadie laughed, but he only winced. "Sorry. Sometimes I forget I'm in public."

"I noticed," she teased, even though it was one of the things she liked about him. Guillermo never forgot.

"So, anyway," he continued, "my parents had me and Jake, and then my mom left." Sadie nodded. *The long story.* "My dad got remarried and they had four more kids: Lauren, Drew, Mike, and towheaded Katie who's ten and looks a lot like Sophie there."

Little Sophie grinned, pleased to have his attention back momentarily. At the same time, Sadie suddenly took an accounting of their position. Without her realizing it, they'd been moving forward, bringing them dangerously close to the lift. Time to find Trevor.

"What about you?" Josh asked. "Any siblings?"

"One." It was impossible to go on tiptoes when she was strapped into stupid skis, but she tried anyway. "Damien. He lives in San Diego. A computer guy." *Come on, Trevor. Where are you?* It was bad enough that Trevor had seen her snowboard. There was no way she was letting Josh see her ski. But with only a few more people in front of them, she only had a few minutes before she had to get on the lift. Her search doubled.

Then she spotted him. Not Trevor, but the man from the restaurant. He was a ways off, watching her quietly like before. Instantly she remembered where she had seen him. It hadn't been in the club, or at the party, but the day before, when she'd been trying to figure out which road led to Sam's cabin. She had stopped at a gas station to fill up and that guy had been in one of the other cars. Watching her. Just like he had been at the restaurant. Just like he was now.

A sudden chill ripped through her. *Have you ever felt like you were being watched?*

CHAPTER 27

Josh nudged Sadie forward. "I doubt Trevor's skiing on this hill. It's a little beneath him." Still, she continued to search. The closer they got to the front of the line, the paler she became. "And I don't think Kevin or Sam are back, either," he continued, "so you're just going to have to ride up the mountain and actually ski."

She finally looked up and saw little Sophie pushing forward into the next chair. She was suddenly digging in her skis. "What happens if I can't ski? Can I ride the lift back down?"

Josh was amused, but persistent. "No. Come one, you're not going to die. But you need to move. We're next."

She followed him into the loading station, yet as the next chair swung around, she looked over her shoulder, still searching for Trevor. "I'm telling you, Sadie, he's not there. If you're that bad, you can always—"

There was whoosh of air, and suddenly Sadie was gone.

"Ow!" she cried below him.

She'd gone down. How, Josh couldn't figure out, nor did he have time. "Duck!" he said, pushing himself out of the way. She did just as their chair passed over her head.

The lift operator finally woke up and stopped the ski lift. Josh surveyed the scene. Sadie's skis were twisted, her poles lying haphazardly beside her on the ground. He couldn't help it. He laughed, matching those of the kids in line behind them.

He didn't need to remember any high school Spanish to catch the gist of her subsequent speech. "Sorry," he said, wiping the grin from his face. "Let me help."

Grabbing Sadie's hand, he pulled upward. Once again, all chaos erupted. Her left ski went out, followed by the right and she went down again. The problem was the warm weather and the crowds. Everything below the chair was pure slush. So he did the only thing he knew. "Hold my poles," he said, handing them down.

"Are you serious?" Her own were sprawled across her lap, but she took them anyway.

He yanked off his gloves, reached down, and scooped her up—skis, poles, and all. She was so tiny it took no effort whatsoever, but the look she shot him was priceless as she stared across the six inches that separated them.

"Are you okay?" he asked. "Did you hurt anything? Well . . . besides your pride?"

She folded her arms. "Will you please put me down?"

He ignored her request, enjoying the moment a little too much. Sure, he was pushing the boundaries he'd set up that morning, but he was having too much fun. He twisted around to address the crowd. "Sorry for the disruption, folks. I have everything in control now."

Sadie laughed in spite of herself. "Josh!" she cried. "Put me down!"

"Oh, all right." With exaggerated gentleness, he set her in the next chair. "You know, that was very nice of you to give those kids some entertainment. That line is *way* too long."

"You're terrible. Can't I have a little dignity?"

"Apparently not." And he erupted for a second time.

Though her eyes were smiling, she kept her expression stern. "You could have helped me *before* I fell, you know. Wouldn't that have been the more gentlemanly thing to do?"

"Had I known how challenging it was for you to get on a ski lift, I would have. But then again . . . I would have missed the show."

As they started their slow ascent up the mountain, she reached down to fix her skis. "Why do you like to tease me so much, Josh?"

Because you're adorable, he nearly said. And really, teasing her was better than the alternative of moping and pouting. If it wasn't for this morning, he might have been moping even now, avoiding her like he'd tried to at the party, but he'd finally figured it out. He'd finally solved the Sadie mess.

Sadie had been sent to him as a test.

It was so logical—and a test she had been, but no more. She no longer had to be a temptation for him. They were to be good friends, purely platonic as it had been in the beginning and as it should have stayed. That way he didn't have to lose her. Or Megan. A win-win.

That was the theory, at least. In practice it hadn't been quite so easy. Several times he'd caught himself staring at her, and more than a few of those times she'd caught him staring as well. Being alone with her again didn't help. Nor did sitting so close to her. Or having her look like that. But he was trying. He really was.

She twisted around and searched the crowds again. He did, too, wondering why she was still searching for Trevor. Their feet were dangling twenty feet in the air. There was no way to get out of skiing now.

With her turned around, the mountain breeze swirled her hair in front of him. It glowed a beautiful auburn in the bright Montana sun. It looked incredibly soft and smelled like—

He winced. *A test.* He quickly reminded himself of the "platonic" part of the platonic relationship, determined to make it work. But the longer she stayed twisted in her seat, the more he began to worry that she wasn't searching for Trevor at all, but was avoiding him instead. *Great. Now I'm making her uncomfortable.*

He nearly said something, but then he noticed her expression. She wasn't mad. She wasn't even frustrated. She was . . . disturbed. Almost frightened. "What's wrong?" he asked.

She turned back around. "Nothing."

But with her facing forward in full view, he was certain. If she'd been mad, he would have let it go, but she wasn't mad. She was scared. A mirror of the woman he met at the cabin. "What's wrong, Sadie?"

She stared at her hands. "Have you ever felt like someone's following you?"

"No. Why?"

"Nothing. Never mind."

It took a moment for her words to sink in, and then his mouth fell open. "Someone's following you?" He spun around, but they'd already crested a small hill, hiding the crowd from them. "Who?" he asked, searching every chair behind them instead. Everyone was either kids or parents of kids. Hardly what he considered threatening. "Who's following you?"

"Just some guy."

"A guy? Which one? Is he on the lift?" Because if so, they were in serious trouble. They were stuck in the air, going two miles an hour, with nowhere to run. They might as well have had a target on their backs.

"No. He's down there in the middle of everyone else, not skiing or anything." She shook her head. "I don't know. Maybe it's just in my head."

She was trying hard to act nonchalant, but Josh didn't buy it. Not for a second.

"What makes you think he's following you?"

"Well . . . I saw him yesterday when I was at the gas station. He was filling up his car like I was, but he kept looking at me. I didn't think anything of it at the time, but then I saw him in The Blue Moose earlier, just kind of watching me. And when I was looking for Trevor . . . and just before I fell down . . ." She hugged herself. "That's four times. It's starting to creep me out."

Josh whirled again, not sure what he'd see, but needing to see it anyway. "And he wasn't skiing," he said, pulse quickening. "What does he look like?"

She shrugged. "Late fifties, black hair, wearing a brown leather coat."

"And you'd never seen him before yesterday?"

"I don't think so. I'm sorry, it's probably nothing. My self-defense class just taught me to be paranoid."

Life experience should have taught her to be paranoid. As it was, his mind raced through the possibilities. First, that she'd caught the fancy of an older sicko who started following her. It was possible with Sadie, who seemed to draw a lot of male attention. Second, that Guillermo had one of his "friends" keeping tabs on her, but why? Josh pushed the anger aside to consider a less threatening possibility. That it was the FBI. But that still left the why. There was a fourth option, though he didn't trust it. That it was just like she said. Nothing. But she'd seen the guy four different times, in three different places. With crowds this big what was the chance of that?

"Josh? What are you thinking? You're scaring me."

He looked down, realizing he was tensed from fists to jaw. "Sorry," he said, loosening his grip on his poles. "Having a cop for a dad makes me a little paranoid, too."

She slugged him. "You're supposed to say, 'Don't worry, Sadie. You *are* just being paranoid.'"

He rubbed his arm. "Sorry. You asked."

"So what do you think I should do, if you don't think I'm being paranoid?"

"Call the FBI," he said without hesitation.

The look she gave him caused the hair on the back of his neck to stand on end. However, he didn't think she'd like his next idea any better. It involved her packing a bag, changing her name, and moving to the Louisiana bayou, so he chose a less-dramatic approach. "Just stay by one of us, and if you see the guy in the leather coat again, let me know."

"Man, you really know how to give a girl warm fuzzies, don't you?"

Obviously not. He should have been easing her concern, not adding to it. Yet if she was right and someone really was following her, then they should be taking it seriously. Right there, he decided to talk to the guys to make sure she was watched at all times. And if the older man showed up again, he was calling that FBI agent whether she wanted him to or not. But in the meantime, whoever he was, that guy was at the bottom without skis and they were headed up.

"Maybe we should talk about something else," he said. "What were we talking about before? Your brother or something?" She eyed him skeptically, so he tried a better distraction. "Or how about music? Besides your own songs, what do you like to play?"

It seemed to work. Her eyes lit up. "Well, I love musicals a lot—I'm kind of a sap that way—but mostly I love the classics: Debussy, Mozart. Chopin's my favorite right now."

"Musicals, Debussy, *and* Chopin? You're definitely a sap."

"Really? What about you? Rachmaninoff's not exactly the cheery, peppy type. What does that say about you?"

He laughed. "Quite a bit, actually."

She laughed as well. "At least you're honest enough to admit it. By the way, I meant it when I said you play well. I was very impressed, Josh. I wish I could have heard more."

The sudden memory of being at the piano with Sadie sobered him to the core. "Thanks. For some reason, Rachmaninoff clears my head, especially when I'm in a bad mood. I can sit at the piano for hours and pound out my frustrations."

Her eyes lowered. "Like last night?"

He stared at her, guilty as charged. It was sheer frustration that had driven him to the piano, and he'd played for half an hour trying to work through it. Then she appeared, plunging him back into the very torment he was trying to escape.

"I think you owe me all of 'C-sharp Minor'," she said softly.

"Sure. As soon as I hear another one of your songs."

Her chin came up. "You don't play fair, do you? After the stunt you pulled last night—and at lunch—I think you owe me the whole song right after skiing, no strings attached."

"You're right." He owed her that much at least. Condition number two. Losing himself in the depths of her eyes, he added, "And I'm really, *really* sorry I broke our deal last night." *Please, just don't ask me why I had to leave.*

She studied him a moment, then smiled broadly, demonstrating her quickness to forgive. "Good. Now I hate to disappoint you, but I really don't want to look like a fool again. How do I get off this stupid thing?"

Josh looked around and saw that they were approaching the end of their ride. "Just put your skis down flat. The hill will do the rest."

"You make it sound easy. Remember who you're dealing with."

"True," he grinned. "But don't worry. I'm prepared this time. Just hold onto me, focus on staying upright, and I'll pull you behind."

He took her ski poles in his left hand, and grabbed her hand with his right. It was such a natural thing to do, driven by purely unselfish motives, but the response he got was anything but unselfish. Electricity coursed through him as her cold skin touched his, speeding the pulse in his veins. He watched her glance from his face down to their hands, then freeze.

She knows, he breathed. *She knows what this does to me.* Just like she'd known he wanted to kiss her at the piano, just like she'd known he had been staring at her all day.

Suddenly he didn't care. He wanted her to know what she was doing to him. Maybe then she'd stay away from him for good.

With a quick breath, he faced her head on: the dark hair blowing in the breeze, the soft lips parted in surprise, and the large eyes that refused to blink.

Just like that, all resolve was gone.

Instinctively, his thumb stroked hers. Her skin was so smooth, so soft, and even though ice cold, it somehow sent heat back to him. His grip tightened around her hand as if she were his lifeline keeping him afloat, when in reality she was only plunging him deeper.

He waited for her to pull her hand away, he braced himself for a rejection or, at the very least, a slap in the face, but it didn't come. Instead she lowered her lashes in a shy smile.

Is it possible . . . ?

On pure impulse, he slid his fingers around, interlocking with hers, leaving all thoughts of a platonic relationship behind. Then he held his breath. Once again her eyes dropped to their hands, very much aware of the moment as he was. Slowly, almost imperceptibly, a smile started, first in her eyes, then spreading across her face in a way that took his breath away.

He was barely aware that his skis hit the snow; he just let them glide down the small hill as he pulled her behind him easily, effortlessly. It took a moment for him to find his voice, and then he said, "There, that wasn't so bad, was it?"

She squeezed his hand. "Not bad at all."

CHAPTER 28

Josh grasped onto Sadie's hand well after the time she needed help. It was no longer an act of chivalry, it was an act of selfish indulgence. He couldn't find the energy to release her, nor did he want to anymore. They were fused together now, and it felt only right.

She tipped her head back and flashed him another of her stunning smiles. He was smiling, too—grinning actually—and had to remind himself to breathe. His eyes took in every feature of her face, stopping on her lips. He was ready. Committed. And suddenly interrupted.

"Josh! Sadie!"

Sam's voice brought him back to the world around him, a world full of other people. He pulled his eyes unwillingly away from Sadie to see Sam and Kevin skiing across the mountain toward them.

"What are you guys still doing up here?" she asked, almost sounding perturbed.

Sam pushed himself over to her. "We decided to wait for you guys. We figured it'd be too hard to find each other again in these crowds."

"Oh. That's nice." Only that time she didn't sound irritated at all.

As she recounted her mishap on the ski lift, Kevin cleared his throat exaggeratedly on the other side of Josh. Josh turned to see his friend bug-eyed. Kevin didn't say a word, but with a slow nod, he motioned down to Josh's hand, which was still entwined with Sadie's.

Josh dropped her hand and ran through the last two minutes. *What just happened?*

Kevin's smile grew.

Sadie stayed unaware of the little exchange as she talked to Sam, leaving Josh time to frantically regroup his thoughts. Three reasons. Three! He just chucked the first two out the window—they both had—but he couldn't ignore the third. He hoped it had just been in his head, at the same time knowing it hadn't.

He surfaced in time to hear Sam say, "My brother took out three people coming off the lift once. Don't worry about it, Sadie."

"I guess." She laughed once more and then turned back to Josh. "So now what?"

Good question.

"Let's ski!" Sam offered when no one else did.

"Right," she agreed, her eyes still locked on Josh. "Ski."

She held out her hand to him, the same one he had just been grasping with childlike delight. He felt a burst of excitement; it hadn't been just in his head. Her eyes danced in amusement, but it wasn't until she asked quietly, "Can I have my poles back, Josh?" that he figured out why.

Completely flustered, he looked down and sheepishly handed over her poles. Kevin burst out laughing, aware of more than Josh wanted him to be.

"I'm sorry, Sadie, about . . ." Josh cleared his throat, finding it suddenly full of cotton. *Haven't I already done this once?* "About that," he tried anyway. "I was . . . I mean . . ."

Her smile began to fade, muddling his thoughts. He really, *really* needed to talk to her, but being alone with her wasn't something he could handle anymore. Obviously.

"You know what," he said to Sam instead, "you and Sadie go ahead. I need to talk to Kev for a sec. We'll catch up in a minute."

SADIE

Sam looked a little too excited by that prospect. Josh didn't know Sadie's reaction since he didn't dare look at her. She and Sam started down the hill in snowplow form.

Josh waited a moment before turning back to Kevin, who for some reason was still grinning. *Oh man,* Josh groaned. This was going to be bad. Waiting until Sam and Sadie were well out of earshot, he said, "I think Sadie has an unwanted admirer."

"Who, Sam?" Kevin said. "He's harmless. Just a little crush. He'll get over it."

"No. Not Sam!" Josh watched the two retreating figures. He shook his head to focus on the real issue. "Sadie thinks she's being followed by someone. A man."

Kevin was sufficiently diverted. "Really?"

Josh quickly recounted what she told him, while checking the skiers getting off the lift and those on the mountain. "So we all need to keep our eyes peeled today," he finished.

"Okay. Will do. Who do you think it is?"

Josh thought through the four possibilities, not sure he'd narrowed them down any. "I don't know, but I don't like it."

"Agreed. Older guy. Leather coat. Got it."

"Now I just need to tell Sam and Trevor—assuming we see Trevor again." Josh checked the hill again. No Trevor. No leather-coat guy. Then he checked on Sadie and Sam again, just to be sure. Sam was in front of her skiing backward. Though Sadie was slow, she had managed to stay upright. Her laughter carried up the hill to them.

"So, Josh, when were you planning on telling me about you and Sadie? The wedding?"

Josh whirled. "What? We're not—"

Kevin held up a glove. "Please. I knew something was up when she ditched me and Sam in line down there. Or when the two of you snuck out of the party together. Or heck, clear back when you drove her to the lodge. Just exactly how long have you two—"

"There's nothing going on," Josh interrupted angrily. "We're. Just. Friends." he said, forcing the words.

"I see. And you were holding her hand because . . ."

"I was helping her off the lift," he replied weakly.

Kevin snorted. "How noble of you. How do you explain the look on your face when you got caught?"

Josh punched the snow with his poles, furious at himself more than anyone. "You're reading way too much into it, Kev. *Way* too much."

"Enough!" Kevin bellowed. "Admit it!"

"Admit what?"

"Admit to me why even as we speak you're staring after her like a lovesick puppy."

Josh grunted, grabbed his goggles, and yanked them over his eyes.

Kevin laughed. "At least be honest enough to admit it to yourself. You've got it bad."

Josh threw his hands up. "Fine! I"—he swallowed hard, trying to digest the truth—"did. But now I don't."

"What the heck's that supposed to mean?"

"After last night, I realized things were getting out of hand—*I* was letting things get out of hand—so this morning I did a lot of thinking. That's when it finally hit me . . ." He watched Sam and Sadie, wondering if it was still true.

Kevin smacked his coat. "What?"

"Well, you're going to think I'm crazy, but I decided Sadie was sent to me as a test. To see how much I loved Megan . . ." He choked on her name—feeling a six-year relationship go down the drain—". . . and my church." An even longer relationship, betrayed.

Without warning, a ski pole collided with his head. "Are you nuts?"

Josh rubbed his head. "Maybe. You're the only one married here. What do you think?"

"I think you *are* crazy!" Then Kevin's mouth fell open. "So that's why you *suddenly* decided to propose to Megan? She's been ready for years, and now all of a sudden you are because you're falling for another girl?"

"Man, when you put it that way it sounds terrible."

"Because it *is* terrible! There wasn't a girl in the world who could turn my head when I was dating Amy. Still isn't."

The guilt soared—*Megan*—but Josh held tight to his reasoning. "This just has to be different then. I think I needed Sadie to convince me it was time to settle down with Megan. I've put it off long enough."

"Your logic has a few holes in it, as does your head."

"Thanks," Josh muttered. This conversation was going nowhere.

"Tell me, Josh, if you don't have feelings for Sadie, then why are you *still* staring at her? And why did it take you a month to drop her hand after so-called helping her off the lift?"

Josh dropped his eyes and punched more holes in the snow.

"What's with you and Sam anyway? You're both gaga over Sadie, and you guys just don't seem the type. I mean, Trevor, I totally expect this from, but you . . . ?" Kevin shook his head. "I've never seen you like this before. Not even for Megan."

Not even for . . . Kevin couldn't have chosen four more painful words.

"Well, where's Trevor?" Kevin asked, searching the hill behind them. "Might as well get his confession about Sadie so we can start group therapy."

It was Josh's turn to smack Kevin with his pole.

"Ow! That was a lot harder than I hit you."

Josh ignored him and looked down the hill. Sam and Sadie were nearly out of sight, but it didn't look like she was enjoying herself any more or any less than when she'd been with Josh. "It's good she has Guillermo then," he said, "so she doesn't notice any of us idiots."

"Maybe . . . ," Kevin said slowly. "I told Sam today—more like ten minutes ago when he wouldn't shut up about her—that he was crazy and needed to get back to that girl in California."

"Yes, he does. The sooner the better."

"And . . ."

Josh eyed him warily. "And?"

"I don't know if I'd tell you the same." Josh blew out his breath in exasperation, but Kevin held up a hand. "Now wait. I'm not the one who's been dragging his feet with Megan for two years. You want to know what I think? I think you've been pigeonholed in that relationship so long you don't know how to get out. But for a minute at least, humor me and leave Megan out of this. If you weren't dating anyone right now, where would that leave you with Sadie?"

"The same place, Kev. Sadie's not someone I would—or should—consider dating."

"Why? The Mormon thing? You'd push someone like her away over something like that? What's wrong with you?"

"Plenty, but I'd like to think I'm the kind of person who keeps commitments to myself, a person that doesn't go back on promises—promises made for a good reason, Kev. I can't walk away from a lifelong commitment to my beliefs for some girl."

"This isn't just *some* girl. This is Sadie. Come on!"

Josh pinched the rim of his nose. "Look, I just got this all worked out in my head this morning. I'm over it—over Sadie—and even if I weren't, it's not a relationship that could ever work out anyway—assuming the relationship exists in the first place, which it doesn't—but even if it did, it can't. I can't let it." He stopped, trying desperately to form a coherent sentence. "This little infatuation has gone on long enough and it ends now!"

"Well, that's too bad," Kevin said flatly. "Because I don't think your 'little infatuation' is just one-sided. Sadie seems to have the same problem you do; having eyes only for one person. And unfortunately for Guillermo, it ain't him."

Josh looked up. "No. She can't . . ."

"Like at the party when she first saw us, I swear she wanted to see you, Josh. Not us. And when Trevor told her you'd left, you should have seen her face. And then again today at lunch. I'm telling you, she follows your every—"

"Please!" Josh interrupted. "Seriously, Kev. I can't take anymore."

"Fine. I'm the only one married here. What do I know?"

Josh whirled around and skied down a different run, getting away from Kevin, Sam, and all thoughts of Sadie.

CHAPTER 29

Kevin swore loudly. He'd wasted a half an hour with Sam waiting for Josh and Sadie so they could "all stick together." Now he stood alone at the top of the mountain. He wanted to kick something—preferably Josh. He hated when his friend turned Mormon zealot on him.

He took off. It didn't take long to catch up with Sam and Sadie. At their speed he probably could have skied to the bottom, stood in the huge line, rode the slow lift, and still beat the two of them back down. Regardless, he called out, "Hey girl, you're doing great!"

Sadie slowed to a stop, which took absolutely no effort. "Thanks. Sam's been nice enough to help me out."

"And Sadie's been nice enough to help me brush up on my Spanish."

Kevin rolled his eyes. Even as Sadie was not-so-inconspicuously searching for Josh, Sam was still giving it his all. "Hey, Sam," Kevin said, "Josh is at the bottom and needs to talk to you. I can take over here."

Sadie did a one-eighty from the waist up, nearly knocking herself over. Kevin shook his head. *I hate it when I'm right.* But Sam was disappointed for his own reasons.

"Oh. Okay. See ya in a little bit, Sadie."

"Hey, Sam," Kevin called. "Watch your head."

"Huh?"

"Never mind." Let the Mormons duke it out on their own.

Once Sam was gone, Sadie said, "Okay, Kev. I'll apologize right now. I'm *very* slow."

"I noticed."

Just as she'd warned, she started skiing at a snail's pace. All of her attention was focused on keeping her skis pointed together. They were the slowest people on the hill, which was really saying something, considering the group of underdeveloped humans around them.

"You know," he said, "you're actually pretty steady on your skis. If you could just pick up your speed a little, you'd be doing pretty good." When her speed remained unchanged, he tried again. "Seriously, do you see how many kids are passing you up?"

"I'm fully aware of that. Why do you think I hate skiing?"

He waited another torturous minute. She hadn't wobbled even once. There was absolutely no reason for her to be *soooo* slow. "You know," he said, trying a different tactic, "I woulda thought you'd be in a hurry to get to the bottom."

"Why is that?" The line was delivered like a well-rehearsed actress, but at the same time her skis straightened, kicking up her speed a few notches.

"No reason." And without missing a beat, he added, "So, Sadie, what do you think of us guys by now?"

"Oh . . . you're all so great." She flashed him a quick smile. "I love you guys."

"Any of us in particular?" No need to beat around the bush. If he got his way, they would be at the bottom soon, and she needed to be warned of what was awaiting her.

The tips of her skis came together, stopping her abruptly. "What are you getting at, Kev?"

"Just wondering if Guillermo has your *whole* heart."

For a minute she said nothing. She checked the base of the mountain again, then asked softly, "What's Josh's girlfriend like?"

Bingo! Kevin took his time answering, especially knowing where the conversation needed to head. "She's kinda quiet—especially compared to us guys. Amy calls her 'The world's nicest person.'" *That's it,* he suddenly realized. That's why Josh and Megan had been stuck in limbo so long. They were both too nice to end it when they should have. "Megan and Amy are friends," he continued, "but that's mostly because Josh and I are friends. Megan's a Mormon like Josh is, which matters a lot to him."

Sadie looked up in surprise. "Really?"

"A lot. Like, obsessively a lot."

Her lips pressed into a thoughtful line. "I guess that makes sense. A lot of people want to be with someone who shares their beliefs. So I guess Josh would . . . want . . . some-one . . ." Each word took longer than the previous as her mind slowed to process, and in the end she wasn't even aware she hadn't finished. He stayed quiet to give her time to mull it over.

Her head finally came up. "I know Sam and Josh don't drink or anything, but are they really that . . ."

"Obsessed?" he offered. *You have no idea.* "You know what they did after you left the cabin Sunday? They went to church."

She stared at him. "Seriously?"

"Yep. They dropped Trevor and me at the slopes and drove into town. After church they went back to the cabin, even though there was still plenty of ski time left in the day."

With both of them stopped, kids were whizzing past, but he no longer cared. He wanted to give her time to weigh the full implications of what he was saying. "But that's just one example, Sadie. Their religion is their whole life, a whole way of looking at the world. It drives every decision, every thought." *Too bad it doesn't drive their hormones.* "So even though I don't always understand it, they both love it. They've even tried to get me and Trevor to join."

"That doesn't seem very likely," she quipped.

He laughed. He liked Sadie. A girl like her could do Josh some good.

Looking downhill, he spotted Josh and Sam, watching him and Sadie like a pair of hawks. It was hard to tell which was more anxious for them to start skiing again. "Don't get me wrong," he said, "Josh is one of the best guys on the planet—Sam, too—but in a lot of ways their religion is a whole world unto itself, a mini-culture within the larger one, and their culture isn't always compatible with ours. Especially . . ." He paused, ". . . when it comes to dating. Sorry, Sadie," he finished softly.

For a long time, she played with the zipper on her coat. "I'm that obvious?"

He didn't answer, but was grateful they were finally on the same page.

"Oh, man!" she suddenly burst. "You must think I'm so stupid, Kevin—*he* must think I'm so stupid. Even after his little announcement today, I was still throwing myself at him . . ."

"Hey, slow down. Don't worry about it. Josh is completely clueless"— *and stupid!*—"believe me. It's just a vibe I picked up on."

Still, she refused to meet his eyes and instead stole a glance toward the bottom of the hill, finally spotting her two admirers. Flushing, she looked back at the snow. "The sad thing is that I still love Guillermo. Pretty pathetic, huh?"

"Nah." *Josh still loves Megan, so you're pretty much even on that one.*

"So I guess your little Mormon spiel was my hint? I'm obviously not someone Josh would . . . I mean, he already has a . . ." Once again she didn't finish. Her eyes wandered to the ski lift. "It's just that I thought maybe he might . . ."

Kevin cursed Josh again. And his stupid religion.

Squeezing her eyes shut, she took in a slow, deep breath. "Maybe it's time for me to see if Guillermo's done working."

"Sorry, Sadie. It's just . . . he is what he is, you know? Personally, I think he's crazy."

She smiled sadly. "Me, too."

Once they made it to the bottom of the hill, Sadie was resolved to avoid Josh at all costs, grateful for the first time that the guys were heading home in the morning. So she had completely forgotten about her previous conversation with him, until he skied up behind her and asked, "Do you see that guy anywhere?"

Even in her angered state, her heart fluttered to have him next to her, hoping somehow Kevin was wrong. There had been a connection there on the lift, just like there had been at the piano, but he never reached for her hand, never even so much as looked her direction as he searched the crowds. "No. Like I said, Josh, I was just being paranoid. Sorry to have worried you." Then she skied a short distance away and whipped out her phone.

Normally she didn't bother Guillermo when he was working, but she needed him. Now. With each ring, she begged him to pick up. When his voicemail came on she slammed the phone shut. "He's not back," she told Kevin.

Kevin nodded in understanding and put an arm around her shoulders. "Well, I'm ready for a real hill and so are you. We're heading over to Pine Hollow."

Less than a thousand feet away, Guillermo stared at his unanswered phone. There were times in his life when things were going well: business was good, personal life was fantastic, and all the stars aligned to perfection. That had been the state of his life two weeks ago. Not now. True, he had felt glimpses of it in the last few days, but now it was slipping through his fingers. Again. Yet he had to know where Augustina's allegiance was, once and for all. So he waited.

"Aren't you supposed to be working?" his younger brother asked.

Guillermo looked down at the papers in his hand. Shipping information. Inventory. Nothing that couldn't wait. He threw them across the mahogany desk and stared at his phone, trying to maintain his resolve. She needed more time. *He* needed more time. It was a dangerous game he was playing. One wrong move and the whole thing could blow up in his face.

"How many times does she have to prove herself?" Manuel asked, irritated. "It's obvious she wants nothing to do with them."

"Maybe it is not the FBI I am worried about."

Manuel grunted angrily. "You don't deserve her." With that, he stormed out of the room.

Guillermo ignored his brother—like he always did—and instead spoke to Salvador. "Something is amiss with Augustina. She has never needed friends before. Is it possi—"

"No, sir," Salvador cut in. "It's not possible. If she were having an affair with this Kevin Hancock, she would never have invited him to the party last night."

"I wonder what his little wife would think of this holiday escapade," he muttered.

"Sir . . ."

"I know. I know." Guillermo ran a hand through his jet-black hair, knowing that jumping to conclusions had ruined his life twice in the past week. This time he would wait. And wait. And then wait some more. But not patiently.

"So you think this Mr. Hancock is just a friend?" he spat, hating the sound of that word. "A friend who let her use his phone last week, a friend she invited to the party, and a friend she now spent the entire day with—and possibly last week with? Just a *friend*?"

"Yes. And need I remind you, she has spent almost as much time with the others."

"For her sake—and *his*—I hope you are right."

"I am. Just let her ski. Let the FBI track her. And by tonight you may have the answers to all your questions."

Guillermo's eyes narrowed on his assistant. "And what if I don't like those answers?"

"You will. She is yours. I am sure of it."

She is mine. He found little comfort in those words. If that were true, then life truly was good—*if* that were true. "I cannot shake this feeling that something is not right. And if I have learned anything in my thirty-five years, it is never to ignore intuition when it speaks to me."

"And what does it say to you now?" Salvador asked.

Guillermo looked out his large office window, the one that gave him a perfect view of his magnificent investment and the New Year's Day crowd. "It says that maybe it is time to speak to Special Agent Stephen Dubois."

Salvador's eyes widened, but Guillermo nodded, liking the idea more by the second. When it came to matters of love, he hesitated, hemmed and hawed, and often lost confidence. But business . . . well . . . business was easy. "When Señor Dubois is finished out there, invite him in. It is time we had another chat."

CHAPTER 30

There was no way Josh could avoid Sadie anymore. Kevin and Sam had done their share taking her on the easier hills, but it wasn't fair to make them miss out on their last day of skiing just because he was losing his mind. The sun was lowering in the western sky, and in another hour he could say he was tired and bug out, but for now, he asked, "Which run?"

Sadie surveyed their surroundings, looking just as unhappy to be abandoned by the others as he was. "Actually, Josh, my feet are killing me. You go ahead and ski with the others. I'm going to sit this one out."

It was tempting to take her up on her offer—very tempting—but he wasn't comfortable leaving her alone. Not with the chance of the guy in the leather coat surfacing again. "That's okay. I'm ready for a break, too."

With a sigh, she pushed her way over to an empty bench. Then she proceeded to take off her scarf, gloves, and skis, giving the distinct impression she was done for the day. Josh sat as well and followed suit. He was ready to be done as well. Done with skiing. Done with the trip. And done with Montana.

She leaned back against the bench, letting her dark hair fall behind, and closed her eyes against the bright sunshine. Her arms were folded and both feet were planted firmly on the ground. Not the friendliest of postures. He thought about striking up a conversation, but all things considered, silence was probably best.

Out of habit, he searched the crowd again, but he didn't see anyone resembling Sadie's description of the man. In the process, he found Trevor by the lodge talking excitedly to a new girl. The way his friend stood hunched over her was so Trevor, like he was interested in her and only her. Then again, Trevor could flirt with anything female; it didn't matter who, what, when, or where. Sadie was like that in a way, flirting with everything male, though he imagined her flirting to be more unintentional. There was no way she realized her power of men—over him.

"I did it again," she said softly.

Josh glanced sideways, surprised to hear from her. "Did what?"

"Ruined your good mood." She kept her eyes closed as she spoke. "Every time I see you, you're in a great mood. At the cabin. At the bonfire. At the piano, at lunch. You were in a great mood today, but I ruined it. Just like I always do. Some friend I am."

He shook his head. Now his behavior wasn't just affecting him. "It's not your fault."

"Yeah? Well, it feels like it's my fault."

"It's not. Trust me."

She was quiet for only a second before dropping the next bombshell. "What does Megan look like?"

He groaned inwardly. Sadie was literally the last person on earth he wanted to discuss his girlfriend with. "I don't know," he finally said.

She cracked an eye open. "You don't know? You've dated her for how long and you don't know what she looks like?"

Suddenly, having Megan in his thoughts seemed like a good idea, so he conjured up her image as best he could. "She's about five-seven. Blonde hair. Fair skin. "

"Figures. Why do men always go for the tall blondes?"

He laughed. He couldn't help it, but the irony of the statement was too much. Treating her question as rhetorical, he continued. "She has blue eyes . . ."

"Like you?"

"Yeah."

"And you dated in high school, right?" she asked, still behind closed eyes.

"Yeah."

"Is she pretty?"

His leg began bouncing nervously. "Very."

"And she's a Mormon like you are, right?"

"Yes." *Oh, please, make it stop.*

"Do you know how to give more than a one-word answer?"

He looked at her and smiled. It was nice to see her humor return, even if only momentarily. "Yes," he responded.

She peeked out of one eye and slapped his coat. "Come on. Tell me about her. I'm curious. Is she musical? How long have you dated? Share."

This time when he answered, it was harder to look away from the olive skin, nearly translucent in the late afternoon sun. He skipped the music question, thinking it unfair to tone-deaf Megan, and instead answered her second. "We met our junior year of high school and then she waited for me on my mission."

"Waited for you? What does that mean?"

"Missionaries in our church aren't allowed to date or socialize during the two years we're gone. We can't call anyone, not even our families except on Mother's Day and Christmas."

"Really?" She sat up a little, finally looking at him. "I could never go a week, let alone a year, without talking to my mom. We talk almost every day."

"It was hard," he admitted, "but I was so busy I didn't mind."

"Did Megan mind?"

Another interesting question. He had written Megan early on, asking her to date others while he was gone. She never did. And again after his mission he tried to give her—and himself—some much needed space. But she didn't want space, she wanted a ring, so she waited . . . again. "I don't know," he finally answered. "Her older brothers served missions, so I think she knew what to expect. We wrote letters the whole two years, though."

"Two years," Sadie repeated. "That's so long. How did you do it?"

He leaned forward, placing his elbows on his knees to force his eyes downward. "I love my church. A lot. It's brought me a lot of peace and happiness over the years. It's brought me closer to God. He's helped me through some really hard times, times when I thought there was no way out, when there was no solution—"

Like right now? his thoughts unexpectedly interrupted. He stopped. That's exactly where he was, falling for a girl he could never be with, while breaking the heart of another who didn't deserve it. Sadie was still watching him, sensing he hadn't finished, so he continued. "I guess I wanted to share that peace and happiness with other people."

Peace and happiness? Once again his words seemed to be just that. Words. Never in his life had he been further away from peace and happiness. *So what am I missing here?*

It only took a second to figure it out. He was trying to solve the Sadie issue on his own, too embarrassed to take it to a higher power. And without help, he was failing miserably.

"Wow, Josh," Sadie said, pulling his thoughts back to her. "Kevin was right about you."

"About what?"

She went on to stare at him in a way that tore at his heart. Her large eyes, so intently focused on him seemed to look through him right to the core. There was something there, a connection he'd never had with Megan. *Why can't I just be with her?* he begged silently.

"Nothing," she finally managed.

She laid her head against the bench and closed her eyes again, and after a minute her breathing slowed to a restful state. She was asleep. Josh had spent an unusual amount of time watching Sadie sleep, the last time had been on his shoulder. *La Bella Durmiente.* At the time it seemed innocent enough to let her head rest against him. He'd even leaned closer to prop up her neck. But things had changed since that ride from Deer Basin—*he* had changed—and it wouldn't be so innocent if he let it happen again. Quietly, he slid himself a safe distance away and dragged his thoughts to their surroundings. Still crowded. Still no leather-coat guy. So he copied her stance: feet planted, head resting on the warm bench, eyes closed.

His mind was a jumble of thoughts as he laid there, ranging from religious commitments to Megan back home, from bits and pieces of his childhood to conversations he'd had with Sadie about Guillermo. Each subject spurred him to the next, yet in completely random order. He didn't stop to organize or analyze; he just let them tumble around.

After it slowed some, he took control again, dragging his choice of memories forward. Sadie kissing Guillermo, sipping champagne. His mom. Megan. All brought to the forefront to battle against the unwanted attraction. But like all good battles, tides turned, and his mind fought back, taking him up the hill to his conversation with Kevin. The last thing Kevin said bothered Josh. Bothered him and intrigued him. *Sadie following my every move? Eyes only for me?*

Kevin was wrong, he decided. Girls like Sadie flirted with everyone, they batted their big, brown eyes at everyone, leaving men in their wake. The whole time they were completely unaware. Unaware of Sam. Unaware of Trevor. *Unaware of me.*

Suddenly tired of it all, he scanned the mobs again, trying to spot Kevin or Sam to watch her. *Heck, I'd even take Trevor at this point.*

It was then that Josh noticed a guy sitting on a bench across from them. It wasn't the leather-coat guy. In fact, it wasn't anyone of consequence at all. Just a thirty-something skier in gray. But the problem was that Josh had already seen that guy a couple of times that day. Each time, he'd been watching their small group like he was now. Overly aware of them. *Not us,* Josh corrected with a sinking thought. *Overly aware of her!*

He bolted upright as Sadie's words came barreling back. Someone was following her—check that: two people were following her. He had no doubt of that now. The skier noticed Josh looking at him and calmly turned away. But it was beyond coincidence now. Josh just needed to prove it.

With pulse pounding, he turned his attention to the lodge and started counting the number of people coming and going in. Each number upped his anxiety, but he worked to keep his face impassive. When he reached one hundred, he whirled back to the skier in gray. The man was as he had first seen him. Staring right at him.

Not staring at me, Josh corrected. *Staring at Sadie!*

Chapter 31

A group of skiers moved in front of Josh, blocking his view of the skier. By the time they cleared out, the guy was gone. Josh shot to his feet. His eyes flew through the hundreds of people, but the guy had disappeared in seconds. He was gone.

"Oh no," Sadie mumbled next to him. "I dozed off."

Josh didn't even glance at her, not caring that his sudden movement had woken her. He was frantically trying to decide if he should chase the guy down. But that would leave Sadie alone. Not something he was willing to do. His search doubled, then tripled.

I need Kevin. Now!

"Sorry," she yawned. "I didn't fall asleep until four this morning. How long was I out?"

"Just a few minutes," he answered, blood boiling. *Who is he—who are they? What do they want with her?* The last question was a hundred times more disturbing than the others.

"I think I slept longer than just a few minutes," she said with a little stretch. "Oh, man, I'm gonna be so sore tomorrow. I don't think I've ever used some of these muscles before."

Josh stepped away from the bench, trying to see around a group of teenagers. When that didn't produce the skier in gray, he took three more steps, searching past the nearest line of skiers.

"You could have gone skiing, Josh. You didn't have to stay behind and watch me sleep."

"I'm glad I did," he muttered, furious he'd ever considered leaving her alone before.

Sadie stood next to him. "Hey, are you okay? You seem a little tense."

"I'm fine. Hey, do you remember seeing a skier in gray earlier? Younger guy, in his thirties. He was on the last run with us."

"I don't know. Why?"

I can't believe it! he yelled at himself. *Why did I scare him away? Now he's nowhere!*

"Josh?"

He ignored the warning tone in her voice. "How about the guy from before?" he asked instead. "The older guy in brown?"

"No."

He broke off his search to look at Sadie. She'd barely even skimmed the crowd. There was no way she could know that fast. "Are you sure? Please, Sadie. This is important."

"Yes. I'm sure."

"Let's walk around then. I need to know if you recognize this new guy."

She stepped in front of him, pulling his eyes downward. But only for a second. She was short—very short—and he just continued searching over the top of her head.

Frustrated, she went on tiptoes. "Look, Josh, I'm really, really, *really* sorry I said anything about that guy before. Would you stop freaking out, please? I was just freaked out earlier because of a stupid dream. It was nothing. Seriously."

"A dream? What dream?"

She diverted her eyes, suddenly avoiding him. He waited patiently for her to answer, but instead of answering, her dark eyes began to pool. Tears were the absolute last thing Josh expected. "Sadie?" he said, even more concerned.

"That's my lake down there," she smiled sadly. "My heaven on earth."

Confused, Josh followed her gaze past the lodge, out of the mountains, to the sprawling, white valley below. Nestled in the hills was a large, frozen lake. "Whitefish?"

Her head snapped up. "You know it?"

"Yeah. I've been with Sam's family a couple of times in the summer, but that's beside the point. Why did your dream freak you out this morning?"

Her jaw tightened, and she stepped away from him. "I dreamed a friend of mine got shot—which was horrible and . . ." She shuddered. "But it was just a dream. It didn't mean anything."

"Then why did it convince you someone was following you?"

"Because . . ." Her voice dropped in volume. "The shooter was coming for me next."

His muscles tensed. "And the shooter was the guy you saw before?"

"No . . ."

"Who was it?" he asked gently. "Who was coming after you?"

Her gaze finally lifted to his. "Guillermo," she stated in a flat, emotionless tone, but the same flicker of fear was back, the same haunting terror flashed in her large eyes.

His stomach dropped. All sorts of ideas ran wild in his head, none of them rational. He quickly scanned the skin on her face and neck. Her eye looked better now, and as far as he could tell there weren't any new bruises, but who knew what she was hiding from him or what that jerk of a boyfriend had threatened her with now.

He closed his eyes, bracing himself. "What did he do to you, Sadie?"

"Nothing!" she snapped.

He was only slightly relieved. "Then why would you dream something like that?"

"You're going to think it's stupid, but . . ." With a quick breath, she went on in a rush. "I saw a gun in his office yesterday. It's no big deal. It was in one of his desk drawers. I don't even think he knows I saw it."

"A gun?" Josh wanted to shake some common sense into her naïve brain. Not wanting to fight, but knowing full well they were headed that way, he prepared his speech well. This time she *would* listen. This was her life she wasn't taking seriously and he couldn't let her brush it aside anymore. "What kind of gun was it?" he asked. "A handgun? A semi-automatic? Or something larger?" Not that it really mattered. Her boyfriend was a creep and was now verifiably dangerous.

"Like I would even know, Josh. A small one, okay? People can own guns. It's perfectly legal. It just surprised me. That's all."

"But why would he need a handgun in an office where he does real estate business, Sadie? It's just another thing that doesn't add up."

"I said it's no big deal, and it isn't."

He just stared at her. "So you dream your boyfriend is coming after you. With a gun. He's going to *kill* you, and this is after he already shot and killed one of your friends. This is the same guy who beat you to unconsciousness, the same guy who has the FBI on his tail, the same guy who was ready to tear my arms off at the party, and the same guy who keeps a gun in his business office . . . well, just in case. And you think it's *no big deal*?"

Sadie's expression hardened. Her only response.

"Well, at least some part of your brain disagrees with you," he said bitterly.

"And what's that supposed to mean?" she challenged.

"It means that maybe your dream is trying to tell you something, Sadie, and maybe it's time you finally listened."

She flinched as if he'd slapped her. Instantly her eyes were glistening in the late sun. But only for a second. Then they turned rock hard. "Dreams. Mean. Nothing. Good-bye, Josh."

And with that, she whirled around and started down the hill.

CHAPTER 32

Sadie hurried down the hill away from the crowds, the view, and most importantly Josh. The snow wasn't packed down on the lower trail, making it hard to traverse in heavy boots, but she didn't care. She had to get away. She ducked around trees, boulders, anything to lose him. He was calling her name, but she picked up her speed, rounding a group of pines.

"Sadie," he tried again. "I'm sorry. I can't help myself. I'm an over-reactive, overprotective, overbearing—"

"Okay. I get it," she snapped over her shoulder, but at the same time, her pace increased.

He ran at full speed and stopped abruptly in front of her, forcing her to stop as well. She was ready to lash out at him, to take out every one of her frustrations on him, but the sight of him took the wind out of her sails. His face, his expression, everything about him was in agony. And when his blue eyes finally met hers, they were pleading for mercy.

"I'm done, Sadie," he said softly.

"What do you mean *you're done?*"

"I'm done worrying about you, I'm done bugging you, and I'm done fighting with you—with myself—I'm just done. You can take care of yourself. You are smart, and strong, and you . . . are . . . fine." He said each word, as if he was trying to convince himself at the same time he was convincing her. But his words weren't comforting and instead sliced to the core as she realized what he was really saying.

Good-bye.

The one he had denied her at the party was finally here and while she had been begging for it seconds ago, now that it was official, she was devastated.

"Like you said that first day," he continued, "it was never any of my business, and I've just been bugging you by butting in ever since. But I want to let you know that I'm done now. I'm not going to bother you again. So you do what you need to, and I'll—"

No! Her hands flew to his mouth, covering the words she couldn't bear to hear. It wasn't supposed to end like this. Not with Josh. Her throat was burning, her eyes were turning to liquid, and she was seconds away from losing it completely.

His eyes widened at her bold move, but she held tight like an insolent child. There had to be some way to stop him. He told her to listen to her dream, and she was ready. Josh belonged with her—she knew that now. It wasn't supposed to end like this. Not with Josh.

Yet . . . looking into those tortured eyes, she knew she was being selfish. "I'm sorry," she whispered, letting her hands drop away. "I just—"

He grabbed her hands before they could fall, closed his eyes, and with a slow, deep breath, pressed the tips of her fingers against his lips.

The move startled her. She couldn't move. Couldn't breathe. It was so contrary to what she was expecting—so opposite of what she deserved—her mind was racing to find a logical explanation. She only found one.

He loves me.

Just like she thought, just like she knew, Josh loved her.

"Josh?" she whispered.

He flinched at the sound of her voice, finally releasing her. Her fingers lingered a moment longer, savoring the feel of his warm lips against her cold skin—a first kiss—before lifting away. Her hands didn't go far, though, and settled on his chest. His eyes flew open, but she knew if she thought twice about it she'd never get up the nerve again.

Carefully, her hands slid up his chest to the back of his neck, letting her fingers run through the dark waves of his hair. Then slowly, she pulled his face down to hers.

Please, she begged silently, *don't run away. Not this time.*

His hands cradled her face, his eyes searched hers, almost asking for permission. Her heart was pounding, her stomach doing nervous flips, but she simply closed her eyes and waited.

She didn't have to wait long.

He closed the distance and his lips met hers. His kiss was soft and filled with incredible sadness. Yet it was perfect, gentle, and very, very Josh.

When he pulled back, he didn't go far. His forehead simply fell against hers. "I'm in love with you, Sadie," he whispered. "I'm sorry, but it's true. I've totally and completely fallen for you."

CHAPTER 33

Josh didn't dare open his eyes, wishing he could stop time. Everything was perfect in that moment: the small breeze, the few trees hiding them from the world, and Sadie. His forehead was still leaning against hers, her soft lips inches from his, calling him back. Her fingers ran lightly through the hair at the base of his neck, and his thumbs stroked her face, willing the moment to last forever.

"Josh?"

He didn't respond, afraid reality would break through the emotions holding him captive.

"Josh?" Her voice was strained. "Please look at me."

He opened his eyes to find her own swimming in the filtered sunlight. As she blinked, a few tears escaped down her soft cheeks. "Why are you sorry that you love me?"

Knowing that he was the cause of those tears was more than he could bear. "I can't fight it anymore, Sadie. I'm yours."

He grabbed her and kissed her again, this time holding nothing back. Not thinking, just feeling. Letting go of all the guilt and pain and allowing himself to love her for the first time. The whole time all he could think was that she was there with him—choosing *him.*

A smile broke through, interrupting the kiss. He couldn't help it.

She tilted her head back and looked up at him, breaking into a smile that lit her entire face. "I love you, Josh."

The reality of those words hit him. He pulled her into his chest and rested his chin on her head. She pulled her arms in, allowing him to completely envelope her like he had once before. It was like coming home. She belonged there in his arms.

For a long time, they stayed that way as he began putting her into his vision of the future, all his plans changed to include her. Work. School. Washington or Montana. It didn't matter. He needed her with him forever.

Forever . . .

The word jolted him momentarily. He quickly pushed it aside to focus on the present. Maybe she could move to Washington while he finished school, or they could date long distance. In time he would propose, and if he was the luckiest man alive, she would say yes, and then . . .

For time only.

Three small words, powerful enough to carve a hole in his chest. There were reasons he had resisted Sadie, reasons based on his view of forever. Not just this life, but the next. Things he spent his life dreaming about—holding hands in prayer, marriage in the temple, going on a mission with his wife—were all things she wouldn't understand or want. He couldn't change who he was anymore than she could. Not even for love.

No!

His grip loosened, though he couldn't give her up yet. There had to be a way to make it work. Yet he'd lived a life that proved otherwise. He refused to make the mistakes of others, refused to let his future children spend a single second wondering why their own mother hated them.

Sadie leaned back, her eyes searching his. "Why won't you tell me? Why are you sorry that you love me?"

He had to look away as he struggled to explain something so deeply rooted in who he was. But the emotions tearing him apart were also clouding rational thought. "Because I can't be who you need me to be, and—" He looked up, realizing what he'd almost said.

Not that it mattered. She finished it for him. "And I can't be who you need me to be."

When he couldn't deny it, she nodded slowly.

She stepped away from him and faced the trees. "Is this seriously about religion, Josh? Is that why you keep pushing me away?"

He just looked at her. She knew more than she'd let on. He tried to form an answer in his head, but nothing sounded right. "Yes," he said simply.

She turned. "You love Kevin and Trevor, don't you? Why them, but not me?"

"Because it's different. My religion goes way beyond something I do. It's in every part of me, everything I do, and if I can't share that with you, then you won't really know who I am. Does that make sense?" he asked weakly, even as she stared at him in disbelief. She didn't understand, which only proved his point. She never would.

"I'll change then, Josh. I don't care which church I go to. Your religion seems nice enough, so what if I just go to church with you? I've been thinking I need to find God again anyway. If that's what it takes to be with you, I'll do it." She stepped forward and wrapped her arms around him. "Just let me be with you," she said into his chest. "You're what I want."

Josh stayed perfectly still. Could it be that easy? Was that the answer he'd been desperately searching for? Let Sadie put herself into his world and leave hers behind? It would solve all his problems, giving him more joy than he could imagine. Sadie. Forever. But . . .

No matter how much he wanted it, it wasn't realistic. His religion wasn't one someone could—or should—jump into because of love. He knew only too painfully it wouldn't last. And in the end, she would hate him for it. *Better now than later.*

"Tell me that you love me, Josh." She clasped him tighter. "That you choose me, too."

He took her arms from around him and put them back down at her sides. "I can't, Sadie. I am so . . . *so* sorry."

CHAPTER 34

"Estas bien, hermosa?"

"No," Sadie answered honestly, she wasn't okay. Not by any stretch of the imagination.

Guillermo studied her across the dinner table, looking truly concerned.

Her eyes went to the grand piano without thinking. Tears pricked her eyes. She pushed her dinner around before setting her fork down. "I think I'm still tired from the party last night. Would you mind if I went back to my room and slept?"

He smiled warmly. "No, of course not. Sleep well. I will see you in the morning. Maybe we can do something wonderful tomorrow. Go shopping, yes?"

She nodded and stood to leave. Guillermo stood as well and leaned toward her. She recoiled back instinctively. His goodnight kiss landed on her ear. Her eyes flew to his, horrified. "Sorry, I . . ." She grabbed her purse and darted past the piano and out the glass doors.

She stumbled into her room and was met by a dresser full of white roses. So much had happened since that morning, and yet she was back where she started. Nothing changed.

The tears started, the ones she'd held back all evening with Guillermo. She lay on her bed, curled up into a ball, and quietly cried herself to sleep.

Kevin glanced over the seat of the extended cab at Josh, who was staring blankly out the side window. Josh hadn't said more than ten words in the last twenty hours. Sam questioned him earlier and bought his weak excuse about being stressed for grad school. Kevin wasn't dense. Something had happened with Sadie. So Josh sat avoiding Kevin on the four-hour drive home like he had avoided him the past sixteen hours at the cabin.

When they stopped for gas in Idaho, Trevor hopped out for snacks while Sam filled up the truck. Seeing his chance, Kevin turned. "All right. Time's up. What happened?"

Josh didn't move. "With what?"

Kevin glared at him. "How about you tell me what happened before I climb back there and pound it out of you. I care about Sadie, too."

Josh jerked around sharply. "Who said anything about her?"

"How stupid do you think I am? I leave you guys alone for five minutes and next thing I know she's gone and you're Mr. Silent. So quit the act and tell me what happened."

Josh glanced over his shoulder at Sam.

"He can handle it," Kevin said. "He may like Sadie, but he likes you more."

"He shouldn't," Josh said under his breath. "I hate myself. In one short week, I've ruined everyone's life."

"Including your own?"

Josh didn't answer. Instead he turned back to stare out the window.

Sam finished paying at the pump and opened the driver's door. Kevin whipped out his wallet and threw a five at him. "Hey, Sam, get me something to eat, would ya?"

Sam stopped mid-sit. "Umm . . . okay. What do you want?"

"I don't care. Something salty."

Sam glanced back and forth at the two friends, smart enough to know he was missing something, but not quite sure what. He took the money and headed into the station.

"I rejected her, Kev," Josh said the second he disappeared. "I kissed her . . . and then I rejected her."

Kevin's jaw gaped open. "You kissed Sadie?"

Josh glared at him. "You're not listening. I rejected her!"

Finally understanding, Kevin exploded. "What did you do? What were you thinking!"

Josh banged his head against the side window. "I don't know. I hate myself."

"Then why'd you do it? Why'd you kiss her?"

"Well, technically she started it, but I wanted her to. And once we started I couldn't think of anything else."

"You mean anyone else?" Kevin clarified, anger rising like bile in his throat.

"Yes." Josh hit his head against the window again. "Oh, man, I hate myself."

"Why? It's not like you and Megan are married."

"As if that makes it any better! I just announced to everyone at lunch—including Sadie, need I remind you—that I was going to propose. Yet somehow, I end up kissing another girl four hours later. What kind of a guy does that?"

Kevin didn't answer. It was Josh's own fault for not listening to him. He punched the dashboard, letting out a long stream of profanities in the process. Josh was right. He had ruined everything! "How could you do this to her? You said you were gonna stay away from her! I told her to stay away from *you*!" Kevin swore again. "What were you thinking?"

Josh lay against the seat. "I don't know. I just started picturing our life together and—"

"Oh, man," Kevin groaned. "Why do you always do that? Why couldn't you just enjoy the moment for what it was?"

"I think I did. That's the problem."

"I don't see that as a problem. I see you as being one of the luckiest men alive. Think about it. You beat out Mr. Venezuelan-million-dollar-Armani-suit man."

Josh's head fell against the frosted window again.

Just then, Kevin spotted Sam coming out of the station, bag of Doritos in hand. Kevin swore again and rolled down the window. Normally he curbed his language around his two buddies, but ticking off a couple of Mormons right now felt too good. "I hate that kind, Sam. Get me something else."

Sam stopped dead in his tracks and held up the bag. "I thought these were your favorite."

Leave it to Sam to know something like that. But Kevin wasn't finished with Josh yet. Not even close. "Just get me a Coke."

Sam didn't look nearly as happy to serve the second time, but with him taken care of, Kevin turned back to Josh. "What happened to you being paranoid about her safety and all that? Someone watching her? What was all that about?"

A sudden shadow crossed Josh's face. "I tried to tell her she wasn't safe, to convince her to call someone—the FBI, the cops—but at that point, she wouldn't listen to a word I said. She ran into the lodge before I could finish."

"Do you think it was someone working for Guillermo?" Kevin asked, softening.

"I don't know. *I don't know!* But she'll figure it out. I just have to stay away from her."

Josh turned back to his window, and the two were silent for a time while Kevin mulled over the damage. He'd seen Sadie's face on the hill; he could only imagine how she was feeling now. Josh rejected her because of his church?

"Let me ask you something, Josh. Why is it okay for you to be friends with me and Trevor, but not for you to date Sadie? Why such a difference?"

Josh closed his eyes. "That's the same thing she asked me. But I don't want to marry you or Trevor. And I'm at a point in my life where I don't want to date just for the sake of dating. I want to find someone to be with me forever."

"Right . . ." Kevin continued carefully, "so why can't Sadie be that? I mean, I know you're into your church and all, but why be so exclusive? I'm sure she'd get used to it. We did."

"I don't want someone to just *get used to it,* and I don't want someone who just tolerates it, like you guys. I want . . ." Josh shook his head. "Never mind. You just don't get it."

"Well, that's something we both agree on," Kevin shot back. "Maybe you should be talking to Sam instead."

"I can't do that. Sam should be punching me, not helping me."

"Yes . . . but Sadie chose *you.* Sam's just going to have to deal with that. Besides, you need his advice right now."

"Why? It's over and done. The decision's been made. Final."

Kevin always knew Josh was stubborn, but never to the point of absurdity. Frustrated, he leaned back and tried to imagine something big—equivalent of Josh's religion—that he didn't share with Amy. Josh had been his best friend for almost two decades, and yet in all honesty, Kevin knew very little about his religion. He knew the basics: Joseph Smith, the Book of Mormon—those had been hounded into him long enough—but beyond that was a blur. *But would that work in a marriage?* he wondered. People did it all the time. Maybe not easily, but thousands of people made it work. *But at what cost? Especially with a guy like Josh?* He shook his head without an answer.

"I wish I could have stopped time," Josh said softly. "Kissing her was . . . I don't know . . . like nothing else."

"I don't know how you walked away from her. It's probably a first for Sadie."

"Thanks. As if I don't hate myself enough already."

"That's okay. I kind of hate you too right now."

Josh lifted his head and looked at Kevin, looking like he'd been through the war and then some. "How do I go back to Megan now? How do I even begin to repair something like this?"

"That's easy. Don't."

"You can say that even though Megan and Amy are friends?"

"That's exactly why I can say it. Tell me, why have you never proposed to Megan?"

"It just never seemed . . ." Josh paused, realizing the trap he'd walked into, ". . . right."

"Exactly. It wasn't. I know you love Megan, but it never really got down into your gut. Megan deserves someone who not only loves her, but is *in* love with her, and despite what you think, you're not." He waited for Josh to argue, but for the first time it looked like something was finally sinking in, so he went on. "You need someone you love from your gut to your soul, so turn the truck around and go get the girl. The right girl."

Sam and Trevor walked out of the gas station together, both with an armful of junk food. "I can't," Josh whispered.

Kevin couldn't believe it. Nothing had sunk in after all. "Then talk to Sam. He's the only one that has a chance of understanding what the heck you just did back there."

"It doesn't matter anyway." Josh's head fell against the window. "It's over."

No! No! NO! Josh moaned as Sam pulled onto his parent's street. Megan's car. It was bad enough she was at his house, but her car was the only one in the driveway. His family was gone.

He climbed out of the truck, his feet like lead. Kevin hopped out as well to help him with his gear. "You want to come inside, Kev?" Josh asked.

"Nope."

"Just a few minutes? Please?" He wasn't ready.

Just then, Megan peeked out the front window. Kevin waved at her with mock enthusiasm before turning to Josh and patting him on the back. "Good luck."

Josh's gear seemed twenty pounds heavier than when he left, and each of the front steps took longer than the previous to climb. Megan pulled open the door before he made it to the top and threw her arms around him. Josh was spared returning the hug since his arms were loaded. Using the excuse that he needed to drop off his stuff, he left her and ran downstairs to his old room.

Normally he would have waited to unpack, but he needed a few minutes to gather his thoughts. First gloves, then socks, scriptures, and navy sports coat were put exactly where they belonged. It was tempting to dust his room and clean the cobwebs from under his bed, but with a final pep talk to himself, he made the long journey up to where Megan was waiting.

She crossed the room and threw her arms around him again. "How was it this year?"

His first thought was that she was taller than he remembered. A strange thought, considering how long they'd dated. Then he realized why. Megan wasn't taller. Sadie was just shorter. The shame washed over him. He hadn't even lasted five seconds before his thoughts had wandered back to Sadie. His arms fell away from her, feeling like he'd betrayed both.

It went unnoticed. Megan walked over and sat on the couch. "So, did Trevor get his way and get you back on a snowboard?"

Josh sat as well, though as far from her as possible. She quickly slid over next to him. He stared straight ahead at the upright piano. That didn't help. "Yeah," he said.

"Was there enough snow to snowshoe this year?"

Each question brought with it more memories. And pain. "Yeah."

Megan turned his face toward her. "Are you okay? You seem quiet."

I hate myself, he thought for the millionth time, as if that justified everything. Finally with a slow, deep breath, he started. "Megan . . ." That's as far as he got.

She knew him too well not to notice. "What's wrong?"

"I . . ." Again he struggled.

"You're scaring me, Josh. What happened?"

"I met someone." It was so cliché, such a terrible way to start, but his mind was too garbled to come up with anything else.

She straightened. "What do you mean you met someone?"

"There was this girl . . ."

She started to stand, but Josh grabbed her hand. "Please, I need to do this. I met someone, but . . ." His eyes closed, bracing himself for the pain that was sure to accompany the words. "It's over now."

"Then why are you telling me?" she whispered.

"Because you deserve to know. She was in a bad situation and needed help so she stayed at the cabin a few days. I didn't realize I was having feelings for her until—"

"Please. I really don't want to hear this."

"I kissed her," he blurted, deciding to skip the details.

She blinked slowly, taking the hit internally. He wished she would take it out on him. Yell. Scream. Anything. But that just wasn't Megan.

She cleared her throat. "I appreciate your honesty. I think I'd better go."

He didn't stop her as she stood again. When she reached for the front door, he called her name, "Megan?"

"Yes?" she asked, without turning.

"I'm sorry."

She nodded softly, opened the door, and walked out of his life.

Chapter 35

Sadie bolted upright. The gunshot had been so vivid, so piercing, it still rang in her ears. Disoriented, confused, and still half-asleep, she waited for another. The only sound in Guillermo's cabin was her heavy breathing in rhythm with the pounding of her heart.

Just another nightmare, she soothed, laying a hand on her chest.

Although she couldn't remember the particulars, she could guess. People were getting shot all the time in her dreams now. It was horrible. Mostly it was her or Josh, but a few terrifying times it had been her mom. And the shooter was always Guillermo. It was awful. It couldn't be healthy, running for your life every night—even if it was just in your dreams. No wonder she'd been so exhausted lately. She'd been so tired she conked out at the beginning of the movie.

She looked around the room, wondering where Guillermo was. The screen was still on—blue, but silent—as were the lights, and there was a blanket over her shoulders. But no Guillermo.

She glanced up at the clock on the wall. 12:28. Either he'd gone to bed or back to work, trying to catch up on all the hours he'd wasted pampering her. In the last two days, they'd gone shopping, soaked in the hot tub, eaten amazing food, and watched movies in his personal theater. They'd even sampled a few wines, trying to pick the one that would be his newest investment. She didn't know when he slept, if at all. Although with the nightmares, she was ready to—

Another shot fired off, just outside.

Sadie jumped, adrenaline rushing through her tired veins. *That one I heard.* Her mind raced. Two shots—not a dream—just below her second-story window. Someone was in trouble.

Guillermo? she gasped. Or worse . . . was he the shooter?

Her stomach lurched, but she forced herself to move. Quickly and silently, she inched off the couch and up to the window. Holding her breath, she peeked around the curtains. The area surrounding Guillermo's cabin was well lit by moonlight reflecting off the heavy snow, and she quickly spotted three men standing below her, all with their backs to her. One was definitely Guillermo, another to the left of him was huge—enormous—and the third had a build similar to Guillermo's. She didn't recognize the other two, nor did she try because she suddenly realized the three men were huddled around something in the snow.

A body?

She recoiled back. *A bear? A moose?* she willed, frantically trying to come up with a less devastating possibility. Closing her eyes, she summoned the courage to check. But as she peered around the curtain again, there was no way to see beyond the three men.

The heavy man turned to say something to Guillermo, placing his face in perfect profile. With a start, she realized that if he turned another inch, he would see her in the upstairs, fully lit room, spying. She fell back into the confines of the wall, ears pricked, breathing stopped, as she waited for the slightest hint of what was happening. There should have been shouting, or at the very least talking, but there was absolutely no sound. Nothing!

Another deafening shot rang out. She plunged to the floor, hands over her head, choking back a scream. Whatever was happening was not good. And Guillermo was in the middle of it! She had no idea what was going on, but for now, she could think only of escape. Both Guillermo's mother and brother lived in the cabin with him. And Salvador, she suddenly remembered, plus others on Guillermo's payroll who would see her sneak out.

What if Guillermo comes to check on me? she suddenly thought. Their last violent encounter was enough to have her scrambling along the floor back to the couch. She lay exactly as she had been. The couch faced away from the door, leaving her feeling exposed, but she lay perfectly motionless—except her hands, which shook uncontrollably. Balling them into fists, she jammed them into her stomach while she listened for the tiniest sound.

Why is it so quiet? she wanted to scream. The silence was almost worse than the shots. There had to be a logical explanation. Target practice. Or maybe they were hunting. Outside. In the bitter cold. At midnight. Yet all she could envision was a person lying in the snow with a hole in their stomach.

"Josh!" she cried out. She threw a hand over her mouth, and the tears started. But for the first time since New Year's, she was grateful he had left and was now safely four hours away.

As she lay there tensed and waiting, it suddenly dawned on her that she was a coward. If someone had truly been shot, she should be trying to help them, save them, or at the very least calling the police. Not lying there trying to save herself. She lifted her head to search for her phone. It was clear across the room, past the same revealing win—

The next shot caused every muscle in her body to spasm. A hundred more thoughts ran through her head, most of which involved running. But it was too late now. She was trapped, paralyzed by fear—just like in her dreams—which meant any minute, Guillermo would show up, gun hovered over her, and end it for real.

She waited. Two minutes. Three. Then five. But the next shot never came. Instead, the next sound she heard was just as terrifying. Footsteps. Outside the guest room door.

It's just Guillermo, she told herself. Instead of calming her nerves, it only sped up her pounding heart. Too many nightmares filled with too many footsteps. Too many memories of being locked in a dark room. Reality was mixing with nonreality, and she was terrified of both.

The door creaked open, and the footsteps made their way over to the couch.

"Hermosa?"

Guillermo's voice was calm. Not loud, not harsh, not angry—just . . . calm. Yet she didn't trust it. He sat on the couch next to her and shook her gently. "Hermosa?" he tried more loudly. "Are you awake?"

She stretched exaggeratedly as if she had been asleep a long time, and then, turning, found his face. It looked as calm as his voice had been.

He stroked her cheek lovingly. "You missed the movie."

Everything in the moment spoke tranquility: his voice, his eyes, the way he smiled down at her. She prayed he couldn't see the naked panic in her face.

Focusing on his sentence, she feigned surprise. "I did? Sorry. I'm just so tired." She rolled back onto her side and pulled the covers up to hide her face. As unnerving as it was to have her back to him, there was no other choice. She was trembling again.

For a long time they stayed that way, Guillermo sitting on the edge of the couch, her pretending to fall back asleep. She forced each breath to get slower and more pronounced, even though her lungs begged for more air. Finally he moved off the couch, but he still didn't leave.

What is he doing? she cried silently. Checking his gun? Taking aim?

After what felt like an eternity, she heard him scribbling something on a paper. Then once again the cabin fell silent. *Just breathe,* she told herself. *In. Out. Slowly.* Her skin was crawling, every instinct telling her to run, but she stayed a sleeping statue.

Then he moved. She could feel his weight again on the couch, then his breath next to her ear. "*Te quiero, Augustina,*" he whispered. "*Sólo el tiempo dirá.*" With that, he flipped off the lights and left the room.

I love you, Augustina? Only time will tell? The only thing that registered in his cryptic message was that he hadn't used any of his dozen pet names for her. First time.

Minutes later, she heard his Range Rover drive away.

CHAPTER 36

Sadie watched the hands on the clock click slowly by. Any hope of sleep was gone. Half a dozen times she thought of ways to escape—out the window like she had before, or just darting out the front door like a normal person—but she wasn't sure what she was escaping from. Plus, as far as she knew she wasn't even a prisoner, so *escaping* seemed a little dramatic. She wasn't hurt. She wasn't even threatened. Just . . . petrified.

Around two she got up the courage to read the note Guillermo left for her. The only light in the room came from the blue screen, but it gave enough illumination to make out his handwriting. It said what she expected it to. He had to leave for business unexpectedly, and he would meet her for dinner later that evening. She was glad he wasn't coming back until evening. That would give her plenty of time to pack her things and leave.

It hadn't taken long for Sadie to realize that whatever feelings she had for Guillermo had melted away when Josh came into her life. When Josh walked out, she tried to throw herself back into Guillermo's willing arms. But it hadn't worked, and instead she found herself resenting him for not being the man she wanted.

Mostly though, she was tired of being freaked out. The nightmares. The strange coincidences. They were easy to dismiss when she loved him, but now she was just done. She kept having visions of him dumping a body somewhere, like something from a low-budget horror movie. She even got up the courage to creep back to the window and peek out, as if she'd find blood on the snow. She saw nothing, of course, but the fact that she thought she might was enough to convince her it was time to be done with Guillermo Vasquez once and for all.

The sleepless hours also gave her time to think, and by four o'clock, she knew there was one last thing to do before she left Guillermo behind her for good. The FBI. It went against every instinct she had, but it seemed like the right thing. Maybe the FBI would find something from tonight, maybe they wouldn't, but it would clear her conscience so she could start fresh.

Her mind went over the phone number the older agent made her memorize on Christmas Day. He asked her to use it if she ever saw or heard anything suspicious. At the time she tried to ignore it, but he wouldn't let her leave until she could recite it perfectly. Now that she had both seen *and* heard something suspicious, she wanted to make sure the number was still there at her disposal. *In the morning,* she vowed. *Then I'm out of here for good.*

As sleep began to tug on her eyelids, she allowed herself to relive her last day with Josh. Just the good parts. The kiss especially played over and over in her head. So many times she tried to come up with another ending to that day, something that ended with a "Happily Ever After," but there was nothing.

Around four-thirty, she fell asleep and, ironically, slept dreamlessly for the rest of the night.

The forecast in Spokane was for heavy snow beginning at noon, yet the heavy flakes started just past dawn. Josh watched them land on the windowsill and melt into nothingness. Up in the mountains, the snow had been everywhere, covering signs, trees, and the roads. On the day they'd found Sadie, the snow was so thick he still couldn't figure out how she had made it so far without boots, a coat, or gloves. She had insisted it was pure survival instinct. Now that he knew her, he was convinced it was her pure stubborn willpower.

Sam's truck pulled up and Josh grabbed his basketball. "I'll be back in an hour, Mom."

"Hey, Josh," she called from the kitchen, "the kids will be at their friends if you want to talk when you get home."

It was only the hundredth time she'd asked, but he understood her concern. Everyone knew he was a mess now, only nobody knew why. "I can't. I told Randy I'd work today."

"Oh," she said, clearly disappointed. "Okay. Have fun."

The air outside was refreshing, and the stairs were already turning to slush as he ran down to Sam's truck. As he pulled open the door, he asked, "Where's Trevor and Kev?"

"They're meeting us at the church."

Sam pulled out of the driveway and cranked up the volume on his favorite station. Country. Josh had never liked country before, but he was ready to chuck the radio out the window as song after song dredged up the pain of a broken heart.

"So what do you think Sadie's doing right now?" Sam asked casually.

It was like being punched in the gut, hearing her name so out of the blue. Josh quickly recovered and focused on the cars passing by. "I don't know."

"I was . . . thinking about calling her."

"You have her number?" Josh had forgotten that small detail.

"Yeah. You think I'm stupid, don't you?"

Josh took a deep breath. It was going to be another miserable day. "Don't hate me, Sam, but there's something I should probably tell you."

Kevin and Trevor were late, giving Josh plenty of time to unburden his soul. But even after he was through, Sam still said nothing. "Can't you just yell at me or something? Please!"

Sam traced a line on his steering wheel. "Stop beating yourself up. It's fine. It's over."

"I can't," Josh whispered.

It was quiet a minute, before Sam sighed. "Why didn't you just tell me on the deck?"

"I didn't know then."

Sam smiled sadly. "I did. How many girls have you dated that weren't Mormon?"

"None."

"Hmm. Me neither. But I think I would have given her a chance. You know, Sadie and I actually talked about religion a few times. She had some issues understanding God, but doesn't everyone at one time or another? You should have heard her describe her experience in the storm. It was amazing. She felt something, I could tell. You never know, she could be pretty open to the gospel."

The pain sliced again, knowing she wasn't just open, but willing. But that led to the never-ending circle of questions in his head, questions that had no acceptable solution. Yet Sam was willing to give her a chance, Sadie was willing to give Josh a chance, *so why am I stuck?* The question baffled him.

It was in his nature to plan. Since he was little, he had it all figured out: go on a mission, date a pretty girl, and then get his engineering degree from Washington State. After college, he'd marry that same girl in the temple and have six kids, the picture-perfect Mormon family sitting in a row each week at church. They were lofty goals, but so far he was on track. It had taken a lot to break from the plan and move up the marriage by a year or two. But other than that, things were on target. That is . . . until Sadie. And try as he might, she didn't fit into any of those goals, nor could he imagine her ever wanting to.

He realized Sam was waiting for a response. "You're just an optimist. You can't take a risk like that when your heart's involved and hope it'll turn out the way you want. I made a commitment, and I'm sticking to it.

Even if it means I lose both Megan *and* Sadie. Put God first and everything else will fall into place."

He shook his head and sat up. "I don't want to wait for the guys. Let's play now."

"Okay." But Sam didn't move. Instead he smiled again. "I still can't believe you kissed her. You're stronger than I am. I don't think I could have walked away."

"I don't feel strong," Josh muttered.

Sam's smile grew. "Good. Then it's time for some one-on-one."

"You're leaving?"

Sadie jumped, cheeks flushing, and stepped away from the window. Manuel stood in the hallway, morning coffee in hand, watching her curiously. There was nothing to see outside in the snow, so there was no reason she should be checking again. But that hadn't stopped her.

"Yeah," she said. "I'm going to hang out at the lodge today." No need to alert Guillermo's little brother, and thus Guillermo, that she was never coming back.

"Oh. You need a ride?"

Sadie nearly smiled. Manuel was younger than Guillermo by a few years, placing him closer in age to her. He wasn't the charismatic type his older brother was, but she suspected that he'd had a bit of a crush on her. "Salvador said he would drive me, Manuel, but thanks anyway."

The ride with Salvador was a quiet one as the heaviness of leaving everything and everyone behind set in. Guillermo. Her job—since seeing Guillermo everyday at the lodge would only complicate things. And with her deep loathing of all winter sports—now a hundred times worse than pre-Josh—there was no reason for her to ever step foot on that mountain again.

Salvador pulled up just outside the lodge. "Would you like me to wait for you, *señorita?*"

"No. Just have Guillermo call me when he gets back."

Sadie left the Mercedes and walked slowly to her room, the dreaded phone call slowing her pace. Once in her room she found several things to postpone the FBI. The first being her mom. She grabbed her phone and slumped into a chair.

"*Hola,* Augustina," her mom answered happily. Something about hearing her mom's voice put a lump in her throat. "Augustina?"

"Hey, Mom," she finally responded.

"What's wrong, *hija mia*? You sound tired."

"I am." Sadie didn't bother mentioning she'd been up half the night. "Can I come over tonight? I think I'm going to be depressed." *Going to be?* she scoffed. *I already am.*

"Why? What's wrong?" Her mom's voice suddenly hardened. "Did Guillermo do something to you?"

"No!" It was annoying how much her mom could sound like Josh sometimes. "But . . . I'm breaking up with him tonight."

The other end went silent for far too long. Sadie could envision her mom breathing a sigh of relief, but being the friend she was, she refused to celebrate openly.

"I'm just ready to start over," Sadie explained.

"Is this about Josh?"

Sadie didn't know what to say. In a lot of ways it was, but she had hidden the whole FBI investigation of Guillermo from her mom, and she didn't have the energy to go into it now.

"Don't worry," her mom went on. "You'll find someone who will love you for who you are without forcing you to be something you're not."

"Josh wasn't trying to change me, Mom. In fact, he didn't want me to change. Not even when I said I would. Why would he do that?" Her voice cracked as the pain ripped through her.

"Maybe he knows you won't like his church."

"Maybe he doesn't think I'm good enough," she muttered quietly. "But it doesn't matter. It's over. So can I come over tonight? I don't want to think about Guillermo or Josh anymore."

"You bet. How about a girl's movie night?"

"No romances!" Sadie insisted a little too desperately.

"No romances," her mom agreed. "And we'll eat ourselves silly—popcorn and ice cream and every other wonderful thing to blow my diet. How does that sound?"

If Sadie hadn't been on the verge of tears, she would have laughed. "Perfect. I love you."

"I love you, too, *querida*. Don't worry. It will be all right. Men are *so* overrated."

That time Sadie did laugh. "You're the best, Mamá. See you tonight."

Feeling worse and better at the same time, Sadie held her phone, grateful she still had one friend left in the world. It was tempting to stay there for hours. She could think of a hundred reasons to put off calling the FBI. Things that had freaked her out last night were easily dismissed in the full light of day, and she had all but rationalized it away. Guillermo could have just been showing off a new gun for all she knew. But if she didn't call, it would continue to nag at her, and she wanted as few reminders from this hellish Christmas break as possible. So before she could change her mind, she dialed the number.

Two rings in and suddenly she couldn't remember the name of the agent. Either one of them. Too late.

"Hello?"

The simple greeting startled her. Not only was the voice unfamiliar, she'd expected more than a simple "hello" from the FBI. Maybe she hadn't remembered the phone number after all.

"Hello?" the man repeated.

"Y-yes . . ." she stuttered. "This is Sadie Dawson. I, uh . . . spoke to an agent recently."

"Yes?"

"I'm sorry, but is this the FBI?" *Nice,* she growled to herself. *What kind of question is that?*

"Yes, ma'am."

"Oh. Sorry." Totally flustered, she struggled to remember why she called. "I was questioned two weeks ago . . . about a man named Guillermo Vasquez."

"Just a moment, please." There were a few clicks and then silence. Sadie was just about ready to hang up when she heard a final click followed by a familiar voice.

"Miss Dawson. This is Agent Madsen"—the name she'd forgotten—"Is there something I can help you with?"

Sadie bit her lip. "I don't know. I guess I just wanted to let you know about something that happened last night . . ." She closed her eyes tightly. ". . . at Guillermo's cabin."

"All right. Are you in any current danger?"

"No."

"Are you hurt?"

She grit her teeth. "No."

"Has he made any threats to your safety, or to anyone else's you're aware of?" Madsen's casual tone contradicted his concerned questions, as if he were reading them from a card.

"No!" She cursed herself for ever listening to Josh. There were reasons she couldn't stand that agent.

"Fine. I'll be there in a few minutes."

"What? No! That's okay. I'd rather talk over the phone if you don't mind."

There was no response.

"Hello?" she asked quietly. "Are you still there?"

Dead silence. The line clicked off.

Sadie looked wildly around her room. She didn't want to see Madsen again. Not here. Not now. Not ever! *And how does he even know where I am?* she wanted to scream.

All the anxiety, all the fear and anger from the last two weeks combined into one overwhelming emotion that suddenly exploded. She hurled her phone across the room and sank to the floor.

CHAPTER 37

Sadie flinched at the soft knock on her door. *Three minutes!* It was bad enough Madsen had known where she was, but it had only taken him three minutes to get to her room. *Three!*

She took her time answering the door, letting Josh convince her in her mind that the FBI were the good guys. Still unconvinced, her muscles tensed as she pulled it open, ready to bolt past the agent at the first sign of trouble.

With Madsen's dark suit and long coat, he seemed more businessman than law enforcer—nothing to alert anyone to who he actually was. He entered her room uninvited, just as he had on Christmas. No greeting, no soothing smile. He just sauntered in as if it were his own. At least he was alone this time. She had liked his younger partner—and his million phone messages—even less than him.

Sadie refused to sit, but neither did she invite him to sit, wanting to be rid of him as soon as possible. So the two of them stood awkwardly facing each other.

Madsen looked around her small room. "Do you mind if we talk in my car?"

"Yes!" she burst out.

His expression hardened in response and she sighed. "Fine. I'll get my coat."

He led her through the lobby that had once been jammed packed with people and was now emptying of the last straggling vacationers. Neither spoke. He went outside and stopped by an unmarked navy sedan. Again, nothing to alert you that the FBI was at your doorstep.

Sadie sat in the front passenger seat, and he sat in the driver's, somewhat facing her. Swallowing quickly, she tried out the line she had practiced. "I have some information for you."

"Good. I was hoping you did."

"But before I tell you anything, I want answers." And without waiting, she plunged in. "Which one of you planted the bug in my purse?"

Madsen's brows furrowed slightly. "What do you mean?"

"The listening device or whatever you call it. On Christmas. Who put it in my purse after I specifically told you not to?"

"I'm not sure what you're talking about, Miss Dawson."

She gave him a curt nod. "Fine. Then I have nothing more to say to you."

She yanked on the door handle, but nothing happened. She tried it again and again, searching for a lock. There was none. "Let me out! Now!"

"Just a moment. I didn't authorize anyone to plant a listening device in your purse."

She whirled on him. "So that's your game? You didn't *authorize* it, so you can pretend it didn't happen? I just want to know who I have to thank for this!" she cried, pointing to her eye and hoping for the first time the bruise was still visible.

"Your boyfriend," he said, unimpressed, "from what my sources tell me."

Her hands balled into fists, her knuckles pure white. *I can't believe I am doing this! I can't believe I am helping him!*

"I'll take your silence as confirmation. Good. Something concrete to prosecute."

Her mouth opened to respond, but seized with indignation. This was just a game to Madsen. To Guillermo. And somehow she was caught in the middle of it all. *No more!*

"I'd like to leave, please," she said, dead calm.

"Sorry to be so direct, Miss Dawson, but that's the truth. We need some hard evidence against Mr. Vasquez to lock him up. Even if it is just domestic violence."

"Just domestic violence? *Just* domestic violence!"

Madsen's calm exterior began to melt. "Tell me what you know and then we can decide what needs to happen from here. Don't forget," he added when her lips tightened rebelliously, "you called me. Not the other way around."

"As if your partner hasn't been harassing me all week," she shot back angrily.

Madsen made no move to deny it and instead picked some lint from his pant leg.

"And how do I know Guillermo isn't going to find out about this meeting and hit me again?" she challenged.

"You don't."

His blunt reply cut off hers. "Vasquez's organization is growing quickly," he went on. "He has a lot of money—and influence—and unfortunately money can corrupt even the best of people." He paused. "Even *my* people."

"Your people? Are you serious?" As if she needed another reason to turn tail and run. "Why are you telling me this?"

"Because you need to know how dangerous he is. You may have survived his temper once . . ." He motioned to her eye. "But that doesn't mean you'll survive it again."

The vision of Guillermo looking down at a dead body took the words from her lips. It was possible Madsen was right, but it pained her to give him anything useful. Yet, she reasoned, this was the only way that she was going to be able to make a clean break. So she started, keeping it brief. Waking up to four shots. The three men.

"One was tall," she said, "maybe six-four or five, and big, like four hundred pounds or something. The other guy was older and a little smaller than Guillermo. I've never seen either of them before. And all three were staring down at something on the ground."

"A body?" Madsen asked, leaning forward.

It was a relief to know his mind had gone to the same place as hers. "I don't know. They had their backs to me. I couldn't see much."

"What about a flash of color. A shape? Anything?"

She shook her head. "It seriously looked like they were staring at the snow." Madsen frowned but said nothing more, so she continued, telling him about Guillermo coming in and his brief note. "He's been gone ever since," she finished.

Madsen pulled on his graying goatee, visibly processing it all. "And you're sure you didn't see what they were shooting at?"

"Yes."

"Okay. Would you be willing to state that in court if needed?"

"State what? I didn't see anything."

"Yes, you did. You saw the place. You heard the shots. You can identify the three people involved. It's not everything I'd hoped for, but it's a start. And hopefully with some time, I'll have enough to pull a case together against him. It is time for Guillermo Vasquez to pay. And believe me," he added darkly, "he will pay. Dearly."

A chill ran down her spine. "What did he do?" she asked quietly.

Madsen no longer met her questioning gaze and instead watched some skiers in the parking lot. For the first time since meeting him, he looked visibly shaken. He finally turned back to her. "What about Christmas Day? Are you willing to press charges?"

"Answer my question," she said. "What did Guillermo do last night?"

He inhaled heavily through his nose, then released it slowly. "No. Not until I piece more together."

She stared at him in disbelief. After all the information she had given him, after taking another chance on his worthless hide, he refused to give back anything in return. Not who planted the bug in her purse. Not what Guillermo had done. Nothing. And in return he had the gall to ask her to testify. "Open the door," she said more calmly than intended. "I need to finish packing before I break up with Guillermo."

"Pack? I thought you were staying up here through the weekend?"

"Stop doing that!" she exploded. "How do you know everything about me?" But before he could answer, her jaw dropped. "It was you," she whispered. "You've been following me."

"Yes."

She didn't know whether to hit him or scream. She chose the second. "Why?"

"To keep you alive actually. You're welcome."

"You're *welcome!* Are you serious? You think I should be thanking you! You had my mom and I totally freaked out and you want me to sit here and *thank* you?"

His arms folded, as if waiting for her to do just that.

The nerve . . . the utter arrogance . . . "How dare you! I told you to leave me alone!"

Madsen didn't move. Didn't apologize. Nothing.

"I saw your guy on New Year's," she said to provoke him. "I saw him following me."

It worked. "You saw Dubois? When?"

"No, not your partner. Another guy. I knew he was there the whole time. Great job on the undercover bit. He stuck out like a sore thumb."

"When?" Madsen barked.

"When I was skiing. He was following me around like a lost puppy. The only one not skiing. Very subtle. I'd think the FBI could do better than that, but obviously not."

Madsen's face darkened. "That wasn't my guy."

"Don't lie to me. You just said you had someone following me. I saw him. Old guy. Leather coat. Four different times. And he was—"

"The only one who was supposed to watch you was Dubois, and he is thirty-three and looks even younger than that," he cut in. "And on New Year's he was skiing, not standing around."

"No," she insisted, losing confidence. "The guy I saw was older. Definitely older."

"That . . . was . . . not . . . my . . . guy," Madsen said, accentuating each word.

"Then who was he?" she nearly screamed.

He rubbed temples tiredly. "Go ask your boyfriend."

Her chest heaved, her jaw clenched. "I can't wait to be done with you. All of you!"

"Miss Dawson, I wouldn't recommend breaking up with Mr. Vasquez tonight. If he went upstairs to check on you, then he's suspicious you know something. It would be highly dangerous to break up with him now."

"And testifying against him wouldn't be? Open the door!" she demanded.

"At least consider my offer. You would be taken care of. Kept out of sight and—"

"Now!" she shouted.

When she tried the handle again, it opened easily. "Don't contact me again," she said as she slid out. Then she slammed the door shut with all the force her body could muster.

CHAPTER 38

Sadie's foul mood lasted the rest of the morning and into the afternoon as she packed. It didn't help that there wasn't enough room in her two bags for everything. In the time they'd dated, Guillermo had given her lots of gifts, most in the form of clothing. She didn't want any of it anymore, but neither could she throw away a five-hundred-dollar sweater. Setting the extra things on top of her bag, she dropped the diamond necklace and matching earrings into her purse. They would be returned to Guillermo at dinner, a small gesture to let him know it was over.

Guillermo called around five and offered to make her dinner at his cabin. She convinced him she was in the mood to eat at Mariposas—a nice public place—and they agreed to meet in the lobby at six-thirty.

With everything taken care of, she lay on her bed to wait, exhausted physically and emotionally. She didn't quite fall asleep, but allowed her mind to wander where it wanted. Josh. She wondered what he was up to, if he thought of her at all, or if he would mention her to Megan. Knowing Josh, he probably would. It was tempting to work on the lyrics to her newest depressing song, but she couldn't find the strength to get off her bed.

Sadie glanced at her clock. 6:15. Almost time for the final good-bye on the mountain. Normally she would have tried on ten shirts and five skirts before going out to dinner with Guillermo, but she settled on the first thing she grabbed, a white blouse and black pants. Boring and dull, like her life was about to become.

A soft knock on her door brought her head around. Guillermo was early. Smoothing down the front of her blouse, she searched for the strength to walk away from him. As she reached the door, a small envelope was slipped underneath. Curious, she grabbed it and slid it open. The note inside was short.

> G. knows about our meeting. You need to leave now! Call me when you're on the road. I can help.
> —Madsen
> P.S. Don't use your phone!

Sadie had to read the note several times before it registered. Then she froze. *You may have survived Guillermo's temper once . . .*

Suddenly she couldn't breathe. Guillermo knew she had gone to the FBI. This time, by her own choice. *How could you do this to me!* he roared from Christmas. She could feel his fist forming. Hear his footsteps coming.

She whirled around, racing through her options. Not the lobby. He might already be there. Not the window either. He would be expecting it. That left only one option.

Run.

Grabbing her purse, she bolted from her room and flew down the hallway, heading in the opposite direction of the lobby. She didn't look over her shoulder, just ran frantically as she tried to remember where a back exit was. If she could just make it to her car, she could make it anywhere. But that required an exit. And stairs.

The lodge was huge, a maze of hallways, and had she only been paying attention, she would have burst out a fire exit. Instead, she turned a corner and skidded to a stop. It was a dead end. She turned around and around. Trapped. The only doors were guest rooms.

She began trying several. Locked. Locked. She pounded, desperate. "Please!" she begged. But the holidays were over. The rooms were empty.

With her pulse hammering, Sadie searched for a cleaning closet. A back stairwell. An emergency exit. Nothing. Then a smaller door caught her eye. The sign said, "Ice." She quickly darted inside and searched for a corner to hide in. Finding only one, she slid her small body between the ice machine and a candy machine and held her breath, wondering how long she would have to hide before she could safely leave. All night, if necessary.

Guillermo paced the lobby of the ski lodge. He'd shown up early, anxious to get the evening over with. It was going to be bad, possibly the worst of his life, and he was ready to have it over with so he could move on.

He glanced down at his watch—6:34—then paced faster. Augustina was late.

All things considered, he'd taken the news rather well. All his suspicions had been confirmed. He'd set the trap, and she'd taken the bait. There was no need to blow up now. But what hurt the most was that he had actually started to believe in her, to believe she was the perfect woman for him. Unquestioning. Naïve. Loyal. He had been ready to move forward and—

He shoved the thought aside. People who dwelt in the past were liable to be trapped by it. It was time to move on. It was time to be done with Sarah Augustina Dawson once and for all.

6:35.

His shoes clapped against the tile as each second ticked slowly by. At 6:36 he sat in an oversized chair. At 6:37 he glanced toward her room.

Madsen! That was the only explanation.

Standing, he brushed off his dark suit. "Salvador?" he said without turning.

"Sir?"

"Find her."

"Yes, sir."

Then Guillermo walked out the front doors.

Chapter 39

Twenty minutes.

That's all it took for Salvador to follow Guillermo out those same doors, Augustina in tow. Twenty minutes exceeded even Guillermo's expectations. On the spot, he decided to give his assistant a bonus—a hefty bonus. Then Salvador was forgotten completely.

Guillermo watched Augustina as she was escorted to his car. Her eyes were wide, her face pale. *Good,* he thought. *She should be scared.* Salvador pushed her into the backseat next to Guillermo, and got into the driver's seat. Augustina didn't bother meeting Guillermo's challenging gaze. She just stared at the empty leather seat in front of her.

The car was eerily silent as Salvador pulled out of the parking lot. And dark. The sun had set some time ago, and that bothered Guillermo. He wanted to see every bead of sweat forming on her flawless face, wanted to see how her olive skin matched the color of her white blouse. He flipped on an overhead light and smiled. *Much better.*

"I was waiting for you, hermosa," he said gently. "You are late."

She said nothing.

"Where were you, mi amor?" he said, spitting out the last two words. "You think you can run from me again, do you?"

Silence.

Somehow the terror made her lovelier. He pulled a lock of dark hair off her shoulder and rubbed it softly between his fingers. He was going to miss her—at least her beauty. The treachery he was ready to be done with. The lies. The deceit. But her beauty . . . *Such a waste!*

He held her hair to his nose and inhaled. The scent of roses. Her favorite. It used to be his favorite too. "You were the world to me," he said softly. "I loved you, hermosa. More than I have loved anyone. I always treated you well, did I not?"

Her ability to remain impassive was impressive. Surely she knew what was in store. Yet she didn't blink. Didn't flinch. Instead, she had turned into a statue next to him.

"I gave you many presents. Did you not like your flowers?"

When she still said nothing, he took more of her long hair and twirled it around the palm of his hand gently. Sadness threatened to creep back in, but he pushed it aside to allow another emotion in its place. Rage. Sadness was useless, but rage . . . rage was power. And like lava bubbling below the surface, his was threatening to erupt.

"What am I going to do with you? Now you have betrayed me. Twice!" He yanked on her hair, pulling her head toward him. "You are not leaving me many choices, are you?" he hissed in her ear. "I think we could have worked things out if you had not had your little meeting today, but now there is no way to convince my colleagues you are safe to have around anymore."

Augustina's eyes squeezed shut, though whether from pain or fear he wasn't sure. It didn't matter. Both would come soon enough. He wrenched her hair down until her face was smashed against the seat in front of her. Her eyes flew open in surprise. In pain.

Now she is ready. With his free hand, he reached into his suit pocket and clutched the object, wavering momentarily. *Has it really come to this?* he wondered. When the answer came back in the affirmative, he pulled out the knife. He let the razor-sharp blade gleam in the light, making sure it was in her line of vision. It was. She blinked rapidly as her eyes filled with silent tears.

"A gift from my father," he explained, admiring the fine craftsmanship. "For my fifteenth birthday. A tribute to my entering manhood. It has been my constant companion ever since. Constant. Faithful. Enduring. All things you lack, I might add."

With exaggerated ease, he brought the knife to his favorite part of her neck, right above the collarbone. She winced even before it touched her delicate skin. He liked that. He pressed the razor-sharp blade in enough to let her know he was serious, but not enough to draw any real amount of blood. Her breaths came out in short bursts, but somehow she remained stubbornly mute. *Ironic,* he thought, considering she had so much to say to the FBI.

"What to do, what to do?" It was taking every bit of self-restraint to leave his knife where it was and not end it right there. But he wasn't finished with Augustina. Not even close.

In one swift movement, he turned the knife's blade and shoved her back up, cutting the long hair he had gripped so tightly nearly at the scalp. The air rushed out of her as she saw her life flash before her eyes.

He held the thick curls to his face. "Hmmm, something to remember you by, I think." But no sooner had he caught the scent of roses than it disgusted him. He dropped the dark curls at her feet. She didn't watch them fall. Already, her breathing returned to normal, and she had become still once again.

In anticipation of his next surprise, he turned his whole body to face her. "You know, I had the opportunity to read a journal recently. It made for interesting reading. Very interesting indeed."

Her head came around for the first time, her eyes wide with horror, and he smiled. It was nice to have finally broken through her calm façade.

Making sure he still had her attention, he pulled out the small blue book. "I didn't realize your passing flirtation had become the romance you had always dreamed about."

She swallowed hard and faced forward again, though she wasn't exactly motionless anymore. Her head swayed, and she had to grab the door to steady herself.

He flipped slowly through her journal, purposely taking his time finding the spot, while loving that she was watching him out of the corner of her eye. As he neared the page he began humming a song of hers. Not his favorite. No. But another song he had recently been reminded of. It was a lovely song, he admitted, even without lyrics.

"Ah," he said, finding the page at last. "This was my personal favorite." Then in his best Augustina impersonation he quoted, "'I will never meet Josh's equal. His kiss is forever burned in my memory, erasing all others. I will love him until the day I die.'"

He slammed the book shut. "This is the man I met New Year's Eve, yes?"

When she still refused to speak, he yelled, "Answer me!"

She shuddered under his eruption, but said nothing.

Guillermo nodded, letting his patience return to him again—at least on the surface. "Okay then, let's try this another way." He reached in his suit and pulled out another object. He didn't bother showing her the gun since he knew she already knew what it looked like—another betrayal. Instead he held it up by her ear. Waiting until his voice was prepared to obey his command, he asked gently, "Tell me, hermosa. Was the man of your dreams the one I met New Year's Eve? At the very party I had planned for *you*?"

"Yes," she squeaked. It barely cleared her throat.

He returned the gun to his suit. "That is what I thought. He is a handsome man, this Josh. I will agree with you on that. I am sorry to have interrupted your moment."

She blinked slowly and, for a second, looked like she was going to pass out.

"I wish I had known then what I know now. I would have finished him off right then, although"—he chuckled sadly—"I shall truly enjoy the game of hunting him down."

"He didn't do anything!" she choked. She turned to face him. "Please . . . don't."

Guillermo snapped. The temper he fought to control was unleashed in his fist. The first blow caught her on the back of the head, slamming her against the window. Instinctively, she pulled her arms up to brace herself for the next one, but he redirected, hitting closer to her nose.

"*Señor,*" Salvador said from the front seat. "She is not a man. You could kill her."

Guillermo stopped before his third blow. Salvador was right and unfortunately she needed to be conscious for the next part. "Well," he said, breathing heavily, "I think it fitting for you to die in the place you 'came alive.' Don't you?"

Augustina continued rocking back and forth, cradling her face. For a moment he wondered if she'd heard him at all, but then her head came up slowly as his words sunk in. She turned to stare out the now-stationary Mercedes. Guillermo laughed heartily.

"She didn't know where we were, Salvador. How wonderful!"

Salvador nodded in the rearview mirror.

"Will you to do one last thing for me, Sadie? Sa-die . . . ," Guillermo repeated, trying out her English name for the first time. "A horrible name. Fitting, I suppose, for the horrible woman you are. But . . ." He smiled, feeling quite delirious, "I have one last request for you, Sa-die. Actually, it is more for your mother than for me. That is, if you don't want her to join you in heaven shortly. Oh, wait," he laughed bitterly, "your new boyfriend thinks you are going to hell."

CHAPTER 40

Josh lay in bed until well after nine. It had been five days since he had left Montana. Five days of misery and worry. His mom was about ready to call a counselor, but it didn't matter how hard he tried, he couldn't escape Sadie. Or the dread he felt at having left her.

He turned up the volume on his laptop, trying to drown his thoughts with a collection of teenage-drama songs his sister, Lauren, had given him for Christmas. Most were fairly cheesy and therefore tolerable. To add to the ruckus, his youngest sister, Katie, was playing Christmas songs on the piano upstairs, even though it was a few days into January.

The door to his room opened, and Drew peeked in. "Hey, Mom wanted me to tell you we're going to the pool. You wanna come?"

"No," Josh said, "I've got a pile of laundry to do before I leave for school tomorrow."

"Laundry?" Drew pulled a face. "Whatever. See ya."

As soon as his little brother left, thoughts of Sadie took over. Josh grabbed his headphones and turned on the song he'd listened to after the party.

While it started playing, he reached over to his nightstand for the stack of pictures Kevin had given him. There were ten or so, mostly of the guys skiing, but Kevin had purposely put the most painful one on top. The back of it read: TO MY FRIEND, THE IDIOT.

Originally there had been three people in the picture, sitting by the bonfire, but to make his point, Kevin had cropped out Sam, making it look like Josh and Sadie were a couple. Staring at the picture, it felt like they were. She was leaning toward Josh, his coat wrapped snugly around her shoulders, and both of them were smiling, almost laughing. But instead of studying Sadie's face like he had so many times, Josh studied his own. He looked happy sitting there. Incredibly so. He missed smiling, he missed being happy, and he missed Sadie fiercely.

The song ended. He set the pictures aside and gathered his laundry, stopping when he reached his gray sweats. She was everywhere. He threw them in the basket and headed upstairs.

The house was finally quiet, and his feet didn't make it past the living room. Setting his laundry down, he wandered over to the piano in desperate need of a jam session. For a minute, his hands rested on the keys, feeling lost. Normally he would have gone right to Rachmaninoff, yet when his fingers found the keys, they began sounding out a simple melody. A melody that had plagued him since New Year's. With a little effort, he started sounding out the accompaniment as well.

He closed his eyes, and soon Sadie was playing her song instead of him. He could hear her voice in his mind, feel her arm next to him on the bench, smell her perfume in the air, and see the dark curl dancing on her—

"Josh?"

He stopped, eyes flying open. His dad was watching him curiously. "Oh, hey, Dad," he said, standing quickly. "You're home early."

His dad loosened his tie. "Slow day. You the only one home?"

"Yeah."

Josh followed him into the kitchen, where his dad started making a sandwich. With four kids living at home, the Young home was rarely quiet, and Josh decided to take advantage of the moment. He struggled for a good way to broach the subject and then decided just to hit it head on.

"Why did you and Mom break up?"

His dad looked up in surprise. "Where'd that come from?"

Josh shrugged, not ready to explain himself.

"Well, there were a lot of things. I don't remember everything she listed. It was a long time ago." He walked around to a stool and started eating his sandwich, appearing to be done with that particular conversation.

"Religion?" Josh asked casually.

"Yeah. That was one."

"What about the Church bothered her?"

"I don't know. The rules. The time commitment. A lot of things."

"And . . . how long did she . . . ," Josh's knee started to bounce, "go to church with you?"

The sandwich was forgotten as his father looked at him. "Not even a year. It didn't take long for her testimony to fade, and soon she couldn't remember why she had joined in the first place."

"For you?" Josh ventured.

"I didn't think so at the time, but maybe." Peter Young pushed his plate away. "Why the sudden interest in your mom, Josh?"

"I've just always wondered why she left." It wasn't true, though. He knew exactly why she had left, could still hear every word through his five-year-old ears as he huddled, unseen, in a corner of the upstairs hallway. *I hate you! I hate them! And I hate that church that turned you all against me!*

"She had a lot of problems, Josh. Not just with me or the Church. She wasn't a happy person. Truth is, I don't think even she knew why she left. She just did."

"Do you ever wish . . ." He struggled. "Well, if you could go back, would you do it all the same? Would you still marry her, knowing what you know now?"

"She gave me you and Jake," Peter responded easily. "I'll always love her for that."

"Oh."

Josh knew his face must be showing more of his thoughts than he wanted it to. Thankfully, the doorbell rang, releasing him. "Kevin's early," he said, jumping off his stool.

"Hey, Josh," his dad called, "When you're ready to tell me what's going on, you can. I know something happened with Megan and you don't want to talk about it. I can understand. I just hope you'll come to us when you are ready. Okay?"

"Thanks, Dad."

Josh walked down the hallway and looked out the side window. His heart stopped. It wasn't Kevin. And his life was about to get a whole lot worse. He pulled the door open slowly.

"Hi, Josh," Megan said quietly. "Can I come in?" Her blonde hair was down and curled the way he liked it, and she had on a blue sweater he'd never seen before, which matched her large eyes perfectly.

He opened the door and watched her sit on the same couch she had before. He didn't move, just stood holding the door while cold air rushed into his house. He was trying to figure out why she was there. Looking nice. Trying to impress him.

His dad came into the hallway and stopped in surprise. "Well, hi, Megan. How are you?"

She forced a smile. "Good, Brother Young. And you?"

"I'm doing great. Really great. Really, really—" He shook his head. "Wow. It's nice to see you again."

"You, too," she said, and then there was nothing left to say. They both looked at Josh. But Josh still couldn't move. For the life of him, he couldn't find any reason why Megan had forgiven him for what he'd done. He hadn't.

His dad clapped him on the back. "Hey, Josh, I need to get some things at the hardware store. I'll be back a little later, okay?" When Josh said nothing, he turned to Megan. "It's nice to see you again, Megan." Then he left and suddenly the two of them were alone.

"Josh?" Megan tried again. "Please . . ."

Hearing his name finally snapped him out of his stupor. He shut the front door and made his way to the living room. He chose the chair across from Megan, finding it safest.

"You don't look so good, Josh."

"Thanks. You look good, too. Really good."

It wasn't until she laughed that he realized he'd heard her wrong. He should have apologized or something, but he was past the ability to think through social niceties.

"Why are you here?" he asked, point blank.

She ducked her head and twisted the strap of her purse. "I've been thinking a lot about what you said. I put myself in your shoes and realized how difficult it was for you to—"

"Don't!" he broke in. "Don't try to make me feel better. You're the kind of person who takes all the responsibility on yourself, but you're not taking this one. This was me. All of it."

She played with the seam of her new sweater a moment. "Do you still love me?"

He looked up in surprise. Of course he did. Not like he had before, and probably not like he should, but he still did. "Yes," he finally managed.

"Enough?"

That question was harder. Was it enough to mostly love someone? Was it enough to care about one person while thinking about another? Of course not, but then what? Where did that leave him? Leave them?

She stood slowly. "I think that's my answer."

"Wait, Megan. I just don't get why you're here, giving me another chance."

"I don't know either. I just . . ." She took a quick breath. "Do you love her, Josh?"

"Yes."

He realized a little too late that he'd answered too quickly. He should have hesitated, paused, or at least shrugged, but it blurted out of him, desperate for escape. Just when he thought he couldn't hurt anyone anymore . . .

"Wow," she whispered. "Couldn't you have lied a little? I mean, I know we've been drifting apart, but . . . you barely know her!"

Josh stared at the floor.

She clutched her purse, speaking almost to herself. "I came here thinking we could work this out, forgive and forget, pretend you never went on that ski trip, but . . . do you really expect me to just forget something like this?"

"No."

She looked surprised by his candidness. "And do you . . . want to forget?"

Before he could consider her question, they were interrupted by the onslaught of his family, home from swimming. "Josh! Josh!" Katie came bounding in the room like only a ten-year old girl could. "I did it! I jumped off the high—" She skidded to a stop. "Megan." She glanced back and forth between the two of them. "You're here."

Megan glared at Josh. "Do you?"

Josh couldn't look away from Katie, from the blonde curls so much like little Sophie's. A thousand memories washed over him, and in that instant he knew.

He turned back to her. "No. I'm sorry."

Megan shook her head over and over again. "No, *I'm* the one that's sorry. Sorry I came back. Sorry I didn't listen to my parents!" She picked up her purse and walked hastily toward the door. "Don't bother calling me when you change your mind. We're through!"

As she shut the door, Josh's head dropped into his hands.

Chapter 41

Josh found his way back into the kitchen. Groceries covered every bit of counter space and his three youngest siblings were emptying bags. But his stepmom was leaned against the counter, trying to read his expression. It must have been bad because she did something completely uncharacteristic. "You kids go downstairs. I'll take care of the rest."

Everyone stopped. "Really?"

Kathy Young didn't take her eyes off Josh. "Yes. I want to talk to Josh alone. You guys give us some space."

They didn't have to be told twice. The three of them flew into the basement. Josh reached into the nearest bag, still reeling from what just happened. There was no going back now.

Kathy folded her arms. "Are you ready to tell me what's going on?"

He took a carton of eggs to the fridge.

"Come on, Josh. You've been silent since you got home, and suddenly Megan's nowhere to be found. Now she shows up and you're still silent? I don't think I can wait until you're ready to talk. I'm going crazy here!"

"But you love Megan, don't you?" he said carefully.

"Yes, I do." He waited for her to say what she always did, *but I would love her better as a daughter-in-law.* Instead her mouth fell open. "*You broke up with her?*"

"Well, no. I don't know. I guess in a way."

"Why?" she cried.

He grabbed a box of crackers. He only got two steps before she grabbed his arm and pulled him toward the couch. "The rest of this can wait."

As Josh sat, he turned the box of crackers over and over in his hands, still hesitating. No one knew the whole story. Sam knew some. Kevin knew most. But each had parts they either didn't know or couldn't understand.

"Please," she begged.

So he started, going back to the very beginning and the moment they found a strange girl in Sam's truck. He went through every detail at the cabin, and his mom, being the ever-patient woman, listened quietly while he unloaded his crushing burden. A few times she interrupted to clarify something, but the rest of the time she stayed quiet.

When he got to the party, he slowed his narrative. Talking about how Sadie found him at the piano, her song, and how close he'd come to kissing her. And then the FBI. How she had willfully chosen to stay with Guillermo and how he just couldn't stand to sit around and watch.

"I barely slept that night," he explained, "but the next morning it finally hit me." He paused. When his mom nodded her encouragement, he continued. "I decided Sadie had been sent to me as a test. Do you think it's possible?"

"It's *possible*," she said carefully, "but it doesn't seem that way to me, to be honest."

He frowned. "That's what Kevin said the next day, except he wasn't quite that diplomatic. Unfortunately, I was convinced of the theory and spent the morning preparing myself in case we ran into her again. I was sure I could now think of her as just a good friend. Of course she found us—because she always finds me—and we all went to lunch at the lodge. That's when, like a complete moron, I announced I was going to propose to Megan."

His mom jerked up. "What?"

"Yeah. Not one of my finer moments."

He watched her expression, but she restrained any comment, so he continued. Skiing. The ski lift. When he reached the actual kiss, he braced himself, sure she would hate him as much as he hated himself, but she said nothing.

"I told Sadie I couldn't walk away from everything I was, not even for her." He stopped, shaking his head. "I can't believe after everything Sadie had been through—everything I'd watched her go through—I ended up causing her more pain."

"What did she do?" she asked gently.

"She told me she would do anything to be with me, even change her religion, but I knew that wouldn't work."

"Why?" she suddenly burst. "She was giving you a chance at everything you want."

"Because I don't want her to join the Church for me. That doesn't work."

"Ohhhh," she said slowly. "I see. Finish your story, then we can talk."

He did as best he could, pushing through the pain of leaving Sadie to explain what happened minutes ago with Megan. When he finished, he waited for her to say something, anything, to alleviate the pain. But instead of responding, her gaze dropped to the box of crackers—now mutilated in his hands. He quickly set it aside. "Sorry," he whispered.

"I hate to see you like this, Josh. It's not you. So . . ." she leaned forward, "how about I ask you a few questions. I want you to really think about them before you answer. I want your deep-down honest answer and not just what you think you should say. Okay?"

He nodded.

"How do you feel when you're with Sadie? When you're not beating yourself up with guilt."

"I feel like I'm myself, for better or worse. Sadie doesn't put up with my garbage and I like that. But she's fun, too, with a sense of humor to rival any of us guys. That's the other thing. She's a part of the guys now. It's awesome! She even loves classical music like you."

"And you," his mom inserted with a smile.

"Yeah." Josh laid back on the couch, losing himself in memories of marshmallows and Kermit the frog. "When I'm with her, I laugh a lot. And she's the most beautiful thing I've ever seen—just ask any of the guys. I wish you could hear her song, though. It was amazing."

"I'd like that."

Realizing his thoughts had run away from him, he quickly reeled it in with a dose of reality. "But as soon as I realize how happy I am—how attracted I am—I start feeling guilty and end up mad or frustrated, which sadly didn't go unnoticed. She must think I'm a psychopath."

"I'm sure she understands," his mom responded, unaware that only a mother is that understanding. "And how do you feel with Megan?"

"I can't even see her without thinking about Sadie."

"And the same didn't happen in reverse, right?"

"Right," he responded, glad someone finally understood his predicament.

"Well, at least we know who you love."

He threw his hands in the air. He already knew who he loved. That was the problem. "What do I do then? Throw away a temple marriage? When I kissed Sadie, I decided I would walk away from it all just to be with her. But then I pictured our wedding in a chapel, for time only. I pictured myself taking our kids to church by myself, a family home evening where I was the only one there, and having arguments with teenagers who wanted to stay home from church with their mom. I've been taught my whole life, *temple marriage, temple marriage,* and that's what I want. A true partnership in God, where you kneel and pray together, a team every morning and night. I want what you and Dad have and not—" He stopped himself abruptly.

"—what he had with your mom?" she finished. "Is that what this is about? Do you think Sadie would do to you what your mom did to Dad?"

He didn't respond. He didn't have to.

"Dad called me and told me you were asking about them—about why she left. Josh, you have to know their marriage had a lot more problems than just religion. Your mom had some serious issues that she refused to deal with. She took it out on your dad, on you and Jake, and eventually on herself. But that was her. *Not* Sadie."

He stared at his hands.

"Didn't you say Sadie was willing to join the church?"

"Yes, but she was willing to join it without knowing anything about it. Not a single bit of doctrine. Doesn't that bother you a little?"

"That wouldn't work, now would it? But aren't you going to give her a chance to try it?"

He shook his head. "I can't. I can't get my hopes up. It nearly killed me to walk away from her once. How would I be able to do it again if I got more emotionally involved? I would pressure her into it without even trying to." He exhaled heavily. It always came back to this, the never-ending circle. "I just have to live with it. I have to get over her."

His mom reached out and took his hand. "Have you prayed about this, Josh?"

"Yes. Finally. And over and over my answer is that God loves all His children and Sadie has just as much right to be happy as I do."

Her face lit up. "So if that's your answer, why are you fighting it?"

"I'm not. Sadie deserves to be happy and not tormented by someone who's obsessed by something she doesn't believe in. She deserves someone who will love her without guilting her into being something she's not. She deserves the best."

"Ohhhh," his mom said slowly, "but I see your answer differently. Sadie deserves to be happy and what would make her happiest is to grow closer to God, the source of real happiness."

"Yes, but—"

She held up a finger. "And though she may not be a member of the Church—*yet,*" she let the word hang a moment, "our Heavenly Father loves her every bit as much as He loves you." She squeezed his hand. "Have you felt any peace since you made your decision?"

"No. I can't remember a time when I've been more miserable."

"That's what I thought and that's why I think you're wrong. I think if God was trying to tell you to stay away from her, your decision would still have been hard, but you would have found some peace and assurance that you're on the right path."

Josh stared at her, stunned by the direction she'd gone. He held his breath, anticipating every word. It was so dangerously close to hope, he was afraid to move.

"Our Father knows the end from the beginning. He knows Sadie better than you do, and He knows *you* better than you do. Maybe He has a different plan for you both, something neither of you originally thought. Maybe He put Sadie in your life in a way you could get to know her without breaking your commitment to only date members. Maybe He led Sadie to a place where she could not only escape a horrible man, but find happiness with another. Maybe, just maybe," she smiled, "He knows what Sadie will choose for her religion more than you do."

A spark lit. At first Josh didn't recognize it for what it was, but as it grew, his mind raced with the potential of what was being offered.

"Let me ask you one final question. If Sadie was a member of the Church already, someone you met in a singles ward, would you have any reservation about being with her?"

"No. None whatsoever."

"Then what are you waiting for? Go get the girl."

Go get the girl. The same phrase Kevin had used. That was it. That was his answer.

Kathy Young sat back and watched the transformation take place on her son's face, one from tormented agony to pure joy. The previously dull eyes had their luster back, the corners of his mouth started to pull up, and suddenly the son she lost on the ski trip was back.

"You found it, didn't you?" she whispered through the tears. "The peace you were looking for?"

"Yes," he smiled. Then he jumped to his feet. "I gotta go, and I'm not really sure when I'll be back."

She stood as well, tears flowing freely.

Josh swept her off the floor in a giant bear hug. "Thank you for saving me."

"It wasn't me. Remember, God gave you a head to think and that's good, but He also gave you heart to feel and this time your heart was right."

A grin took over his entire body as he flew down the stairs to his room. He grabbed his coat, his keys, and the top picture from the stack, and made it back upstairs in record time. In his race to get out the door, he nearly knocked over Kevin.

"Hey!" Kevin cried. "What the heck?"

"Sorry, Kev," Josh said, throwing on his coat. "I have to go."

"What? This is our last day! You and Sam are leaving tomorrow."

Josh handed the picture to his mom and announced excitedly, "I'm going back!"

It took a second for Kevin to understand, and then he slapped him on the back. "So you finally got your head on straight. Get outta here already," he said, kicking him out the door.

Kevin laughed as Josh sprinted down the hallway, out the door, and to his car. "He's going back?" he said, with a shake of his head. "It's about time."

Josh's mom laid a hand on his arm, crying and smiling simultaneously. "So, Kevin," she said, holding a photo. "Tell me everything you know about a girl named Sadie."

CHAPTER 42

"Blue Ridge Lodge. May I help you?"

"Yes. May I have Sadie Dawson's room, please?"

Josh heard a click as the call was transferred. He hadn't stopped smiling since he left the house. His first call had been to Sam to get Sadie's cell number. That had been his second call, but her phone went straight to her voicemail. There was no way he could leave that kind of a message, so his next call was the lodge. He still had no clue what he was going to say to her, or what her reaction would be, but it didn't matter anymore. He was going back.

After eight unanswered rings he hung up. It was the middle of the day and Sadie could have been anywhere. Unwilling to give up so easily, he tried the number again.

"Blue Ridge Lodge. May I help you?"

"Yeah. Sorry. Can I have Sadie Dawson's room again?"

"Yes. Just a moment."

For a moment, he wondered if Sadie was purposely avoiding his call. But after the third ring, the phone was answered.

"Hello?"

Josh startled a little. It wasn't Sadie. It was a man. Only it didn't sound like Guillermo.

"Hello?" the man repeated.

"Um . . . yeah," Josh said. "Can I speak with Sadie, please?"

"Who is this?" the voice asked curtly.

"This is Josh. Who is *this*?"

"Josh?"

"Yes. Josh Young. A friend of Sadie's. Who is this?" Josh demanded.

"Mr. Young, this is Agent Madsen from the Federal Bureau of Investigation."

Josh's car nearly ran off the side of the road, finally recognizing the voice. He quickly swerved back into his lane, getting an angry honk from behind him. "Well, can I speak with Sadie, please?"

"Miss Dawson is not here."

It finally clicked. The FBI. In Sadie's room. "Where is she?" Josh asked half as loud.

The FBI agent hesitated. "Mr. Young, can you come to Montana?"

"I'm on my way to Montana right now. Why? What's going on?"

"Just come to Miss Dawson's room—room 208—and we'll discuss what happened."

"No! Please tell me what's going on! Where is Sadie?"

The other line went dead.

Josh made the four-hour trip in less than three. He hadn't come up with any logical explanation except that something was terribly, terribly wrong. By the time he reached the lodge, he nearly knocked over a group of kids running around inside.

"Room 208?" he asked at the front desk. The man pointed down the hall, and Josh sprinted the whole way, pounding on the door before his feet stopped.

When Madsen pulled it open, his eyes shot up in immediate recognition. "You're Josh?"

Josh pushed past him into Sadie's small room, hoping against hope. She wasn't there. Her room wasn't empty, though. There were three other people there—two in suits like Madsen and the third a woman, mid-fifties, sobbing quietly in one corner.

Josh's pounding heart suddenly stopped. "What happened?"

A badge flashed in his face. "I'm Special Agent Bruce Madsen, Mr. Young. We spoke on the phone earlier, and if you recall, we also met briefly on New Year's Eve."

Josh couldn't drag his eyes away from the sobbing woman. "Where . . . is . . . Sadie?"

"Sit down, please."

His knees buckled. "What happened?"

"Miss Dawson is missing," the agent said without emotion. "She's been gone two days."

"Missing?" In a split-second Josh's thoughts went from zero to sixty. "Guillermo!" He spun around. "Where is he? Has anyone checked his cabin? What about her mom's place? Have you checked there? Or her apartment? Or—"

"Mr. Young!" the agent broke in. "Sit." He motioned to the bed, but Josh didn't want to sit. He needed to stand. To pace. As he did, the woman stopped crying to stare at him—glare at him, actually. Her eyes were red and swollen, and filled with pure hatred, yet there was something familiar in those eyes. In her small build.

"Sadie's mom?" he realized.

A stream of angry Spanish erupted from her, spewing words at him like daggers. Josh didn't catch a single word until she switched to English. Then he only heard three.

"You killed her!"

He felt the blow to his lungs. *Sadie's dead?* He staggered to her bed.

"Get her out of here!" Madsen yelled to one of the other agents. The agent complied, gently propelling Sadie's mother to her feet and out the door. Her blazing eyes never left Josh as she was escorted out. With her gone, Madsen turned back to Josh. "When was the last time you spoke with Miss Dawson?"

Josh couldn't find air. Sadie was dead. Not missing. Dead! He clutched her bedspread, trying to make it untrue.

The agent had to repeat his question before Josh looked up. "New Year's Day," he whispered. "Please . . . *please* tell me what's going on. I can take it. Just . . . is she . . . ?"

"Honestly, we don't know." Madsen picked up a small blue book and handed it to Josh. "Miss Dawson's journal. We found it on her bed after she went missing. Read."

Though Josh wasn't ready, he took the journal and forced his eyes downward.

January 4th,   My last entry.

I love Josh and I always will. I cannot live without him, yet he chooses to live without me, so what else can I do? The memories of our time on this mountain are more than I am able to bear, which leaves only one choice. It is time to burn the memories for good. I am so sorry, Mom. Please forgive me.

As each word sunk in, Josh started shaking his head. "No. No. NO!" He looked up at the agent, tears blurring his face beyond recognition. "I killed her?"

"Just a minute, Mr. Young. I need you to stay with me. What do you know about Guillermo Vasquez?"

Josh traced the devastating lines, feeling the world shatter around him.

"Mr. Young?"

"Some," he whispered.

"Vasquez has been setting himself up as a major player in a transnational drug ring. Because of the proximity to the Canadian border, this area has become a hotbed for drug activity. He's still new and building up his contacts—both in and out of the government—but so far he has proved very cunning and difficult to . . ." Madsen stopped, peering at Josh. "Are you listening?"

"I . . . I just can't believe she's gone. I was coming . . ." The words barely passed his lips. "I was coming to tell her . . ."

"Mr. Young, look at me now!"

The shouting brought Josh's head up.

"I don't think Miss Dawson's dead. Not yet. I have a hunch Vasquez has her on the run, but I need you. I need your head and any information you can give me. Can you do that?"

The small ray of hope gave Josh sudden focus. He nodded. And for the next several minutes, Madsen pieced Sadie's story together, starting in mid-December when Guillermo started prepping her for entrance into his secluded society. "For her safety and potential assistance in the investigation," Madsen explained, he and his partner approached her Christmas Day. Josh could still feel Sadie's revulsion about that meeting, but Madsen sounded convinced it was solely for her own benefit.

"When she stormed out, my partner followed her to the Vasquez cabin in hopes of deducing which key players would be at that Christmas dinner. Unbeknownst to me," Madsen said, "he placed a listening device in her purse and was listening to everything just outside."

"Your partner?" Josh blurted.

"Yes. An amateur move. Vasquez's lawyers would have thrown out any evidence in court."

"So everything that happened to Sadie . . . ?" Josh pictured her battered face, her lifeless eyes, feeling sick.

Madsen rushed on. "My partner lost transmission and decided to patrol the area around the cabin with another agent. He heard shouting and doors slamming, then silence. It wasn't until morning that, in the middle of a blizzard, they saw an object fall from an upper window."

"Sadie," Josh breathed.

Madsen nodded. "At the time, Dubois didn't know what—or who—it was, but I told him to investigate. By the time he reached the area under the window, small footprints were barely discernible. Figuring they must be Miss Dawson's, they began following her."

Madsen's words began to mix with Sadie's now. The two agents tracking her, shouting for her to stop. "Dubois had pieced together enough of the story to realize if he didn't find Miss Dawson before Vasquez did, she was as good as dead. However, their shouting alerted Vasquez to the fact that she had fled. He sent his men into the storm as well. I'm surprised there wasn't an altercation between his men and mine," Madsen added tiredly.

Josh nodded, sobered by the memory of Guillermo's threat on New Year's. *Step aside, little agent, before you can step no more.*

"By the time the storm ended and we had reasonable visibility," Madsen said, "the wind and snow had covered her tracks. She was gone. In all honesty, when she didn't surface again, I figured Guillermo's men had found her and finished the job."

It was like reliving that first day in the cabin for Josh. Her face. Her fear. Like the hunted animal she was. Josh could feel every petrified second as his own now that she had vanished again. Feeling the responsibility shift to his shoulders, he took over her story. Finding her. Her injuries and her description of being locked up at Guillermo's. Everything that had happened at the cabin or any tiny bits of information Sadie had told him, he now told Madsen, praying it might possibly help her now.

Once Josh got her to the lodge, Madsen picked up again. "From the moment she returned, she dodged every attempt we made to contact her. Yet Vasquez trusted her less than ever. This, combined with the knowledge of his violent tendencies, convinced me it was time to start round-the-clock surveillance on Miss Dawson."

As Josh digested the words "violent tendencies," Madsen grabbed a manila folder. He handed Josh a photograph of a man in his early thirties.

"The skier in gray," Josh said, recognizing his face immediately.

Madsen nodded. "My partner, Stephen Dubois."

Josh studied the picture again. "But Sadie said there was another man following her, an older guy in a leather coat, but I never saw him."

"Yes. That was one of Vasquez's men. He had a couple of men

watching her that day, actually. I don't know if it was because of you, or me, or simply because she'd already run from him once, but Vasquez was watching her every move. Her phone. Her purse. He even tapped her bedroom here. He knew everything going on in her life the last week— possibly sooner. He even invited us to the party, as you may remember, just to let us know he was aware of our presence."

Everything . . . Josh closed his eyes, stomach churning, and every sentence out of Madsen's mouth only sunk him further. After she ran into the lodge, she had run right back into Guillermo's arms and had been at his cabin where she heard gunshots two nights ago. The three men. A possible body. Madsen never gave Josh time to recover; he just kept delivering one blow after another.

Madsen stopped his narrative unexpectedly. It took a second for Josh to notice and then he looked up. "We have reason to believe the person shot and killed that night was Agent Dubois."

"Your partner?" Josh blurted.

"He was monitoring Guillermo's cabin, and we've not heard from him since."

Josh swallowed hard, thinking of Sadie's dream. "Who shot him?"

"Technically, there's not a shred of evidence he was even killed, but assuming he was, Miss Dawson identified it was one of these three men: Glummer, a large man I've yet to identify, and the third"—Madsen pulled another picture from his file—"is this guy."

"The ranger!" Josh cried.

"Who?"

Though the man hadn't been at the cabin long, Josh knew that weathered face. "That's the guy who said he worked for the National Forest Service. He said his name was . . . ah, I can't remember. He gave us her missing person flyer. Sadie hid in the bedroom, so he never saw her, and we never told him she was with us. She called the Forest Service the next day, but they had no idea . . ." Josh couldn't finish. "If the ranger would have seen her that day . . ." he tried again.

Madsen handed the picture to the other agent who had quietly been taking notes the whole time. The agent left without a word, and Madsen turned back to finish the rest of the details. Guillermo checking on Sadie after the shots, her decision to finally go to the FBI and to break up with Guillermo—which should have made Josh rejoice, but knowing where the story was headed, only filled him with a deep foreboding.

"She called her mom but didn't mention anything that had happened," Madsen said. "She gave her mom the impression that she was depressed because of certain things that had happened with you, which"—he motioned to the journal—"understandably has her mom quite distraught."

Josh nodded blankly. The suicide note.

"Around six that evening," Madsen continued, "we got a tip from an inside source saying Vasquez found out about her meeting with me and planned to dispose of her."

"Dis-pose?" Josh repeated with difficulty.

"Yes. I'm sorry."

A wave of nausea hit Josh. He squeezed his eyes shut to block it out, but Sadie was there, unconscious in the back of Sam's truck . . . black eye . . . bruised shoulder . . . running blindly into the storm . . . *Sadie* . . . he groaned.

"My agents at the lodge were *conveniently* detained, so I sent her a message through the front desk. By the time my other men got here, Miss Dawson was gone. That's the last anyone has seen or heard from her. Almost two days without a word."

"The cabin!" Josh shot to his feet. "She promised me she would go back if Guillermo ever . . ." He started for the door. "She has to be there."

Madsen stepped in front of him. "I'm not done yet, Mr. Young."

"I don't care. I have to check Sam's cabin."

Madsen grabbed his arm. "One of my agents searched your friend's cabin this morning. There's no sign anyone has been there since you left."

"The Jackson cabin? Are you sure?"

"Yes."

Josh pushed past him anyway. "I don't care. She has to be there now. I have to check."

"Mr. Young," Madsen said, blocking the door with a chilling air of authority. "I will send Agent Griffin back to check out the cabin again, but right now I need you here. I need any information you can give me."

"But—"

Madsen held up a hand while he whipped out his phone.

"Inside and out," Josh shouted into Madsen's phone "Especially the trail out back. Look for any—"

Madsen shot him a look that shut him up.

When the call was done, Madsen sat on Sadie's bed. Devastated, Josh sat as well. "What about Guillermo?" he asked. "He knows where she is. Can't you force him to talk? Arrest him? Anything?"

"I was at his cabin with a search warrant within two hours that evening," Madsen said. "I personally interrogated him and searched his place inside and out—including his cars. I'm afraid there was no sign of Miss Dawson. She's gone."

Josh's head dropped into his hands.

"Vasquez insists that, after ending their relationship, she left his cabin in a rage and took off into the mountains. Her car is gone and her purse, so it's possible. There's not a single fingerprint on her journal besides her own. I've checked his place twice since, and there's simply nothing to find." Madsen shook his head. "He's covered all his bases. She's vanished. Dubois has vanished. And now Vasquez has vanished as well."

"What?" Josh cried. "Where? When?"

"He took off for Canada this morning, although I doubt he's still in Canada now. His official story is that he was only staying in Montana to be with Miss Dawson anyway. Now that she broke up with him, he says he has business to attend to out of the country."

"No! Why did you let him go? Couldn't you find some reason to keep him here?"

"I held him as long as I could, but there's simply no evidence. He has no criminal record, a handful of alibis, and at least three judges, a district attorney, and a couple of mayors who will vouch for his integrity. My guess is he called out a favor and all of northwest Montana jumped up to help him. I simply couldn't keep him here."

"No . . . ," Josh moaned into his hands. Nothing felt real anymore.

"After reading her journal," Madsen continued, "I knew I needed to get a hold of you. It was obvious you knew enough of the story to be of some help. However Mrs. Dawson didn't appear to know your last name or where you lived beyond the Spokane area. I was in the process of contacting the owners of the cabin for your information when you called. I had hoped the two of you had spoken more recently. Maybe give us something more to go on."

"No," Josh whispered. "We hadn't."

The air around them was heavy and thick, and yet utterly empty and devoid of Sadie.

Josh picked up the journal and traced her words again.

My last entry . . . cannot live without him . . . Please forgive me . . .

Madsen watched him. "Did Sadie ever seem suicidal to you?"

Even as Josh thought about it, he knew. "No. It's just the opposite. She's a fighter."

"That's what I thought. I'm sure Vasquez made her write the note."

Josh's fingers stopped on his own name, a lump forming in his throat. "Are you sure it's her handwriting?"

"Yes," Madsen answered at the same time his phone rang. Checking the number, he stood. "Excuse me, but I need to take this. If you get a chance, please talk to Mrs. Dawson—Marcela. I need her to calm down so I can get something coherent out of her." Then Madsen walked out of Sadie's room, leaving Josh alone on Sadie's bed.

Josh's eyes roamed her room for answers. There was a bag overflowing in a corner, with a few sweaters folded neatly on top. A packed bag.

No one packs to commit suicide, he reasoned. *She was going home. Leaving Guillermo. The note had to have been forced.*

He read the journal again, this time looking for clues. After a minute, he realized the words didn't sound like Sadie at all.

I cannot live . . . more than I am able to bear . . . It is time to burn . . .

The English was too stiff. Like Guillermo's . . . He was positive Guillermo made her write it. *But why?* he questioned. The answer was devastatingly obvious. Guillermo wanted her dead. By her own hand to clear his tracks. *Dispose.*

Josh pulled out his phone. "Katie," he said, "I need to talk to Dad. Can you put him on?"

He spent the next several minutes trying to explain everything as quickly as he could. A few times he had to stop and gather his emotions, but talking it through helped to organize the information into more logical pieces. By the end of the conversation, his dad was heading to Montana to offer up his twenty-five years of experience. His mom was staying behind, offering up every prayer of the heart.

Josh asked for one last thing before hanging up, and that was for his mom to call Kevin, Sam, and Trevor. He couldn't handle going through the story another time—let alone three—but they all deserved to know. He wasn't the only one who loved Sadie.

When he hung up, he racked his brain for something more he could do. Using the only thing he had left, he fell to his knees and poured out his heart.

CHAPTER 43

Sadie glared at Mr. Ugly. That's the name she'd given the man who stood guard over her because she hated him, and he *was* ugly. A big, fat, ugly man. When she'd first awoken to his scarred face she had been terrified of him. He was the same man she'd seen in the snow with Guillermo—enormous both vertically and horizontally—but that was forever ago. Now she just despised the beast. He was sitting on Sam's couch, dinner and beer in hand, rubbing it in that he was eating and she wasn't. Little did he know. She was well beyond hunger.

"What are you waiting for?" she growled. "Can't you just get it over with?" For all she could figure, it had been two days since she'd been in Guillermo's car, two days of lying on a cold hardwood floor, arched backward with her hands taped agonizingly to her ankles. She was in such pain she wasn't sure she'd even be able to move if he did cut her loose. Not only that, but Mr. Ugly hadn't turned on the heat, leaving her frozen as well. And with the stench of gasoline that now permeated the Jackson's cabin, any desire for food had long since been replaced with a stabbing headache. She was done with it all. "Guillermo couldn't kill me," she goaded. "He had to leave. Maybe you're a coward like he is!"

He took a bite that could have fed a small army. "I'm just waiting for the order, princess. That's all. Guillermo wanted to give it time after he

291

left the country, so, we have to wait. Why are you in a hurry to die anyway? Maybe you can't live without him?"

Sadie spat at him. It didn't have a prayer making it the eight feet it needed to go, but she didn't care. He'd get the message.

He laughed, showing all the food in his mouth. "I don't enjoy this anymore than you. I'm ready to be back in warm Belize with my own little beauty."

"You'll never make it there. I told the FBI you were shooting someone. They'll be coming after you, too."

He stared at her a moment, then erupted again. "You really are stupid, aren't you? We didn't kill anyone. Guillermo was testing you. And guess what . . . you failed!" He threw back his head again, letting some of the food fall down his shirt.

Sadie shut her eyes, nauseated for more than one reason. Guillermo set her up. The self-loathing was more unbearable than the pain. Everyone saw it coming but her. Even her mom.

Mamá, she cried, imagining her reaction to the suicide note. Over and over, Sadie tried to convince herself that it was better to have her mother believe the lies than to know what actually had happened to her only daughter. But deep down, she knew her mom would be devastated—and probably find a way to blame herself. Not that Sadie had been given a choice. "Either write what I say and shatter her heart," Guillermo had said, "or not, and I will shatter her body."

Even Salvador had said as much by the ice machine, when she was ready to bolt past him. *It's you or your mom. Your choice.* After which he informed Sadie of her mom's precise location, right down to the movie she'd rented for their girl's night. Sadie had no choice, but it didn't change the fact that the suicide note would destroy her mom.

Surely Madsen, though, she reasoned. Surely he would have seen through the lies. But if that was the case, he would have found her in hours, not days. Either way, she had to face the truth. No one knew where she was. No one was coming.

Her eyes gravitated to Sam's family picture as they had so many times now. Guillermo couldn't have picked a more painful place for her to die. His torture was to be all-inclusive, punishing everyone who ever meant anything to her, including people she'd never met. She looked into the smiling faces of the Jackson family, still unable to believe they were about to lose a place that meant so much to them. All because they had taken in and sheltered an unknown woman. But worse was knowing that when they found out, Sam would tell Kevin, Trevor . . . and . . . and . . .

Josh!

His name broke through her reserve and she started to writhe on the floor, bringing a curious glance from the brute on the couch. But Guillermo's threats in the car weren't empty ones, and if he had planned this for her, she could only imagine what he had planned for Josh. *Or has already done. Because of me.* Her grief spilled onto the cold floor in the form of hot tears.

But then he came. Clear as ever, Josh sat on the hearth next to her, smiling as he made a fire to warm her in the freezing cabin. Her vision of him was so clear—no doubt helped by the strong fumes—and her shivering body relaxed under his care. Josh blew gently on the flames, bringing her the warmth and comfort she didn't deserve.

Sadie squeezed out the last of her tears, promising they would be the last of her life. She took her and Josh to an even happier place. Whitefish Lake. She pictured them walking hand in hand across the rock-lined shore and her breathing slowed. They stopped—Josh's arms around her—to admire the spectacular sunset, filled with every shade from orange to purple. And in the last rays of day, Sadie tipped her head back and gazed into his blue eyes. *This is where I want to be when I die,* she would say. *Right here. In your arms.*

"Hey, princess, you aren't actually sleeping again, are you?"

Sadie opened her eyes to glare at the man who ruined her peaceful vision. He laughed and then turned to the window. "Well, well, well . . . today might be your lucky day after all."

Within seconds, there was a soft knock on the door. Mr. Ugly set his plate aside to answer it. Sadie tried to twist around on the floor to see the visitor. If it was Guillermo, she had a mouthful of spit waiting. But her awkwardly arched body barely budged.

"It's time, Luis," the visitor said. "Get it over with."

The pain slashed through her. It wasn't Guillermo. It was worse. It was his little brother, Manuel. She fought back the emotions threatening to destroy her carefully controlled front.

Mr. Ugly shot her a smile. "Great. I have a few things to finish up and I'll be out."

He shut the door, sauntered back to the couch, picked up his plate, and shoved another enormous bite in his mouth. Sadie wanted to scream. For the past hour, she had watched him pour gasoline everywhere—walls, couches, tables, and everything else in sight. She thought it was finally over then, but no. He had plopped himself back down on the couch with more food. But now that Manuel was ready, Guillermo was ready, and she was more than ready, all Mr. Ugly could think of was to shove food in his stupid face! "Don't you have something better to be doing?" she shrieked.

His eyes grazed over her, head to toe, in a way that made her skin crawl. "Possibly."

Finally after squeezing the last four bites into one, he set the plate down and looked out the window. "I think I'll take you upstairs."

Upstairs? Strangely she had never stepped foot upstairs in Sam's cabin, and she had a sinking feeling she didn't want to.

"I got to thinking," he said, picking his teeth with his fingernail, "when the fire starts down here, I'd like you to have time to hear my hard work. You know, add to the suspense and all. Besides, don't you think a bed would be a little more . . ." A new fear jumped into her throat and the room began to spin around as she waited for him to finish. He never did. Instead, he broke out in a deep, guttural laugh.

No fear, she chanted to herself. *No tears. I'm dead already.*

Luis lumbered off the couch and whipped out a knife. She screamed, but the knife went to her ankles, not her throat, and suddenly she was free.

She should have reacted, grabbed the knife, or ran for the door, but her limbs didn't move. They had been stretched awkwardly for so long, she was paralyzed.

"Hmm," he frowned. "I figured you for a fighter. That's disappointing. Oh well."

He picked her up, tossed her over his shoulder, and grabbed the last canister of gasoline. The jerky movement finally released her limbs. She started kicking, screaming, biting, and clawing as he headed for the stairs. She got a few good chunks of skin under her nails before he stopped on a step.

"There. That's more like it," he replied.

Luis grabbed hold of both her wrists and dropped the rest of her body, full force, against the stairs. Sadie had no time to register the pain, too terrified of what lay ahead. She flailed with every available body part, but nothing affected him as he dragged her up the stairs. He outweighed her four pounds to one. "Let me go!" she screamed.

"Why? You're going to be dead soon anyway."

In a sudden burst of terrorized anger, she threw all her energy into one leg. The toe of her shoe rammed into the back of his thigh. He stumbled, nearly dropping her down the flight of stairs. Then suddenly he whirled. She saw his boot a second too late. It hit her ribs and sent her sailing against the wall. The air whooshed out of her. Pain engulfed her. She gasped and wheezed. Air. It felt like his four hundred pounds were kneeling on her chest, when in reality, he was leering at her from across the stairs.

"Come now, beautiful," he said through clenched teeth, "no more of that. You're going to be in enough pain as it is."

Breathe! she demanded her oxygen-deprived body. When the first breath came, it threw her back against the banister, starting the whole cycle over again. Screaming. Gasping for air. And writhing in agony.

In a whirl, she was off the stairs and over his shoulder. Sadie had no fight left. She was losing the battle with consciousness. Her vision was closing in on itself. White becoming black. She was drifting. Flying.

"Luis!" someone bellowed. A gun fired, spraying wood chips everywhere. "Drop her!"

Mr. Ugly obeyed, dropping her in an agonizing thud.

"Now get outside, Luis, before I shoot you myself. And you better run fast. I don't know how long I can restrain myself."

Sadie didn't have time to register what was happening. Her ribs were one giant explosion of pain. She cradled them in her arms, rolling around, trying desperately to inhale. Her ears were filled with screaming—her own—and she realized it was robbing her of the last of her oxygen. She forced her screams to groans and finally soft crying as she focused on taking each breath.

By the time her ears cleared, all was quiet around her. Her eyes cracked open. Manuel was kneeling beside her in Sam's upstairs hallway. "Are you okay?"

Her teeth were clenched too tightly to give any answer but a tear-drenched moan.

"Luis is a pig," he hissed. "Guillermo will make him pay for this."

As she found more air, a sob erupted. She couldn't help it. The sob sent her back into excruciating convulsions, starting the cycle all over again.

"He will pay dearly," Manuel muttered darkly. "I will see to it myself."

Manuel watched her as she, muscle by muscle, brought her body to a state of complete stillness. By the time she opened her eyes again, the reality of the moment hit her. Manuel was saving her. She wouldn't die. She wouldn't burn. She would live. Relief flooded over her. She'd always known Manuel wasn't capable of Guillermo's treachery.

"Thank you," she managed. "For saving . . . me."

He looked as though he'd been electrocuted. His hand flew off her and he stood. "I . . . Sadie, I . . . ."

Whatever brief glimpse of hope she had was shattered when his eyes could no longer meet hers. "Come," he said, pulling her up and carrying her weight with his arm. "It's time."

"Why?" she cried.

"I'm sorry, but I just can't do any more for you. Not this time. This cabin has to burn, and you must be in it. There is nothing I can do to stop that now."

"Please . . . just let me go. Guillermo won't know . . . I'll disappear . . . he'll think I'm dead . . . just please . . ." The tears flowed as she begged for her life.

Manuel stopped in the hallway, hesitating.

"Don't be what he is," she whispered. "You're better . . . better than this."

He studied her long enough for her to contemplate what it would mean to live, to see her mom again, her brother. But, with a glance out the window, he shook his head angrily. "Not anymore." And in one swift movement, he opened a door and dropped her on hard tile.

Sadie cried out as the floor aggravated her previous injuries. By the time she recovered, Manuel taped her up again, but instead of arching her hands behind her back, he taped them to the front of her ankles, being ironically compassionate one last time before she died.

"Manuel," she choked as he stood to leave. "For Guillermo . . ." Then she spat as far as she could.

He nodded sadly and shut the bathroom door, leaving her in total darkness. The closed door took every bit of light with it, and even more, accentuated the awareness that she was nearing the end of her life. Although she had tried to prepare herself, had spent two days convincing herself she was ready to die, she broke down. *Please!* she begged. *I don't want to die!*

CHAPTER 44

Josh looked up at the sound of a soft knock on Sadie's door. He didn't know how long he'd knelt on the floor, but before he could stand, Sadie's mom walked back in the room. She looked terrible—eyes puffy and red, her face etched in deep lines—and yet he searched beyond all that, desperate to find every resemblance she shared with her daughter.

For a long time, the two stared at each other, before Marcela whispered, "I'm sorry about before. I'm just not ready to accept . . ." Her hands covered her face as the emotions took over.

Josh stood and went to her. "Don't be sorry, Mrs. Dawson. This *is* my fault. If I hadn't left, none of this would have happened."

"No. You would just be missing as well."

"That would be better than being stuck here," he said softly, "not knowing what to do."

Her dark eyes met his, no longer filled with hatred, but carrying sorrow like he'd never seen. Knowing that he was the cause of such grief was more than he could bear. As he turned to leave, she said, "Do you think it is possible that Augustina didn't—"

"Yes," he interjected, before she could say the words neither of them wanted to hear. "Actually I think it's *impossible*. There's no way Sadie wrote that note on her own."

"She's never talked about death before, but she sounded so, so sad on the phone . . . and . . . ," her voice cracked. "I didn't help her. I could have stopped her, and I didn't do anything."

Josh went to Sadie's mom and took her by the shoulders. "Mrs. Dawson, there is absolutely, positively no way Sadie wrote those words on her own. They aren't hers. I'm sure of it." He waited until she looked up before finishing softly, "That wasn't Sadie."

She buried her face again. "*Oh, mi hija querida.* What has he done to you?"

Josh felt his chest cave, his throat swell without an answer.

"I never saw her the first time Guillermo hit her," she sniffed, "but she told me she looked awful."

"She did," Josh said, still haunted by the memory. "It wasn't just her eye, though. Her whole face was lifeless, so . . . not Sadie. But she wouldn't let us call anyone—not a doctor or the police or you. We felt so helpless."

Marcela gave him a weak smile. "You took care of her when I couldn't, Josh. My Augustina told me how you all took her in, cared for her, and kept her safe all those days. She told me how wonderful you were to her."

"Not wonderful," he corrected softly. "Horrible."

She didn't bother denying what they both knew. "Why were you coming back?" she asked in a whisper.

He couldn't respond immediately. "I was coming back to see if she would"—he shook his head angrily—"if she could take me back."

"Oh, Josh." Marcela laid a hand on his cheek. "My Augustina loves you. She told me. That's why she was leaving Guillermo."

"She shouldn't. She should hate me."

"Well . . ." A smile lit her dark eyes. "She may have said something about that, too."

He laughed in spite of himself. That was Sadie.

Marcela went to Sadie's bed and picked up the journal. "She has written in a journal since the time she was a little girl. And now that she's gone," she stroked the blue cover, "at least I have this much of her."

"Sadie's not gone, Mrs. Dawson," Josh said firmly. "We'll find her, don't worry. She's a fighter. She's probably fighting her way back to us right now. She'll know what to do. I only wish *I* knew what to do," he added quietly.

The door opened and Agent Madsen stormed back in. Josh crossed the room. "Was she at the cabin? Did they check the trail out back? Any sign of her anywhere?"

"No. Agent Griffin searched inside and out. The Jackson cabin is completely deserted."

"But . . ." Josh felt himself sink with his hopes. "But that can't be!"

Madsen's gaze flickered to Marcela. "May I speak with you alone a minute, Mr. Young?"

Josh nodded and quietly followed him into the hall, shutting the door behind them, and dreading what was so bad Sadie's mother couldn't hear.

"Guillermo's cabin is on fire," Madsen said without preamble.

Josh shook his head, not sure if he heard right. "What?"

"It's burning as we speak. The fire started twenty minutes ago and from the sounds of it, it's going to be a complete loss." Madsen turned and threw a fist against the wall.

"I'm sorry," Josh said, head spinning. "I can't keep up. Why would Guillermo's cabin . . . be . . ." He stopped, remembering. *It is time I burn the memories for good.* "Oh, no!" He started backing away from the images forming in his head. "No. NO!"

"I'm heading over there right now to check it out," Madsen said.

"I'm coming with you." And without waiting for approval, Josh ran back in Sadie's room and grabbed his coat.

In the cold darkness of the bathroom, Sadie was furiously trying to bite through the tape. She had no idea how much time she had before the fire reached her. She didn't know if Manuel had even set Sam's cabin on fire yet. She knew nothing except that she needed to get free. Her ribs burned with pain as she bent in half, and it took every ounce of strength to fight against her body's natural desire to flee pain, but she had to get low enough to her ankles to reach the tape with her teeth.

With another centimeter cut, she looked under the bathroom door. Still clear of smoke. The best she could hope was that Manuel had changed his mind. The worst was that the cabin was already burning, slowly creeping toward her just like Luis hoped. All she knew was—

A sudden explosion rocked the tile, answering all questions.

In a burst of sheer adrenaline, she yanked her hands back and ripped through the last inch of tape. She tore the tape from her ankles as well, and jumped up without thinking. It was like being hit by a semitruck. The pain knocked her backward. There was no time to recover.

She groped around the darkness and flipped on the light switch. She turned, searching. No window. She began pushing against the door, shoving, kicking, but whatever Manuel jammed up against the handle had her trapped.

"Help!" she screamed. She searched the cupboards for anything big and heavy to break down the door. Nothing but towels. She gave the door another painful kick. Nothing.

The first of the smoke began to seep under the door and what had been sheer terror turned into blood-curdling fear. She whirled around, grabbed the towels, and shoved them in the sink. *Faster!* she begged and hurled them into the tub. Every second it took the water to run, the smoke crept into the room. She swallowed several times in anticipation, and shoved the first sopping wet towel under the door. Too late. A cough erupted, exploding against her ribs.

She cried out. Drinking furious handfuls of water, she tried to wash away the irritation. The next towel went over her face, soaking her blouse with freezing water. She didn't have time to care. When the last towel was drenched, she doubled it over the first, hoping to buy some time before the smoke invaded her small corner of the cabin.

Now what? she begged the heavens.

There was a large crash downstairs and within seconds black haze was oozing through the heating vents as well.

Damien.

Her brother's name came from nowhere, but she spun around, searching the walls. Two were log; two were painted. She tapped on a smooth one, listening.

Taking a large step back, she kicked the wall with all her might. Though she was adding to her injuries, the shout that escaped her lips was one of joy. She'd made a hole. A small one, but it was enough to energize her to kick again with adrenaline-powered force. The hole grew and she ripped off a large chunk of the wall before kicking again. When she got through the bathroom layer, she started on the second. The first kick brought a glimpse of daylight.

"A window!" she cried out. She was going to make it. But with the hole came thick plumes of black smoke. The smoke burned her lungs and eyes, but she was almost free. She pressed the soaking towel over her face and kicked blindly. When the second hole was big enough, she hunched down and ripped like crazy—punching and tearing her way through.

One final blow and she fell halfway through the hole. The full onslaught of smoke entered the bathroom. She couldn't see a thing. Squeezing her body between the studs, she stumbled into the blackened bedroom. She stayed low and scrambled along the floor toward the dimming light.

She had one last thought before she unlatched the window. She dropped the soaking towel, grabbed the nearest blanket off the bed, and hefted the window wide open. The smoke came at her full force, happy for release. And the heat. Oppressive. Demanding.

Coughing and wheezing, she had to turn back one last time. She watched the flames engulfing Sam's beautiful hallway. "I'm so sorry," she whispered. With a cry of anguish, she lowered herself out the window, hung a brief second, and then let go.

From inside Agent Madsen's car, Josh watched the black smoke swirling in the sky. They were still a mile away, yet the thick plumes rising from Guillermo's cabin erased the setting sun.

Madsen was on the phone again, yelling. From the little Josh had gathered, Guillermo's cabin was for sale, supposedly listed a month earlier, though there was no prior record. Madsen insisted it was lies, lies, and more lies. When he hung up he let out a stream of profanities worthy of a biker brigade. "There's going to be nothing left!" Madsen fumed.

"Why?" Josh asked. "If Guillermo's behind the whole thing, why burn his own cabin?"

"Insurance money. Implicate Miss Dawson. Any number of reasons. The most devastating to us is wiping out any evidence."

Josh grew quiet, each word taking longer than the previous. "And you think . . . Sadie . . . could . . . have . . . been . . ."

Madsen didn't look away from the snowy road. "Yes."

Josh pinched his eyes shut and added to the never-ending prayer in his head.

The cell phone rang again and Madsen scowled before he even answered it. "Yes," he barked. "Yes, I'm almost there now." His brows pulled down heavily. He was quiet a moment before glancing over at Josh. "Are you sure?" Another pause. "Agreed."

As he snapped his phone shut, Josh asked, "What now?"

"There's another cabin burning. On the south side of the mountain."

"Another? Do you think it's somehow connected?"

"Yes." Madsen gripped the steering wheel. "It's your friend's cabin."

Josh's mind went blank. "Sam's cabin?" He yanked off his seatbelt and twisted around, trying to see out the back window. He searched every hill, every mountainside in hopes of finding another trail of smoke. It was too far. Too far!

"I'm sorry, Mr. Young. By the time we send over the remaining fire trucks, it will be another complete loss. We'll head over there as soon as I check out this one."

"No!" Josh cried. "I have to go there now!"

"Right after I check out the Vasquez cabin."

Josh grabbed the door handle and yanked it open.

Madsen slammed on the brakes, sending the navy sedan sliding on the snow. "Are you crazy?"

"Look, I have to get there now, so either you take me or I find it myself."

Agent Madsen watched him carefully, then swearing under his breath, he flipped the car around and sped back the way they'd come.

CHAPTER 45

There was nothing left. Just a shell of blackened logs and the large stone fireplace. Josh couldn't take his eyes off the horrific scene. Even several hours after the last of the flames had been extinguished, Sam's cabin was still smoldering heavily. A few pines closest to the cabin had been lost, but because of the heavy snow, the rest of the Jacksons' property had been saved. Josh spent two hours searching the trees and woods with a group of officers and a large searchlight. They stayed close to the trail out back, calling Sadie's name, but there was no sign of her anywhere. So he watched the cabin smolder, unable to accept what his eyes told him to be true.

Someone laid a hand on his arm. His dad. He'd just arrived from Spokane and received a briefing from people who spoke the same police language as him. "I'm going up to her car. Do you want to come?"

"No," Josh said. He'd already seen Sadie's car pulled off into the woods just up the road. His hopes had soared and sunk in a matter of seconds. Sadie wasn't in the car, nor anywhere around. Her tiny footsteps lead directly to Sam's cabin but not beyond. What had only been a small possibility of her being in the burning wreckage, suddenly became an inevitability and the overwhelming sense of dread grew into an all-consuming grief. Sadie's mom finally had to be given a sedative.

Just like the cabin, Josh hadn't been allowed inside Sadie's car nor anywhere near it, but supposedly the interior reeked of gasoline. And her credit card had been charged at the gas station down the road just five hours before. Five! As if that wasn't enough, a torn-up picture of Guillermo was also found inside her car. With that and the suicide note, everything was made to appear that she was responsible for both fires, taking revenge on the two men she hated. Josh refused to believe it. Thankfully, so did Madsen. So Josh stood, completely numb—not from the temperature, but from the day.

"Sir?" someone said from behind. "Mr. Young?"

"Yes," he said, without turning.

"It's going to be several hours, possibly longer, before we can search the ruins. Please, go back to the lodge and get some sleep. We'll call you in the morning when it's safe."

Josh shook his head. He wasn't going anywhere. Not without Sadie.

The officer watched him another moment, but like everyone else, he walked away.

As dawn broke in the Montana mountains, six men huddled in the cold, still somewhat in shock. Sam was talking softly to Kevin, Trevor, and his dad, all of whom had arrived from Washington to see what was left of the Jackson cabin. Peter Young, however, stayed close to his son, who was becoming more and more withdrawn.

"I'm so sorry, Dr. Jackson," Kevin was saying.

"It's okay," Sam's dad replied, though his voice spoke otherwise. "It's just a cabin."

"There's no way she was here," Trevor added. "No way. That jerk has her somewhere. I'm sure of it! They need to track him down, figure out where he—"

Josh left the five of them, passing Sam's mom who had an arm wrapped tightly around Marcela, and went straight to Madsen. The FBI agent had been bouncing back and forth between the two cabins all night, and was just now arriving back at Sam's. Madsen was hunched over with a mug of steaming coffee. "Any news?" Josh asked.

"Not much. Guillermo flew from Canada to France and then chartered a private jet from there. My best guess is that he'll hop countries until he disappears. He's not going to resurface anytime soon."

It was like Josh was on autopilot. His mouth asked the questions he needed to know, without any effort or emotion whatsoever. "Any sign he took Sadie with him?"

"None. We're working with the Canadian and French authorities as well as our own. I'm still hopeful we'll find something at his cabin to help, but quite frankly, there's not much left."

Another agent approached them. Madsen excused himself and moved away. There wasn't a single thought in Josh's head as he stared at the wreckage. He wouldn't allow it. He had shut down mentally, finding safety there.

Someone put an arm around his waist. Sam's mom. "You look exhausted, Josh. Did you sleep at all last night?"

He shook his head imperceptibly.

"You're going to collapse. You need to sleep. Why don't you lie down in the truck for a minute. Take a quick nap. That way you're still around if we hear anything."

"No. I'm okay."

"What about to warm up then? You must be freezing. You've been outside all night."

"I'm not cold."

She looked at him in disbelief.

"Hey," Kevin said, coming up behind them. "I'm heading to the lodge. You guys want some breakfast?"

Sam's mom looked up at Josh. "That's a good idea. Thanks, Kevin."

As Kevin walked away, she tried again. "Look, Josh, I'm here if anything happens. Why don't you go lay down in your dad's . . ."

Her words faded as Josh watched Kevin open the driver's door of

Sam's truck. Rocky was inside barking wildly, and Kevin had to grab his collar before he could escape.

Josh's previously shutdown brain kicked into gear. "Hey, Sister Jackson," he interrupted, "can I borrow Rocky for a minute?"

She followed his gaze. "Umm, sure. Go ahead."

Josh sprinted through the maze of police cars to Sam's truck and pounded on the passenger window. Kevin flinched and then cracked the window. "Yeah?" he shouted over the barking.

"I'll keep Rocky," Josh said without further explanation.

"I don't know if that's a good idea. Rocky's really freaked out by the fire. We're trying to keep him away from . . ." Whatever Kevin saw in Josh's face was enough to change his mind. "Okay. Sure."

Josh opened the passenger door slowly and caught Rocky by the collar before he could break free. Rocky was barking, jumping, and thrashing—a powerful dog when he wanted to be—and Josh struggled to keep hold of him.

Kevin jumped out of the truck. "Here's his leash. You're gonna need it."

With the leash hooked, Josh knelt in the snow in front of the black lab. Rocky quieted momentarily, surprised to have Josh nose to nose with him. "You have to help me find her," Josh whispered. "Can you do that? I know she's out there somewhere. Please."

Rocky started backing away from him, trying to break free. When he couldn't, he lowered his head and began to growl. Josh rubbed him between the eyes to calm him down. It worked. For a split second. Then Rocky took off. He was headed down the driveway on a dead run. In the wrong direction.

Josh yanked back on the leash, stopping Rocky's fast progression. The dog yelped, but Josh began dragging him up the snowy driveway, furiously trying to redirect Sam's dog. They needed to search the trail behind the cabin, but Rocky wanted nothing to do with anything by the cabin, and instead was throwing his full weight against the leash.

"Rocky!" Kevin yelled. "Sorry, Josh. He's been acting like this since we pulled up."

The dog was howling and moaning in protest, but Josh was determined. And desperate. He kept pulling the leash, hand over hand.

"Rocky!" Sam shouted from by the cabin. "Sit!"

With a whine of defeat, the dog dropped to its haunches.

Josh started down the driveway, wondering if this whole thing was a bad idea. He had no idea how to get Rocky to comply. The beast only listened to Sam any—

Rocky bolted. When Josh was just a few feet away, the dog jumped up and took off, yanking the leash clear from Josh's hands. Within seconds, he was down the driveway, on the road, and sprinting back toward the main road.

"Rocky!" Josh and several others shouted.

The dog was long gone.

"I'll get him, Josh," Kevin called.

Josh waved him off, already racing down the snowy road after him. He kept calling Rocky's name, but it didn't do any good. The dog was headed for home.

"Rocky! Sit!" Josh yelled as he slipped and slid down the ice. He rounded a curve and just got the black fur in sight again when the dog unexpectedly broke from the road, leaped over a snowbank, and disappeared behind a patch of trees. Out of breath, Josh plunged in after him.

Rocky's barking doubled, as did his speed, but at least Josh had tracks. Still calling out, he wound around the snow-covered trees, trying to spot anything black.

"Rocky! Come! Now! ROCKY!"

The dog finally obeyed, emerging from under a thick group of pines. Josh was about to give him a piece of his mind when he saw that he had something in his jaws. He dragged the object toward Josh, making Josh think that they were snow-covered and breathless all for some stupid squirrel. But the object in Rocky's jaws was too big for an animal. And it was checkered.

Checkered?

Josh covered the remaining distance as Rocky dropped the checkered object on the snow. Josh picked it up in surprise. It was a blanket. From an upstairs room in Sam's cabin.

Barking excitedly, Rocky took off again. Josh didn't stop him. Instead, he chased him full speed as the dog darted under the branches of a huge pine tree. Josh pulled up the lowest branches and followed him under. It took a second for his eyes to adjust and then he froze. There was a wet heap on the dirt.

"Sadie?"

In one giant leap he was to her side. Her body was curled in a ball, and she was completely motionless. "Sadie?" He knelt beside her and gathered her into his arms. Then he turned her face. He gasped. Any skin that wasn't soot-covered and bloody was pure gray.

He put his face to hers, cringing when her icy skin brushed against his. Holding his breath, he listened for anything, any sign of life. Nothing. Yanking off his coat, he wrapped it around her, and then he grabbed her ice-cold hand and began blowing warm air on it.

"Come on. Please wake up. Please. Breathe. Something!"

He checked her breathing again, even laying his fingers on the side of her neck for a pulse. When both came back with nothing, he frantically yelled over his shoulder. "HELP! Please help me!" His voice echoed off the trees, with little chance of carrying.

Tucking her gray face into his chest, he picked up her still, small form and darted back under the branches. Then he half-ran, half-stumbled through the deep snow, covering the same distance he'd just come in half the time. "Dad!" he yelled.

Chapter 46

Josh laid Sadie on a blanket, and Sam piled several others from squad cars on top of her. Marcela draped herself over it all, sobbing, while Sam's father listened for a pulse.

Sadie looked ten times worse in the full light of day. Her face was a sickening gray, her lips and ears, a pale blue. Every part of her was covered in black smears, dried blood, and ashes, including what remained of her hair. Josh couldn't allow himself to imagine what she'd been through, or what was to come. He just kept her icy hand by his mouth, willing her to breathe.

When Sam's dad looked up, his expression was grim. "She's breathing—barely—but severely hypothermic. Stage two, maybe three," he added to Sam.

Peter Young put a hand on Josh's shoulder. "She needs a blessing."

Josh shook his head. "I—I'm not sure if I can," he stuttered, too overwhelmed to think.

"You can," his dad said. "She needs you. You need to do this for her." Dr. Jackson and Sam were nodding in agreement. Even Marcela stopped crying and looked up.

Josh could barely choke out the words, "Can I . . ." before she broke down again.

"Yes! Anything. Help her. Please!"

Josh looked from Sam, to the doctor, then to his dad. With a nod, each quickly closed the distance and put their hands on Sadie's cold, damp head.

The water on Whitefish Lake wasn't the clear glass Sadie was used to. It was dark and violent, as if she were in a bad storm. Looking up to the blackened sky, she realized she *was* in a bad storm. Her clothes were wet and heavy against her body, making movement difficult. Still, she walked swiftly, hoping to make it to safety before the rain started.

Too late.

The first raindrop hit her arm with a sizzling sensation. The second was so hot it scorched her cheek. And with each subsequent drop, the heat increased, until it felt like she was on fire from head to toe. She began to run, trying to escape the acid rain, but the stinging droplets only pelted against her harder and harder, burning her flesh.

It registered that there was something very wrong with this dream. It shouldn't have been this painful—*it shouldn't have been painful at all!*—but from her fingers to her toes, it felt like she was being sprayed with boiling water.

She screamed out. At the same, precise moment the bullet hit her, penetrating deep into her lungs. Her body collapsed, wheezing and writhing, as the sharp rocks lining the shore tore into her flesh. *This is just a dream. Just a dream! Wake up!* But she couldn't. The darkness was pulling in around her. Only this time it was a darkness of the mind. Clouding. Hovering. And she could feel herself slipping. Losing herself to it.

Josh! she tried to shout. Nothing crossed her parched lips.

"It's over now," he said in response.

Over, she repeated. She could feel his calm words release her. She gave up the fight. It was over now. Her limbs went slack, her muscles relaxed, and immediately, the pain was gone. Her skin. Her lungs. Everything felt whole. *It's over,* she said again in awe, and then she closed her eyes and welcomed the blackness that swallowed her up.

"Mrs. Dawson, please!" Josh shouted. "Let the paramedics work."

Marcela tried to shove him away. "No! Let go of me! Augustina!" she wailed.

He tugged harder on her shoulders. She broke free and threw herself over her daughter's now-still form. "Augustina! Don't leave me! NO!" She'd watched her daughter go from writhing, to screaming, to absolutely nothing at all.

It took both Dr. Jackson and Josh to drag her away. Then Josh locked her in a long, hard embrace. She pounded her fists against his chest. "Stop! Let me see her! You can't do this!"

"Mrs. Dawson," Josh said firmly. "It's okay. Sadie's going to be okay. Look . . ." He turned her face with his hand. "Look at the blankets . . . and her face . . ."

Marcela wiped her eyes, doing as commanded. Through the rush of medics, she saw the blankets that covered Augustina were moving with each breath. Not only that, but already the gruesome gray lips were fading into a life-giving pink.

"She's going to be okay," Josh insisted quietly.

Marcela crumpled against his chest in a great sobbing heap, grieving for what almost was. Josh simply stroked her hair. "*Está bien,*" he whispered. "She's okay."

CHAPTER 47

Sadie woke to a loud beeping next to her head. Her eyelids were heavy—too heavy—but she forced them open enough to look around. She was in a semidark room. A small fluorescent light shined in one corner and for some reason her mom was asleep on a cot next to her. Stranger still, an unfamiliar woman hovered over her, pressing buttons on a loud machine.

"Where—" Sadie cleared her voice, finding it soft and scratchy. "Where am I?"

"Hillside Terrace," the woman whispered back.

Though she had never heard of it, Sadie took in the woman's scrubs, the white blanket covering her legs, the uncomfortable IV strapped to her arm, and the tremendous pain stretching from her ribs to her feet and figured she was in a hospital—though why, she wasn't sure.

Her lids began to droop again. Blinking quickly, she asked, "What happened?"

The nurse smiled. "A lot of people are wondering the same thing. You're one lucky lady, Kristina."

Sadie didn't have time to correct her as it registered that someone was squeezing her hand on the other side of her bed. She mustered up enough energy to move her head around. The man sitting beside her squeezed her hand again. "Hello, beautiful."

She fought against her eyelids, wanting to see his face. *Josh?* Though she couldn't remember why, she knew Josh didn't belong in this strange place. Of course, neither did she. Her mind was mush, trying to figure out why she was there, in a hospital. Broken.

Suddenly her eyes flew open, remembering the last time she'd seen that face. New Year's Day. Josh's rejection was still fresh in her mind. As was the Guillermo rebound. *Guillermo?* The memories flowed faster and faster until she remembered exactly why she was strapped to a hospital bed, broken. Her mind was a torrent of emotion, and she couldn't think beyond one fact. She didn't want Josh there.

She slipped her hand from his. "Why are you here?"

His brows raised in shock. "I . . ."

"Please leave," she said, trying to keep control over her voice.

The nurse quickly busied herself with paperwork. Sadie waited for Josh to argue, but instead he stood slowly and walked to the door. She couldn't help but watch him go.

When the light from the hallway hit the cot next to her, her mom rolled over. "Oh, dear. I dozed off again." Then she saw him holding the door and sat up. "Did you finally decide to eat?"

Josh's gaze went back to Sadie. She pretended not to notice. But her mom nearly fell off the cot. "She's awake?" she cried.

"Yes," Josh answered. "I'll be out here if you need me, Marcela."

The nurse quietly made her exit as well, leaving Sadie with her mom, overjoyed and hovering. "You *are* awake, Augustina!"

"Unfortunately," Sadie muttered. Every breath took effort.

Her mom's smile faded. "How do you feel?"

"I hurt. Everywhere."

Marcela patted her arm, as tears cascaded down her cheeks. "Oh, my sweet *hijita*. Do you remember anything?"

Sadie shut her eyes, but only briefly before the memories could consume her. "A little."

"Oh, baby," she sobbed. "What would I have done without you?"

"I'm okay, Mom," Sadie said, rubbing her back. And then it dawned on her. She really *was* okay. She had survived Guillermo. Somehow. *I wonder if he*—her heart leaped into her throat—*knows.* "Mom!" she choked. "Guillermo!" She tried to sit, forgetting her current broken state. She cried out, but continued urgently. "You have to go. If Guillermo knows I'm alive, he'll come after you. Please! You have to go now!"

"No, no, Augustina. Agent Madsen has it all under control. I am safe. You are safe, too. You just need to get better."

Madsen? Hearing the agent's name didn't exactly put her at ease. She fell back against the bed. For the moment, at least, they were safe. Sadie's muscles relaxed against her bed. *And Josh, too,* she realized. He was alive. They all were. Hot tears fell down her cheeks, tears of shame, fear, and pure exhaustion. All of them had survived Guillermo—for now.

Humming softly, her mom brushed some hair from her forehead. "Damien is on his way from California. He should be here in a few hours."

"Damien? Mom . . ." she moaned. "I'm just fine, or"—she shifted her foot, which for some reason was in a cast—"at least I'm going to be. Please. I don't want anyone to see me like this."

"Is that why you sent Josh away?"

"He was here," Sadie said softly, still confused.

"Of course he's here. Why did you send him away? The poor man hasn't left your side for a second."

Her embarrassment quickly turned to anger. "Why is he here? To gloat? To rub it in that he was right and I was wrong? That Guillermo wanted to kill me all along?"

Marcela jerked back, stunned by her daughter's blinding anger. But just as fast, she was patting her hand again. "Oh, *hija,* I understand why you're angry, but so much has happened since New Year's. Josh came back for you. He found you."

"Please, Mom. Not now. Not like this."

Thankfully her mom didn't push, leaving her time to contemplate having Josh back in her life.

There was a soft knock, and they both turned. When Sadie saw the face that peeked in she broke into a smile. "Kevin!" she tried to call, though she couldn't get enough air in her lungs to make it carry. Like Josh, there was no reason for Kevin to be back in Montana, but unlike Josh, she was thrilled to see him.

He crossed the room to her. "Hey, girl, you don't look so good."

"Thanks. Nice to see you, too." But suddenly she wondered how true that was. She hadn't seen a mirror, and this time she didn't want to. "Seems a little familiar, doesn't it?"

His smile faded. "Eerily familiar."

She didn't like seeing Kevin without a smile and so she changed the subject. "Why are you in Montana?"

"Oh, I was just in the neighborhood. Thought I'd stop by."

Sadie laughed. Bad mistake. Her ribs cut into her lungs, which shot a pain down to her broken ankle. Like a chain reaction, one place set off the next, and it took nearly a minute to get back to a spasmless state. Kevin watched it all in wide-eyed horror.

"Oh, I'm sorry, Sadie. Really, really, really sorry. I won't make you laugh anymore."

"It's not that bad," she managed. "Remember . . . I'm Ice Woman."

"I don't think I like that name anymore," he said, barely audible. "We didn't think you were going to make it there for a while. You were so cold and gray. I don't think I've ever been so scared in my life. You looked dead. It wasn't until after Josh did that prayer thing that—"

"Don't," Sadie cut in suddenly.

Kevin looked shocked, but her mom quickly said, "Tell her. Tell her what Josh did."

His eyes widened in sudden understanding. "Oh, Sadie girl, if you only knew what that guy has been through the past few days—longer actually—you'd understand. Don't shut him out. I've never seen a guy so low. He's beat himself enough over this. He blames himself for everything that happened to you."

She closed her eyes, the only way she knew to make it stop.

After a minute, he sighed. "I guess she needs to sleep. Agent Madsen's out there wondering if he can question her yet. What do you want me to tell him?"

"Give her some time," her mother replied quietly, but Sadie spoke over her.

"No. It's okay, Kevin. He can come in. I have some questions of my own."

Kevin nodded. "Okay. I'll be back later."

"Oh, Kevin," her mom called as he opened the door, "Could you send Josh in for me?"

"No!" Sadie shrieked.

Marcela continued, ignoring her eruption. "I need him to get something for me."

"What?" Sadie challenged. Her mom just shrugged.

Kevin chuckled. "I see where you get it from, Sadie."

As he left, suddenly his words played over and over in Sadie's mind. *You don't look so good.* Her eyes took in the ugly hospital gown, while her hand felt around her face. She had no idea how bad it was. Except one thing. Her hand slid around the side of her head. The hair there was short, so incredibly short! "How bad do I look?" she whispered.

"Oh, Augustina! Of all the things to worry about. You look beautiful. Josh hasn't stopped staring at you. I really like him by the way," she added with a grin.

"Mom, please!"

Sadie closed her eyes, wishing to rush sleep. She wasn't ready for him.

Even when she heard the door open, she left her lashes on her red-hot cheeks.

Her mother kissed her forehead and, in an act of pure treason, left her side.

"Just love her," Sadie heard her whisper across the room.

"I do," Josh's soft voice floated back.

Then Sadie listened in horror as her mom walked out of her hospital room, leaving her utterly and completely alone with him.

CHAPTER 48

Sadie refused to open her eyes. She didn't know what to say to Josh, or what to feel or think or do, so she lay there, pretending to sleep. After a minute he sighed and went back to the chair he'd been in before. "How do you feel?" he asked gently.

"Never better," she quipped.

"Wow," he said with a smile in his voice. "You really *are* going to be okay. I mean, if you have enough fight left to fight me, then you're really going to—"

"Please leave, Josh," she whispered. "Please." Her eyes were burning behind her lids, threatening to erupt, but she maintained her resolve.

It took a minute for him to speak, and then it came out in a whisper, "Okay."

She cracked open an eye. His head was down, his shoulders slumped, but he locked eyes with her for the briefest second.

"You look awful!" she blurted.

He smiled weakly. "Thanks."

"No seriously . . ." He had heavy circles under eyes, his dark hair was going every which way—which she'd never seen—and he hadn't shaved in several days. Even his clothes were filthy and wrinkled. And his eyes . . . that was the worst part. The blue had faded to a worn-out gray.

Seeing him in such disarray softened her. Maybe Guillermo had found him after all. "What happened?" she asked gently.

"You're asking what happened to *me*?"

"Yes. Seriously. You look terrible."

He shook his head incredulously. "You."

That wasn't quite the answer she expected. Maybe Kevin was right. She really didn't know what Josh had been through. She propped herself up for a better view of him. Only her body didn't react kindly. It kinked something in her back. Wincing, she shifted to the left but her hand slipped out from under her, jarring her ribs. That time she cried out.

"What can I do?" he asked, instantly beside her. "Do you want me to get you something? Call the nurse? The doctor? What?"

"Nothing," she said through clenched teeth.

"More medicine," he said, pushing the nurse's button.

She continued searching for the painless position from before, but the more she moved, the worse it got. Her legs. Her back. Her ribs. "What happened to me?" she cried in frustration.

Josh fell back in his chair. "Now there's a logical question. What did happen to you? I almost lost you. Again."

His question wasn't one she trusted herself to answer and she hid from the memories before they overwhelmed her. She had been avoiding them, pushing them aside any time they surfaced, and shifting the blame to someone else just to ease the burden. But the alternative was more than she could bear, so she left his question unanswered. Even in her own mind.

Instead, she lost herself in those gray eyes, struck again by the sight of him. She really had no idea what had happened to him or anyone else. Or even the cabin, for that matter. *The cabin,* she cried silently. The last she remembered seeing was an angry mass of red flames.

"How bad is the damage?" she asked.

"Three broken ribs, a broken ankle, a huge lump on the back of your head, a welt next to your nose, cuts and bruises—the most disturbing of which are on your wrists and ankles—and half your beautiful hair is gone."

Sadie stared at him in shock. "That's not what I meant, but, wow, all that?"

He nodded as his gaze fell to her hands. Sadie looked down as well and saw what he did. Ugly red welts like twin bracelets. She quickly pulled her hands under the blankets and ran through his list again. All of it fit her areas of pain, but still . . . that was a lot of "brokens." "No wonder I feel like I'd rather be dead," she muttered.

Josh's head jerked up so fast, she flinched. "Please don't say that."

"I—I'm sorry. I didn't mean it."

"I know. I know." He exhaled a little. "Sorry. It's just kind of a sensitive subject for me."

Her eyes locked on his a moment before she had to turn away. "What I was trying to ask was how bad is the cabin. Was any of it saved?"

"No. Both were destroyed."

"Both?"

His face pulled down in confusion. "Yes. Sam's and Guillermo's."

"What?" She sat up too quickly and was gasping for air again. He punched the nurse's button several more times, and then a few more just to be sure. "What happened to Guillermo's cabin?" she choked out.

"The same thing. It burned to the ground."

"But why? That doesn't make any sense. Sam's was for me. Why the other?"

"I don't know, Sadie. You know more than any of the rest of us. I can't figure out why you were at Sam's cabin, or why that agent didn't find you. I can't figure out why it was on fire or why Guillermo would burn his own. But the most incomprehensible thing is how your beat-up, tied-up, ash-covered body was able to get out. I don't know anything except that you're here, alive, and nothing else matters."

Something finally clicked. Josh was here. In her room. With her. She lay back and closed her eyes. *What must he think of me?* Her breath caught. What if he read the suicide note? Though she couldn't remember the particulars, she remembered enough. She couldn't live without him and had run off to kill herself. No wonder he thought it was all his fault.

His chair squeaked, and she opened her eyes in time to see him make his way around her bed. "I'm going to find a nurse," he said quietly. "You just sleep."

"I'm sorry," she whispered. "For everything."

"Don't, Sadie. Don't apologize. None of this would have happened if I hadn't left."

"That's not true. You'd just be in the next bed down. Or worse. Dead. Look what I've done to you," she said, dissolving into tears. "You were the one who told me—"

He stepped forward and pressed his fingers to her lips. "Really, Sadie. I'm not joking. I need you to keep hating me right now. It will make both of us feel better."

His fingers on her lips, so warm and familiar, had her thinking all sorts of crazy things. *He said he loved me, right?* But as she reached for him, Josh flinched away and shoved his hands in his pockets. "Sorry." And then the nurse poked her head in.

"Did you need something?"

"Nope," Sadie answered. "We're good."

"She needs more meds," Josh said over her. "Something strong."

"No!" Sadie cried a little too desperately. She had way too much to figure out, and drugs would only interfere. "I don't want to feel foggy again. Or sleep anymore. I'm okay. Really."

"Despite what she says," Josh countered, "she's in a lot of pain."

"I can ask the doctor if he has something else," the nurse offered instead.

As the nurse left, Sadie's mom came back in with Agent Madsen on her heels. Sadie groaned for more than one reason. "Is this a bad time?" Madsen asked.

"Yes," Josh and Sadie said together.

Madsen came in anyway. "Mr. Hancock said you were ready to talk, Miss Dawson."

Sadie rolled her eyes. *Nice greeting.* Not a "Hey, Sadie, how are you feeling?" or "Hey, Sadie, I'm really sorry I just about got you killed again." She really couldn't stand that man.

"I can wait if you don't feel well enough," he continued, "but I'd rather not."

"She doesn't," Josh snapped.

Sadie smiled because it sounded like he couldn't stand Madsen either. But at the same time, she was ready to be done. "It's okay, Josh. I want to get this over with."

Madsen pulled a chair to the small table at the foot of her bed. Josh, however, was watching her, trying to ask if she really was up for it. Yet looking into his weary, almost unrecognizable face, she knew it was he who wasn't up for it.

"You should go," she said softly.

A look of pure rejection washed over him, misunderstanding.

"Augustina," her mom chided, "let him stay. He wants to know what happened to you. We all do."

"You, too, Mamá," she added.

Her eyes widened in betrayal. "No. I want to be here. I want to help you through this!"

Josh went to Marcela and, with an arm around her shoulders, began walking her toward the door. Still she protested, tears erupting as she did. "It'll be okay," Josh insisted. "Just let Sadie say what she needs. You don't need any more images haunting you at night."

Sadie watched the two of them, curious. Somehow in the time she'd been fighting for her life, Josh and her mom had bonded—quite strongly from the looks of it. As touching as that was, Sadie suddenly wanted his comfort, too, his strong arm holding her together. The truth was, she was terrified to relive the past four days. And yet, she needed to be done with it all. But not alone. Not anymore. "Josh?" she called softly. Both of them turned. "Stay?"

Josh was dumbfounded, but Marcela looked shattered. He whispered something to her, hugged her briefly, and then let her walk out of the room alone.

Madsen had been waiting semipatiently through the whole exchange and motioned for Josh to sit beside him. Then he pulled out a recorder, looked at Sadie, and said, "Go ahead."

CHAPTER 49

Unable to look at either man, Sadie focused on the three sterile glove dispensers across the room and began where Agent Madsen's knowledge left off. The note. Both Madsen and Josh stayed silent while she spoke, allowing the memories to flow: hiding behind the ice machine, memorizing every turn Salvador took so she could escape and find her way back to the lodge. But the further she got in the story, the harder the words became. Her hand moved with her memories. To the cut on her neck. To what was left of her hair. "I thought Guillermo was going to end it right there," she whispered.

"Did he mention anything about the shots outside his cabin?" Madsen asked. "Surely he read of your suspicion in your journal."

"No, but Luis told me that the whole thing was a setup, to check my loyalty to Guillermo." *You really are stupid,* he laughed from her memories.

Madsen frowned. "I don't buy it. I think Guillermo knew you witnessed a homicide, and he was ready to get rid of you—especially after you came to me with the information. You would be—and now are—the closest thing I have to a witness."

"Who?" she asked softly. "Who did he kill?"

"My partner. Stephen Dubois."

"The one from Christmas?" she cried. Her heart sped up, picturing his young face on the snow below her. Her throat clogged. "I could have saved him," she whispered. "I just stood there. I didn't call the police. I did nothing. I can't . . ." Her stomach rolled. "Oh no . . ."

"Had you acted differently that evening, Miss Dawson, I'm convinced Vasquez would have finished you off as well. The first shot was most likely the one that killed Dubois. He was dead before you could have helped."

What if he wasn't? She pressed the heels of her hands into her eyes.

"Help his family now by finishing your story. Help me put together a case against his murderer. Dubois had no chance that night. Give me a chance now. So let me ask again, did Vasquez mention anything about the shooting when he threatened you in his car?"

Sadie wiped her cheeks. "No. I'm sorry. He was mad about something else."

"What?"

Her eyes flickered to Josh, suddenly remembering he was there, and suddenly thinking that making him stay was a very, *very* bad idea.

"What?" Madsen prodded.

"I think she's done," Josh answered when she didn't. "She needs to sleep."

"No." She closed her eyes. It was inevitable. "Guillermo read things I had written in my journal. Things"—she swallowed—"about Josh." Her gaze went back to Josh. He was staring at her horrified. *It's my fault,* she wanted to say. For showing up at the cabin. For dragging him into her nightmare of a life. For New Year's. For writing about him in her journal. All her fault. Not his. But she could see that he felt the opposite, and she hated herself for it.

"And?" Madsen asked.

She focused on the glove dispensers. *Just get it over with.* "Guillermo asked me if Josh was the same guy he met on New Year's Eve, even though from my journal he must have already known. When I wouldn't answer, he . . . pulled out a gun."

Josh flinched but Madsen was all business. "Did you get a look at the type of gun it was, anything that could identify it?"

"No, but I've seen it before. Maybe with pictures I could identify it."

"Good. Go on."

"So . . . Guillermo asked again if the guy in my journal was the one he met at the party." Josh's head dropped onto the small table, but it was too late. "And . . . and . . ." she tried. Tears erupted, hot and hard. "And I told him yes! I'm sorry, Josh! I'm such a coward! Guillermo said he should have just killed you at the party instead of having to hunt you down later."

"Hunt?" Madsen repeated, leaning forward. "Josh?"

"Yes! He'll go after him and he won't stop. You have to do something! You have to—"

Madsen held up a hand. "I'll take care of it. You're safe. Your mom is safe. And Mr. Young is here." He sighed. "We'll worry about the rest later. For now, just finish."

She waited for Josh to lift his head off the table, to show some sign that he understood her cowardice. He didn't, so she rushed on. The threats. Guillermo forcing her to write the note. "I think he hit me a couple of times, it's a blur, but the next thing I knew, I was on the floor of Sam's cabin, all tied—"

Josh's head jerked up. He stared at her a long moment, before facing Madsen. Madsen, however, kept his eyes on Sadie. "When was that approximately?"

"I don't know. It was dark out, maybe nine o'clock on the same night I talked to you."

"I knew it!" Josh exploded. He jumped to his feet and started pacing. He stopped long enough to shout at Madsen. "I told you!"

Sadie stared at him in shock, but Madsen whipped out his phone. "Mercer . . ." Madsen hissed angrily, "take Agent Griffin into custody . . . I know, I know! Just do it!" Then Madsen slammed the phone shut.

Sadie looked back and forth between the two men. "What? What did I say?"

Neither heard her. "Does this Agent Griffin know she's alive?" Josh said in the agent's face. "Does he know where she is now? Has he already contacted Guillermo? Just how many leaks do you have?"

"No, no, no," Madsen answered, trying to keep up. "No one in my department knows anything for this reason. As far as they know, Miss Dawson's dead and I'm writing up my report."

"Will someone please tell me what's going on?" Sadie shouted over them both.

Madsen folded his arms. "I think we found our leak, Guillermo's little pawn in our department." Sadie waited for more explanation, but he barked at her. "Continue!"

She couldn't, though. She was watching Josh pace. Something she said had him shaking with fury. And then the nurse walked in again, only this time with a doctor. The doctor, oblivious to his tense surroundings, began asking her a series of questions: pain levels, breathing abilities.

Sadie did her best to answer, distracted by the furious whispers taking place at the bottom of her bed. Words like *counseling* and *permanent protection* kept jumping out at her. But it wasn't until the doctor said something about her being the youngest patient he'd ever treated, that she tuned back in. "You put me in a nursing home?" she cried.

Madsen nodded. "Josh's idea."

"Don't worry, Kristina," the doctor continued, "We're well equipped to handle . . ."

His words faded out and eventually he did as well. The war of words had ended at the foot of her bed. Madsen looked ready to continue. Josh, however, looked sick. So she went on in a haze. Freezing on the cabin floor. The gasoline. Mr. Ugly.

"Two days and he wouldn't shut up," she said. "I can tell you every relative in every town he's lived in. He kept saying that it was an art to get a whole cabin to burn, especially before the fire could be put out. But all I could think was, *Not the picture. Not the picture.*"

"What picture?" Josh asked softly.

Surprised, she broke out of her trance. It was the first time Josh had spoken directly to her through her whole narrative. "The Jackson family," she said. "I stared at it the whole two days, thinking it was the most beautiful picture I'd ever seen. I was envious of Sam's parents for their family, their happiness. I couldn't stand the thought of them being burned." Her voice cracked. "Not even in a picture. I can't believe what I've done to them."

Josh left his chair and came to her side. He reached up and brushed the tears from her cheeks. "It wasn't your fault, Sadie. You have to believe that. It's Guillermo's fault. All of it."

She closed her eyes, enjoying the brief physical contact. As he started to pull away, she grabbed his hand. "Stay," she whispered.

A light touched his eyes for the first time. Josh took both her hands in his and faced Madsen. Ready to be done as well, she rushed on. Luis. Manuel. She was on autopilot, letting the memories flow. It wasn't until Josh suddenly stiffened that she stopped. She quickly rewound her last sentence and froze as well.

"Is that why he cut you loose?" Madsen asked, leaning forward.

She thought back to Luis's horrible face, his filthy hands, the unmistakable look of lust in his eyes, and being helpless to it all. Suddenly her body was done. Her breathing accelerated, her mind raced, and in an instant, she was shaking head to toe.

"Sadie?" Josh squeezed her hand. When she couldn't respond, he said, "I think she's done."

"Do you want to continue, Miss Dawson?" Madsen asked.

"Yes." The word formed in her mouth only. There wasn't air enough to push it out. Luis was coming. She was dying. Smoke. Couldn't breathe. Guillermo. The gun. The nightmares would never end. They were only just beginning.

"Miss Dawson?" Madsen said again.

"I think she's done. Sadie?" Josh asked, squeezing her hand again.

The nausea grew as the last two weeks pounded against her. Every event, every memory meshed into one giant explosion of pain. It was all too much. She was losing herself to it.

"What did Luis do?" Madsen pressed.

"I said she's done!" Josh suddenly roared. Her eyes flew open in time to see Josh take a protective stance in front of her, blocking Madsen from her view. "Leave!" Josh ordered.

For a moment the agent didn't move, and then he gathered his things. Sadie watched him as time moved slower and slower. *Sleep,* her survival instinct begged. *Just sleep.* But when Madsen grabbed the handle, she managed one last question. "How did you know?"

Madsen stopped and turned. "What?"

"How did you know Guillermo was coming for me? At the lodge."

"We got a call from someone. He said Guillermo knew you had met with me and was planning to get rid of you."

"It was Manuel, wasn't it?"

Madsen pursed his lips in surprise. "The brother? I don't know. He's called us a few times with information, but never left his name."

"It was Manuel," she insisted quietly. "I'm sure of it. That's twice now."

"Twice?"

Sensing she was ready to finish, Madsen moved back to his chair. Josh was shaking his head furiously. "You don't have to do this, Sadie."

"Yes, I do," she said. Then she began again, slowly and numbly, and finished the rest of her painful story. "So Manuel saved me in a way," she said. "If he had taped me up the way Luis had, I would never have been able to break free in time."

Madsen pulled on his graying goatee. "Interesting. I wonder if it was intentional—a last way to defy Guillermo. I must say I'm impressed, though, Miss Dawson. What possessed you to kick through a wall?"

"I suddenly remembered when my brother was a teenager and kicked a hole in the wall. The bathroom door wasn't budging, so . . ." She shrugged.

Madsen nodded. "Impressive. And once you were outside, you didn't see any cars, anyone by the cabin or on the road? I think Mr. Young and I were there within thirty minutes."

Josh? There were huge parts of the story she didn't know, but she shook her head. "No. I started down the road, but realized Manuel could come back, or Luis, or anyone, so I hid. Even with the blanket, it didn't take long to realize I was going to freeze to death under that tree. If I hadn't been in so much pain, I would have dragged myself back up to the fire just to warm up. I swear," she added softly, "when I get out of here, I'm moving to Florida or somewhere warm. I'm so sick of being cold."

Madsen smiled—his first. "I think that can be arranged. And you think you got some of Luis's skin in your nails?"

She nodded, still sickened by it.

"Good."

As Madsen stood, she breathed a sigh of relief. It was finally done. She looked up at Josh, only he was no longer standing next to her. Confused, she followed her hand still clasping his, and found him at the side of the bed, on his knees. He'd dropped to the floor sometime during her narrative. His face was one of grief, torment, and anger.

"It's okay, Josh. It's done."

She squeezed his hand and asked what she had already guessed, "So who found me?"

"Josh." "Rocky," the two men said, contradicting each other.

Sadie glanced up. "How?"

Josh smiled, eyes moist. "An answer to prayer."

"We weren't sure if you'd make it," Madsen added. "Dr. Jackson worked on you for—"

"Dr. Jackson?" Sadie cut in. "Sam's dad? He's here?"

Josh nodded. "Sam's in the other room with Kevin, Trevor, and his parents."

"Oh, no! Their cabin!" The tears started again. "I'm so sorry."

"Do you really think they care about the cabin?" Josh asked. "It's a building, Sadie."

"But . . . their memories . . ." she cried. "My memories."

Josh leaned down and kissed her forehead. "It's okay," he whispered against her skin. "It's going to be okay."

The longer he stayed, the slower her breathing got, until he brought her back to a painless, tearless state.

"I need to get going on some of this," Madsen said, unaffected. "Can you tell me one last thing, Miss Dawson? How well can you identify the people at Vasquez's Christmas party?"

Even though it felt like an eternity ago, she answered, "Pretty well, I think."

"And New Year's Eve?"

"Yes," she said more confidently. "Guillermo made me spend time with every guest."

"Good. I'll put together a list and by tomorrow, I'm sure I'll have plenty more questions for you. We can also talk about your options once you get out of here."

Sadie nodded tiredly. As long as it involved somewhere warm and the man holding her hand she could handle anything.

CHAPTER 50

As soon as Madsen left, Sadie closed her eyes. Josh continued to grasp her hand so tightly, he worried he was cutting off her circulation. He loosened his grip a little, but not much.

Her eyes fluttered open. "I think I'm a little tired."

"That's okay, you sleep."

"I will if you will," she said, but within seconds she was breathing deeply.

He watched her every movement, too overwhelmed to do otherwise. He stared at their hands, intertwined into one. She needed him now, but what about tomorrow? Or the next day?

The last sixty hours began to tug on his eyelids. He quietly dragged the cot over to the side of her bed and, without breaking his grasp, lay down and instantly fell asleep.

He woke up with one arm draped over his head, the other still amazingly holding Sadie's hand. He heard a soft conversation and rolled over. Sadie was sitting upright in bed and her mother was in a chair next to her. They were both watching him with the same smile.

He sat up quickly and ran his fingers through his disheveled hair. *How long was I out?* He rubbed his heavily stubbled chin and sniffed his clothes, which reeked of smoke. Not cool.

"How are you feeling?" Sadie asked.

"How are *you* feeling?" he shot back.

"Better." And she did look better. Her face. Her color. She looked wonderful.

Marcela stood quickly. "Well, I think I need to check on . . . something." She gave Sadie a kiss on the cheek, winked at Josh, and quietly made her exit.

Josh kept looking at Sadie. Something looked different about her. Then he had it. "You cut the rest of your hair?"

She frowned, tugging on her now-short curls. "My mom tried to fix it for me."

"It looks cute. I like it."

She didn't smile at the compliment. And in fact, she did the thing he feared. She dropped his hand, breaking their long grasp. Josh stared dejectedly at her hands as they began twisting the hospital blanket. "My mom and I were talking just now," she said softly.

"Oh?"

"She filled me in on some of the details, things that happened when I was gone."

Panicked, Josh watched as she worried a corner of the blanket into knots.

A single, solitary tear ran down her olive skin, but her voice stayed calm. "You told me to run, Josh, but I didn't listen. You were trying to tell me about Guillermo the whole time, and now I've ruined a lot of people's lives." She paused and looked up. "Including yours."

He started shaking his head. "Don't do this. None of us had any idea who he really was. But it's over now. He's not going to hurt you ever again. I promise."

Her hand reached out and took his again. It was crazy how that one, small gesture could calm his racing heart. "What did you say in that prayer?" she asked softly.

It took a second before he understood. "Oh, your blessing? The words actually weren't mine, they just flowed, but what I remember is that your body would heal, as would your spirit."

"That's what my mom said," she said softly. "And do you believe that?"

"Yes. But most overwhelming for me was feeling how much the Lord loves you, Sadie. It's hard to describe the surge of emotion at the time, but I think the words were that He's waiting, arms open, to receive you in. And through His love, you'll be made whole again."

"And do you believe that?" she asked, eyes shining.

"Absolutely."

"Through His love . . ." she repeated quietly.

Josh blinked back the sudden emotion. "If you only knew how much He loves you."

"And do you?" She wiped her cheeks angrily. "I mean, why did you come back, Josh? My mom said they were trying to find you and all of a sudden you just called. Out of the blue. Before you even knew I was missing. Before you had any idea anything had happened to me, you were on your way back to Montana. Coming back . . . to me."

"Yes."

Her dark eyes finally met his. "Why?"

"I came back to talk to you." Her eyes narrowed skeptically and he smiled. "I came back to grovel, actually. And beg. I was coming back to ask you to give me another chance. I knew you'd probably refuse me, but I had to at least try."

"What about everything else? I meant what I said before, about your church. I know what it means to you, but . . . but I understand if you don't want me to. I mean, after everything I've done to you—to everyone else—I can't expect you to really think . . ." Her head fell against the bed and Josh tried to cut in, but she rushed on. "I'm no saint, but is it really so horrible for me to want to be with you? I'm a train wreck, I know, but you kind of are, too."

He laughed. "True. Very true."

Her eyes widened. "I'm so sorry. It's not true. You're perfect, actually, and amazing, and I can't believe I'm even selfish enough to ask this, but can't you just give me a chance to show you that I can be the kind of person—"

Josh stopped her ramblings with a kiss. He intended for it to be a short one, just to get her attention, but once there, he ended up lingering longer than intended.

When he finally pulled back, his words were soft, but sure. "God has been trying to give me a gift, Sadie. I don't know why or how I'll ever repay Him, but I'm not going to reject it. I don't want to live without you, Sadie. I've tried and failed. Please don't make me try again. Please let me stay with you. Not just now, but tomorrow, and forever."

Once again he was lost in the depth of those beautiful, dark eyes. "I love you, Sadie Dawson. Totally, completely, and forever love you."

A smile spread across her entire face until she was glowing. He reached up and stroked her cheek, hardly believing she was real, that she could possibly be his. Forever. Not willing to wait another second, he cradled her face, leaned forward, and kissed her again. All the pain was forgotten, all the sadness. Everything was left behind in that perfect moment of her perfect kiss.

ABOUT THE AUTHOR

Rebecca Lund Belliston studied music and information systems at Brigham Young University and Utah State University, where she met her husband, Troy. They now live in Michigan and have five children, ranging from teen to toddler. Besides writing, she also loves to read, do family history work and graphic design, and teach. *Sadie* is her first novel. You can follow her online at www.rebeccabelliston.com.